CONJOINED

By

DEREK CICCONE

This is a work of fiction. All of the characters, organizations, and events portrayed in this novel are either products of the author's imagination or are used fictitiously, any resemblance to actual persons, living or dead, is entirely coincidental.

ISBN: 978-0-9854287-7-8

Keep in touch with
Twitter - @DCicconeBooks
Facebook - Derek Ciccone Book Club
Website - derekciccone.com
Email - Derekbkclb@yahoo.com

OTHER BOOKS BY DEREK CICCONE

JP Warner Series

Officer Jones
Huddled Masses
Psycho Hill
Confederate Gold

Painless Series

Painless
Carolyn Chronicles Vol. 1

Stand Alone

Kristmas Collins
The Trials of Max Q
The Heritage Paper
The Jack Hammer
The Truant Officer

Chapter One

31 Years Ago

Sarah Dunbar couldn't sit still.

She rose from her chair and began to pace. Her husband, Nathan, glanced in her direction, but said nothing. He knew better than attempt another lecture about saving her energy. The surgery would stretch into tomorrow, perhaps taking as many as thirty hours to complete.

She couldn't believe he could remain so calm. He sat with legs crossed, engrossed in his novel. Exactly the type of guy you'd want flying your plane, which was his profession. Sarah was more like the unruly passengers she'd dealt with during her time as a flight attendant; the ones who refused to abide by the *Fasten Seat Belt* sign.

That was a different lifetime. One in which her twin daughters weren't about to be wheeled off into an operating room, where they would literally be cut apart—like a scene out of a horror film. Yet it was the best option. That was the one thing she was sure of.

They were approached by the hospital Media Relations Director, Jennifer Towns. A pretty, perfectly put together woman who smelled of hairspray. She would be providing them updates at each critical juncture. She would also handle briefings for the media, who were camped outside the hospital ready to tell the story of Eliza and Christie Dunbar, the nine-month-old conjoined twins who surgeons would attempt to separate in a rare and risky operation.

Jennifer walked the Dunbars through the steps one final time, even though Sarah had memorized every tiny detail, and they had done a "dress rehearsal" here last month. With so many people and possibilities involved, organization was the key, and each step had been planned to the second.

She concluded by looking Sarah deep in the eyes, and said, "Christie and Elizabeth are in good hands—Dr. Null is the best in the business."

The comment triggered something deep within Sarah. "That's not my daughter," she protested, an edge in her voice.

Nathan stepped in, placing his arm around Sarah. "What's wrong, sweetheart?"

"She called her Elizabeth … our daughter is Eliza."

Sarah needed everyone involved to know that her babies were not a number. They were not patients. They were her daughters, and every little detail counted.

A few minutes later, Dr. Finnegan Null entered the waiting room. He wore blue scrubs and his unkempt salt-and-pepper hair made it appear as if he'd just woken up. He didn't exactly look like one of the world's top pediatric surgeons, which he was.

"How are you doing?" he asked Sarah, his visit likely the result of her mini meltdown.

"Who cares about us—how are *you* doing? You're the one doing the surgery," Nathan said, effectively lightening the mood.

They shared a brief laugh, before Dr. Null asked, "Do you have any questions or requests before we get started?"

Sarah did have one. She wanted each and everyone involved in the surgery—thirty-one in all, including Dr. Null—to introduce themselves to Eliza and Christie. It was important for them to look her daughters in their big brown eyes … to make this personal for them.

The request was fulfilled. Team Eliza wore pink bandanas and scrubs, while Team Christie was in blue. The twins' fingers had similar color-coded tape, as did all the attached tubes and wires.

"Nice to meet you, Eliza—I'm Dr. Smith, and I'm honored to be assisting in your surgery."

"Hello Christie—I'm Dr. Perkins, and I promise that we'll take good care of you."

And so on, all thirty-one—pediatric surgeons, urologists, orthopedics, plastic surgeons, nurses, radiologists, anesthesiologists. By the smiles on the twins' faces, they appeared to be taking this much better than their mother. They had grown accustomed to the attention that had been bestowed upon them the last few crazy months.

At 7:30 am, Eliza and Christie Dunbar were wheeled into the unknown.

The only time Sarah stopped pacing was for her sessions with the filmmakers, who were documenting the surgery. She had initially resisted the idea when presented to her and Nathan. Their first reaction was to shield them. Hide them away from a cruel world that might judge or mock them. But they soon realized that they weren't shielding them for the girls' sake, but to prevent their own embarrassment.

So each hour Sarah would sit with the film crew and share her emotions. It was cathartic, as by the time each new hour arrived, Sarah felt like a powder keg that was about to explode. When they first started filming, three months ago, the cameras felt invasive and she'd analyze every word she uttered. But she barely even noticed them these days.

The tension mounted as they reached the first minefield. Dr. Null believed that the twins had two livers fused together, but wouldn't know for sure until they opened them up. If they shared one liver, they would have to stop the surgery. And the girls would be forced to live as one. A life without freedom, with their possibilities severely limited.

A nurse appeared, dressed in Team Eliza pink. When she approached, Sarah could see tears in her eyes. Her stomach sank, expecting the worst. But the nurse surprised Sarah with a strong hug, and the words she'd hoped to hear, "There are two livers—we can go on."

During their embrace, Sarah realized that this was as emotionally draining for the doctors and nurses as it was for her. This *was* personal for them. And for the first time she believed they might get through this.

But there were more challenges ahead. As thrilled as she was that the surgery could continue, the livers were filled with major blood vessels and separating them risked causing a fatal hemorrhage. All she could do was hold on tight and hope that the doctors could navigate through the treacherous waters.

An hour later, the nurse returned with more good news—the livers had been separated. But no time to celebrate. More minefields were looming.

The updates started coming fast and furious. The gall bladders and bile ducts could be separated, along with the urinary bladders. And each girl's reproductive organs were intact, so Christie and Eliza would be able to bear children if they chose.

"Is it too early to discuss grandchildren?" Sarah joked to the messenger nurse, the stream of positive news slightly loosening her up.

At the twenty-three hour mark, Sarah received the words she'd been praying for, "Your children are separated."

Christie remained in the original OR, while Eliza was moved to a neighboring one. Six more grueling hours later, Christie's team had sewn her up. Ninety minutes after that, Eliza went into recovery.

The surgery officially ended at thirty-one hours, and shortly thereafter, Sarah and Nathan got to visit with their daughters. Sarah was mesmerized, seeing them for the first time as two individual children. Her heart practically exploded with joy.

In the days that followed, Christie healed quicker, while Eliza had to undergo another operation to close her wounds. Sarah noticed that the girls had begun to develop their own personalities. Eliza was more gregarious, while Christie was very suspicious of strangers, and was protective of Eliza. But all things considered, they were in good spirits.

They spent the next few weeks in the hospital, with Sarah and Nathan marking each milestone like they'd won the Super Bowl—*their first solid food, rice cereal, woo-hoo!* All leading up to the day when they were able to return home to Ridgefield. There was a long road ahead of them, and more surgeries on the horizon, but they would take it one day at a time, as a family, and count their blessings.

For the first time in months Sarah felt like she could breathe. It still didn't seem real to her. Who would have thought an innocent trip to the obstetrician's office could lead to this. The doctor telling her, matter-of-factly, "Your babies might be joined."

"They might be what?"

Nathan was away on a flight and she had no idea what she was going to tell him. *We're going to have Siamese twins?* They discussed ending the pregnancy, but it was never a serious consideration. The doctors cautioned them that the babies likely wouldn't survive beyond the first hours. But Christie and Eliza beat those odds, and they'd been beating them ever since.

They had seven months to get ready for the arrival, but seventy years couldn't have prepared them. Just holding the girls was an ordeal, as were most of life's simple tasks. But then came their miracle in Dr. Null, who believed the girls were candidates for separation surgery.

They decided it would best be done when the babies were nine months old, so they'd be able to physically withstand the surgery, but young enough to avoid most of the emotional trauma associated with it. The lead-up was rigorous, filled with endless doctor visits and sleepless nights. Balloons were inserted under the girls' skin, which would slowly be expanded, creating enough skin to cover the wounds. That was the only point along the way in which Sarah questioned what they were doing. *Oh my God—I'm turning my children into Frankenstein!* But Nathan was a rock throughout the entire process, talking her off the ledge numerous times.

Exactly three weeks following their historic surgery, the twins were wheeled through the hospital halls to the cheers of the staff. Upon exiting the hospital they were met by clicking flashbulbs and reporters, all trying to get the first shot of the Conjoined Kids following their separation.

Sarah had been keeping it together pretty well … until they arrived at their car and she saw the *two* car seats. The tears began to flow.

Nathan came up behind her and whispered, "They might be separated, but they'll always be together."

Those were the words she needed to hear. A smile replaced her tears. They had given their children the gift every parent hoped for—the gift of freedom. To be able to pursue whatever they want in this world, and become whomever they chose. And their journey was just beginning.

Chapter 2

March 1st – Present Day

Most milestones are based on even numbers that end in zero. The 50th wedding anniversary, the 40th birthday. But the big date for my sister Chris and me is the 31st.

Which was why I was up at the crack of dawn, long before the Little Macs arose, watching the video documentary that chronicled the months leading up to, and including, the day that changed our lives forever.

I had to hold back the urge to call Chris. While we're identical twins, our sleep patterns—along with pretty much every aspect of our lives—are anything but identical. It would have to wait, even if my rare moment of nostalgia felt empty without her.

Especially since she's the only one besides me who's in on it—the significance of the number 31. Why it represents the unyielding bond between us. It has always been our clandestine code, our version of the secret handshake, our Wonder Twin powers.

It was 31 years ago today when my sister and I were separated in a rare and risky operation, with no guarantees of either of us coming out of it alive. It received much ballyhoo, not just in our hometown of Ridgefield, Connecticut, but across the land—*Would the Conjoined Kids pull through?*

The operation took exactly 31 hours to complete, and there were 31 doctors and medical technicians involved in it. It even took place on March 1st ... 3/1. And while we were separated that day, it bound us together more than ever, and 31 has always been our reminder.

I refocused on the video. Chris and I were considered the "stars" of the documentary, but it was my mother, Sarah Dunbar, who symbolized the emotions felt during that perilous time. The filming began when Chris and I were about six months old, just after the decision had been made to attempt to separate us, and continued through our first birthday, three months following the surgery. And during those six months my mother ran the gamut of emotions from overwhelmed, to scared, to strong, and you could just see the relief spilling out of her when she learned the surgery had been a success. And my favorite moment was when she did her famous "happy dance." It saddened me that she'd never be able to do that dance again.

I've only watched the documentary a handful of times, but when I have, I like to fast-forward to the part that details the day of the surgery and then onto the months that follow. I save the beginning for the end. The part where Chris and I were connected at the hip—pelvis, actually—spending our first months on this planet literally sitting in each other's lap. When you come into this world staring your sibling in the eyes, it makes for a powerful bond.

A floor-shaking noise disturbed my train of thought. As much as I've always dreaded the sound of my alarm clock, it had nothing on my youngest, Kelly, and her recent morning ritual of waking up our household ... and likely our neighbors ... with her guitar. And this was no unplugged acoustic set.

The guitar ... and the dreaded amp ... was a gift from her father, my ex, Kirk McCaffrey. It's the type of gift one would only give when they don't live in the same household. In fact, Kirk doesn't even live on the same continent—he plays basketball professionally in Europe, as he has for most of the girls' lives.

"Mom—can you *please* make her stop?" came the predictable plea from my oldest, Brooke, her whine rising above the earsplitting sound of the guitar.

I shut off the video. My morning had officially begun.

I pushed off the couch and slowly made my way to the stairwell. I shouted up, "Anybody playing a musical instrument of any sort will not be getting any pancakes."

The guitar solo ceased, and Kelly's small voice asked, "Will they be blueberry?"

"It's a surprise—you'll have to come down and see," I replied. We're usually a cereal and toast family, but this was a big day in their mom's life and any big day deserves pancakes, right?

Ten minutes later the Little Macs appeared—showered, smelling good, and wearing their adorable plaid skirt and sweater school uniforms. I wanted to squish them with a hug, but Brooke had recently informed me that they were no longer "cool with that."

Brooke had shot up in height this year, requiring her to have her uniform upgraded two sizes, which was not terribly surprising with her father being six-foot-six. Kelly had received Kirk's curly hair and strong jaw line in the DNA transfer, but was still waiting on that growth spurt. The girls were not conjoined twins like their Aunt Chris and me—they're more along the lines of Irish twins. Brooke is eight, while Kelly will be turning seven next month.

They took a seat at the kitchen table and Brooke performed her morning ritual—a much quieter one—of checking the results of her father's most recent game on the laptop.

Kelly stretched a yawn. "Thank God it's Friday," she announced, as if second grade was such a grind.

"Don't you think you have better things to thank God for than that?" I asked, completing the first batch and sliding plates in front of the girls.

"Oh yeah—I should thank him mostly for pancakes."

That's my girl.

A quizzical look spread over Brooke's face; her focus remaining on the computer screen. "They won, but Dad's name isn't mentioned again."

I didn't want to let her in on the secret that her father's temper and general hardheadedness often resulted in run-ins with coaches and management, leading to suspensions, and eventually firings. Which explained why he'd been on five teams in seven years, from France to Italy to Spain, and this year Turkey.

I went with, "I spoke to him the other day. He mentioned that he'd sprained his ankle and might have to sit out a couple weeks until it heals."

Brooke had never been the gullible type, but she seemed to buy my answer. And for all I knew it could be true—I hadn't spoken to Kirk in over three weeks. But that was neither here nor there; as there were much more important items on the agenda right now—*pancakes!*

After making quick work of breakfast, we headed out into the brisk March morning. We piled into my Honda Pilot and drove off toward another day in the life of Eliza Dunbar ... even though I knew today wasn't just another day.

Chapter 3

I dropped the kids at Saint Francis Elementary. Or Sainty Frank's, as we used to call it when I attended back in the day.

My longtime friend, and current neighbor, Connie Marchand, met me in the parking lot. She didn't seem overly offended that she was likely awakened by Kelly Van Halen this morning.

Her husband was the one who provided the tip on the cozy house on Candlewood Lake in Danbury, which the girls and I have lived in the last three years, and doing our best to turn into a home. So the Marchands knew what they were getting into when they pushed for me to buy ... although, perhaps not the guitar part.

Connie gave up a promising photography career in New York to stay home with her three children, but she still occasionally freelanced. She noticed that I was staring at her camera equipment and informed me, "It's school picture day."

My heart dropped. What kind of mother forgets picture day, and doesn't have their children unnaturally primped and dressed? Looking like they almost never do?

Connie read my dread. "Don't sweat it, Eliza—today is just for the make-ups. Your girls came out great the first time, as usual. Unlike my boys they actually smile for the camera, so consider yourself ahead of the game."

She was in a hurry and I didn't want to keep her. She made her way toward the front entrance, but not before reminding me that she'd see me later this afternoon at Dirty Martini Friday. Our end-of-the-week get-together where Connie and I, along with our friend Jillian, meet at a local bar for drinks. Suddenly I agreed with Kelly—thank God it was Friday.

I walked across the street from the school to my favorite coffee house, Luke & Jack's, and purchased the strongest cup they could legally make. *Happy anniversary to me!*

I still had a half hour until my meeting with my editor so I thought it was time to call Chris. But just as I was about to click her number, I was startled by my ringtone, and the caller ID told me that my sister beat me to it.

"I was just about to call you," I answered.

"I know," she said, and we shared a laugh at our intuitive powers.

"Happy anniversary!" I exclaimed.

"The big one … I can't believe it's actually here."

We'd talked about it for years. I'd never been sentimental about the annual anniversary date—most times I tried to distance myself from the whole conjoined thing—but there was something about this one that was special. And it had seemed so far in the future that it was almost surreal that the day had come.

"I thought such a monumental day deserves a little more than our usual, so I'll be cooking up my famous marinated flank steak tonight, with brownies and ice cream for dessert. The kids are spending the night at Mom and Dad's."

Our "usual" was just the two of us toasting with a glass of champagne … maybe a couple of glasses. Last year my parents hosted a party to mark the 30th anniversary and invited pretty much everyone we'd ever known. But number 31 was just about us.

I could feel Chris grow distant. "That's partly why I called—I can't make it tonight. I'm in Miami."

A wave of disappointment rushed over me. "Miami?"

"Sorry to drop it on you like this, but Norby sent me down here last minute."

While this news didn't thrill me, I was glad that Chris seemed to have finally found her niche working for Norby.

I felt like Chris and I had lived two lives already, and we were now headed into our third act. Our first sixteen years of life we were known as the "Conjoined Kids." In the beginning I loved the attention—*what kid wouldn't?* But that changed when I grew into my teen years and I couldn't run away from it fast enough. As things turned out I wouldn't have to run for very long, because that was about the time I became known solely as Chris Dunbar's sister—the start of my second life.

If you believe every life-event is a zero sum game with a winner and loser, then there is no doubt that Chris "won" our surgery, at least from the physical standpoint. She came out of it with a full set of tools, including two healthy legs. We were born sharing three legs and it was known going into it that one of us would lose out. I drew the short straw.

I tended to make up for this—some would say overcompensate—with my cult of personality. I was even nicknamed "The Mayor" back in high school, as they said it was like I knew everybody in town.

Chris put her healthy legs to good use and became one of the most highly recruited basketball players in state history. It was such a big deal that when she made her college choice to attend the University of Connecticut, ESPN showed up at our high school to cover it.

And when she hit the game winning shot to beat Tennessee in the Final Four, one reporter quipped that she would never have to pay for a drink in the state ever again. The statement was prophetic and eventually problematic.

She was expected to have similar success at the professional level, and was the first female athlete to sign on with super-agent Norby Weinberg. But before her career began she tore her knee for the second time. Then during her rehabilitation from that injury, it happened again. The third time was not a charm, as the doctors told her she would never be able to play again.

Basketball had always been the glue in her life and she was aimless without it. She capitalized on her local fame for a while—she would do endorsements and make appearances for shopping malls, banks, etc. But that couldn't fill the void and she eventually turned to alcohol. When she got her second DUI, almost killing herself in the process, her endorsement days were over.

Another problematic issue was the arrogance she displayed on the court. It helped to make her the great player she was, but it also rubbed a lot of people the wrong way, burning a lot of bridges in the process, and limited her options going forward.

I thought many of those people who took shots at her on her way down, should have first walked in her shoes. It can't be easy for someone to live their first twenty-plus years of life being adored and showered with attention, only to have the faucet suddenly turned off. And besides, they didn't know her like I did. Nobody did.

"Well, that sucks," I said, never very skilled at holding my tongue.

"It's not like I had a choice in the matter. This job might be my last chance at making something of myself—I can't screw it up."

"I understand," I said, and I did, but that didn't mean I had to be happy about it.

"You're upset … I can tell," she said.

"No, your job is priority. You did the right thing."

"C'mon, Eliza—you can't fool me. But I'll tell you what, when I get back I'll make it up to you."

"A month's worth of babysitting—31 days?"

"Much better—Baskin-Robbins ice cream. We'll eat all 31 flavors, or until we throw up, whichever comes first."

I smiled. "How can I turn that down? You've got a deal."

"Can't wait," she said; her tone turning serious. "I know I haven't always been the best sister, Eliza, but I hope you know I love you."

She was right—you can't fool a conjoined twin. I could tell she meant every word of it. "I love you too, sis."

After we ended the call I headed for my meeting. But suddenly it just seemed like any other day.

Chapter 4

The *Danbury Ledger* newspaper was headquartered in a three-story brick building along Main Street. It was built in the 1800s and was recently designated a historic site. That meant it couldn't be torn down, so it would likely outlive the fledgling newspaper that has called it home for 150 years.

I entered the office of my editor, Bob Hurlbert, and took a seat facing his desk. Bob was a grizzled newspaper veteran with a shock of white hair that I'm convinced was brown when I started here full-time, five years ago. His wardrobe consisted of Oxford shirt, suspenders, no tie, with his reading glasses perched precariously on the end of his nose. His sleeves were always rolled up, ready to work.

Newspapers were his life, and he planned to go down with the ship. That's not to say he hasn't nudged me to get myself into a lifeboat before it's too late. "Eliza," he would say in his gruff voice. "With the risk of sounding sexist, it seems like such a waste for you to hide that pretty face behind a byline." It was his subtle way of trying to push me toward TV, radio, or even, gasp, Internet blogging. All of which have better long-term outlooks than newspapers.

My first year out of Northwestern University I was offered job that combined two of my loves—journalism and sports—covering the Chicago Cubs baseball team for their television network. It wasn't exactly hard news—I'd basically interview players before and after the game with a smile plastered on my face: *How did it feel to strike out and lose the game?* To which the player provided a cliché-filled response, but you could tell he was thinking: *How do you think it felt, you dumb I won't say the word.* But for a first job you couldn't beat it. I got to travel the country and watch baseball, all while most of my classmates were stuck in a cubicle under the halogen lights of an office.

Attending college in Chicago was a great decision. For the first time in my life I wasn't one of the Conjoined Kids, or Chris Dunbar's sister … I was just Eliza. And I would have stayed there if it weren't for my mother's health issues. Great city, great friends, great job. But with that said, I would have preferred to be covering the Cubs for the *Chicago Tribune*, and not television. I was willing to go down with the newspaper ship as well. So there was no way I was getting in that lifeboat.

Bob leaned back in his chair. "So whatchya got for me, kid?"

We met every Friday to review the week, and make sure everything was prepared for the profitable Sunday edition, which might be the one thing keeping us employed at the moment. Yet I still got nervous when he'd stare at me like that, awaiting my answer.

I checked my pad, even though the only notes I had were in my head. "Well, I've finally heard back from the mayor's office, regarding my request to interview him about his proposed immigration law."

Bob flashed a smug smile "Let me guess—he had a change of heart, and has suddenly found the time to do a sit-down with you early next week."

"Monday morning."

"Funny how that works."

Danbury might not be the most glamorous city, but it's one of the more diverse places you'll find, made up of an eclectic mix of ethnic cultures. Much different from Ridgefield, the neighboring town where I was raised. Don't get me wrong it was a nice place to grow up, but it tended to have one flavor—creamy rich vanilla.

But the diversity has sometimes led to tension, which was behind the mayor's proposed law. The law has been panned by critics and led to daily protests outside of his office, so after initially refusing to talk to us—still angered we endorsed his opponent in the last election—he now wanted to use me and our newspaper to spin some good PR ... er ... get his side of the story out.

Bob maintained his smile. "I think our esteemed mayor believes you to be a pushover, Ms. Dunbar. Which has all the makings of another poor decision on his part. Any news on the bank robbery?"

"I'm following up with Detective Ruiz later this morning."

He nodded. "I'm guessing that will be a short meeting. If we had dedicated our front page to all their hot leads, we'd have saved a hell of a lot of money on ink."

I'm sort of the AP around here—all purpose, not Associated Press—and cover everything from politics to bank robberies to sports. And my baby, the Arts & Culture section that appears in the Sunday edition. Besides Bob and myself, the rest of the writing staff consists of three journalism interns from the local university and a handful of freelancers.

"Then later this afternoon I'll be meeting with a couple of board members for the Danbury Culture Center to go over a few events they're planning for the spring, which I plan to highlight in next week's A&C section."

He laughed. "How come I never get invited to Dirty Martini Friday?"

"I don't know what you're talking about," I replied sheepishly.

"I've only been a reporter for forty years, give me a little credit."

"Well, Connie and Jillian are on the DCC board, so I'm not making that up. And it's girls only ... not to mention, after dealing with you and my kids all week I'm in dire need of that martini."

He grinned. "I'm a scotch man, anyway. What about *this week's* Arts section?"

"I will be including my review, and interview, with Elvis Costello. I attended his show at the Ridgefield Playhouse last week … on my own dime, I might add," I stated proudly. I took Kelly and Brooke with me— *their first real concert!*—figuring you're never too young to be exposed to good music, and some peace, love, and understanding.

"What about sports?" Bob asked, moving on. I was pretty certain he'd never heard of Elvis Costello. His musical taste was more Big Band era.

"Monday night, Danbury Catholic has a state tournament basketball game. I'll be there to cover it."

"Isn't that the high school you went to?"

"It is."

"Then I better not see any favoritism in your reporting, got it?"

I nodded with the solemn seriousness he was seeking, as if anyone would care if I skewed the narrative in favor of the home squad.

Bob reached for his coffee mug, which served as his signal that the meeting was adjourned. His version of banging the gavel. I stood and headed for the door.

"One more thing, Eliza."

I turned back to face him.

"Happy anniversary."

I smiled, surprised he remembered. "Thank you."

"Since last year was the big three-oh, I guess we can spare you another retrospective this year. You know how people like those big even numbers that end in zero."

If only he knew. But while today started out by looking backward, I decided that the rest of the day would be dedicated to what was ahead of me. I walked through the door and into the future.

Chapter 5

Police headquarters was a short walk from the *Ledger.*

As had become custom, I stepped into Detective Ruiz's office with barely a knock. But I was immediately apologizing, having interrupted a discussion he was having with a fellow police officer. A very blonde and pretty police officer, I noted.

"I'm sorry—I didn't know you were in a meeting," I said and began to retreat.

Tim waved me to come in. "Not a problem, Eliza—we were just finishing up here."

He introduced me to Officer Annie Sampson, the residue of laughter still on her face. We engaged in a friendly handshake, and she said, "From the *Ledger,* right?"

I thought of claiming to be a different Eliza Dunbar, since our coverage of the "Marilyn Heist" hadn't exactly been favorable to the Danbury PD. But I owned it, "That would be me."

She surprised me with a smile, adding, "I enjoy your work," She then looked back to Detective Ruiz. "I'll see you tonight, Tim."

She shut the door behind her as she left, and Tim looked at me. "What's with the grin?"

"She likes you."

He shook his head as he took a seat behind the neatest desk you'd ever find in a police station. "So you're writing a gossip column now?"

"We haven't sunk that low … yet. Just sometimes my journalistic eye and woman's intuition come together in perfect harmony, and I can see things."

"I think it led you astray this time. Annie hopes to make detective one day, and she comes to me seeking advice. That's where her interest lies."

Tim would be a good place to go for that advice. He's the youngest detective in history of the Danbury PD. Which isn't a shocker, since his family has been an institution on the force going back a century. And with his athletic build, golden skin and short-cropped dark hair, word on the street is that the ladies around town call him Hottie Five-O. Which quality Officer Annie was more interested in was still to be determined.

Our history stretches beyond the crime beat. Tim is kind of a hand-me-down from my sister. He first met Chris through their shared love of basketball, back when we were in middle school. They would travel around to different courts in the area and hustle people for money. It worked in their favor that they were normally underestimated, based on their age and that Chris was a girl.

During the summers they would attend basketball camps together, which included long car rides to places like Syracuse and Providence. My parents would often drive them and I was deemed too young to stay home alone.

We hit it off on those long trips and became best buddies. And we were in every sense of the word—inside jokes, sharing each other's hopes and dreams, long phone conversations when that was still a thing—until Layna Bryant entered the picture with her micro mini-skirts and wiggle walk, and I got unceremoniously pushed to the curb.

But that was a long time ago, and I was over it. We've worked professionally together for the last couple years. Occasionally a glimpse back to our BFF days will arise, but the moments quickly grow awkward and we retreat to the comfort of business. And today would be no different.

"Your paper has really been beating us up on this bank robbery," Tim got right to the point.

The robbery in question took place at the Easton Bank, which happened to be right across the street from police headquarters on Main Street—*talk about brazen!* And it wasn't your typical ski mask and gun robbery. The robber was dressed in a blonde wig, sunglasses, and a pink satin dress, appearing to be a Marilyn Monroe impersonator.

The headline in our paper the next day was *Diamonds Are a Girl's Best Friend.* And keeping with the Marilyn theme, when a week had passed with no arrest in sight, and the natives were starting to get restless, we went with *Seven Day Itch.* With ten days gone by, and Bob having written a scathing editorial on how he believed the police bungled the case, the headline referred to them as *The Misfits.*

"You know I don't write the headlines and I had nothing to do with Bob's editorial. My articles have been fair," I defended.

Surprisingly, he agreed, "You're the only journalist in town that I trust, Eliza. Which is why I need you to run with a new lead ... but you didn't hear it from me."

I liked the sound of this. "Go on."

Tim pulled out a folder and took out several photos. They were ones taken of "Marilyn" by onlookers after she left the bank. She didn't dash into a getaway car and flee. She took her time and waved to the crowd as if she truly was a movie star walking the red carpet. The last thing on anyone's mind was that she'd just robbed the bank. Brilliant, really.

I shrugged. "I've already seen these."

"Right up until she stepped into the black SUV with tinted windows— a Suburban with fake New York plates—and they drove off. That's the last we've seen of her or the vehicle."

"I don't understand how this is a new lead."

"Have you ever heard of black dome security cameras?"

I shook my head.

"It's advanced optical vision technology that has the ability to photograph through tinted windows. Our department had been selected by the state as one of their test groups, to see if this could be a helpful tool for law enforcement."

"You mean like violate people's privacy and get all 1984 on the citizens you're supposed to be protecting?"

"I'm just a cop who uses whatever is given to me, hoping to get the bad guys off the street. And I recently found out that we've been testing this technology here at the station—

"You mean spying."

He sighed. "It's hush-hush. So if it wasn't for the heat they were catching from your paper, the higher-ups probably wouldn't even have let me in on it. But basically it's been attached to the front of our building shooting cars along Main Street, and it captured our suspects that day of the robbery."

He took out more photos. These were shot through the tinted back window of the SUV as it pulled away. The getaway car. And it caught the back of the bank robber's head as she sat in the backseat.

"Seems that Marilyn couldn't wait to get her wig off," he said.

I viewed the photo. She had short brown hair, almost like a …

"I think our suspect is actually a man," Tim said with a proud look. "Goodbye Norma Jean … hello Norm."

I thought of the bank security video that had been made public, and come to think of it, the suspect did walk awkwardly in the dress and heels like it was a new experience for her.

"All we have is the back of the head, so we had a sketch artist combine it with the stills of the security video and put together a composite of our suspect."

He handed a drawing that looked like a generic everyman. I doubted it would be very helpful.

"So you want me to run with the sketch ... but leave out the part that your department has been spying on the citizens of Danbury?"

"It will be a scoop for your paper, and it might help us to catch a crook. Everybody wins."

Except perhaps the future of our society. "Do you have a description?"

"Caucasian, about 5-10' with brown hair."

"Like half the city. And you're sure the suspect is a male this time?"

"You saw the photos."

I took another look at the stills from the security cameras, and I wasn't completely convinced, but he was the expert.

Tim's desk phone buzzed, followed by a woman's voice, "Detective Ruiz—Chief Wallach wants to see you."

That was my signal. I stood. "Thanks for the tip, appreciate it." I began to walk away, but if he thought he was getting off easy he'd forgotten who he was dealing with. "So what's 'see you tonight' about? You and Officer Annie have a date?"

He shook his head. "Jeff Hardy is retiring—we're all going out for a drink to celebrate it. How about you, any big Friday night plans?"

"It's my anniversary."

"Aren't you divorced?"

"Marriages come and go, but sisters are forever."

"Oh, I totally forgot—congratulations. So are you and Chris doing something to celebrate?"

"She's in Miami, so looks like I'll be spending it with my two favorite girls instead."

"Miami … I'm jealous. How's she doing with the new job?"

"Sounds like things are going well—I'm hoping she's finally found her niche."

"That's good to hear—I was worried about her there for a while. We should get together sometime—the three of us—for old times' sake."

I smiled. "As long as that doesn't mean that I'm stuck between you two in the back of my parents' car on a trip to Syracuse."

He smiled back. "It wasn't so bad, was it?"

I thought for a moment. "No—it was actually pretty great."

Tim caught himself and snapped back to the present; as if he feared lingering too long in the glimpse would turn him to stone. "Well, have a good weekend, Eliza … and hopefully next week you'll be writing a story about an arrest."

"We've been saving the ink," I said with a smile.

Chapter 6

At 2:45 I arrived at the one appointment I couldn't afford to be late for. When you have a three o'clock with trainer James "Beef" Wellington, it means that you're dressed and ready to work at 2:55. Being on time is the same as being late.

I changed into my workout clothes in the dingy locker-room of Beef's gym on White Street, and met him as he finished up with another victim.

His nickname dates back to our high school days when he was north of three hundred pounds—*that was a lot of Beef!* But those days were long gone and he was now a chiseled, gluten-free statue of health. He was part of the trio, along with my sister and Tim Ruiz, which led Danbury Catholic to back-to-back state championships in basketball. Beef controlled the inside with his massive girth, while Tim was a lethal shot from the outside. The three of them together were like a symphony orchestra, with Chris acting as the conductor. She so dominated her freshman year playing girl's basketball that she petitioned to play with the boys. Everyone thought that was cute and fun, and oh so progressive, until she started beating them, and that's when the complaining began.

They called themselves the "Mickey D's Gang," because their diversity could only be matched by the politically correct McDonald's commercials that were popular during their teenage years. My sister was a white upper-class, quasi-famous girl from Ridgefield. Tim grew up in a working class police family, a mixture of Irish and Puerto Rican, while Beef was the black kid from the Danbury hood. He actually grew up in a middle-class neighborhood off East Meadowbrook, but he liked people to think he's from the hood ... and his secret is safe with me.

"You going to the game Monday?" he greeted me. He never led with hello, as if it were a waste of time. The game was more than nostalgia for him—his son Terrell played varsity as a freshman, which was impressive, although, the real headline should be: *How the hell does someone in my class have a kid in high school!?* And here I thought I started early.

"I will be covering it for the paper."

"That editor of yours going to force you to be unbiased?"

"My article will be, but I'll be wearing my DCHS sweatshirt and cheering them on like crazy."

"Good answer—because if you said anything else, you were going to be doing burpees until you begged for mercy."

"Burpees?"

"You don't want to know."

"So what do you have planned for me today?" I asked, slight dread in my voice.

"I've cooked up a special anniversary workout for you."

"Aww ... you remembered. That's sweet."

"Let's see if you're still saying that an hour from now."

The Beef workout was old school—blood, sweat, and more blood. He's lived through all the trends—spinning, Tae Bo, P90X, and don't get him going on CrossFit.

But before we got down to business we got down to his other business. They might call me The Mayor, but nobody knows more people in this town than Beef. He isn't technically a private investigator, but he is a capitalist, and always willing to accept "donations" for information he knows ... or is able to find out ... and is my best source at the paper.

"Any news on the robbery?" I asked.

He just shook his head. "It wasn't someone local, that I'm sure of."

I studied the puzzled look on his face.

"What is it?"

"Usually dudes who are ballsy enough to pull off a bank robbery don't just stop there. It's just as much about the thrill as it is the money. If they needed ten grand so bad, they could have gone over to Ridgefield and pulled a gun on some rich dude. No cameras that way."

"And there haven't been any more robberies in the area."

"Exactly."

"The police confirmed to me today your original thought—that it was a man dressed as a woman."

He shrugged his sculpted shoulders. "Once you've been fooled by that, you never fall for it again."

"I don't even want to know."

We began with sit-ups and the row machine, before moving on to an intense set of pistols, which are basically one-legged squats.

I started to have severe back pain a few years ago. I thought it was just the result of carrying around the girls, but found that it was related to my leg, or rather, my missing one. I tend to get out of alignment, much like a car. I also deal with balance issues, and I fall much more than a normal person, which takes a toll. And even though the technology has improved greatly with my prosthetic, so much so that I can go swimming or wear shorts without anyone even noticing, it's heavy—over ten pounds—and lugging it around all day can put a strain on you.

So I come here three days a week, and Beef and I meet up on Sunday mornings for a cardio workout. Given the choice, I'd skip working out altogether, go home and hug my girls, then make a batch of extra cheesy macaroni and cheese. But I've seen how hard it is for my mom, not being able to be up and around, so I know the importance of maintaining my health.

And Beef hooks me up with a deal. I pay for the sessions with everything from cooking meals for him to babysitting his pit bull, Boss, when he's out of town. This remains controversial with the other mothers in my circle, but Boss has proven safe, and pit bulls sometimes get a bad rap—I've always had a soft spot for those with bad raps. And because my kids are my kids, and make no sense, they adore the supposedly menacing Boss, yet are deathly afraid of cats.

I've received many positive comments about my sleeker, athletic body resulting from the workout regime. I was always a little self-conscious about my looks growing up, due to the obvious leg issue, and it probably didn't help me that my best friend was Jillian Donnelly, who cast a lot of shade with her cheerleader big hair and megawatt smile.

I started to gain confidence during my year on TV in Chicago. My fan mail was filled with flattering comments, albeit some of them a little creepy, and I even received a few marriage proposals. I had blogs and websites devoted to me, usually centered around the "sexiness-level" of the outfits I wore that day. *Seriously, that happened!*

But I'm a reporter, so I feel I can give a fair assessment of myself. I would say my best features are a pretty face, surrounded by straight, shoulder-length chestnut hair, which highlights my deep brown eyes. And I'm not afraid to say that my boobs have always been an asset, and have held up miraculously well after nursing two kids. On the downside I am missing a leg, and have numerous scars from the many surgeries I had *after* the big one. So my bikini-modeling career ended long before it even got started.

We ended the workout where we always do—in the boxing ring. I don't have a lot of mobility, but I do pack a mean punch. And Beef doesn't take it easy on me, with the one caveat that he never hits me in the face, with hopes that it stays one of my better features.

But that rule doesn't work both ways. He sent a punch toward my midsection, which I blocked, and returned a right hook that caught the bridge of his nose.

He stopped, wincing the tears from his eyes. Once he gathered himself, he smiled from ear to ear. "That's what I like about you, Dunbar— you're a fighter."

I smiled back. When you have two kids and one leg, you sure as hell better be.

Chapter 7

I parked in the back of Wojo's, a hole-in-the-wall sports bar on South Street. If you can properly spell the owner's full name—Sam Wojichienski—you drink for free for the night. But since we've been coming here every Friday for the last five years, the Dirty Martini group was ineligible.

I noticed Jillian's Mercedes parked right next to Connie's mini van, realizing they'd beaten me here—I had a few leads that came in just before five that I needed to follow up on, resulting in my tardiness.

I found them tucked away in a corner booth and, by the grins on their faces, I could tell they had already begun to get their dirty on … martini that is.

Jillian looked as stylish as she has since I met her as a Daisy Scout, when we were selling thin-mint cookies to unsuspecting strangers. Even back then her uniform was perfect, and nobody could resist her. Her current uniform was an expensive, power pantsuit, as she was a bigwig at a well-known ad agency in Westport—and it really does list Big Wig as the title on her business card.

She also is afflicted with "pretty girl syndrome," in that, because she doesn't quickly warm to strangers, she has often been labeled as aloof, thinks she's "too good" for people, and of course, the obligatory B-word.

For those who are less attractive, the words are shy and cautious. But as I've mentioned, I've always had a soft spot for those who get a bad rap.

Beside her sat Connie Marchand, looking a complete contrast in the same sweater and jeans she wore when I ran into her this morning. As much time as Jillian spends on cultivating her outward image, Connie was the most secure in her own skin of anyone I'd ever met, and has never given a rat's patootie what anyone thinks.

But that's not to say all was paradise in the Dirty Martini world. Jillian and I had long been best friends. But over time I've grown closer to Connie, and I think she feels a little threatened by it. Although really, it's just that we just have much more in common with our kids being the same age. Plus, we're neighbors, so we see each other almost every day.

And to further complicate matters, there was an undertone of rivalry between Jillian and Connie when it came to the age-old "working woman versus stay home mom" argument. As someone who's lived both sides, I think there's enough room on the bus for everyone. I also know it's a good idea to stay out of it.

Jillian lives in Fairfield with her boyfriend Maxwell, a wealthy hedge fund manager. The only time we've ever met him was during a trip to the Mohegan Sun Casino last year when he spent most of the time acting like Mr. Big Shot, and lecturing Connie and her husband on how they're wrongly investing their money. The only investments I make these days are in more clothes for my girls, so his advice didn't do much for me.

But while there might be a few cracks in our fault line, I've learned that things are never perfect in life and you can't let that threaten what's good. And our friendship, along with these Friday soirees, are firmly on the good side of the ledger.

Wojo arrived with my martini, stirred, not shaken. But heavy on the olive juice, and low on vermouth, which wasn't very James Bondish.

Jillian couldn't hold back her smile. She held up a handful of tickets. "Guess what I got?"

"You didn't," I said, my excitement matching hers.

"Oh, yes I did … one of our clients is a big sponsor of their tour."

All of us at once, "Chilli Peppers!"

We screamed like teenage girls, receiving dirty looks from the other patrons, before morphing into a much more mature adult response—a three-martini toast. Followed by a predictable request that I tell "the story" once again.

My claim to fame—at least one unrelated to my being born connected to my sister—when I got pulled up on stage at a Red Hot Chilli Peppers concert, thirteen years ago, as they sung "Give it Away". I danced with Anthony and Flea. On stage. That really happened!

Wojo returned to our table with a fruity looking drink that was not a martini. He slid it in front of me, "Courtesy of the gentleman at the bar."

I craned my neck and laid eyes on the man who'd just bought me a drink. I recognized him as someone I'd seen in here before, but had never met. I flashed him an awkward smile and wave, which he returned.

"Why don't you go say hello?" Jillian pushed.

"You never know—he could be Mr. Right … or at least Mr. Right Now," Connie added.

"Or he could be a serial killer," I said.

Jillian rolled her eyes, which annoyed me. I was tempted to remind her of the flaws in her own relationship, and offer to help her get off her high horse. But I understood the way society thought—an uninspired relationship was still better than no relationship. As usual, I disagreed with society.

"When was the last time you actually went out with someone?" Jillian continued.

I thought for a second—not exactly a sign that I've been doing a lot of dating—and replied, "New Years—I went to that party with that guy who worked for the telephone company ... Keith."

"Not a date ... I mean a relationship."

"How exactly would you define a relationship?"

"Let's start with baby steps. How about a date that was followed up with a second date within a reasonable time frame?"

"And when exactly would I do this; those few minutes of solace I have between my job and the kids?"

"I forgot—you're the first single mom in the history of society. The problem is, you're just too picky."

I'm picky, agreed, and I was picky long before jobs and kids. But I'd disagree that I'm *too* picky. My mother once told me that I would have to settle on a lot of things in this world, but I should never settle when it comes to love. I thought it was great advice, but I also couldn't shake the idea that she was referring to my father when she said it.

"Don't you know that Eliza is waiting for her true love to become free ... that news anchor from Channel-8, Joe Capozzi," Connie said with a laugh.

Jillian joined her laughter, "Oh yeah, I forgot about that. She's obsessed with his hands or something like that."

"Come to think of it, didn't Kirk have really big hands?" Connie said.

This conversation was not trending in my favor.

"You know what they say about men with big hands," Jillian added.

"I never said anything about the *size* of Joe Capozzi's hands," I interjected. "Just that he has really sexy hands. And I think that hand size stuff is a myth, anyway."

"It sure wasn't a myth when it came to Kirk," Jillian said with an inebriated grin. "They don't call him Big Mac for nothing."

I knew where they were going with this. Last year while playing for a team in Spain, for reasons only known to him, my ex decided to do a full nude layout in a Spanish magazine. And thanks to the Internet, one day I'll get to try to explain it to our daughters.

I needed to get off this subject ASAP, so I agreed to go talk to the guy at the bar. He seemed nice enough, a chiropractor named Don, but don't all the serial killers seem nice? At least that's what the neighbors always say after they find the bodies in his basement. That, and they kept to themselves. Come to think of it, Don was sitting at the bar alone.

We traded numbers and he mentioned possibly going out to that new Italian place in Brewster. I doubted such a dinner would actually materialize, but it was a successful trip just to get my friends off my back. When I returned the conversation turned to our kids' latest school project, and another over-scheduled weekend that included a birthday party—*it seemed like we attended one every week!* Sunday I would get a brief reprieve, as my parents planned to take the girls to see the new penguin exhibit at the Maritime Aquarium. Since none of this pertained to Jillian I noticed her starting to drift off, and then began checking her phone.

Just when it seemed that things were winding down, the fourth member of our group entered Wojo's. We turned and looked, as did everyone in the place. And the way Don the Chiropractor was ogling her, our potential date seemed to be in jeopardy.

Chapter 8

Bringing Alexis Tskitapolis into the group was a risky move on my part, and I had to go into full "Mayor mode" to convince Jillian and Connie to agree. Her family had lived down the street from mine when we were kids. She was my first friend, before she moved back to Greece when we were in elementary school. Alexis returned with her family a few years back as an adult, but both of her parents had died under tragic circumstances about a year ago and I thought she could use some dirty martinis in her life at the moment.

She made her way across the bar, her thick, curly hair appearing heavy on her head as it bounced. She wore a tight sweater and jeans, and even her curves had curves. Jillian was most the strident critic of her joining, I think because she had always been the undisputed babe of the group and didn't want to invite competition. But Alexis now ran the family restaurant business, including the well known—and near impossible to get a table at—Skita's, in Ridgefield. She provided us VIP treatment there anytime we chose, which Jillian has taken advantage of to impress some of her business clients. This of course won her over.

And it was fun to live vicariously through Alexis, which sometimes came in handy when I was having a Walter Mitty moment while attending *another* birthday party. She would frequently jet off to France with a mysterious older companion—I like her, so I won't use the term "sugar daddy"—and she'd often start a story with something along the lines of, "And then the Count flew us to Monaco in his helicopter …" I didn't know people like that really existed outside the movies.

And she normally didn't show up until at least halfway through our get-together anyway, so it wasn't like her inclusion was disrupting our routine.

Today she brought an accessory. "Who is that?" Jillian asked what we all were thinking.

"I think that might be one of those Greek gods from mythology class," Connie said.

"Does he meet your picky standards?" Jillian said to me with a sly smirk.

"I think I could fit him in between birthday parties," I said.

Alexis reached our table, and introduced the gorgeous creature on her arm as Niko.

He looked like he'd just leaped off the cover of a romance novel. And with the exception of the thick, dark stubble on his face, he very much resembled Alexis. So I first thought they might be related, but he was clutching her in a not-very-family way. Alexis referred to him as a "friend" that was visiting her from Greece. I got the idea that we had different definitions of what a friend was.

He spoke in broken English, "You no tell me, Alexis, you had such beautiful friends. Had I know, I come to America more often."

Group swoon.

Alexis informed Niko that this table was "girls only," and he willingly went to the bar and took a seat next to Don the Chiropractor. Although, if there was a vote as to whether we should make an exception this one time, I'm fairly certain it would have been unanimous.

After twenty minutes or so of us trying to get the scoop on Niko, while Alexis remained coy—only adding to our interest—Jillian looked at her watch and said, "I've got to be going. Max has a work thing tonight we have to go to."

Alexis seconded, adding that she and Niko were going to a lavish party in Manhattan tonight. Of course they were.

This left Connie and me. She invited me over to watch a movie after dinner, but I decided that if I couldn't spend the anniversary with Chris, I would spend it alone. Connie seemed to understand, and offered to take the kids off my hands for a few hours—an offer I accepted.

And when she drove off in her mini van, I was just a party of one. For someone who came into this world attached to another person solitude was an unnatural feeling for me, and even more so on this day.

Chapter 9

My father looked surprised when he opened the door.

"Hey Dad," I said, and kissed him on the cheek as I entered.

"Did we get our signals crossed? I thought you had plans tonight?"

"I did, but Chris had to travel on business to Miami, so you and Mom have been paroled from babysitting duties."

"Chris is on a business trip?"

I didn't know why he sounded surprised—Chris had been constantly on the road since she started working for Norby.

"What is it?" I asked, reading his expression.

He waved me off. "It's nothing. I'm just surprised she didn't give you more notice, being your anniversary and all."

Nice try, Dad, but that wasn't it.

"The girls are with your mother in the kitchen," he quickly changed the subject, and I followed him through the Great Room. While his response to Chris' trip was odd, everything else appeared normal. My father looked as he always did—the king of the sweater vest, his graying hair parted neatly to the side, and his skin slightly sun-kissed from his travels. He looked like he should be perpetually golfing.

The hallway that connected the Great Room to the kitchen was what we affectionately called the Dunbar Wall of Fame. It was lined with family photos and wall-hangings, and was currently dominated by pictures of the grandchildren; my two girls and my sister Karen's three boys.

Karen, five years my senior, lives with her family on a ranch in Wyoming. They come east every year around the Fourth of July. And during those visits it's mandatory to take a "stairway photo" of the kids. The photos were hung in the hallway in chronological order, and as I glanced at them on my way by, it struck me how quickly they'd all grown up.

Chris was displayed prominently on the wall as well, most of the photos from her basketball days. There were many of me with Brooke and Kelly, but my lone solo shot was from my graduation from Northwestern, dressed in purple cap and gown. A few of my wedding photos once hung here, but my father couldn't get them down soon enough after Kirk and I split—he was never a big fan.

My relationship with my father has always been a mixed bag. There are times when he's completely engaged and I feel connected to him. And then there's the other side, when he seems distant. I never noticed that side when it came to Chris—he displayed an enthusiasm for her that I've never felt. I was never jealous of it, but was often confused.

I like to know where I stand with people. With my father, I feel like I'm guessing—which one is he going to be today? It's probably why I've always had a closer connection with my mother.

And of course it wouldn't be the Dunbar Wall of Fame if it didn't include an ode to the Conjoined Kids. There was no shortage of framed newspaper clippings and magazine covers.

Some would say my parents exploited our situation, but I like to think they made the best out of a bad one—it's not like they were selling drugs or duping old ladies out of their savings. There were the books, the TV appearances, the "where are they now" anniversaries for five years, ten, fifteen ... thankfully, by the twentieth, Chris and I were off at college and unavailable.

My father made a good living as a commercial pilot. So add in what they earned off of us being conjoined, and a few wise investments, and you get this McMansion in Ridgefield where I grew up.

"Look who I found," my father exclaimed as we entered the kitchen. He had morphed into cheery-grandpa mode.

I don't know who looked more surprised to see me—my kids or my mother. I walked directly to Mom, leaned down to give her a kiss as she sat in her wheelchair.

"Happy anniversary, my sweet Eliza," she said out of the side of her mouth.

I'd just finished my first year on the job with the Cubs when I got the call about the accident. It was one of those early New England snowstorms in November, and while returning home from dinner my parents skidded off the slick road. The car was totaled, but they were both fine, "No reason for you to worry, Eliza."

But eight days later that proved to be anything but the case. My mother had suffered a vascular injury to her neck during the accident, forming a blood clot that went undetected, leading to a stroke. It left her paralyzed on one side of her body, which was why she now talked like Rocky Balboa.

I returned home to help out, fully expecting to return to Chicago in February, and resume my duties when the Cubbies headed off to spring training. But you know what they say about plans … it's been almost ten years and I'm still here. Getting pregnant was also a factor in my stay, but that's another story for another day.

"Thanks," I said, and kissed her again … just because.

"We're playing Monopoly," Kelly announced, the three of them huddled around the kitchen table.

The sight of my kids playing … and enjoying … an old school board game warmed my heart. I'd settle for anything that didn't require a screen or some form of technology! Bob Hurlbert has described me as an old soul. I'm not sure exactly what that means, but as long as it has nothing to do with sagging or wrinkles then I'm cool with it. And I think it might be connected to my love of board games.

"So who's winning?" I asked.

"Kelly's cheating," Brooke informed me.

"And she was properly penalized for her indiscretions, so I think it's best we focus on the future," my mother said. Just because her words were slow and slightly slurred didn't mean she had any less to say. And if you listened closely there were usually a couple of good nuggets of wisdom in there.

"She got evicted from Park Place and Broadway," Brooke said.

Kelly sighed theatrically. "Life just isn't fair."

My mother added, "And what lesson have we learned?"

Both girls at once, "Winners never cheat, and cheaters never win!"

More good advice from Gram. And how I wished that were actually true.

My mother had a good laugh with the girls. It was a happy moment, and as I looked down at her, hunched in her chair, with her short haircut and extra weight, I still saw the slim woman with the long flowing mane who would practically float around the room like a butterfly. The biggest compliment I ever receive is when someone says I remind them of her, or "you look so much like your mother." And even if it's unspoken, they're referring to how she once was.

The thing that's most vivid to me about pre-stroke Mom was how freely she strutted through life as if nothing bothered her. For me, each day feels like an uphill climb, but for her, there was nothing that she couldn't face. She had been to the brink and looked into the abyss, and her babies made it through.

Part of me wished that Brooke and Kelly would have gotten to see that Gram, but this one wasn't too shabby, and some kids don't ever get the chance to play Monopoly with their grandmother. So I found my happy face.

"What happened to your plans?" my mother asked in her methodical cadence.

"Chris had to go out of town unexpectedly. So we'll do it when she gets back."

I caught my father out of the corner of my eye, and once again a strange look came over his face. I wasn't sure what it was about, but I needed to get to the bottom of it.

"Sorry to break up your game, but we need to get home so I can make dinner. And let Gram and Gramp have some peace," I said.

"What are we having?" Brooke asked.

"My famous marinated flank steak … and brownies for dessert!" I sold it hard.

They didn't look enthused. "Gramp was going to order pizza."

I couldn't believe my flesh and blood would trade a homemade steak dinner for some bread and melted cheese. Actually, I could. So I continued to sell, "Then after dinner you can go over to the Marchands and go hot-tubbing."

That did the trick. Within a blink of an eye they had their coats on, ready to go. I instructed to help Gram clean up the game, but the three of them decided to leave it out so they could resume at their next get-together.

I leaned down again and gave my mother a kiss goodbye. "I love you, Mom," I said, feeling myself getting emotional.

She patted my hand. "I love you too, sweet Eliza. And don't you ever forget it."

I wouldn't.

The kids ran ahead to the car, which gave me a moment to talk to my dad alone. "What's going on with Chris? You have this weird reaction every time I bring up her name."

He paused for a long moment. "Just the business trip—I thought that something might have happened with her job."

"What do you mean?"

He appeared to be debating whether to tell me, then finally gave in, "She came over recently, very out-of-sorts, and asking to borrow money. More like demanding. I got the impression that she might be back to her drinking ways, so I refused. This set her off, and when I continued to resist she made a bunch of threats and stormed out. I figured something must have happened with her job, which was why she needed the money, but I'm relieved to hear that everything seems to be all right now. She was probably just having a bad day."

That sounded like a lot more than a bad day. And it was about as close as my father has ever come to saying anything negative about my twin sister. Even during her, to use his words, "drinking ways," my father still blamed that on Kirk being a bad influence on her.

"How did she sound to you when you spoke?" he asked.

I shrugged. "Normal, I guess."

He smiled. "Like I said, it was probably nothing."

Chapter 10

"So why did Chris have to go on a trip?" Kelly asked. They don't refer to her as Aunt Chris because my sister doesn't believe in titles.

"For work," Brooke filled her in.

"That stinks! I was going to play a new song for her on my guitar."

And finally I found some good concerning Chris' absence.

The three of us sat around the kitchen table eating our dinner of steak and brownies. Kelly had wondered why we would choose to eat the steak first and then have the brownies for dessert.

"Because all good things come to those who wait," I busted out some motherly philosophy.

Her face crinkled in thought. "Why would you wait for the good things if you can have them right now?"

She was right—life was too short to wait for the good things, and this big anniversary would only come around once, so the brownies would be the co-entrée.

After we finished, Connie came by to take them off my hands for a bit and they headed next door. I grabbed our celebratory bottle of champagne—the good stuff this year—and took it with me to the living room. I then picked up where I'd left off on the documentary video.

I fast-forwarded it to the post-surgery part. They had just brought us home, and my sister Karen wandered into the room and asked the most simple, but symbolic question, "Where is Eliza's leg?"

It marked the change in our reality, and foreshadowed the challenges ahead. The only way we had known had been altered—mostly for the good, but not without cost. Sometimes, like that moment, we can plan for these life-changing events, but more times than not they strike like a lightning bolt on a sunny day.

My mother's stroke came to mind.

With my thoughts on her, I rewound the video to the time leading up to the surgery. My parents were in the doctor's office, and Dr. Null was making it sound rather simple—"It's as if we're doing fifty minor surgeries, which each doctor has successfully performed hundreds of times. The only difference being that we will be performing them in one operation."

My mother wasn't buying it. Society might have viewed Chris and me as some sort of circus freaks, but we were her children and we weren't going to be medical guinea pigs. She made the doctor look her in the eyes and guarantee that we *both* would make it. There would be no sacrificing one of us to provide full life for the other.

I'd venture a guess that doctors don't usually make those types of guarantees, but in this case he did, and only then did she officially sign off on the surgery. And she continued to fight for us right up until the moment we were wheeled into the operating room.

As I continued to watch, it struck me how lucky Chris and I were to even be alive. Conjoined twins are the result of a very rare congenital defect, and the life span of those afflicted is usually measured in hours. Ischiopagus Tripus, the type Chris and I were born with, which connected us at the pelvis and lower breastbone, is even rarer.

We were delivered at thirty-eight weeks via C-section and weighed 13 pounds 3 ounces. We spent ten days in the neonatal intensive care unit before being brought home.

I thought back to when Brooke was born and how overwhelmed I felt the first few months. But that was nothing compared to what my parents went through. Just trying to hold us was a struggle, and they didn't exactly sell conjoined twin clothing at Baby Gap—my grandmother sewed together a couple baby gowns so that there were two openings for our heads, which became our go-to outfit. They couldn't get us to nurse and sleep at the same time, so it was a lot like living with a roommate who stayed up all hours.

But here we were over thirty years later, maybe a little battered and bruised by life, but still standing together and ready to face that next lightning bolt whenever it strikes.

Connie returned my children around ten. I tucked them in and settled in to watch Joe Capozzi deliver the local news, followed by a re-run of *The Good Wife,* while working on my bottle of champagne. I was all alone, but as I drifted off to sleep on the couch, I felt really lucky.

Chapter 11

I woke up to the sound of knocking in my head.

I pried my eyes open—it took me a moment to focus having slept in my contact lenses—and noticed the half-empty bottle on the coffee table. My head was reminding me that I sure couldn't drink the way I could back in my college days … probably a good thing. A martini with the girls and a couple of glasses of champagne would have been the warm-up act in those days.

As I pulled myself to my feet I realized that the knocking wasn't just in my head. Someone was at the front door. I slowly made my way to it, unconcerned about my appearance, figuring it was just Connie.

When I checked the peephole, there were two men in suits standing outside, both of whom I recognized. What was going on?

I swung the door open, and standing before me was the intimidatingly tall and heavily-mustached Chief Bernard Wallach, along with Tim Ruiz— the police. Their faces were serious, so I was pretty sure I hadn't won the Publisher Clearing House sweepstakes, and they weren't here to present me one of those big cardboard checks.

"If this is about the article, I haven't even finished it, so you have nothing to complain about yet," I said.

"That's not why we're here," Wallach replied in a polite but firm tone.

I looked to Tim, hoping to find some clue of what was going on, but he also had his all-business cop-face on. I thought of a possible prank involving Chris, connected to our anniversary, but Wallach wouldn't be involved in something like that.

"Is it illegal to have a pathetic Friday night at home by myself watching videos?" I tried to joke, but was unable to cut the tension.

"We're going to need you need to come with us, Eliza," Tim said.

I looked at them incredulously. "I can't just leave my kids."

"Connie Marchand has agreed to come over and watch them," Wallach said.

Whatever this was, it was no joke. "Fine, just give me a minute to throw on some clothes," I said and made my way upstairs.

I took my contacts out and put on a pair of glasses, then tied my hair into a ponytail. I kept on the sweatshirt I'd slept in, but replaced my pajama pants with a pair of jeans and heeled boots. I tossed on my favorite pea coat and I was ready to go. Where I was going was another story, and one that had me slightly worried.

As I tiptoed by the girls' room I heard Brooke's soft voice, "Is someone here?"

I stepped inside—Brooke was sitting up, wide-awake, while Kelly was still in a deep sleep. "It's Detective Ruiz. I've got to go with him … for work. Mrs. Marchand is coming over to watch you and Kelly. I shouldn't be long."

"Why would you go with a policeman for work?"

"Sometimes the police and newspaper people work together on a story. I'll be back soon." I kissed her on top of the head and got out of there before she had more questions that I didn't have answers for.

When I returned downstairs Connie had arrived, and I could tell she was as much in the dark as I was.

She forced a smile. "The things you'll do to get out of a birthday party, Eliza."

Which made me think. "How long will this take?"

Wallach shook his head. "I'm not sure."

Connie interjected, "Don't worry—I'll make sure they get to the party if you run late."

I thanked her, informed her that the birthday gifts were all wrapped and stored in the upstairs closet, then followed Wallach and Tim out of my house. I got into the backseat of the large, black Chevy Tahoe with tinted windows—the Chief's vehicle. The two men got into the front seat and Wallach drove off.

"So what's this about?" I asked, my frustration growing.

"We'll explain in a few minutes," Tim said, and I detected a shake in his voice. Not a good sign, and it was clear they wanted me alone when they told me.

I recognized the route—it was the one I took most mornings with the girls, and sure enough we soon pulled into the empty parking lot of their school. Without the usual morning chaos, it didn't even appear to be the same place. I got the idea that's why they chose it.

Tim turned back to me and I braced. If it were good news Wallach would have delivered it. That's how politicians work. And for all intents and purposes, the police chief is a political job.

"There was a break-in at your parents' home last night," Tim said. He fought to keep his tone even, but his eyes gave him away.

Visions of horror swept through my mind. "They were robbed?"

"We received a call at 1:15 this morning from a neighbor," Tim said. "They reported hearing loud voices and fighting coming from the house … and a gunshot. Followed by the sound of people running through their yard—we believe fleeing the crime scene."

I was focused on one word, and my stomach gripped. *Gunshot.* I struggled to get the words out, "Oh my God, are they alright?"

Tim's expression practically slapped me across the face—it was a look I would remember for the rest of my life. "Please no," I pleaded.

"By the time we arrived your mother was already gone. There was nothing we could do," Tim said. It looked like he felt the pain of a thousand knives stabbing him as he said it.

"What do you mean gone?" I asked, even though I knew exactly what he meant.

"Your mother is dead ... I'm so sorry, Eliza."

My world began spinning out of control. "No, that can't be," I said.

Wallach now had his chance to supply the "good" news. "Your father was shot in the abdomen. He lost a lot of blood, but paramedics were able to get him to the hospital in time."

Certainly better than the alternative, but right now I could only focus on my mother. My poor, sweet mother.

"Please open the window," I said.

When my request was met, I stuck my head out into the cool morning. I then threw up champagne and steak all over the parking lot. And I didn't stop heaving until I was completely hollow inside.

Tim handed me a roll of paper towel to clean myself up. "My mother was shot by an intruder?" I asked, but it was still not computing.

"Your mother's death appears to be a drowning, but we won't know for sure until the report from the medical examiner comes back."

"Drowning? I thought you said it happened in the house?" This didn't make sense—their pool had been closed for winter.

"We found her in a bathtub."

The image seared my mind. The thought of her being shot was bad enough, but this was a violent and cruel way to die. I felt lightheaded.

"Your father was able to give us a brief statement before being taken to the hospital," Tim continued. "He told us that three men had broken in and were demanding money. They threatened to kill your mother unless their demands were met. When he was unable to comply, they took her into the bathroom, filled the tub, and forced her into it. Your father tried to rescue her … that's when he was shot."

I just kept shaking my head, desperately trying to wake up from this nightmare. That's what this must be. The only explanation.

"I can't even begin to express how sorry I am," Tim reiterated.

Wallach added, "As you probably know, the Ridgefield police force is now under the umbrella of the Danbury PD, so I will personally see to it that whoever is behind this will be brought to justice."

My body was completely zapped of energy. I collapsed to a laying position and stared up at the roof. Wallach was still talking, but it was if I'd hit the mute button on the world. All I could think about was how much my mother had sacrificed for us, and the one damn time she needed us we couldn't help her!

I felt a burst of strength and sat up in my seat. "Has anyone called Chris?"

"We tried, but were unable to get hold of her. Same with your sister Karen," Tim said.

Karen didn't surprise me, as she basically lived off the grid. But Chris was a different story. "She's in Miami on business. Did you try her cell?"

"We did."

Maybe she didn't recognize the number—she'd recognize mine. But I also received no answer. I was about to leave a voice mail, but what exactly would I say?

I decided against it—I'd try her later when I could somehow speak coherently about what happened. As if that would ever be the case.

I worried about how Chris and Karen might hear the news. As torturous as this was, it would have been a lot worse to hear about it from the television.

"Who knows about this?" I asked.

Wallach answered, "Word is starting to trickle out—the local Connecticut media has been reporting on the home invasion, but haven't been able to confirm your mother's death, or your father's condition yet. It's just a matter of time. That's why we chose to tell you in this manner."

I nodded my thanks. But then the world began to spin again. I had nothing left to puke up, and lying down didn't work this time. I felt like my insides were on fire and I couldn't escape. I had to get out of here.

I opened the door and stepped out. I began walking as fast as I could. I had no idea where I was going, but I determined to get there. I trudged through the parking lot and then along the quiet Great Plain Road, before I felt a strong hand on my shoulder.

"Where are you going?" Tim asked.

"I need to be alone," I said and pushed away from him.

"Are you sure that's the best thing right now?"

"I'm almost thirty-two years old, I think I know what's best for me."

"Fair enough, but perhaps you'd be better off being alone somewhere warmer. You're not going to do your kids any good if you catch pneumonia."

I just kept walking.

Tim grabbed me and pulled me back. This time I buried my head in his chest and sobbed.

"Let me know what we can do for you, Eliza. Just name it and I'll make sure it happens."

I pulled away and wiped the cold tears from my face. "I need to go to the house. I need to see where my mother died."

Chapter 12

The news trucks were parked along the street I'd grown up on.

The story might not have gone national yet, but I wasn't naïve enough to think it didn't have legs. The murder of a woman in upper-class Ridgefield where such things were not supposed to happen, would be a huge story in itself. Add to it my family's local celebrity due to the conjoined twins saga and Chris' basketball exploits, and you had a salacious blockbuster on your hands.

Wallach drove the Tahoe into my parents' driveway. He and Tim then helped me out of the vehicle and shielded me from the photographers as we entered through the garage.

The house was full of police collecting evidence, so we could only walk in certain areas. I expected the place to appear as if it had been burglarized. A couch tipped over or maybe some broken glass. But it looked the way it always did.

Tim met up with a couple of colleagues to get an update; one being the woman from Tim's office yesterday, Annie Sampson. Both offered me condolences.

I tried to present an image of strength. I wasn't a victim that needed to be treated like fine china. I could assist them in their investigation.

"There was no forced entry," Tim said. "So it was likely that your parents knew the person or persons. Our initial guess is they came to the door and were let in."

That didn't sound right. "You said it was after midnight—by that time they would usually be in bed. They kept a steady routine, falling asleep after the local news. So it would be abnormal for a neighbor or a friend to drop by at that hour."

The police walked me through the house—they asked me to be on the lookout for anything that seemed out of place. I was holding it together pretty well—I was numb at this point—until I came to the kitchen and saw the box from the Monopoly game still sitting on the table.

I gulped back tears. The idea that Brooke and Kelly would never play with their Gram again was like a flaming spear through the heart. How could I possibly tell them? To see the looks on their faces—the innocence being drained from them. I bent over in pain.

Tim put his arm around me. "Maybe we should go."

"No—I'm fine," I lied. I steadied myself and viewed the room. "Everything appears as it was when I left last night."

"What time did you leave?" Officer Annie asked.

"I picked up my kids around six. My parents were going to baby-sit them last night, but my plans fell through."

"And what were those plans?" she followed up.

"It was the anniversary ... of me and my sister being separated."

"Separated?"

"They were conjoined twins," Tim filled in.

Annie must be new to these parts, because her look said *for real?"*

"Chris and I celebrate it every year, but she had to go away on business this year to Miami."

"Being that it was the anniversary, do you think there could be a connection?" Tim asked.

I hadn't thought about that. "We did attract some weirdos when we were kids. I remember this one crazy woman who thought we had been part of God's plan to bring people together, and separating us was the work of the devil. So she wanted to put Chris and me back together again."

I had no idea how she planned to do this—*glue? Velcro?* It was probably best that I didn't know.

"Do you remember her name?" Officer Annie asked.

"Margaret Burns, but she's been dead for years. I think she killed herself in whatever institution she ended up in."

I doubted there was a connection. Nor did I think this was related to the Conjoined Kids—that business had been dead for years. The only reason the *Danbury Ledger* ran the article on the thirty-year anniversary last year was because I worked there.

We continued to walk through the house. "What about the security system?" Annie asked.

"With my father away so much for his job, and my mother being vulnerable because of her health, security was always important to them. They had a high-level system put in some years back, but I'm not familiar with the details."

"We would like to look at the security video. We can get a warrant, but that will take time, and every second counts when it comes to catching whoever did this, so I'm asking your permission."

"That's fine by me, but I'm not sure I have a say in something like that."

"You actually do—you have power of attorney if your parents ever become incapacitated, or die."

This was news to me. "In that case, go ahead. If you need me to sign something …"

"Thank you—we appreciate your cooperation. Did your father own a gun?"

Her question caught me off guard. "Not that I know of, but like I said, security was very important to him and my mother, so it wouldn't shock me if he did."

As Annie continued to pepper me with questions, I was doing my own investigation in my head. Someone showed up after midnight. Perhaps someone they knew. Although, when the police say "no forced entry" that can be a little vague. It just meant they didn't break down the door or smash open a window. It could have been someone claiming to have car issues and asking to use their phone, and when my father let him in the person pulled a gun. So it wasn't necessarily someone they knew.

I was led into the hallway that connected the living room and kitchen—the Dunbar Wall of Fame. The photos had been taken down, and the safe hidden behind them was open.

"Do you know what might have been inside it?" Tim asked, pointing at the empty safe.

"Usually just small amounts of cash and fake jewelry. Nothing overly valuable," I said.

I once asked my father why he didn't keep valuables in the hallway safe, and he told me that it was just a diversion. So if our house was ever burglarized the robbers would think they cleaned out the safe, but the true valuables were in the "real" safe in a different part of the house.

When I asked where the real safe was, he refused to tell me. With a smile on his face, he'd say, "If I told you, Eliza, then where would we hide all your Christmas gifts?"

It didn't stop me from searching, but I never found it. Did the intruder have knowledge of it? That would mean they had a connection to my parents. Not random.

Tim nodded. "When we spoke to your father at the scene, before he fell unconscious, he said there was nothing in the safe. When he opened it, proving so, the attackers grew incensed."

I shrugged. "I'd like to be able to shed some light on that, but I have no idea," I said, and took note that he didn't mention another safe.

Tim could sense my pain was boiling over. "You've been a big help, Eliza. Now I think we should get you home."

I wasn't going anywhere just yet. "I need to see the bathtub."

The police looked at each other, before Tim said, "The investigators are in there right now."

"I need to see where my mother was murdered."

The firmness of my voice left no doubt. I wasn't asking.

But I was willing to compromise. I wouldn't go in, and potentially contaminate the investigation—I would view it from the doorway. When I looked inside the bathroom, one of the investigators was joking to his partner that if you're going to drown, my parents' natural stone, luxury tub was the way to go.

Tim's horrified expression said he wanted to add to the body count. He pulled the officers off to the side and had heated words with them.

I was too sick to be offended. I stood in the doorway, trying to imagine how things unfolded last night. The tub was still full of water and I couldn't help but to visualize my mother struggling for her life.

There was blood on the floor—the first sign I'd seen of a brutal crime. There was also two markings. A large one that I assumed represented where my father was found, along with a smaller outline next to it. I asked Tim, "What does that indicate?"

"The gun. The one that was used to shoot your father was left behind."

My journalist instincts kicked in. "That makes no sense. Why would they leave it behind?"

"They may have panicked. Perhaps the plan was to threaten your parents, not kill them. But when your father forced the action, and they shot him, they made a run for it." He pointed at the open window that was the likely escape hatch. "In their haste, they forgot the gun."

If that were the case, then these guys were amateurs. That wouldn't add up with the rest of what I'd seen—the break-in, the kill, and the escape … it seemed clinical. Professional.

I started feeling wobbly again and grabbed on to the sides of the doorframe. "I'm going to take you home," Tim said.

"I need to go to the hospital," I countered.

"Your father is unconscious. Why don't you get some rest and then see him later? Maybe he'll be awake by then."

"Not him—I need to see my mother."

"Your mother?"

"My mother needs me right now."

Chapter 13

I waited in the backseat of the Tahoe.

The delay was the result of Wallach holding an impromptu press conference with the reporters in front of the house.

As he'd mentioned, the Danbury PD was now in charge of policing Ridgefield. It was one of those great plans *on paper.* The small town could shed the expense, while adding more manpower from the neighboring city. And Danbury would take a nice share of large property taxes from Ridgefield's seven-figure homes, with very little increase to their crime docket. I doubt they ever imagined their highest profile murder in years would take place there.

While this was going on, I attempted to reach my sister. *C'mon, Chris, answer ... I need you right now!* But the call again went to voice mail. This time I left a brief, desperate message, "Call me. It's urgent."

Wallach eventually returned and we drove away. He dropped us off at the police station, before heading off to important business—a weekend ski trip in Vermont. Seriously.

At the station we switched to Tim's car, a 1969 Camaro that he'd restored back when we were teenagers. Tim had always been a "car guy," who grew excited at the mere mention of carburetors and front-end alignment, while I mainly see them as a way to get from here to there.

"You still have the Camaro?" I asked, anything to change the subject.

He looked confused; as if getting rid of his pride and joy was ever an option. "Yeah, I only bring her out on weekends—I had no idea today would be anything but a typical Saturday."

Preaching to the choir.

We drove to Danbury Hospital.

"Your father already identified her body at the scene. You don't have to do this," Tim cautioned.

"Yes I do," I said, and I think he understood.

We were met in the hospital morgue by a medical examiner, an older man named Dr. Edwin Morris. He explained that my mother's body would be here only temporarily before being shipped to Hartford, where the Connecticut State Medical Examiner would perform an autopsy. This was going to be a high profile case and I could tell no detail would be overlooked. Everything would be by the book.

"How long will this process take?" I asked.

"It's been fast-tracked so I would expect that it to be completed by early next week. Toxicology reports might take longer, but you will have a good idea of the cause of death by then."

"And you believe that she drowned?"

"She definitely drowned. The question is: was she forced under the water? My initial report didn't find any wounds or signs of a struggle."

It was actually comforting news—the possibility she wasn't awake during her final moments. Because the alternative was horrifying.

When I requested to see her, Dr. Morris suggested that it might be better for me to view photos of her body instead, but I was determined.

And I was still hoping for a miracle. Like in those TV dramas where they pull the sheet off the corpse and the character is overcome with relief, as it isn't their loved one. "It's not her!" they exclaim, cue the dramatic music.

But there would be no such moment here. It was my mother, Sarah Dunbar, and she was dead. She looked peaceful, like she was enjoying an afternoon nap. I hoped that one day I could take some solace in that. This would not be that day.

They gave me a moment to be alone with her, and I grabbed her cold hand.

I knew it was selfish of me to want her back. She'd sacrificed everything for us, and had been trapped in her failing body for almost a decade. She was free now.

I couldn't get my mind around the idea that she wouldn't be there anymore. She had been at almost every big moment of my life. From our famous surgery to my first lost tooth to the first day she put me on a bus to school. I remember searching the crowd at my college graduation until I found her—as if it wasn't real until I did—and the same at my wedding, which she put on her best smile, even though she believed I was making a mistake.

I thought of her with the girls—it seemed like yesterday she was holding Brooke in this very hospital. And she and Kelly had that bond of fellow free spirits. They so got each other. I should have been be happy for the time they were able to spend together, and how it would help shape their futures, but right now all I could think about was what had been taken away. And I was angry.

I owed everything to this woman. But that's not to say we never had our typical mother/daughter tiffs and fights, especially during my teenage years. Including her many "suggestions" about my choice of clothing, hairstyles, and boyfriends. I also carried resentment in those days about the Conjoined Kids publicity, which made it a constant struggle to find my own identity. But I realized now, if I hadn't already, that it wasn't about the attention or the money for her—it was about celebrating us. To show the world how proud she was of Chris and me. And it came out of the guilt she felt about our condition, which I couldn't fully understand until I had children of my own.

My phone rang. Wouldn't it be so Chris to call at this exact moment, I thought. But when I checked the number it wasn't her, or Karen. It was a reporter from Channel-3 News seeking a quote from me about the murder. *I'll give you a quote ...*

I returned my attention to my mother. I didn't tell her that I would dedicate my life to finding out who did this to her, and get her justice. Because she would not have approved. She would have thought it to be a waste of precious time. So instead I promised to make any and every sacrifice for my children, just as she had for us. And to be strong for them in that moment when called upon, just as she had been for us.

For the second time today I felt the hand of Tim Ruiz on the back of my shoulder. "What do you say we get out of here?"

I nodded through tears. "I don't think I can pull myself away," I said, feeling my body going limp.

"Just lean on me, Eliza. I'm here for you."

And I did.

Chapter 14

I stood in my father's room on the seventh floor, in the Critical Care Unit. He was hooked up to tubes and a ventilator—the only sound was the beeping of the machines monitoring his vital signs.

He looked so old and vulnerable as he lay in the hospital bed—two things that I'd never associated with my father. I grabbed his hand and I took solace in its warmth.

"I can't lose you both," I whispered. "What will the girls do without their Gramp? Who will go to Grandparents Day at their school next month?"

They had never missed one. In fact, I had them penciled in for all the girls' big life events. Their graduations. And weddings. Doting over their first great-grandchild.

I was about to ask him what happened—not that he could answer—when a nurse came in to check the bandages on his abdomen.

"That's good what you were telling him—he needs a reason to keep up the fight," she said, as she worked on the bandages. "He lost a lot last night, and sometimes when you lose a lot you forget what you still have."

She left with a smile for me, and was soon replaced by a Dr. Kendall. At this point I was beyond bedside manner and hopeful talk. *Give it to me straight, Doc.*

Dr. Kendall spoke like a med school professor, explaining that they performed an exploratory laparotomy on my father last night. He'd suffered severe abdominal trauma and lost a lot of blood, but thankfully the bullet missed all the vital organs.

"What's his prognosis?" I asked.

"I'd give him a better than 50/50 shot, which is far greater than when they wheeled him in last night. He's not a young man, and it doesn't mean there won't be complications along the way, but he's one of the lucky ones."

"That said, he has a long road ahead," he cautioned.

We all did, but I thought it would be much longer if he didn't walk out of here. The daughter in me feared losing both my parents, while the journalist couldn't help but to think that if he didn't make it, the answers to what happened last night would die with him.

Chapter 15

Tim met me outside my father's room with a steaming cup of coffee.

"How is he?" he asked.

"The doctor was cautiously optimistic."

"That's good news," he said, but something was distracting him. "Can we go somewhere and talk?"

I didn't like the sound of that, but agreed, "Yeah, sure, of course."

He took me down the hallway until we found an empty room. He shut the door behind us and forced a smile at me.

"I was just thinking about those car rides to basketball camp with your family. The thing I most remember is your mother. She's what kept us all from killing each other. Got us all to sing."

Before the stroke my mother loved to sing, anytime, anywhere. And she was able to convince others to sing along with her. Kind of like that old Coke commercial.

Tim began to softly sing one of her favorites, taking me back in time. "This land is your land, this land is my land, from California to New York Island …"

"You must have thought we were insane."

"The opposite. I was always jealous of the Dunbars and how tight you were. I know we haven't been as close as we once were, Eliza, but your family still holds a big place in my heart, and I'm going to get whoever did this to her."

"I trust that you will," I said. "You meant a lot to her too. She always asked about you."

He nodded. I could tell that mattered to him. "But I just need you to know that I have to be a police officer now, more so than a friend."

"I understand—I wouldn't expect anything different."

I had the feeling that a line in the sand was about to be drawn, and that I wasn't going to like it.

"The gun they found at the scene—the one that shot your father—was registered to Nathan Dunbar."

So that's why Officer Annie was asking me about whether my father owned a gun.

"It changes things … how we look at the case," Tim continued.

"How so?"

"Just that it creates many questions. And since his prognosis has been upgraded, hopefully he can answer them when he wakes and put any suspicion to rest."

Suspicion? Only one shot was fired and he was the one who was hit. He was the victim … unless Tim thinks …

"What was their relationship like … your parents?" he asked, as if he was reading my mind.

"You know them."

"I did, but that was a long time ago. People change, relationships change," he said, holding a hard gaze on me.

I let out a deep breath; reminded that my father never looked at my mother the same way in recent years. "It's been different since my mother's health issues. It wasn't easy for them. It was like starting over—and I don't deny there was strain at times. But you can't possibly think he would do this to her. And then what? Shoot himself to back up his story?"

"I didn't say that. I'm just covering all possibilities, Eliza, no matter how unlikely—if you feel uncomfortable with my involvement I can request that someone else be put on the case."

That was the last thing I wanted. "I'm sorry—it's just been a really crappy day," I said, feeling my tears ready to erupt again.

"I was over there last night—there's no way the people I saw would harm each other. Not to mention, the neighbors heard people leaving the house."

"We haven't been able to confirm who made that call. It came from a burner phone traced to New Jersey. That doesn't sound like the type of phone one of your neighbors would use."

My frustration grew. "So now my father made that call himself, and then went with the brilliant plan of hiding the phone, but not the gun? All while being badly wounded? C'mon, Tim."

"There are a few other things about your father."

I stiffened, not liking where this was headed.

"Did you know he's been having financial difficulties?"

"I wasn't aware, no."

"Investments gone bad, behind with creditors. Bankruptcy a possibility."

"And my mother's health issues are a financial burden. So since this is turning into a bad movie of the week, let me guess, he just took out a life insurance policy on her?"

"They recently cashed in on their policy, looking to pay off debts. That's actually good news."

"Best I've heard all day."

"There's something else about your father."

I again braced.

"I want to caution that this is just speculation, and I have no evidence to back it up, but the word on the street is that he's been seeing someone."

"As in another woman?"

He nodded somberly.

This news didn't shock me as much as it should have. I wanted to give a strong denial and vouch that he would never even consider cheating on my mother, but I couldn't.

That didn't mean I wasn't hurt, which brought out my defensiveness. "Anything else? Is he behind the JFK assassination? 9/11?"

"Eliza, I'm not accusing him of anything. But if something was going on it will come out at some point, and the press will have a field day with it. The best thing that can happen is that he wakes up and puts all this speculation to rest. So let's just hope and pray that happens sooner rather than later."

My leg grew wobbly once more, and I grabbed hold of Detective Ruiz. And when I did, he turned back into Tim. I again buried my face into his chest. But this time I couldn't find the tears.

Chapter 16

It was late afternoon when Tim dropped me back at my house.

I walked inside, and the first thing I saw was the champagne bottle from last night. It made me think of our big 31st anniversary and how much Chris and I used to look forward to it. Would we have thought about it with such enthusiasm if we knew what would happen the following day? Not a chance. Another reminder that you shouldn't waste time thinking too far into the future, because you never know what's lurking around the next corner. Robin Williams tried to teach us that in *Dead Poet's Society*—carpe diem—but we didn't listen.

I tried Chris one more time, and when I was sent to voice mail I let out all my frustrations in one primal scream.

Where the hell are you, Chris!?

I wanted to curl up in my bed and threaten to never come out of my room, but I'd given up that right once I chose to become a mother. So I marched out of the house and across the street, prepared for my toughest test yet.

Connie greeted me with a warm hug. Word spreads quickly in a place like this. "I'm so sorry, sweetie."

"Do they know?" I asked, picturing some loudmouth parent spouting off at the birthday party, unaware that Brooke and Kelly were there.

"No—we've been keeping them busy. First the party, and now they're with my boys, playing street hockey."

That was good, in the sense that I wanted them to hear it from me. But now I had to find the best way to tell them.

A Mercedes SUV pulled into Connie's driveway and Jillian got out. She rushed inside the house. "Please tell me this is a bad dream," she said, but she recognized the reality in my eyes.

We embraced. "I came as soon as I heard—I didn't know what else to do so I brought you this."

It was dinner from our favorite Korean restaurant in Westport, HJ Park's. It felt like the nicest gift I'd ever received.

Connie called the kids in. Mine were less than thrilled to be pulled out of their game, but the sight and smell of HJ Park's lessened the blow. I walked them home and we took a seat on the couch. "I have something important to tell you before we eat," I said, my voice shaking.

They sensed something was wrong, and Brooke asked, "Are you alright, Mom?"

"Whenever I'm with you two I am," I said and squished them with a hug, whether they were "cool with it" or not.

I've always preached honesty and that would be my approach here. Of course, as we get older the truth becomes more complicated, so I left out parts like drowning, guns, financial issues, and possible affairs.

Brooke always connected with the emotions of the room and she began to tremble. She understood that she wouldn't see her grandmother alive again.

Kelly had always found a way to get what she wanted. She didn't yet believe in limitations. We would find a way to get Gram back because that's what she wanted, and she wouldn't be deterred.

They had many questions—they're my daughters, of course they did!

How did she die? I went with that she had an accident in the bathtub and Gramp got hurt trying to help her. Vague, but not a complete fabrication.

"You can die in the bathtub?" Kelly asked, and I was pretty sure she'd taken her last bath.

"Nothing will happen to you, honey. It was just that it was her time to go to heaven and be one of God's angels. It could have happened anywhere."

A nice comeback, I thought, until Brooke asked, "How do you know she's in heaven?"

With all the money spent on Catholic school you would think they would have covered that one.

I didn't have an answer, but luckily Kelly did, "If Gram wouldn't get into heaven, then who would? She's like the best person ever!"

She wasn't going to get an argument from me.

Now to the lightning round. Who is going to play Monopoly with us now? *I am always available!* Are you going to die, Mommy? *Not for a very, very long time!* If you die, Mommy, would we get to live with Daddy? *Not if you want me to ever rest in peace!* Will Gram have to use her wheelchair in heaven? *That's the great thing about heaven, not only will she not need her chair, but she will be able to fly.* They thought that one was pretty cool.

Later that evening Karen called. Her questions always had a way of getting right to the heart of the matter, and this time would be no different. "How could this happen?"

That one I had no answer for. We discussed Dad's condition, and then we compared the talks we had with our kids. Her boys seemed to take it okay—they have been around animals since they were born, so they had a better understanding of death.

She offered to be on the next plane out, but there was really nothing she could do until Mom's body was released and we could make plans for the funeral. I agreed to keep her informed, and we could go from there.

The topic then turned to Chris.

"You haven't heard from her?" Karen asked, sounding perplexed.

"I talked to her yesterday morning—she was in Miami on business. But I haven't been able to get hold of her today."

"She's probably been in transit and hasn't got the messages," Karen said, but didn't sound convinced.

A terrible thought flew into my mind. Thinking back to Tim's question about the anniversary date possibly being connected … what if this was an act against our entire family? Not just our parents. Perhaps Chris was also in danger.

I kept my thoughts to myself, but said to Karen, "Just make sure your family is safe." I think she thought I meant in general terms.

She chuckled. "If anyone tried to break in here the critters would get them, and if they made it past them, Trent is real good with a shotgun."

"Did you know Dad owned a gun?"

She thought about it. "No, but he did ask Trent a lot of questions on the subject last summer when we were visiting. Dad mentioned that he didn't feel comfortable with Mom being alone when he was away."

The irony of that statement hung over us for a long moment.

After we ended the call I made my way upstairs. I peeked in the girls' room, but stayed out of sight. In a few years this would be considered invading their privacy and I was determined not to be one of those mothers.

They were sitting on Brooke's bed, surrounded by their favorite stuffed animals. They weren't crying, or scared, or freaked out. They were just talking to each other about Gram, and all the fun things they did together. And how they were going to miss her. My presence was not needed.

I returned downstairs and called Bob Hurlbert, to ask him if I could get a story in by deadline for the Sunday edition. He told me he'd save a spot on the front page, and ended the call with, "Hang in there, kid." It was about as sentimental as he got.

So I sat at my laptop and wrote the most important story of my life. A retrospective on the life of Sarah Dunbar. My father was the breadwinner, Karen was the firstborn, and the Conjoined Kids got all the publicity. In all of this, my mother was the overlooked one. But she was the one that held everything together, and without her around, I worried things might get pulled apart.

Chapter 17

The sun did come out tomorrow. And I wasn't sure how I felt about that.

The cold morning air had a sharp bite to it, but a strong sun brightened it.

I had arrived at the Danbury Catholic High track decked out in my Spandex running suit, to meet Beef for our cardio workout. But the man who considered five minutes early being late was nowhere to be found.

After leaving him a few *Where the hell are ya?* messages, he finally showed up at 8:30, and he didn't look thrilled about it.

"I was under the impression that our session was canceled," he said.

"I never canceled it."

He held up a newspaper and pushed it toward my face. "Then maybe you should start reading your own articles. Now go home."

I stared at the picture of my mother on the front page—a stock photo from years ago at a signing for one of the Conjoined Kids books. Bob wrote the nuts-and-bolts news story himself. Next to it was my retrospective on the life of my mother.

As if they could sense I needed them, the Little Macs came running toward us—they had been kicking around a ball on the football field that the track encircles. Brooke ran ahead, long-legged and athletic like her father. But Kelly was able to stay close behind, and had that determined look on her face that said she wouldn't be denied.

They weren't in a hurry to see me, or Beef. Their interest was in Boss, Beef's pit bull. The dog looked just as excited to see them. It was a true love fest. I've always been amazed how kids can put things into boxes—they were deeply saddened by the loss of their Gram, but it didn't consume them or keep them from living.

"Why don't you three go play—your Mom and I need to get to work," Beef said, and the kids ran with Boss out onto the field.

I turned to him and said, "There's nothing I can do except be sad. I need to keep a sense of normalcy for the kids."

"This isn't about the kids. And it sure as hell ain't normal."

"I just need to be a reporter right now, not a daughter, okay?"

Because if I was, I would be curled up on the floor in a puddle of my own tears.

"Go home."

"I pay you to be my trainer, not my therapist," I said.

He let out a frustrated sigh—he'd never won an argument with me in eighteen years, and he had no shot today. "Just remember that you asked for it," was all he said.

I rode my hand-cycle around the track, while Beef jogged beside me, barking at me like a drill-sergeant. My bike had two rear wheels and a steerable front wheel, powered by hand cranks. Sort of like an overgrown tricycle. It was a Lean Steer type, which allowed me to shift my body weight when leaning into a turn, and took a lot of practice to master. I can run on my prosthetic when need be, but the hand-cycle allows me to get a good workout without adding undo pressure to my leg. When you only have one you need to take extra good care of it.

No words were spoken during our first loop around the track. Just a lot of huffing and puffing. I tried to keep my focus on the steering and cranking, but my attention kept going to Brooke and Kelly, who ran freely around the field with Boss. Their laughter spurred me on.

"She was a great lady," Beef finally said, as we began our second loop.

"The best."

"So have you heard from Chris?"

"I left messages, but she hasn't called me back."

Beef looked confused. "I thought you two had some conjoined-twins power. Like if one of you whispered in the Himalayas the other would hear it on the other side of the world … or some shit like that."

"I wish—it would sure save me on my phone plan."

"Knowing Chris, she just needs to get things right in her head before she faces you. She can go inward like that."

She could, and that was my hope as well. The theory that she was traveling and hadn't received the news was no longer viable. The story had hit the national news by now.

"So have you heard anything?" I asked.

He shook his head, but I wasn't buying it.

"I know you have police sources, Beef. So you know all about my father's financial problems, and the gun … and the possible girlfriend. I'm a big girl—I can handle the truth."

"Are you really asking me if I think your father killed your mother because she was a financial burden, and then planned to run off with his lover? And shot himself to make it look like there was a break-in?"

"That's exactly what I'm asking."

"He did seem like the type."

My head almost exploded. "You think my father was the *type* that would kill his wife?"

"I thought you wanted it straight."

"On second thought, maybe I could use a little chaser."

"I don't know if he was capable of killing your mother, or anyone for that matter. But he's one of those dudes who would be your best friend when he was getting something out of it, and then toss you out when he no longer needed you. When I was helping Chris win those basketball games … and getting noticed by those college recruiters … he was my best bud. But once basketball ended, and Chris was on her way, it was like I didn't exist."

"So you think it's possible that …?"

"No chance he killed her," he cut me off.

"But you just said …"

"I know what I said, but there's no way anyone who helped create such a fine woman like Eliza Dunbar could do something so heinous."

"That's sweet, Beef, thanks."

"That's what they all say, until they realize I charge extra for the mushy stuff."

Beef has always been a savvy judge of people, and brutally honest, so it was a good sign that he didn't think my father could have been behind this … not that it ever made sense. But that didn't mean I didn't have other questions.

"Whatever my father's financial situation was, or the results of the ballistics tests on the gun, it's going to come out. It's out of our hands. But I need to know who this woman is … the one he's supposedly seeing."

His face creased. "You really want to know? Or you want me to confirm nothing's going on to make you feel better?"

"What I want and what I need, are two very different things," I said, looking out at my children.

Beef nodded astutely. "If that's what you need, then what do you want?"

"What I want is a time-machine that will take me back to before any of this happened."

"Why does everybody always want to go back in time? Just gonna go through the same shit twice."

"Or get it right the second time."

"You might not like the truth."

"I rarely do, but I believe in it. Do the police think my father is involved in some way?"

"They don't know what to think. But the only prints they found in the house were from your family. Your parents, you, Chris. So if it was someone from the outside, then they were pros."

"Leaving the gun behind wouldn't be consistent with a professional hit."

"Unless they were looking to frame your father for it."

"And why would they want to do that?"

"No idea."

One thing that was clear was the importance of the phone call. Did someone really hear the intruders running away from the house? "I need to know who made that 911 call. Was it one of the neighbors like they claimed?"

"I'll do my best, but Ridgefield isn't really my home turf."

"This is my mother we're talking about, Beef."

I could tell he understood. "Consider it done," he said, and then retook his drill instructor position, "Now stop yapping, and start cranking, or I'm going to make your life a living hell!"

Too late.

Chapter 18

I took the girls to Luke & Jack's, who besides their super duper coffee make an exquisite grease-soaked breakfast sandwich. I didn't know if I was defeating the purpose or balancing things out, when it came to my morning workout.

When I asked them what they wanted to do today, their answer was to get a dog like Boss. It wasn't the first time I'd heard the request, and it was usually a non-starter, but I was in a vulnerable state at the moment and might have agreed to getting them ten pit bulls, a horse, and a flock of sheep. But I found surprising strength and held firm.

I asked again, and this time they said, "We want to visit Gramp!"

I thought of the beeping machines and the tubes. I tried to discourage it, "He's going to be sleeping all day, so you won't be able to talk. Why don't we wait until next week when he feels better?"

But then I wondered—*what if there is no next week?* And I deprived them of seeing him for the last time.

I began to reconsider, but I don't know if it mattered anyway, because they weren't taking no for an answer. I like to think they got their stubbornness from their father, but their resourcefulness from me.

The hospital it would be. And besides, Gramp could use the good vibes the Little Macs would bring. He'd had a tough couple of days with more on the way.

We stopped home to change. Kelly suggested, "Maybe I can play my guitar for him. That could wake him up."

It would probably wake up Rip Van Winkle. This request was not hard to fight off, and I quickly put the kibosh on it.

While I was changing, the girls gathered a couple of small model airplanes they had made with Gramp, and decided that they would bring them to decorate his room. Along with a framed photo of Gram, because "he probably really misses her *a lot*."

We all do.

As we made our way through the halls of the hospital I thought of my mother. Was she still on that cold slab in the basement, or had she been moved to Hartford? I tried to tell myself that she was no longer in that body, and was off flapping her angel wings like nobody was watching, but it was hard for me to disconnect her from the body that once trapped her.

My father looked just as bad as he had the previous day. According to Dr. Kendall there was no change in his condition. But he cautioned me to be patient, and that it was a good sign that he hadn't taken any downswings or dealt with any infection, which was a common problem in these type of wounds.

When I returned my attention to the girls, Kelly wondered, "If Gramp doesn't wake up, who's going to take us to the Aquarium today?"

"What?" I asked.

"We were supposed to go to the Maritime Aquarium today with Gram and Gramp to see the penguin exhibit, remember?" Brooke added.

I'd forgotten about that. Understandably so, I'd like to think. The answer was that I would. As my mother once told me: life goes on, and it's a mother's job to make sure it does.

So we said our goodbyes to the unconscious Gramp and left the hospital. We had just passed the mall, and were about to pick up Route-7 toward Norwalk, when I heard the sirens behind us.

Chapter 19

I watched in the rear-view mirror as Tim Ruiz stepped out of the police car and walked toward us.

I rolled down my window. "Was I breaking the law?"

"I'm not here on business—just making sure you're okay."

"I'm hanging in there, thank you."

"How about your father?"

"He's the same—if you're wondering if he's awakened so you can grill him, I'm sure the hospital will keep you informed."

"I also wanted to let you know that we assigned an armed guard on his floor. We don't believe he's in any imminent danger, but until we rule it out, better safe than sorry."

"And you needed to pull me over to tell me this?"

He'd made it clear he was going to be a policeman first when it came to this case, so that's the way I would treat it.

He was getting the hint. "I'm sorry, Eliza, I obviously miscalculated, and I apologize. Have a good day."

As he took a step away from my vehicle, I blew out a heavy breath. "I'm sorry, Tim, I didn't mean to be like that. Do you remember our meeting Friday morning when you wished me a good weekend? Well, it hasn't exactly been the best."

He stopped. "It's been bad for all of us, but I'm sure that doesn't compare to what your family is dealing with. How did Chris take the news?"

"I don't know—I haven't heard back from her."

His expression turned quizzical. "Is that normal ... to not hear from her when she goes on a business trip?"

"I don't know what normal is anymore."

He nodded with understanding. "Well, I've taken up too much of your time. I'll let you go ... wherever you're headed."

"We're going to the Maritime Aquarium!" Brooke spoke up from the backseat, excitement in her voice.

Tim smiled at her. "I love the Aquarium. That sounds like a fun day."

Kelly looked to me. "Can Detective Ruiz come with us, Mom?"

"Detective Ruiz is busy keeping Danbury safe, sweetie," I said.

"Maybe next time," Tim added.

"I'm going to hold you to that," Kelly said.

He smiled. "I don't doubt you for a second."

We spent the afternoon in Norwalk at the Maritime Aquarium. The penguins were a hit with the girls, and we visited some of their old favorites like the otters, jellyfish, and loggerhead turtles. We also viewed an IMAX movie on the humpback whale. It was good to take our minds off of reality for a few hours.

Before we returned home, we made a stop at nearby Calf Pasture Beach. There's something about a cold, windy day at the beach that provided me calm, and if ever I needed that it was this day.

The girls asked me for quarters, which they then sent into Long Island Sound with passionate but uncoordinated throws. They must have missed my lecture on valuing money.

"What are you doing? I asked.

"People throw quarters into the fountain at the mall for good luck," Brooke said.

"Throwing them into the ocean is like triple good luck," Kelly added.

"But you have to make a wish first," Brooke said.

So I emptied the change in my purse and we tossed it into the rough seas. We made wishes for Gramp to be better and for Gram to be having fun in heaven. If I haven't mentioned it—I love these kids!

The skies turned dark as we turned into our driveway back in Danbury. Home sweet home, in what turned out to be the best possible day I could have expected under the circumstances.

But then I saw the headlights of the van pulling in behind us.

Chapter 20

This is it.

That was my first thought when the van came to a stop behind us. We were trapped. Whoever had come for my parents—and possibly Chris—were now going to finish off the rest of the Dunbar family.

But then I recognized the woman getting out of the van, and let out the biggest sigh of relief ever. My imagination was really running rampant.

Alexis looked ready for a magazine cover, even though she was wearing a pair of overalls and her thick dark curls were tied up. It appeared she'd just come from a long day working at the restaurant.

"I hope I didn't scare you, driving behind you like that," she said.

"Not at all," I said with a dismissive wave, but my shaking hands likely gave me away.

She wrapped her arms around me. "I just heard—I can't believe it."

"Thank you," I replied, still feeling awkward with the condolences.

"I figured that you're going to be busy the next week with the arrangements and all … I know with my mother …"

Her words trailed off, but she gathered herself, "Anyway, we have so much leftover food each night at the restaurant that I thought I'd bring it to you. Cooking is the last thing you're going to have time for."

The girls joined us. "You remember Alexis, right? We ate at her restaurant for Brooke's birthday."

"The opa place?" Kelly said.

It was tradition at Skita's for everyone to shout "opa!" when the saganaki cheese is flambeed at the table, right before the flames are extinguished with a squeeze of fresh lemon juice. No surprise, my girls enjoyed this much more than the meal.

They helped carry in the boxes of food, which might have been enough to feed a small village. "You didn't have to do this," I said guiltily.

"I wanted to. And as you know, my new quest is to make sure none of the food goes to waste."

She was planning on setting up a company that would efficiently get the extras from local restaurants to soup kitchens and homeless shelters, and I had agreed to do an article on it to get them publicity.

We unloaded the boxes on the kitchen counter—souvlaki, gyros, and baklava.

"Looks like we know what we're having for dinner, girls," I commented.

"Opa!" they replied.

They went upstairs to wash up, while Alexis and I took a seat on the couch. Many people over the coming days and weeks would do their best to try to understand what I was going through, but Alexis understood the pain and loss better than anyone.

After her family returned from Greece a few years back, they had a lot of success re-opening Skita's and their other restaurants. When I attended the grand re-opening, I remember seeing her mother, Macaela, for the first time since their return. She was still a striking figure, but she seemed different. I couldn't put my finger on it, but since I hadn't seen her since I was Brooke's age, it was quite possible that I didn't have as good of a handle on her as I thought I did. Time has a way of skewering our memories to make things properly fit.

That was the last time I saw her. Just over a year ago, they found her in the barn of a large farm they own in Roxbury. She had hung herself.

The loss hit her father hard. And two months later, he sailed his boat out into Long Island Sound with no plans to return. Within a matter of months, both of Alexis' parents had committed suicide.

"How is your father?" she asked, concern in her voice.

"He's stable, but still unconscious. I took the girls to see him today—the doctors seem to believe it helped lift his spirits."

"That's good," she said. "Be sure to focus on him as much as you can. My mistake was getting so caught up in the loss of my mother that I didn't realize that my father was the one who needed me. If I could do it over …"

"I'm sorry," she said, wiping away a tear. "I can't believe I made this about me. Some friend I am."

"It's fine," I said, and thought a subject-change could do us both good. "So how are things going with Niko?"

She shrugged—not the excitement I expected. "There was a time when we'd never leave the bedroom during a visit, but things are different these days."

"Believe it or not, I do understand the Europe/United States relationship all too well. It's not easy."

"Speaking of, how is Kirk? Is he still in Spain?"

"This year is Turkey. At least it was … he hasn't played in a couple of weeks and I'm starting to wonder if something happened."

"He hasn't been in touch with you? Are you concerned?"

"Not really—sometimes we go weeks without talking. I'm sure he's fine. It's just that he tends to get kicked off teams a lot."

"That surprises me … that he wouldn't be in touch more. I know how much he loves his children."

I looked at her strangely, and she amended, "I'm just assuming he does. I mean, how couldn't he—they're such amazing children, no?"

I couldn't disagree with that. Although, I wasn't sure how this turned into a discussion of my ex-husband. But I didn't have time to ponder it, as my ringing phone interrupted our conversation.

I eagerly reached for it, hoping it was Chris. But it was a number I didn't recognize, and I let it go to voice mail—probably another reporter. I wondered if I was ever this insensitive when working on a story. I sure hoped not.

"What's wrong?" Alexis asked.

"It's just that I haven't been able to get in touch with my sister since this all happened."

"Chris is a wanderer—she's been like that since we were little. But she always finds her way back home," she said.

I sure hoped so. Mention of Chris seemed to spark something in Alexis, and she ran outside. She returned with a photo—an old Polaroid. "I found this when I was cleaning out my mother's things, and I thought you'd like to see it."

It was a picture of our families having a picnic in the impressive backyard of the Tskitapolis' estate, back when we were children. I smiled—those were good times. An era of innocence before friends started moving away, divorces, suicide, murder, and all the fun stuff that life has to offer.

"I love it—I don't think I have any pictures from those days. Can I get a copy?"

"Absolutely. I'll scan it and email it to you."

"That's great—I think Brooke and Kelly would get a kick out of it."

She laughed. "Maybe they'll go as us for Halloween next year."

As I handed the photo back to her, I caught another glimpse of it. I thought I noticed something, but decided that my mind was playing tricks on me.

Alexis had to get back to the restaurant. It was good to talk to someone who got what I was going through, but I still needed the one person in this world who truly understood me, inside and out.

But I was done waiting for her to come to me. Tomorrow I would find her.

Chapter 21

Monday morning, I thought about not sending the girls to school. It would be understandable, obviously, and Connie suggested that they should take the entire week off.

Rumors were flying around about what happened to their grandparents, and I cringed at the thought of Brooke or Kelly having to deal with insensitive comments or accusations.

But I trusted St. Francis school and their teachers, and the close-knit group of children who attended. Just as it was when Chris and I went there, and while we dealt with the occasional teasing about our conjoined status, the school and our fellow classmates always stuck up for us. That's why I fought Kirk to send them there—he was a big believer in the girls attending public school, since they would have to deal with all types in life. Money has always been an issue with Kirk as well, and more so now that he has it, so that also factored in.

I dressed professionally, as today was all about business—a white button down and black slacks, with my favorite blazer over the top. But I wore sneakers, choosing to carry a pair of heels in my bag. I learned this trick during my job for the Cubs, when I spent half my days running through airports trying to make my flight.

I dropped the kids at school, trying to act like this was any other day, before heading to the train station.

While I waited for my train, I purchased a copy of each of the newspapers they sold. *The Danbury Ledger*, *Stamford Advocate*, *Connecticut Post.* My own paper was the only one not to name my father as the lead suspect and splash his photo all over the front page. The articles mentioned the gun, along with the financial problems and speculation about a tawdry affair.

There was such a rush to be first these days in journalism. And while they used terms like *alleged* and *yet to be confirmed* to cover themselves, the articles strongly implied that he did it. And of course all of these papers will send my father an apology when it becomes clear that he didn't kill his wife. *Yeah right!*

I tossed them in the garbage and boarded the train. I rode it the short distance from Danbury to Norwalk, where I picked up another train to Grand Central Station. Forty-five minutes later I had arrived in the heart of Manhattan.

Stepping off the train, I checked my messages—two from my boss— "We need to meet pronto, Eliza." But I had a more pressing matter to take care of before I got bogged down with Bob.

I stopped at a store inside Grand Central to purchase my morning coffee. I glanced at a copy of the *New York Globe* on the counter and felt like I'd been smacked in the face. I was suddenly back in the doorway of my parents' bathroom.

On the cover was a photo of my mother, taken from above, while she was submerged under the water of the bathtub. Her eyes blank—dead. The headline was *Cold Bath.*

The cashier noticed my stare, and commented, "Just horrible—I can't believe that sicko would drown his wife."

I also thought it was horrible, but for different reasons. I couldn't decide if I was more outraged that someone would leak the crime-scene photo of my dead mother, or that a newspaper—and I use that term loosely—would choose to print it.

That was probably the reason Bob wanted to speak to me—to warn me. My impulse was to buy all the copies and throw them away, as if there weren't tens of thousands of copies at newsstands around the city, and spread across the world on the Internet. My stomach clenched.

I steadied myself. "I can't believe he would drown his wife either," I replied. I paid for my coffee and then set out to find the one person who could help me make some sense of this.

Chapter 22

The last thing I needed at this point was to be recognized. *There she is—the daughter of the bathtub murderer!* So I strolled into one of the many touristy shops along Lexington Avenue and purchased a midnight-blue winter cap with a New York Yankees logo on it, and the biggest pair of sunglasses I could find. Think 1970s Elton John.

I took a cab to the Midtown office of Norby Weinberg, making a quick change into my heels along the way. It was located on the 22nd floor of an imposing glass skyscraper. On the elevator ride I removed the cap and shook my hair back to life. My fellow elevator mates didn't seem to recognize me.

The receptionist looked like she'd stepped off the cover of Vogue. "Can I help you?" she asked in a condescending tone, as if I must be lost.

"I'm here to see Chris Dunbar," I said.

She looked confused by the request. "And may I ask who wants to see her?"

"Eliza Dunbar … her sister."

Her confusion deepened. "And what is this pertaining to?"

"Sister business."

She pressed a button and spoke into an intercom. "I have a woman claiming to be Chris Dunbar's sister here with me, an Eliza Dunbar."

She picked up the receiver and listened for a long moment. She then looked up at me with a forced smile. "Someone will be out to meet you in a minute. You can take a seat over there," she pointed to a waiting area.

"Thank you," I said, but didn't even make it to my seat when I heard my name, "Eliza?"

I turned to see a man in a sharp black suit and slicked back hair. He approached with a friendly smile, but was gauging me closely. It appeared that my arrival had upset the apple cart.

"Chris talked a lot about you," he said as we shook hands. "I'm Daniel Ryan, an associate of Mr. Weinberg."

"I'm sorry to have barged in here during business hours, but I wouldn't have if it wasn't important."

He looked momentarily puzzled, before it hit him. "Your parents … I'm so sorry. I saw it on the news. My condolences to your family."

"Thank you. I appreciate that. Is Chris in the office today? I really need to see her."

"Why don't you come with me," he said, and led me down a hallway. People in professional suits and expensive haircuts passed us by in each direction, scurrying to their next meeting like rats hopped up on energy drinks.

Norby Weinberg was a big-time sports agent. Chris was his first female client and, despite Norby's public reputation of being a heartless shark, he remained loyal to Chris after the injuries ended her basketball career. The latest example was hiring her as a recruiter. Her job was to help sell the agency to targeted athletes. As a former star athlete herself, she could theoretically relate to the young player, and showcase her own experiences with Norby.

Daniel pulled me into an office that had a spectacular view of the New York skyline. He took a seat behind a glass desk, and pointed for me to take a seat facing him.

"I'm from Chicago, so I'm familiar with your work … with the Cubs," he surprised me.

I smiled. "Thank you … that was a long time ago."

"Clubhouse reporter is pretty much an eye candy job, but you brought something more to the medium. Don't get me wrong, you're a very attractive girl, but you also have brains, and knew the game. It was refreshing."

"Thanks … I think."

He pushed a card across the table. "If you're ever looking to get back into the game, we've started a sports television division and I would love to represent you."

"I appreciate it," I said, looking at the card, "but right now I'm focused on finding Chris."

Just as he was about to reply, an older man bounced into the room. He wore a pinstriped shirt, no jacket or tie. His salt-and-pepper hair was neatly swept to the side with a hunk of gel in it. Normally to get an audience with Norby Weinberg without an appointment you better run a 4.3 40-yard dash or be able to hit a baseball 500 feet. So it was curious that he'd take time for me.

"I'll take it from here, Daniel," he said.

Daniel nodded a goodbye at me and couldn't run out of the room fast enough.

Norby took a seat behind the desk and smiled, flashing his capped bright teeth. "They tell me you're here to see Chris?"

"That's correct."

"She's not here."

"I'm aware that she went on a business trip to Miami, but I haven't been able to contact her. And as you might have heard, our mother recently passed, so it's important that I speak with her."

"I did hear that and I'm deeply sorry. From what I've read, she was an extraordinary woman."

He stared at me for a moment, as if he were solving a puzzle. "You do know that Chris doesn't work here anymore, correct?"

"I'm not sure I understand."

"She hasn't worked here in a month. I don't know anything about her trip to Miami, but it certainly didn't have any connection to this office."

I gathered myself. "Was she fired?"

"Quite the opposite—we did everything we could to change her mind, but she said this just wasn't for her."

I looked straight ahead, focusing on the skyline, my mind spinning. *What is going on, Chris?*

Norby stood, eager to return to his busy day. "I'm sorry that I couldn't be of more help, but if I can assist you in any way, Eliza, please don't hesitate to ask."

There wasn't anything he could do. It was becoming very clear that I was all on my own when it came to saving my family.

Chapter 23

Chris' apartment was on 92nd Street on the Upper West Side. It never seemed like much to me—with the exception of its nice view of Central Park—but the monthly rent was higher than my mortgage payment. I was pretty sure Dad helped her with it.

I climbed the narrow staircase to the third floor. When I knocked, I could hear a stirring inside the apartment. I wasn't sure what I would do when I saw her—hug her, or punch her in the mouth.

To my surprise a woman answered, wearing just a towel. She was blonde and in her early twenties—it definitely wasn't Chris.

"Can I help you?" she asked, sounding indignant.

For a moment I thought I might have knocked on the wrong apartment, but I re-checked the number on the door—303—it was the right place. "I'm looking for Chris Dunbar."

She looked at me like I had two heads. She turned and shouted into the apartment, "Do you know a Chris Dunbar?"

"I'll take it," a man's voice called out. The girl slipped away, replaced by a tall, smiling man, also wearing just a towel.

But when he realized who it was, his smile ran for safety.

"What the hell are you doing here, Eliza?"

"What am I doing here? You're the one who's supposed to be in Europe playing basketball," I said to my ex-husband. I had officially entered the theater of the absurd.

The blonde had seen enough. She'd thrown her clothes back on—not that there was a lot of them to put on—and pushed passed us, out the door. But she did have a few parting words for Kirk, "At least wait until I leave before you have your other bimbos come over. *Chris Dunbar?* What is that, like, your alias? More like Chris Dumb-bar."

Kirk appeared to be amused by her exit, flashing that boyish grin that had got me too many times to count.

He retreated into the apartment and I followed.

He began, "She was just—"

"Selling Girl Scout cookies?"

"Something like that." He looked me up and down. "You look good."

He always looked good, but I wasn't going to give him the satisfaction. "Go put on some clothes so we can talk."

He shrugged and disappeared into a bedroom. He returned a few minutes later in a T-shirt and sweats, barefoot. At his height, it gave the illusion that he would scrape his head on the low ceiling of the apartment.

He made a stop in the kitchen and pulled two bottles out of the refrigerator. "Beer?" he offered.

"It's a little early."

"I'm still on Turkey time—it feels like the middle of the night."

He plopped down on the couch and put his feet up on the coffee table. "Sit wherever you want," he said as if he owned the place.

I chose to remain standing. This shouldn't take long.

I waited for Kirk to start, and he finally said, "Listen, Eliza, I'm so sorry about your mother. I know things soured with me and your parents at the end, but they were the first people to really take me in. I'll never forget how they had me up for Thanksgiving when I had nowhere to go."

"Yet you were here, just an hour away, and you chose not to say anything until I showed up."

"I mean I was here, but I wasn't really here."

"What does that even mean?"

"Chris was the only one who knew I was in New York. I was keeping a low profile until I got things together."

"Got what together?"

He inhaled a deep breath and blew it out. "I was released, Eliza. Turkey was my last shot, so my career is basically over. I came back to the States to figure out what my next move was and Chris took me in … like she always has."

It did explain why Brooke hadn't seen his name in the box scores. So there was that. "When did this happen?"

"Three weeks ago."

I almost burst a blood vessel. "You've been here for three weeks and you didn't come to see your daughters one time!?"

"Like I said, I was here, but I wasn't …"

"Just save it. I've been telling Brooke that you have a sprained ankle, which is why you haven't been playing, but it turns out you've been suffering from brain damage."

He shook his head like I just didn't get it. "You're right, you're always right, Eliza." He took another deep breath to calm himself. "The fact is, I was embarrassed. I want them to be proud of me and I just didn't want them to see me like this."

"Like what?"

"Like a loser. And I can't deal with how you're looking at me right now—I shouldn't care what you think anymore, but it still matters."

I sighed. "All they care about is that you're their father. They adore you whether you play basketball or not."

I noticed that he had that puppy dog look in his eyes. I looked away—those eyes had been trouble from the beginning.

Chapter 24

Chris brought her friend from college to Thanksgiving dinner, since he didn't have any family of his own. I hadn't thought much about it, as I was too busy trying to survive my first semester at Northwestern, not to mention the holiday travelers at O'Hare. But once I laid eyes on Kirk McCaffrey I couldn't stop thinking about him.

He was tall and handsome with a confident smile that masked his vulnerability. One accidental touch of hands while the passing of the cranberry sauce and I knew I was in big trouble.

I only saw Kirk a handful of times over the next five years, when he would visit Chris during holidays or summer break. But I did admire him from afar, because he took my place as Chris' protector.

Outwardly, you would think the last thing my sister would need was protection. But her tough outer shell covered up the fact that she'd always been the more fragile of the two of us.

She took a lot of crap in high school from the other players; a lone girl playing in a boy's world. And the fans of other schools liked to taunt her about our conjoined status. I was always there, sitting in that first row behind the bench, so whenever the taunts began to overwhelm Chris, she could look over to me and pull strength from our bond.

I had a pit in my stomach the entire summer leading up to college. We had once been famously separated, but never by distance. So it was a relief for me that she met Kirk McCaffrey, the star of the school's men's basketball team, who not only became her close confidante, but also took over my job of protector ... and she would need it.

Chris returned to the women's game in college, and for those of us who like to think we're the more civilized of the sexes, it didn't turn out to be so in this case. The attacks on my sister turned nasty, focusing on her gender, including the spreading of rumors that Chris was an asexual creature, having lost her reproductive organs in our surgery. For the record, our vaginas are in perfect working order ... just so you know.

The first sign that Chris might not fit the mold was during our childhood when she refused to use her given name of Christie because "it's a girl's name." And when a neighbor told her that she had "the prettiest eyelashes" they'd ever seen, she attempted to pluck them out. She was a tomboy obsessed with sports, and the joke was that she was the son that my father always wanted.

The thought was that she'd grow out of it, but into our teenage years she continued to cut her hair boyishly short, wore no makeup, and refused to wear dresses.

She was very much a girl, identified with being a girl, and liked being a girl. Her problem was with the society that was attempting to tell her what it meant to be female by jamming her into high-heels and smearing lipstick on her face. Taking issue with society's expectations was something we had in common.

Their senior year, the UConn men's basketball team won the national championship on a Monday, which Kirk celebrated by driving through the night to Indianapolis to support Chris, as she led the women's team to the title the next night. They had gone from sharing Thanksgiving dinner at our home to sharing the cover of *Sports Illustrated.* It seemed like a fairytale ending, but the story was just getting started.

Like myself, Kirk spent his first year after college working in professional sports. Except, he wasn't covering them for a TV network, he was playing for the Boston Celtics. But his college exploits never fully transferred to the NBA level, and he was released the next summer, with no other team picking him up.

He moved in with Chris, who was renting an apartment in Danbury. Chris was dealing with the physical pain of her knee surgery, while Kirk was trying to come back from the emotional pain of, for the first time in his life ... at least when it came to basketball ... being told he wasn't good enough. The two of them planned to push each other back to their previous heights. But things changed that November when my mother had her stroke.

I don't know if it was that we were both feeling vulnerable, or we really were in love, but after I returned home to help out with Mom, Kirk and I began a whirlwind romance the likes of which I've never experienced before, or since.

Six months later I was pregnant with Brooke. Most people assume that the pregnancy was the reason we got married, but we had discussed eloping well before. Just months after Brooke was born we doubled down, as I was happily pregnant again.

So there we were, two kids in our early twenties, married, with two kids of our own, and not a clue what we were doing. My life had done a complete one-eighty, but I was happy. We were happy. At least I thought so.

We were getting by financially with a big assist from my parents, which drove Kirk crazy. He always had a big chip on his shoulder about money, having grown up in foster homes. And it was the trigger that began most of our fights.

That's when he got the offer to play overseas in Italy. It would include a six-figure salary, a leased car, and a lot of perks. It would have been perfect ... except for the distance.

There was no way I could jet off to Europe with two children under the age of two. So I stayed behind. We discussed that if things worked out and it became a regular gig, we could move there full time the next year.

Looking back, I think he really resented my decision to stay behind. It was also the first time he'd met Pragmatic Eliza—he'd only known her alter ego, "throw caution to the wind" Eliza. She had a short shelf life. And it was pretty obvious which one Kirk preferred.

Things worked out in a big way for him in Europe, but when I talked about moving there for year two, this time he discouraged me. He said it was best not to displace the girls at such a young age, but the truth was he had a new rock star life overseas and his wife and kids didn't fit into it.

I caught myself being bogged down by the murky past once again, and got back to my original reason for coming here, "Where is Chris?"

"I have no idea—I figured she'd be with you and your family, after what happened."

"When was the last time you saw her?"

"Thursday night. She'd met this guy last week when we were out, and he invited Chris to Miami for the weekend."

I read the look on Kirk's face. "You seem surprised by this. I mean, she is a single woman."

"It's just that he didn't seem like her type."

"Why not?"

"First off, he was this loudmouthed, muscled-up gym guy. And he was hitting on her with these cheesy lines that she'd never go for. Things like: *Every heart sings a song, incomplete, until another heart whispers back.."* He rolled his eyes. "I mean, was this dude serious with that?"

"Plato," I said.

Kirk looked intently at me. "How do you know his name—did Chris tell you?"

"No—but that so-called pickup line was from Plato, the Greek philosopher. Is that the name he used?"

"Yeah, which makes him an even bigger cheese ball."

"If he was so bad why'd Chris leave with him?"

"I think she wanted to show up the other high-class society babes in the bar that night, who were fighting to get with this douche-bag—just to say she beat them. You know Chris, when her competitive juices take over."

Despite Chris' best attempts to scare off the opposite sex, she'd never had any problem attracting men. It sounds self-serving to say she has a pretty face with delicate features—since it's, well, my face—but it would have to be to pull off the severe haircut, no makeup look. And her toned, athletic body was always a draw. So it didn't surprise me that this "in-demand" guy would hit on her. But it did surprise me a little that she'd go home with him that night, as that's never really been her style, at least when she's not drinking.

But if the description was accurate, Kirk was right about this guy not being her type. Chris preferred her guys a little bookish and slightly nerdy. I was willing to buy the competitive angle for that night, but that doesn't explain why a week later she'd be going away with him. Maybe there was more to this guy, and I wasn't ruling out the possibility that she'd fallen off the wagon, but it still seemed a little fishy, especially in the context of all that's gone on the last few days. I couldn't help but to think that maybe when she called me last Friday, and told me she was in Miami, that she was leaving me a clue.

"Did you know she left her job?"

"Yeah."

"Guess I'm the last one to know, as usual."

"Or maybe I'm not the only one that keeps bad news from you. We all want Saint Eliza to see us in a good light."

There was a message in his statement, a sarcastic one at that, but I chose to ignore. It was clear that Kirk wasn't in the loop—so there was no point in me sticking around. "Will you call me if you hear from Chris?"

"Of course."

As I headed for the door, I got in the last word, "If you want to see your children sometime before they graduate from college, you know where to find them."

"I plan on it. We should do something as a family."

This caused me to turn back. And just so we're clear, "We're not a family, Kirk."

My family was actually a bigger mess right now than my relationship with my ex-husband. And that was saying something.

Chapter 25

Mission *not* accomplished.

There was a time where I would have searched every crevice of Manhattan Island from Harlem to Battery Park until I found my sister. But I'd learned to cut my losses, discretion is the better part of valor, know when to hold 'em know when to fold 'em, and all those soul-crushing pearls of wisdom that are sadly true.

And I had no hand to play. Chris had recently moved to the city due to her job with Norby, and spent most of her time working. When she did go out socially it was usually with someone from work or a client. Or, I guess, with her mystery roommate Kirk … I couldn't even go there. And who knows how this Plato guy fit. But Chris had quit her job, and I couldn't say for sure that she was even in New York. I wouldn't even know where to begin to look. So I called off the search and caught the next train back home.

I drove directly from the train station to the office, having received two more messages from Bob during my trek back from the city.

"Take a seat," he said. He looked concerned—I could tell that he'd taken the leaked photo of my mother personally. I also realized that this was the first time we'd talked in person since my life flew out of orbit.

"First off, I want you to know how sorry I am about your mother. Are you doing okay? Have you been sleeping?"

"I'm hanging in there."

"Just remember to take care of yourself, and if people offer to help you, take it. And if you need any time off just let me know."

"That's the last thing I need. The less I think about things the better."

Bob cleared his throat. "I also want you to know that under no circumstances would this paper ever print such an insensitive photo."

"Thank you—I wouldn't expect anything different. And I'm sorry that I didn't get back to you sooner this morning. I had a family emergency to deal with."

"Your life is one big family emergency right now, Eliza—no fault of your own. But I have to do what's best for the paper, and that means take you off the story."

It took a moment for his words to compute, but once they did, my blood began to boil. "Take me off the story? I'm not *on* the story—I'm living it!"

"Exactly—you're too close."

"There's no such thing."

"You're as fair of a reporter as I've ever been around, but there are built-in biases that you can't overcome. And even if you were able to, the perception of the readers will be that you're protecting your family."

"I can separate the two, and the readers can always sense the truth. You taught me that."

"If that's the case, how come our competitors are all over your father as the number one suspect?" He held up a handful of newspapers as evidence. "But my lead reporter is writing retrospectives about the victim?"

I said nothing.

Bob continued, "It was beautiful and eloquent, and any parent would want a daughter like you, Eliza. But while your mother might be your story, she isn't *the* story."

"I wasn't holding anything back. It's not my style to run with something just to be first."

"I'm not asking you to send your father to the gas chamber without a fair trial like some of the other clowns in this business, but there are facts to be presented. Such as no outside prints found in the house, that the police can't confirm that it was actually a neighbor who made that 911 call, or that your father was shot with his own gun."

"I'm your only full-time reporter. Even if you wanted to take me off the story, there wouldn't be time to hire someone else."

He grinned. "I have covered a story or two in my career if you haven't forgotten, including a couple of wars. I'll take the lead, while you continue to handle everything else—business as usual."

I wasn't going down without a fight—so I played my last card, "People will be drawn to my perspective. The daughter of the victim bringing the reader into the dark soul of the tragedy. It's all about human-interest stories these days, and my presence will double your readers. They won't be able to look away."

"I could care less about human interest—I'm only interested in getting the story right."

"Look at this place falling apart—it's pretty obvious you don't care what the readers want!"

I regretted my words the moment they left my lips, but I was at my wit's end, and taking me off the story was the final slap in the face.

Bob didn't seem to take offense—he'd always thought a little conflict was good for the process. He took a seat behind his desk and looked down at a yellow legal pad. "So you'll be covering the state basketball game tonight?"

Before I could jump down his throat once more, I received a text. I read it, then looked to Bob. "I'll be there—no bias. But first I have an interview with the main suspect in my mother's murder. Let's see if our competitors can top that."

The text was from the hospital: my father was awake.

Chapter 26

I passed Tim in the hallway on my father's floor. We held a gaze on each other for a moment, but didn't speak.

The nurse provided me instructions as I entered the room. She informed me that he was fragile, and further worn down by the police ambushing him the moment his eyes opened. So she suggested I be short and to the point, and keep it positive. She would have to settle for two out of three.

He looked frail and old, same as my previous visits. The machines still beeped and buzzed; the only difference being that he was awake this time.

He forced a smile at me. "I see someone has done some decorating in here," he said, his eyes going to the model airplanes. I took note that he seemed to be avoiding the picture of my mother that they'd set up on the bedside table.

I remained stone faced. "I'd like to take credit, but that's the work of Brooke and Kelly."

He continued smiling. "They're such great kids—you must be so proud, Eliza."

"Tell me what happened, Dad."

"I'm really tired. Can we do this tomorrow?"

"We're going to do it now."

He appeared caught-off-guard by my aggressive tone. He cleared his throat and spoke slowly, "Friday night, we were in bed. We'd just finished watching the news, and the kid who replaced Jay Leno was on. Your mother was thirsty so I went to the kitchen to get her something to drink. That's when I heard a knock on the back door."

"At that hour? And you just let this person in?"

"I was surprised, but I assumed it was Chris."

"Why would you think it was Chris?"

"Like I'd told you the other night, she'd come over at a strange hour the week before."

And if I recalled correctly, she was demanding money. And knowing what I know now, there was a good chance my father didn't have any money to give her. It also made sense that Chris might need money, since she'd quit her job.

"It was dark. I looked out, and I saw a figure in a hooded sweatshirt and assumed it was Chris. But when I opened the door, three men barged in, guns blazing. It wasn't Chris."

"Did you recognize them?"

He shook his head. "Their faces were covered with masks. They were all big, over six feet and well built. I detected an accent in their voices."

"What type of accent?"

"You would think with all my layovers in Europe that I would be an expert on accents, but I couldn't place them. I'd say Russian or Eastern European, but I can't say for sure."

"What did they want?"

"They demanded money. I told them that I didn't keep any valuables in the house, but they called me a liar and took your mother out of bed at gunpoint." He grew emotional. "She was so scared."

Tears filled both our eyes, but I remained vigilant, "The police told me that you're having financial problems."

"Just a cash flow issue—a lot of our money has been tied up in investments. It's nothing we haven't been through before."

I was skeptical, but moved on, "If they knew where your safe was, it had to be someone who had knowledge of you and your home. It wasn't some random break-in."

"I don't think they knew anything. They tore down all the paintings and photos off the walls until they found the safe in the downstairs hallway. They demanded I open it, and when they found it empty the threats increased. They kept saying we were rich and rich people always have money, and if I didn't turn it over to them they were going to …" his voice trailed off.

"So what did you do?"

"The only thing I could think of. I told them about the second safe in our bedroom."

So that's where it was. And I doubted it was filled with Christmas gifts.

"Did you keep valuables in there?"

"It was more for security purposes than valuables."

I put the pieces together. "That's how your gun got involved. It's where you kept it."

He looked down, as if embarrassed. "I guess I'd seen too many movies. I opened the safe, pulled out the gun, and pointed it at them, yelling something like 'get out of my house before I shoot.'"

"I'm guessing that didn't go so well."

"They practically laughed at me as they wrestled the gun away. All I'd done was piss them off—it was like I'd disturbed a hornets nest. They dragged us into the bathroom, and one of the men began to fill the tub with water. They said that because I didn't meet their demands it was going to cost Sarah her life. I offered to take them to the bank in the morning, or to cash in some of our investments. They could have our cars, the house, it didn't matter at that point, I'd give them anything to save your mother."

He was hitting all the right notes and filling in all the necessary blanks, but I couldn't tell if this was the truth or a well-scripted cover story.

"I wasn't sure if it was just a threat, but when they put your mother in the tub, knowing she wouldn't be able to hold her head above water in her condition, I couldn't take a chance. I rushed to her, hoping to pull her out. I think I surprised them, and the one who was still holding my gun, fired.

"I was paralyzed on the floor, but I could still hear them. They sounded so far away, yet I could almost reach out and touch them. It was surreal. I remember that one of the men started yelling at the shooter. It seemed that the plan wasn't to shoot me, but it changed everything. Believing I was going to die meant they had to get rid of the witness.

"They planned to make it look like I killed her, and planted the gun beside me. My mind was telling me to grab it, but I couldn't move."

"Did you call the police?" I asked.

"How would I do that? I couldn't move."

"Did you hear one of the intruders make the call?"

His confusion intensified. "Why would they do that? I'm guessing they'd want to be as far away as possible when the police arrived."

"Well, somebody did," I said, frustration in my voice.

He closed his eyes for what seemed like a minute. I first thought he'd fallen off to sleep, but he was trying to compose himself. "I just wish it had been in time to save her."

"You said you blacked out, but you gave the police a brief statement at the scene."

"When I came to, I was surrounded by medics. I kept asking about your mother, but they kept avoiding my questions. I could tell from their eyes that it wasn't good. That's all I remember—I barely remember talking to the police."

"Were you seeing another woman?" I couldn't believe those words actually came out of my mouth.

He paused just a bit too long. "Tim asked me the same question, so obviously there must be some rumors going around."

"That's not an answer."

He took a deep breath and slowly blew it out. "I'm not going to lie to you, Eliza, and tell you that I've always been the perfect husband and father. But that was a long time ago, and I swear on the life of my grandchildren that there was nobody else at the time of your mother's death. I don't know how much stronger I can say it."

I was overloaded by emotions, and now faced with another unthinkable question. "You told me that Chris had recently come over in need of money. And a week later you had a break-in, also demanding money. Chris is nowhere to be found, Dad—do you think she possibly could be involved in this?"

My father grabbed my arm with surprising vigor. "Chris is a good kid. No matter what happens to me, the two of you need to stick together. That's how you came into this world, and now you need each other more than ever."

Chapter 27

To review my day.

I learned that my sister had left her job and was "missing." Kirk was back, or back but not really back, or something to that effect. My editor took me off the most important story of my life, and my father basically admitted that he had cheated on my mother. Talk about a case of the Mondays.

I focused on the tasks at hand; the first being to pick up the girls at school. I waited in the parking lot of Sainty Frank's for the kids to file out. And when I laid eyes on my girls, walking side by side, a bounce in their step, backpacks and lunch boxes darting every which way, I lost it.

I scrambled to wipe away the tears before they reached me. I was the general of this bunch, and generals don't cry. I think Patton said that.

They piled into the backseat, talking a mile a minute. There was a drama brewing, but it had nothing to do with what happened to their Gram. It was centered on an incident at recess with their friend Gabrielle, who might not be their friend anymore, but probably would be tomorrow, even if they didn't know it yet. The normalcy of it almost made me smile.

That's the amazing power of kids. They come into your life when you're perfectly sane, and then drive you nuts. But just when you're on the brink of losing your mind, their mere presence is the one thing that can bring you back to sanity.

But as we neared home, reality was there to greet us. Outside our house was a swarm of reporters. They couldn't get into the hospital to hound my father, and Chris must not have been returning their calls either, so they went to Plan-C, which was to pester the murdered woman's daughter and grandchildren. Sometimes I'm not super proud to say I'm part of this profession.

The girls reacted to the mob of reporters just as I expected. Brooke frowned with worry, as she does when her routine has been altered. While Kelly sees a group of strangers and is like "let's party!"

I told the girls to take off their jackets and put them over their faces. It was one of the stranger requests their mother had made of them … and I've made a few. But I wasn't going to make it easy for these leeches to exploit my kids.

As I drove slowly toward our driveway they surrounded the car and started flashing photos. I let them have their fun, but when they didn't back off I laid on the horn, causing the sea to part. Wonder if that's how Moses did it.

We don't have a garage, so I would have to walk with the kids from the car to the house. I didn't want to do it with the jackets over their heads like they were hostages, or we had something to hide. So I had them walk to my side, which allowed me to shield them from the camera lenses.

It turned into an exciting adventure for the girls, and even Brooke had a smile on her face when we "made it" into the house and shut the door behind us.

I continued to focus on the next task. *Keep it normal, Eliza!* And that would be to attend the high school basketball game that I was to cover for the newspaper.

This drew rave reviews. The kids love attending the Danbury Catholic games. Especially the part where I let them wear my old high school sweatshirts, even though they practically come down to their ankles.

While they were upstairs changing, I checked my messages. There was one from Bob, inquiring how my father was doing. In other words: *how'd that interview with the lead suspect go?* I texted him that my memory of my conversation with my father would be better if I was back on the story. But since Bob has little idea how to access a text message, I doubted that he'd ever see it.

I warmed some of the leftover Greek food in the microwave for a quick dinner, and we were off.

The tiny gym at DCHS was packed to the gunnels, and even though the temperatures were near freezing in Danbury tonight, it was like a sauna inside.

Seats weren't easy to come by, but luckily Beef had carved out a section of rickety bleachers for the girls and me. I kept my head down as we made our way up to our seats. Not my usual way, but I didn't want to deal with the suspicious looks, or on the other side of the coin, the sincere condolences about my mother were too hard to take right now.

The game was about to start, so there wasn't much time for small talk with Beef. And once the noise ratcheted up, as the students began to bang their feet against the bleachers—a favorite of Brooke and Kelly—it became impossible to hear.

The noise didn't die down until halftime, when with DCHS up by four points, there was a mass exodus to the bathrooms and snack bar. My kids would not be left out, and summoned me for a few dollars so they could buy some candy.

I've always felt safe here, especially since so many people in town knew us, so I usually let them go by themselves, which makes them feel grown up. But tonight I thought twice about it. Not so much that they would be abducted or something terrible like that, but that they might overhear an insensitive comment about their grandparents. Beef encouraged me to let them go, and I trusted his instincts.

Beef then leaned in close to my ear, and asked, "So you wanna to know?"

"Know what?" I asked, but I had a pretty good idea what he meant.

"You're not gonna to like it."

I was still holding out hope that my father was telling the truth, and whatever did happen took place a long time ago. That he and my mother had worked together to move past it, because as I know all too well, marriage is complicated. But I knew that was just wishful thinking.

"Give it to me straight, doc," I said, putting on a brave face.

"Just remember, you asked for this."

He handed me a photo. It appeared to be a dimly lit parking lot, taken from a security camera. I immediately recognized my father leaning up against a car, his gray hair illuminating in the light.

But I also recognized the car he was leaning up against. And the woman who stood beside him—her thick dark curls and perfect features were unmistakable. I felt sick.

"I warned you," Beef said.

"Alexis," I murmured under my breath.

"I have to say the old man does alright for himself."

I glared at him.

He shrugged and handed me a second photo. My father was still leaning up against her car, but this time they were in an embrace, her curvy body pressed up against him.

I looked to Beef, expecting each photo to get worse. As if easing me into the shock. The next one would probably be kissing, and then …

But those were the only two he had. I began to rationalize—maybe they were just talking. Maybe it was related to … *Oh hell, Eliza, why else would a man meet a beautiful woman half his age in an empty parking lot?*

I tried to hand them back, but Beef wanted no part. "They're all yours—no charge."

Brooke and Kelly returned with their candy, unscathed, and I stuffed the photos into my purse. They were talking to me, but I couldn't hear them. My world had been muted—the only thing I could hear was the pounding of the basketball against the wood floor of the gym, as the second half had started. Taunting me like the beating heart in Poe's *Tell-Tale Heart.*

"Are you okay, Mom?" Brooke tapped me on the shoulder, snapping me out of my trance.

The world had sound again. "I'm fine, sweetie, I'm just a little hot. I need to get some air."

I looked to Beef. "Would you mind watching them until I get back?"

He nodded, knowing it wouldn't be anytime soon.

Chapter 28

I felt disorientated as I arrived at the hospital. I couldn't help but to wonder if he lied to my mother about it, just as he had to me. Or did she know that he was cheating on her? Worse, did he make her believe that it was actually okay because of her condition, and that she was somehow at fault for that?

But what was most striking was how easily he lied to me—his own daughter. Not one nervous twitch, not one suspicious bead of sweat. What type of sociopath does that? Maybe one that would murder his wife to run off with his young girlfriend, so they didn't have to meet in secluded parking lots.

I immediately knew something was wrong. "Ms. Dunbar—we've been trying to reach you," the woman in charge of ID badges said with a distressing urgency in her voice.

I looked at my phone and noticed it had been turned off.

In a flash, I was huddled with Dr. Kendall and a couple of other specialists. They were explaining to me the dangerous infection called Systematic Sepsis, which had begun in my father's small bowel and had spread to other organs. Dr. Kendall spoke of trying to contain it, but his tone was grim.

Suddenly my anger was gone, and I was just a scared little girl who was facing the very real possibility of losing a second parent in a matter of days.

There wasn't anything I could do but wait. If he made it to morning, and they could stabilize him, then he had a fighting chance. Dr. Kendall suggested I go home to get some rest, but I chose to stay.

I called Beef and explained the situation. He would watch the kids overnight, and I could pick them up at his place in the morning.

I sat in the waiting room, reconstructing my entire life and wondering if it was all a lie. I thought back to ways my parents used to look at each other, and how they no longer did so in recent years. And I thought of the distant look in my father's eyes during some of my recent visits. Was he thinking about Alexis? My supposed first friend, who had the nerve to come over and console me just the other day.

I had just settled in for a long night on a short couch, when I received a visitor.

He sat down next to me and I took notice of how good he smelled. He searched through the magazines on the table in front of us. "I was looking for a 1987 *Sports Illustrated*, but these magazines don't seem to be that up to date."

I smiled at Tim, or was it Detective Ruiz? I got confused these days. "Are you here as a friend or on business?"

"A little of both."

"Business before pleasure, that's the rule."

"No, the rule is that first you need to give me the score of the game. I've been working all night."

"DCHS won by eight, but I missed most of the second half."

His joy was tempered, understanding the reason for my early departure. "I'm sorry, Eliza. But he pulled through once before—Dunbars are tough."

I nodded my thanks. "How about we get down to business?"

"Let me start by saying I can't tell you how sorry I am about the photo of your mother being leaked. I know the horse is already out of the barn, but for what it's worth, we did find the person responsible—a crime scene investigator—and he was fired."

"I appreciate that."

"Also, Connie called me about the media hounding your neighborhood. Luckily it's a private road, so we were able to move the herd out of there, and they will be charged with trespassing if they return."

I smiled. "Lucky for them. Because I was about to unleash Kelly on them with her guitar."

He smiled back. "Have you been able to get in touch with Chris?"

"I went to New York to look for her today, but came up empty. I'm starting to get worried. Okay, more than starting."

He didn't look as concerned as I was. "We were able to look at the security tapes from your parents' home."

"What did you find?" I asked. *Please don't let it be my father drowning my mother!*

"Nothing."

"What do you mean nothing?"

"The footage from the night your mother was murdered … it's gone."

"You're saying someone removed it?"

And that someone would have to have intimate knowledge of the security system to do so. Which narrowed it down to my parents, Chris, and me. One of whom was mysteriously missing. This was not good.

"But just that night is missing, so we were able to look at the video going back weeks," Tim continued.

He reached into his bag and took out a tablet. He played the video for me, and it wasn't pretty. It was the night my father had told me about, when Chris had come over seeking money. Chris was screaming at him—the basic gist was that me and her had made my parents their money, but when she needed it, they kept it all for themselves. My father remained under control throughout, trying his best to calm my sister, and keep her from waking my mother. If I was being honest, Chris came off as a desperate addict in need of money.

Tim shut it off. I could tell he saw his old friend Chris on the video, not the person who was rapidly moving up the suspect list. So I tried to reassure him, "You're doing your job, that's what you have to do."

"I've known Chris since middle school. I've seen the good and the bad. I find it incredibly hard to believe she'd be involved in something like this, drugs or no drugs."

"I respect that you're checking out every angle. But that video was from last week—there isn't any proof that Chris was even in the state the night of the murder, much less at my parents' house."

"Actually there is."

My stomach sank. "What do you mean?"

"They found Chris' fingerprints on the gun that shot your father."

"It can't be her," I blurted.

But aren't the family members always the ones in the front row of the courtroom, showing delusional support for the killer right up until they are taken away to prison? And even in the face of overwhelming evidence, they still don't believe the verdict.

"I agree, there has to be some explanation. But she can't explain it away if she's not here. And it looks bad that nobody can get in touch with her."

"We need to find her," I stated the obvious.

"You've always been so close, I suspect she will try to contact you at some point. I need you to let me know when she does."

"Of course."

I leaned my head on Tim's shoulder and it felt good. "I've missed you," I said. It just sort of slipped out.

"We meet practically every week. I thought you'd be sick of seeing me by now."

"I mean I miss my friend—the one who always made me feel like everything would be alright. The one I could tell anything to. Remember how we'd stay on the phone some nights until we fell asleep?"

"That was a long time ago. But yes, I've missed you too, Eliza."

I snapped back to reality. "I didn't mean that."

"So you don't miss me?"

"I do, but I know how that must have come off—I'm not trying to sway you. You have a job to do, and if the evidence leads you to Chris then so be it."

"Well, the good news is we've covered the business part, and now I'm just here as a friend."

Tim and I talked for hours—but nothing about my father's precarious condition or Chris' fingerprints. And then I fell asleep on the hardest couch I'd ever placed my ass on, capping off a big old crapper of a day.

Yet for some reason, for the first time since that terrible morning, I felt like everything was going to be okay.

Chapter 29

I woke up on the same couch, my back aching. Tim was gone, but standing in front of me was Dr. Kendall. *Uh-oh.*

But it was good news. He believed that they'd stopped the spread of the Sepsis, and had it under control for the moment.

"Can I see him?" I asked.

"He's still sedated—it will be hours before he wakes."

I didn't have time to wait around for that. I had to pick up my children and get them off to school. But when I arrived, and scanned Beef's apartment, I noticed that something was missing.

"Brooke and Kelly … where are they?"

"There's been a change of plans."

I was about to blow my stack. "A change of plans? You were supposed to be watching them, and—"

He raised his large arm like a stop sign. "I had no choice—I was outranked."

I walked inside the house to the smell of sizzling butter. I entered the kitchen and Kelly's face exploded with excitement. "Mom—look who's here!?"

"Daddy surprised us," Brooke followed up with equal enthusiasm.

Kirk smiled at me. Not only was he playing the role of "Father of the Year" this morning, but he was also Bobby Flay.

"I got your favorite coming right up, Eliza—chocolate chip pancakes," he said.

I took a deep breath.

"Daddy made me French toast," Brooke informed from her seat at the kitchen table. "He said one day he's going to take me to France so I can have real French toast!"

"That sounds like fun," I said with a forced smile.

"He made me blueberry pancakes ... my fave!" Kelly added.

I took note that the girls were still in their pajamas. "Once you finish, you need to go put on your school uniforms and brush your teeth. We don't have a lot of time."

"Daddy said we could go in late today," Brooke said.

"Oh, he did, did he?" I looked to Kirk.

He tried his boyish grin. "I just figured that we could spend a little time together. It's not like they're not getting into college if they miss a few hours."

My stare drilled a hole through him.

Kirk got the message. "Your mother is right—let's finish up and go get dressed."

"Can Daddy take us to school?" Brooke asked.

I weighed the positives (the girls would really like that) and the negatives (there's a 50/50 shot they wouldn't end up at school) and eventually gave my approval.

This excited Kelly, who exclaimed, "He's going to take us in his new Corvette!"

I'd seen it when I pulled in—it was hard to miss with its canary yellow color. "Leased I'm sure," I said.

"No—I bought it," he said, holding his gaze on me. "I'm fully committed to being here."

Another deep breath.

With Kirk and the kids off to school, it gave me some time to catch up on some things that needed my attention. The laundry being the highest priority. But the first thing I did was listen to the messages on the answering machine, and it was a mistake. I was just glad that Brooke and Kelly were at Beef's last night and didn't have to hear them.

They contained some of the most vile and threatening language I'd ever heard in my life—and I'd spent a year in a baseball locker room! And it's not like me or my girls had anything to do with my mother's murder, or my father's supposed involvement. We were the victims, too.

As I listened to another call from a stranger referring to my family as a bunch of murdering blankety-blanks, the phone rang. It was a number I didn't recognize. I picked up with the intent of telling this person where they could put their insults, and to leave us alone before I called the police. But while I didn't recognize the number, I did the voice.

It was Chris.

Chapter 30

The call was brief. She said to meet her at "our place" and she'd explain everything. That would be a lot of explaining.

I knew exactly where to go. I parked the Pilot along Main Street and crossed through the wrought iron gate and into Ballard Park; a five-acre oasis in the center of Ridgefield. I walked slowly, hoping not to draw attention to myself. My eyes darted in all directions, and I would occasionally look behind me, hoping it didn't look too obvious. I had no idea if I was being followed.

I passed stately trees and formal gardens, which glow with lush greenery in the summer, but are more barren this time of year. There was a sign stating that no pets or animals were allowed, except horses for wedding carriages, which was the most Ridgefield thing ever.

My mother used to bring Chris and me here when we were little, with the intent of spending time with the other children in the playground, but we'd always find our way to the gazebo in the center of the park. Just the two of us—our spot.

When I saw Chris sitting inside the gazebo, dressed in a ski vest and jeans, wool cap and sunglasses, I dashed toward her.

She rose to her feet just before I crashed into her arms, and held on for dear life. "I've been so worried about you!"

In case it wasn't previously clear, I'm the more emotional one. Chris tends to, as my girls might say, have more chill.

In fact, we are almost exact opposites of each other. Like a jigsaw puzzle, where the contrasting shapes were cut to fit perfectly together. I'm no doctor or scientist, but I've always been convinced it relates back to our separation. When we were conjoined, Chris got the majority of the nourishment, so she was the chubbier baby, while I was about half of her. Then after we were separated, it was as if we totally swapped calorie intakes. I'm the people person—the Mayor—while Chris was always more comfortable alone. My love for baseball aside, I was the girly girl who played with dolls, while Chris was the tomboy. She's tall and sleek, I'm medium height with curvier body. She has an incredible ability to focus on one task, and I can be a little scattered, bouncing from one thing to another.

When I finally released the hug, we took a seat on the bench and I inspected her closely. She appeared to be lucid and sober. "Are you okay? Are you injured?"

"I'm fine ... physically anyway."

"So who is setting you up?"

I didn't even think to ask her if she "did it." The idea of my sister murdering my mother, before turning the gun on my father, was off-the-charts absurd. But that didn't mean I didn't have questions. She was there that night, and Dad was protecting her—I needed to find out why, and what happened.

"How's Dad?" she asked, genuine concern in her voice. She'd always been a master at avoiding subjects she didn't want to discuss.

I pondered the question—*how is Dad?* There were all sorts of possible answers. He was doing better than Mom? He wasn't the man we thought? He's in the hospital?

I went with, "He's in stable condition. He had an infection last night and it was touch-and-go for a while, but his doctor thinks he made it through the worst part. We're just taking it day by day, minute by minute."

She buried her head in her hands. "I can't believe this is happening."

I rubbed my hand over her shoulder. She was cold—I could tell she'd been out here for some time. "Where have you been, Chris?"

"Laying low."

"I went by your apartment yesterday. Your house-guest said he hadn't seen you since last Thursday."

"Kirk didn't want anyone to know he was back. I let him stay there until he could get his head together, and he could face you and the girls. He felt like he'd really messed up this time."

He sure had no problem facing them this morning, so he must have gotten over it.

"I'm guessing you also stopped by to see Norby," Chris continued.

"Why'd you leave? I thought you had a good thing going there."

"It just wasn't what I wanted to do with my life. I realized I want to teach and coach. But any career plans are sort of on the back burner for now, obviously."

Enough of the small talk. "What happened, Chris?"

After a long pause, she said, "A few weeks ago, when Kirk first returned, I took him out on the town hoping to cheer him up. He was more in the dumps than I'd ever seen him. We were at this trendy bar in Tribeca, and this guy starts hitting on me."

"Plato ... Kirk told me. Doesn't sound like your type."

She shrugged with a sad grin. "I always give points for creativity, and I'd never heard the Greek philosopher line before. I also had a few drinks, which I know I'm not supposed to do. I guess I learned the hard way again."

She stared out into space for a moment, before continuing, "The guy told me he had an apartment near my place and we could split a cab. But somewhere along the ride, I agreed to go home with him."

"Except there was no home."

She nodded. "He led me into an alley, where another huge Greek guy was waiting for me. This one was even bigger than Plato, and sticking with the theme, he called himself Socrates. I didn't know what they were going to do … rob me, rape me."

Plato … Socrates … could Aristotle be next? Just when I thought this thing couldn't get stranger.

Chris closed her eyes hard, as if it might make this go away—this was as emotional as I'd ever seen her. Soft emotions anyway, different from the outward anger and fights.

"They told me that Dad was in deep with their boss, and they were going to hurt him if I didn't help pay off his debts."

"What was Dad involved with?"

"They didn't say, but I assumed it was gambling. You know how he liked to play the ponies. Anyway, I'm not exactly rolling in dough these days, but I put together five grand for them. They went away, and I thought it was over … until it wasn't."

"And these guys were actually Greek—not just using the names of Greek philosophers?"

Chris nodded, unsure where I was going with that. But the Greek part had set off my alarms. Dad was somehow involved in this, and he was connected to everybody's favorite Greek goddess, Alexis.

"I think Dad is having an affair," I blurted out.

Chris looked surprised. "An affair? With who?"

"Alexis Tskitapolis."

Her face almost fell off. "Alexis? That's crazy."

"I have photos."

"And you think this has something to do with these guys who attacked me? Why, because they were Greek and she's Greek? Is that like all Italians are in the Mafia?"

"I don't know—I'm just throwing stuff against the wall to see what sticks at this point."

"About ten days ago they returned looking for more money. When I told them I was all tapped out, they threatened me."

"They were going to hurt you?"

"No, someone I care about," she said, and stared at me to make her point. "Actually two people we both really care about."

My breathing came to a halt—Brooke and Kelly. "Oh God."

"They had photos of them coming out of school—said they could get to them any time. You see why I had to go along with them, right?"

Boy, did I ever.

"They came up with a way to get the money. They had me rob the bank on Main Street in Danbury last week."

Holy Crapola! "You were Marilyn?"

"I went over the surveillance video in my mind. How she walked, the mannerisms. Combined with Chris' short haircut that, from a distance, shot from behind, might make her to appear male. Oh my God, now that I think about it …

"And a perfect disguise—nobody would ever think to suspect Chris Dunbar in a dress," I tried to lighten the heavy moment, but it fell flat

Chris' face remained stone. "The point is, I took them very seriously. I knew it could land me in prison for a long time, and that their threats would just keep escalating, but I couldn't risk the alternative."

"I would do the same for you," I said.

"They had me and they knew it. They ordered that I go to Dad and demand money. I was told to go at night and to make it appear that I'd fallen off the wagon."

"They were setting you up to be the fall girl in the home invasion. You would be seen on the surveillance video looking like a desperate addict in need of money ... so much so that you'd come back a second time willing to kill for it."

She shook her head sadly. "Which leads us to last Friday night."

Chapter 31

We didn't have much time. With each rustle of the wind Chris looked ready to jump off the bench and make a run for it. She was like a trapped rat, and she was scared.

"The plan was to force our way into the home and demand money."

"It just seems strange to me."

"What does?"

"If these guys wanted money there were a lot more efficient ways to get it—hell, they'd just robbed a bank a week prior. And it's not like Dad ever kept valuables in the house."

"I agree—I don't think it had anything to do with money."

"But you said they were demanding money—I don't get it."

"I could tell what they really wanted was Dad. It was personal for them."

"What could Dad have done to these men to make it personal?"

Chris shrugged. "I have no idea."

I had a few ideas of my own, but didn't share. I recalled a line from a movie; *Money is about business, personal is about a woman.* Which brought me to Alexis—maybe Dad was messing with the wrong man's woman, and he wanted to make him pay. Niko popped into my head.

I got back on track. "So you're saying that they forced you into this?"

"I didn't feel like I had a choice, if that's what you're asking. Obviously I was being set up—it wasn't a coincidence that I was the only one not wearing a ski mask when we went in.

"We met up at the train station in Brewster, then drove to Ridgefield in a van. There was a third man this time—another Greek. I got the idea that he was higher up on the food chain than the others."

"Could you pick these men out of a lineup?"

"Sure—but they're going to have to catch them first. Good luck with that."

"Dad said he heard a knock when he was in the kitchen making tea for Mom, and he *thought* it was you at the door. But when he opened the door, it wasn't you—just the three masked men."

"He's just trying to keep me out of it. I made it clear it was me when I knocked—that was our ticket in. And when Dad opened the door, the three men barged in behind me, so that part was accurate. I was to act like the ringleader—as if it were a continuation of the last time, except I'd brought reinforcements with me.

"I pushed him up against the wall and told him something like he'd had his chance to hand over my money, but now he was really going to pay—like a line out of a bad movie. The first time, when I came alone, he was confused by my actions. But this time there was an understanding in his face. He had seen these guys before—he knew them, and why they were here, even if I didn't.

"The third man—the leader—said things to Dad like nobody walks away from us, our business isn't finished, and your debt is not paid off yet. I didn't know what they meant, but I could tell that Dad did.

"The others dragged Mom from the bedroom. Unlike Dad, she looked shocked—she'd never seen or heard of these people before. She asked me what this was all about, and I ..."

Chris put her head in her hands once again. When I put my hand on her back to comfort her, I could feel her trembling. "I told her to shut up or I'd kill her and Dad. Those were the last words I said to Mom."

She began to lose it, and I could feel myself starting to shake right with her. But I had to keep this moving forward—if I was going to help her, I had to know the details of what happened.

"Dad told me that they forced him to open the hallway safe. When they learned it was empty, and increased their threats, he took them to the safe in the master bedroom."

"His attempt to save the day was high on bravery, but low on intelligence—all it did was piss them off."

"And if you were acting as the ringleader, then I'm sure it was your reaction as well."

"I had to keep playing my role. But once we entered the bathroom, I was no longer needed."

"Because there was no security camera in there. You had already incriminated yourself, and the police would believe you were the one who killed Mom and Dad."

"The moment the door shut the third guy punched my lights out. I went out cold." Chris removed her sunglasses and displayed a black-and-blue eye that was partially closed. She'd absorbed quite a blow—it still looked fresh.

I cringed. "You need to see a doctor."

"That's probably not a good idea."

Something we shared in common was a fierce stubbornness, so I didn't push her. It was no use. "So you don't know what happened next?"

She just shook her head, and I tried to fill in the blanks.

"According to Dad, they filled the bathtub and put Mom in it, threatening to drown her if their demands weren't met. Dad claimed that he tried to save her, which panicked one of the men, who shot him at close range, in the abdomen."

"How do you know it was out of panic, and not intended?"

"He said he heard them fighting about it afterward, and since they believed he was going to die, it changed their plans, sealing Mom's fate. In their eyes, she was a witness to a murder at that point."

"I sensed that they planned to kill her anyway. They really wanted to make Dad suffer for whatever he did to them, and what would cause him more pain than to watch his wife die, and then frame his daughter for it?"

I couldn't get the visual out of my head of my mother struggling in that tub, her body betraying her. And to add insult to injury, her last thoughts were that Chris was involved. Or maybe she had figured it out by that point—she was always savvier than people gave her credit for—and she realized that Chris was just a pawn. I guessed that was the lesser of the evils.

"Speaking of framing you, how did your prints get on Dad's gun?"

"My best guess is that they wiped it clean after they shot him, and then placed it in my hand while I was unconscious."

"So where did you end up?"

"When I regained consciousness early Saturday morning, I was tucked away in one of the Little League dugouts at Rogers Park. I realized I was being set up, and I needed to get out of sight as soon as possible. I couldn't go back to my apartment, and I was too paranoid to use my phone, so it wasn't until Sunday that I learned what happened to Mom."

"Any guesses how you got there?"

"If they were going to frame me, they couldn't have the police find me sprawled out on the bathroom floor like I was also a victim. I think they left me somewhere I'd be found … and eventually charged with Mom's murder."

"Which would explain the neighbors hearing someone fleeing the scene, not long after the gunshots. Is that where you've been, in New York?"

I could tell she didn't want to answer that one. "I've been here and there."

"How can I contact you?"

"It's better for you that you don't know. I'll get in touch with you if we need to talk."

She started getting jumpy, and stood. "I need to get out of here, Eliza."

We hugged tightly. "Take care of yourself."

She started to walk away when something else hit me. "What do you think happened to the security video? The footage from that night is missing. If they wanted to frame you, it seems that they would want the police to find it. And Dad was incapacitated, so he couldn't have removed it."

Chris turned back to me and tossed me what looked like a DVD.

"When I woke up on Saturday, it was stuffed in my pocket. Whoever removed me from the scene planted it on me. Maybe they thought it would make me look even guiltier, I don't know. Just a warning: it's not pretty."

I looked at the video and then back at Chris, who was again on the move. She shouted back to me, "I trust you to do the right thing with it, Eliza—you always do the right thing."

Chapter 32

I still couldn't believe that Bob Hurlbert thought I might have biases when it came to this case. I mean, my twin just admitted to me that she robbed a bank and led a home invasion that resulted in my mother's murder. She had flimsy excuses as to why her fingerprints were on the gun that shot my father, and why she ended up with the security video of that night. And not only did I believe every word, I made her out to be the victim. *Take that, Bob!*

There was a video-player in the backseat of the Pilot. It was usually used by Brooke and Kelly to watch Disney movies on long trips. But today their mother would use it to watch a horror flick.

Chris was right—it was a brutal watch. Similar to when Tim showed me the video of Chris fighting with my father, except multiplied by a gazillion. She claimed she was forced, and didn't have a choice. I believed her, but would the police?

The other possibility was that she was lying. That she was the one behind this, just as it appeared on the video, and now with the cops onto her she sought out the one person on the planet who was gullible enough to believe her.

The quality of the video was good. Voices could be easily made out, along with the shouts and screams. The noise stopped once the bathroom door shut. I felt ill—knowing it symbolized the end of my mother's life.

I focused on my father. I analyzed his expressions and body language. He was never the easiest person to read, and that night was no different. What did he know? What wasn't he telling me?

He was convinced that Chris wasn't behind it, and wanted to protect her. I believed Chris when she suggested that Dad was the target. But why was he the target? What was he the target of? Who did he get in too deep with? And what was the thing they wouldn't let him leave? Chris felt it was personal. That would mean something more than a gambling debt. The only connection I had at the moment was Alexis, but Chris was right, it was nothing more than a wild stab in the dark.

Plato and Socrates came as advertised on the video—big and burly, their job was to provide the muscle. Simpletons … order takers. But the third man, the one who Chris first met that night, had a different vibe about him. He appeared much more complex—someone capable of plotting this scheme. There was also something about him that seemed familiar to me, but I couldn't put my finger on it.

I don't know how I got through the video once, much less the five times I watched it. And when I'd finished, the tears I'd held back to keep things on track with Chris, finally came out.

As I drove to my next appointment, I struggled with what I should do with the video. Chris trusted me to do the "right" thing. I had no idea what that was, but I was leaning toward tossing it into the lake tonight after the sun went down.

By the time I reached the gym, my sadness had turned to anger.

As always, we ended in the boxing ring where I took my frustration out on Beef, surprising him with a flurry of punches, some of which stung him.

We sparred back and forth, Beef relentlessly jabbing me to the midsection, trying to fight the tiger off, but I caught him across the lip with a mean right hook. His eyes turned menacing and gave the impression he would return fire. But he didn't get the chance—I just stopped in the middle of the ring and threw my mouthpiece to the ground.

Beef wasn't sure what to make of my surrender. "What's wrong, Dunbar—can't take what you're dishing out?"

"I saw Chris today."

"You what?"

"Are you sure this place isn't bugged?"

"It's got all sorts of bugs … and rats … and leaks. But not the kind you're talking about."

"She basically confessed to everything."

"She admitted killing your mother?"

"Of course not. She was set up."

"Says everyone in prison."

"You think she did it?"

"Naw … but can you prove it?"

"I have the security video from that night."

"And it clears Chris?"

"Pretty much the opposite. The question is what do I do with it."

Beef thought for a moment. "I'd give it to Ruiz."

The answer surprised me. I was sort of hoping he'd support the "toss it into the lake" option. "But if I hand it over to the police, I'm basically sending my sister to jail."

"I said to give it to Ruiz, not the police."

"If you haven't noticed, Tim *is* the police."

"He can control it. And he'll do right by you. He goes way back with Chris, and he's been in love with you forever."

The last statement took a moment to register. "Hold on—what did you say?"

"Like that's some sort of breaking news? The guy used to follow you around like a puppy dog. "

"We were friends, that's what friends do. Not to mention, that was a really long time ago."

"Sounds like he's still following you around—traffic stops, hanging in hospital waiting rooms."

"He's investigating my mother's murder, not hitting on me. And if he ever did have feelings for me, he sure had a strange way of showing it. He basically pushed me aside once the great Layna showed up. And oh by the way, he married her."

"You're lucky he did."

"What does that mean?"

"The worst thing you can do is find your soul mate when you're a teenager. What you want to do is put that person on layaway until you're less young and stupid. This might just work out perfectly for you two."

"Now he's my soul mate? Are you trying to get me to punch you again?"

"Deny it all you want, but still hand the video over to him. It's Chris' best play—she can't run from this."

He was right about that part. Chris needed to turn herself in and fight the charges. Dunbar girls were fighters, not runners. And just to confirm it, I sent a shot to Beef's midsection, causing him to bend over in pain.

"Hey—what was that for?"

"I hate when you're right."

Chapter 33

I didn't have much time.

I made my way to the Danbury Public Library and began formulating a plan. This included writing an article for the *Ledger,* based on my interview today with the new lead suspect in the case—my sister. Bob could talk tough about taking me off the story, but there was no way he was turning down an exclusive interview with Chris Dunbar.

The words were hard to write, especially the honest truths concerning Chris and her role the night of my mother's death. I felt emotionally drained when I finished, and had lost track of time. It was well past dinnertime when I packed up and headed home.

I found the girls sitting around the kitchen table with their father, playing Monopoly. Just the sight of it gave me eerie flashbacks to last Friday night, when I felt so much joy watching them play the game with my mother.

Kirk smiled at me. "Well hello, miss. My name is Kirk McCaffrey and I own Park Place and Boardwalk."

I was impressed. But more so that he came through in picking the kids up from school on time. I'm always impressed by reliability.

The kids—all three of them—provided me a rundown of their accomplishments. Dinner had been cooked and eaten, dishes were washed, homework was completed. I loved hearing the excitement in the girls' voices after the last few days of sadness. And I couldn't deny that the presence of their father was the main reason why.

Brooke informed me that he had made them a Turkish delicacy for dinner that he'd picked up while playing there this past year.

"Turkey sandwiches!" Kelly exclaimed.

I looked to Kirk who shrugged a smile. I couldn't help but to laugh. "How exotic."

After the game finished up and the girls were put to bed, I flopped down on the couch—a mini pit stop, but my night was just getting started.

Kirk joined me. "Thanks for helping them with their homework," I said.

"No prob—I need to get used to doing it."

"Excuse me?" *Because if you think you're ...*

"I mean that I'm going back to finish my degree at UConn. I'm 33, basketball is likely over, so it's time to start a grown up career."

Who was this guy? Then he put his bare feet up on my clean coffee table and I remembered. That used to drive me crazy. I looked at him quizzically. "Are you moving in?"

"Are you offering?"

"Absolutely not."

He laughed. "I just thought you could use a little help the next few days. I'm sure you're being dragged in a million different directions."

If he only knew the half of it. "A few days would be helpful, thank you. But then you need to find another place—I don't want to confuse them."

"Your wish is my command."

"And I'd appreciate it if you work with me on this, so I don't look like the Wicked Witch of Candlewood Lake when you go."

He nodded.

"Listen, Kirk—I'd be thrilled if you really stick around and are involved in their lives. But we've built something really solid here. They're used to you being away—not bouncing in and out."

"You've done an amazing job with them, and the last thing I'd do is mess that up."

It seemed genuine, and I thanked him. He then changed direction. "So how's your dad doing?"

He read my look and grew concerned. "Did he have another setback? Infection?"

"No, he's stable. It's just that …"

I stopped myself—I was getting too comfortable in this conversation. "C'mon, Eliza, what is it?" he pushed.

I should have kept it to myself, but, "I think he was cheating on my mom."

"Get outta here—your parents? The perfect couple we could never live up to?"

"I'm finding that there's a lot more to my family than I would have ever thought."

"Not to be nosy, but it sounds like you know who he was doing the deed with."

As long as I'd gone this far. "Alexis Tskitapolis."

He looked stunned. "Alexis, your friend from the restaurant? Wow, that's hard to believe, she's—"

"Super young and pretty. Not to mention loaded?"

He continued to look mystified. "I'm having a lot of trouble picturing that."

"I've seen photos."

"Of them in action?"

"Of course not! Well, not exactly the action you're speaking of."

Before this conversation sunk to further depths, I was saved by a knock on the door. Kirk stood protectively. "Are you expecting someone?"

"Actually I am."

When he answered the door, I wasn't sure who was more surprised to see the other—Kirk or Tim.

The two men sized each other up. Kirk broke the stare and turned to me. "You didn't tell me you had a date, Eliza."

I grabbed my coat, and the bag that contained the security video. "It's not a date … and it wouldn't be any of your business if it was."

Chapter 34

I got maybe two hours of sleep, and I was waiting to greet the paperboy when he delivered Wednesday's *Danbury Ledger*. Panic had set in. I had to see what I'd done—what damage I'd caused. I was feeling regret, and I hadn't even seen the article yet.

I sat at the kitchen table and analyzed each word.

No lawyer in their right mind would have put this out there. But I thought it was important that Chris took the "stand" and testified before the court of public opinion. I was confident that the public would see that this woman would never kill her mother, and that she was being set up. This was a society raised watching procedural police dramas on television—they knew what the real killer looked like, and it wasn't Chris Dunbar.

And the longer she was "on the run" the less credibility she'd have. By getting her story out there—the first step in fighting the charges—her words would carry more weight. But it had to be done before she was captured, or then everything she said would be suspect.

Kirk continued with his helpful ways, brewing a pot of coffee. When he brought me a cup, he took note of the article. I could tell that he was biting his tongue, trying to remain in my good graces.

"You don't approve," I said.

"No comment."

"You do know that by not commenting, you're commenting."

"I just don't see how this helps Chris."

"She trusted me to do the right thing, and I believed this was it."

"By the right thing, she probably meant hide the video and get her a fake passport to get out of the country."

I had a snarky comeback on the tip of my tongue, about him being an expert on heading out of the country whenever things got tough, but Kirk took the conversation in another direction. "I didn't get a chance to tell you this last night, with you being out on your date and all."

I sighed. "It was business, as in none of yours."

He smiled, still finding pleasure in getting under my skin. "Anyway, the Medical Examiner's Office called while you were out. They finished their report. It was a drowning. No sign of drugs or trauma. The body is being released to you, and you can pick up their report at the Danbury Police Department."

It was what I expected. But it was still hard to grasp that my mother now had an official cause of death.

"I hope I'm not overstepping my bounds," Kirk continued, as if that had ever stopped him before. "But I began the process of setting up the funeral services for you. You have so much on your plate. I contacted your sister Karen, and she agreed that Friday would be a good day. She and her family are flying in tomorrow."

In another time and place, yes, that would have caused a pretty large brouhaha, but I was too tired to fight, and it actually would be helpful, so I simply said, "Thanks."

We sat in quiet for a moment, before a raucous sound caused Kirk to jump to his feet—it shook the room like we were having an earthquake. I remained calm, sipping my coffee and counting down: *3 ... 2 ... 1 ...* "Mom—Kelly is playing her guitar before she's allowed to."

As if we couldn't figure that out on our own.

"Christ almighty," Kirk said, patting his chest to see if his heart still worked. "I thought that was a car bomb."

I smiled. "The amp really makes it. I wonder where she got it from?"

His guilty look told me that it was coming back to him. You know what they say about karma, and she can be.

I took another glance at the newspaper. "Remember when you wanted the kids to skip school yesterday?"

"Go in a few hours late, not skip."

"I was thinking that today might be a good day for the girls to spend some time with their father."

He saw where I was going with this.

"I'm heading up to UConn to meet with an adviser about resuming my classes. I could take them with me—show them where Chris and I went to school. Maybe get some Willimantic Pizza for lunch."

It sounded good, and was met with approval by the Little Macs. Brooke knew all of Kirk's basketball statistics and had watched every YouTube clip she could find, but she'd never seen where he played in his glory days. *"Can we see where you hit that game winning shot against Georgetown?" "Can we see where you had that dunk against Villanova?"*

Kirk suggested that we switch cars, so that he would drive them in the more secure SUV, while I would take the Corvette. A very pragmatic suggestion, and I agreed, although, bringing more attention to myself wasn't exactly what I needed this morning.

I dressed in my best business suit; the one I wear for job interviews, even though I hadn't been on one in years. I returned to the kitchen and poured a bowl of cereal. I kept telling myself not to turn on the television, but the silence got the best of me.

I clicked on to GNZ cable news, and Chris' face was splashed all over the screen. The anchor was using terms like *lead suspect, brutal murder, bank robbery, history of addiction, believed to be armed and dangerous.*

Still no apology to my father for jumping the gun on his guilt, but at least the media had learned their lesson this time … yeah, right.

There was one thing I noticed to be missing from all the reports. The victim. My mother. Sarah Dunbar had become a footnote in the circus. Yet I knew that she'd end up playing the biggest role in the outcome. Because she was the one who taught Chris and I to remain strong in the toughest of times. And she was the one who instilled in us to stick together no matter what. And right now that bond was the only thing that could save us.

Chapter 35

I pulled up to the *Danbury Ledger* building in the bright yellow Corvette—I could only imagine how that looked. Spoiled daughter dashing around in fancy sports car while her murderous twin remained on the run.

The reporters were blocking my path to the parking garage, so I tried the honk method again, along with some threatening revs of the engine. But they didn't seem as afraid of the Vette as they were of my SUV. They closed in on the car, shouting questions at me. Luckily, a couple of uniformed officers ordered them to move out of the way. And when they did, I entered the parking garage.

I could have taken the back entrance into the building, but I wanted to be seen. Confident in my article, confident in my sister, just being my confident, likable self. So I entered through the front of the building, walking calmly as I was again surrounded—I just smiled at their questions and politely declined comment.

Last night I'd provided Tim the missing security tape, and in return I was granted this meeting. I had then gone to the *Ledger,* where Bob was burning the midnight oil. I submitted my completed article to him, and I was officially back on the story.

All parties were present when I stepped into the conference room. Chief Wallach, Detective Ruiz, along with the political heads of both Danbury and Ridgefield. It wasn't a hard room to read. Tim and Bob had my back, Chief Wallach was my opponent, and the two politicians would go whichever way suited them best politically. They were the swing votes.

There was also a new member of our traveling circus—Morgan Gregson, a lawyer who agreed to represent Chris and the rest of my family, on the condition that I would stop writing articles that can and will be used against Chris in a court of law.

I noticed multiple copies of today's paper on the conference table. All parties were emailed my article last night, along with a copy of the security video. So they were all up on the subject matter when the meeting came to order.

Apparently thinking he was in charge, Chief Wallach began, "You are aware, Ms. Dunbar, that you are interfering with an official police investigation, correct?"

Talk about a loaded question: *when did you stop beating your wife, sir?*

Gregson advised me not to answer, and Bob looked like he wanted to jump in on my behalf, but I had this. "Without me there would be no investigation. Or at least not one that was leading anywhere. I am the person who provided you the security video you couldn't find, and the information about the bank robbery you couldn't solve. But no reward money is necessary, or one of those fancy keys to the city—all I'd like is a simple thank you."

Wallach didn't like the answer. And the Danbury mayor—the real one, not me—backed his police chief, "With all due respect to your article, Eliza, freedoms of the press are not without limits. The reason you were able to provide this information is because of your unique relationship with the suspect. And as long as you continue to hide her, that relationship has moved to the wrong side of the law."

"Are you accusing one of my reporters of a crime?" Bob couldn't help himself. "Because if you are, then you're accusing me too, and you'll have a fight on your hands that you won't win, Mr. Mayor."

Bob had taken my place interviewing the mayor on his immigration bill last week, and word is it didn't go well. I got the feeling we were experiencing some carryover.

The mayor predictably backed down. "I'm not accusing her of anything. But you would have to admit that she has a built-in bias when it comes to this story, and in the name of good journalism you should have her taken off the story."

I expected WWIII to break out, but Bob just smiled. "I have the honor of telling you how to do your job each and every day, Mr. Mayor, so it would be hypocritical of me to take offense when you tell me how to do mine."

Gregson spoke up, "Your focus on Eliza's words and alleged biases are wrongly placed. You should be more concerned with Chris Dunbar's actions. She handed over the video and she agreed to turn herself in. These are the actions of an innocent person, which I'm confident a jury will see."

Wallach would have none of it, "If Chris Dunbar is such a standup gal, why is she still hiding out? Why didn't she turn herself in immediately? And why has she been avoiding questions from the police, but willing to answer them from her twin sister?"

"Chris is willing to answer all your questions after she turns herself in," I said, and then outlined the deal that we agreed on last night. The *when, where, how* of Chris' upcoming surrender. But it's not like we signed a legally binding document, so with a few hours to sleep on it, I wanted to make sure we still had an agreement.

"What I should do is arrest you for obstruction," Wallach provided some bluster, but he really had no choice but to agree to it. The fact was, they had no idea where Chris was, and were no closer to bringing her in than the day of the murder. She could be right under their nose, or in Miami, or Europe. This was the way to arrest her with the least amount of PR hit. It never looks good when the police can't catch the bad guys, since their job is to, well, catch the bad guys.

"Do we have a deal?" Bob always liked to get the final say.

We did, even if some weren't exactly thrilled about it. Chris would turn herself in on her terms.

With that, the police and politicians rose and exited the room. When the door shut, I finally exhaled.

Chapter 36

I was hoping to take a moment to savor my small victory, but that wouldn't be my life. I received the text: *Your father is awake.*

I barreled out of the parking garage. I never thought of myself as a sports car kinda girl, but I was beginning to enjoy the Corvette.

I hurried up to my father's room.

While I was happy he was alive, there would be no loving hugs or "Thank God you made it—you gave us all a scare, Dad" type banter. And when I looked down at him as he lay in the bed, hooked to tubes and wires, I felt sad for him more than anything.

I had many surgeries as a child, and each time I awoke from the anesthesia I was greeted by my smiling family, with Chris front and center. "She's awake!" I would always hear her announce, as I struggled to open my eyes.

It was the same with my mother when she had her stroke. She awoke to all three of her children, who flew in from other parts of the country to be with her, and she smiled. She could only use part of her face when she did, but it was enough for us to know that she felt loved and supported.

But my father was all alone.

"Where's your girlfriend?" I got right to it—this was the first chance I'd had to address him since Beef gave me the news.

"I don't know what you mean, Eliza."

"Sure you do."

"I told you last time—I'm not perfect, and I certainly wasn't a perfect husband. But your mother and I were in the best place we were in years. There was nobody else."

I tossed the photos on his lap. "Then how do you explain these?"

He struggled to reach to the bedside table for his reading glasses.

He studied the photos, before looking up at me. "You think me and Alexis …"

"What else *could* I think?"

"You could have waited to ask me, before jumping to conclusions. We were there on business."

I snickered. "One of those typical business meetings that takes place in a dark parking lot, just the two of you?"

"I understand how it might look, but we met at her restaurant after closing hours. And when I turned down her proposal, she didn't give up and chased me down in the parking lot."

"Because you were so vital to whatever this business was? Spare me."

"I think it more had to do with Alexis' stubbornness—once she has her mind made up about something, she won't give in until she gets it. She's a lot like her mother in that way."

A strange comment, no doubt, and it reminded me of the photo that Alexis had shown me from those days. But her mother, like mine, was dead, while my father was still here lying to me.

"What was this business proposal about?" I asked, unable to hide my skepticism.

"Alexis had this crazy idea—at least I thought it was crazy—to ship the leftover food from her restaurant to Haiti, to help with the disaster relief. She wanted me to be the pilot that flew it there."

"The only thing crazy about that is that you actually think I'd be gullible enough to believe it."

"What you believe is up to you, Eliza. She thought that since I was coming up on retirement age, and with your mother's medical bills, I could use some extra money. Or at least that's how she sold it to me."

I played along, "Why did you turn her down?"

"I was already spread so thin between work and spending time with your mother. Plus, her plan was pie in the sky. The amount of money it would cost to fly the food there, and to refrigerate it, she might as well have opened another Skita's in Haiti. Eventually she decided on a more sensible solution—donate it to a shelter in Danbury. There's plenty of hungry people right here at home."

"What about the hug?" I asked, pointing suspiciously at the photo.

"She's Greek, she's emotional, she was just saying goodbye. Don't you think if there was anything more going on, whoever gave you those photos would have included one to show that?"

It's interesting what and whom we choose to believe. Chris asked me to suspend belief to buy her story, and I did. My father presented me with a logical possibility, and I remained a doubter.

I handed him a copy of today's paper. "Did you see my article?"

"I did, but I was hoping it was just a hallucination caused by my meds."

"Why is that?"

"I told you to stick together at any cost. I don't see how the article accomplishes that."

I moved in, close to his ear. "If we're all in this together, then maybe you should come clean and start telling the whole truth. Instead of letting your wife and daughter take the fall for whatever trouble you got yourself into."

He glared at me, the most passion I'd seen from him in a long time. "I want to confess. I killed your mother and shot myself to cover it up. Get out your pen and tape recorder—you'll have your front-page headlines. And if you want me to make up some juicy details about some affair, I'll do that too."

"It's a little late for your gallantry. The police have already seen the security video—they know Chris was there."

"Then they also know there were others."

"Which would be much more helpful if they didn't appear to be taking orders from Chris. Or if her fingerprints weren't on the gun."

My father hung his head. "This had nothing to do with her. It's all about me."

"Chris told me she thought it was personal. What did you do to make it personal, Dad? Did it have something to do with Alexis?"

His look intensified. "Go home, Eliza. Be with your kids. Make sure they're safe."

"They're with their father. They'll be fine."

"Kirk is back? Is he okay?"

"Why wouldn't he be?"

He began to backtrack. "Just that I'd heard he'd been kicked off another team, and that he was very down about it."

"All of a sudden you're interested in Kirk's well-being?"

"He's the father of my grandchildren. He might not be my favorite person, but I want what's best for them. And children with a father in their life, even if he's flawed, is always best."

He very easily could have been talking about himself. But then something hit me. "How did you know that he'd been released?"

"After the night Chris came by looking for money, the next day, I went down to her apartment hoping to clear the air. To my surprise, Kirk was there. He told me what had happened and that he was staying with Chris until he could get his head back together. He asked me not to tell you or the children, and I kept my word."

Not telling me stuff had become the norm, and I was frankly tired of it. I turned to leave without as much as a goodbye.

As I reached the door, he said, "Life is about second chances, Eliza. Your mother gave me one, and we took advantage of it before it was too late. I hope one day you'll be able to forgive me."

"Maybe she shouldn't have," I said, without looking back.

Chapter 37

The hospital waiting room became my sanctuary.

But this time I wasn't holding a vigil, awaiting word on my father's condition. I knew his condition—he was a self-centered jackass.

I was hiding out from the world. Nobody could get to me in here. The press wasn't allowed in, no angry phone messages, no funeral arrangements. There was even a nice break from the police. Although, there was part of me that hoped that Tim might show up and lend me a smile. He didn't.

So I spent the rest of the afternoon catching up on my interrupted life. I wrote a couple of articles for the paper, paid my bills online, and even checked my social media for the first time in a week.

Everything seemed normal on Facebook—friends posting photos of their pets and their latest meal, along with the never-ending stream of inspirational messages. And of course, the workout people must let you know that they worked out today. My life might have been crumbling around me, but it was business as usual for the rest of the world.

Twitter had decided that Chris was an arrogant jerk back when she played basketball, so therefore she must have murdered our mother. Hashtag no logic. Hashtag clueless idiots. Hashtag I should have stayed off social media.

I did find some supporters in my personal email. Friends who were worried for me and wondering how I was holding up. There were a few emails about upcoming events for the girls' school and Daisy Scouts, which felt gloriously normal.

My work email, which was posted at the bottom of my articles, was not as supportive. Critical response was part of the business, but these were more along the lines of the hate-filled comments that Bob received for his editorial work. He'd always instructed me that moving people to emotion was part of our job. And my coverage of Chris had certainly done that. Not only was I biased in their eyes, but also I was aiding and abetting a murderer. *Was I not the one who broke the bank robbery story?* I made a mental note to forward the emails to Gregson, to make sure these people never get on the jury … or within a hundred yards of my family.

It was already dark when I finally headed home. I was actually in a decent mood, considering the circumstances … until I saw the Skita's van parked in the driveway.

I marched into the house and stared her down. "What the hell are you doing here?"

Alexis looked guilty and nervous. Kirk spoke for her, "After what you told me last night, Eliza, I thought it would be a good idea for you two to talk. So I called her."

I looked at the girls. "Go to your room, and do your homework."

"But we already finished—

"Go!"

They ran up the stairs.

"I'll let you talk," Kirk said, and made his way to safety.

"Talk … that sounds like a great idea … but first let me grab a bite to eat. I'm famished," I said with a fake smile.

I opened the refrigerator and took out a carton of souvlaki, turned, and fired it at her. It bounced off Alexis' shoulder. Strike one.

I grabbed a carton of gyros and threw it. This time I missed. Ball one.

Before her designer clothes were covered in baklava, Alexis made a run for it. I followed her outside. This was the first time I'd seen her since Beef provided me the photos of her and my father, so Kirk was technically right, we did have a few things to discuss.

I reached her as she was about to get into her vehicle "My father!? You can have any man on the planet, and you go after my father?"

"I don't know what you believe is going on, Eliza, but I can assure you it's not what you think," her voice shook as she spoke.

"I saw the photos of you two in the parking lot … getting cozy."

"I don't know what photos you speak of, but unless they were altered in some way, you couldn't have seen anything incriminating between me and your father."

"Then what did I see?"

"I asked your father to come by the restaurant one night, after hours, as I had a business opportunity I hoped he could help me with. One in which I needed a pilot."

"Sounds like you two got your story straight."

"I don't know what you mean. But I do understand what it's like to lose a father."

"He told me about the business meeting."

"He did?"

"How you wanted to fly the leftover food to Haiti."

She looked surprised. "Oh … yes … but he convinced me that I wasn't being logical. So I ended up doing it locally—you know, the article you planned to do for me."

"I can't believe I fell for that—you used me and my job to cover your tracks with my father. That's sick."

"It was business, Eliza, you must believe me."

"I'd like to, except he told me he'd turned down your business offer, so there was no reason for you and him to continue your contact."

She looked really guilty.

"I checked the plane records, Alexis. Every time you've gone to Paris, with your 'sugar daddy', my father was the pilot of your plane. It must be a coincidence."

She wasn't expecting that. And this time there was no scripted response.

I could sense that someone was listening. I turned around. "Close the window, Brooke."

No action.

"I said close it!" This time I could hear it click shut.

"I was on those flights, but it was because I had to be careful when I returned to Europe—the Greek government has tried to hold me responsible for my father's business decisions. If they detained me, I might be forced to sign over my entire estate to them.

"Your father was able to use his connections with the airline to get me onto flights at the last minute. That way my travel plans couldn't be tracked by the Greek law officials. I admit that, when I told you I jetted off with a boyfriend, that was just to divert from the real reason I went."

"And why would my father do this for you? He only knew you as a child, before your family moved back to Greece."

"He contacted me after my mother's death to offer condolences. He told me he had great memories of my mother and my family, and often thought back to those times. He said if there was anything he could ever do to help me out, he would, so I took him up on it."

"Then what was the real reason for these trips to Europe?"

"My father had left me in charge of his estate. But because of the Greek government's witch hunt, business had to be conducted in secrecy."

"The Greek guys—the ones who called themselves Plato and Socrates—who forced Chris to break into my parents' home. Were they part of your business?"

Her face filled with worry. "I can't tell you who your sister encountered, or who attacked your family—I wasn't there. But the men you speak of are the enemies of my family. They are very dangerous."

"But they didn't go after *your* family—they went after *mine.*"

"I would never put your family in danger, if that's what you're implying ... especially your mother." She started to cry.

All her tears did was increase my anger. "The men refused to let my father out of whatever he was involved in. What was he up to? And don't tell me it was about feeding the poor."

She just looked away. She knew the answer—I was convinced of it.

"You and my father deserve each other! Two people willing to do or say anything to save themselves, while my mother is dead, and Chris is going to fry for it!"

"That's not fair, Eliza."

"Your family was taken away from you, so you had to take away mine. Is that how it works? You spoiled little—"

Her head snapped back, as if my cheap shot had landed across the bridge of her nose. "I must go—coming here was a mistake."

Finally we agreed on something.

She took a couple of steps toward her car, before turning back. She reached into her purse. "I made you a copy of that photo you wanted."

She tossed it onto the ground. She then got into the van and sped away.

I picked up the photo of the summer picnic with our two families—the good old days. But as I viewed it, I got the idea that those days might not have been as good as I thought.

Chapter 38

With the way last night ended, and my mother's wake looming later today, it would take a lot for me to see the bright side this morning. But that's exactly what the arrival of my sister Karen and her family accomplished.

Karen was dressed in flannel and jeans—it was always funny to me to see Miss New England preppie now a Wyoming rancher. But the fashion advice she gave me as a kid still held up; the footwear makes the outfit. And the pair of leather, designer boots she wore was the difference between looking country bumpkin or cowboy chic.

Her husband Trent removed his cowboy hat and offered his polite condolences, and her three boys followed their father's lead. His flowing blond "Thor" hair might have been gone, but he still looked good, like one of those hunky country singers.

My three nephews received big hugs from their Aunt Eliza. I couldn't get over how grown up Jed, the oldest, now fourteen, looked. It seemed he'd grown a foot since I last saw him this past summer. He's an up-and-coming rodeo star and I watch all his events online, so I know more about roping a calf than you'd ever expect.

Kyle is the middle child, and Nate the youngest, born three months before Brooke. They were dressed like mini versions of their Dad, which was very cute.

The house began to shake, and for a moment I thought the staircase was going to come crashing down. We turned to see Brooke and Kelly rushing toward us. It was "Cousin Time!"

After their enthusiastic greetings, the girls decided to introduce their cousins to a little New England culture—street hockey—which gave the adults time to talk. Kirk took the lead in preparing the coffee, trying to get back on my good side, knowing he overstepped his bounds by a country mile last night. And don't think I didn't notice my sister's look upon seeing my ex-husband here, appearing very much like he had moved in. But we had enough things to worry about right now without getting into that.

We didn't get caught up in the details of what happened to Mom, the mystery of the case, or the why. Karen was never big on why. *Why are we here? Why me?* In her mind, what's done is done, and it's about looking ahead. That is very much the opposite of myself—I'm all about the why; hence, my choice in professions. But the older I've gotten, the more I see my sister's point of view, and find her pragmatic outlook noble on some level.

Her main focus was on the current condition of our father (stable for the moment) and sister (on the lam, but not for long). It was an improved prognosis for both since we'd last talked, and Karen looked slightly relieved. We then moved on to the nuts and bolts of tonight's wake, and the funeral scheduled for tomorrow morning.

The coffee and conversation stretched to noon, when we rounded up the kids and I whipped up some lunch. In honor of our mother, I made her go-to meal when refrigerator resources were low—grilled cheese sandwiches. They were by no means as good as hers, but they were still a hit with the kids. Then we piled into our vehicles and headed out.

The first stop was the hospital so that Karen could visit with Dad. She went in by herself, and although I wasn't privy to it, I'd bet their conversation was more pleasant than the last one I'd had with him. She was in there for about a half hour, before she summoned Trent and the boys.

Their visit was shorter, perhaps fifteen or twenty minutes. But I could hear laughter coming from the room. It had a soothing sound to it.

I chose not to see him. One of my mother's sayings popped into my head: *If you don't have anything nice to say, Eliza, then don't say anything at all.* I wished I'd taken that advice more often during my life. I made an excuse that Dad needed his rest, but I could tell that Karen wasn't buying it. Years go by, and miles stretch between you, but it was still damn near impossible to fool your older sister.

The next stop was the funeral home, to make sure everything was set for tonight. I didn't really want the girls to come along, and Karen felt the same about her flock. Trent suggested he take them all back to the hotel and let them burn off some energy in the indoor pool, so they weren't too hopped up tonight. We all agreed.

We drove into Ridgefield along the tree-lined Main Street, passing historic homes and charming storefronts. The flags were at half-mast for my mother; an honor usually reserved for politicians or local soldiers who lost their lives in battle. I thought back to just a few months ago when the girls and I joined my parents here for the lighting of the Christmas tree. The place was so alive that evening, and now it felt like all the lights had been turned out.

We arrived at the Lovett Funeral Home, where we were greeted by Mary, a smallish woman in her sixties, who had that perfect balance of somber and peppy; a gift all funeral directors seem to be born with. She ran through the procedure of the wake—doors would open at six, and close at nine. She said they were expecting a high turnout for my mother—I don't know how she would know that—and she assured us that if it ran long they would certainly accommodate.

She then gave us a tour of the room where it would take place. I stopped upon seeing a mounted screen that was looping photos of my mother, accompanied by a James Taylor song.

She looked happy in all the photos, even in later years when her wheelchair restricted her. But the ones with her children, and grandchildren, she was practically beaming through the screen.

She loved our family more than life itself, and it saddened me that not everyone could be here for her final sendoff. The absence of my father and sister left a void. My family had become known for our separation, but this was the first time we were ever truly separated. More like fractured. And it left me with an empty feeling.

Chapter 39

A wooden coffin was stationed at one end of the room, surrounded by what looked like an entire floral shop. Karen went first, to say her private goodbye.

I was dreading this, and seeing Karen constantly wiping tears from her cheeks was not making it any easier. Once she was done, I walked hesitantly toward the coffin. She met me halfway and we hugged. "That was a lot harder than I thought it would be," she whispered in my ear, between sniffles.

I sucked in a deep breath and approached. The biggest shock to me was that it no longer was a shock to see my mother in this manner. Something that a week ago would be unfathomable. It amazed me what you could get used to in this world.

It was as gut-wrenching as I thought it would be. I assumed that some profound last thoughts would come to me, or I'd find the courage to confess some final sin. But it turned out to be just a lot of rambling and tears.

I felt a strong hand on my shoulder. It was Kirk. His touch felt hesitant—Kirk was a lot of things, but unsure was never one of them. I put my hand on his to let him know it was alright.

"You did a great job with all of this. Thank you," I said.

"Just trying to help out. I hope her dress is okay—I found it in her closet. It was the one she wore to our wedding. I remember how beautiful she looked that day."

"She liked the dress better than she did the groom," I said, trying to lighten the mood. Kirk smiled back at me. "But in all seriousness, it was a good choice."

Which was important, since she would have to wear it for eternity. I would prefer to be buried in something more comfortable, like T-shirt and jeans, but the dress worked for my mother.

Kirk exhaled. "That's a relief. But I did bring a few extras just in case we needed to make a last minute costume change."

I smiled. "But is she wearing clean underwear?"

His expression grew confused. "What?"

"My mother used to always tell Chris and me to make sure we always had clean underwear on when we left the house, just in case. And we were always like, in case of what?"

He laughed. "That sounds like her."

"I was just kidding you know, about her disliking you. I think she just knew we were heading down the road we ended up heading down, but we had to find that out on our own."

"Will you say the same thing when Brooke and Kelly get to be that age?"

"Hell no—we're locking them up once they hit the teenage years."

This was turning into a regular party. And I looked down just to see if my mother was laughing with us. She wasn't. But probably was in spirit, saying something like, *Good luck with that, Eliza! Acorn doesn't fall far from the tree.*

Later that afternoon we picked up my kids and returned home for a quick costume change. The three of us girls changed into our dresses, and their father into a dark funeral suit with rigid tie.

The lines were out the door and wrapped around the small building that housed Lovett Funeral Home, stretching down the block. We stood in a receiving line, greeting people as they passed through, some of them I knew, many I didn't. The local politicians, along with my new friend Chief Wallach were present, but also the people my mother had known over the years. Many of our old neighbors, including the Gibson's, some of the other "basketball moms" who used to cheer their butts off at Chris' games back in the day, and helped put on those famous spaghetti suppers for the team the night before the game. People from the many clubs she'd been a part of in recent years—knitting, book, league of women voters.

The outpouring of affection did lift my spirits, and even more so when "my peeps" came through. Connie and Beef, along with Jillian and her boyfriend, Maxwell.

It was also notable who wasn't here—Alexis.

This was my kids' first experience with death, and the traditions of the living when it came to dealing with it. And I thought they handled it as well as could be expected, helped by being in the company of their cousins. We brought them early before the crowd arrived so they could see their Gram. They mostly stared at her, unsure how to act.

But when Brooke added the Monopoly thimble into the coffin because "Gram was always the thimble," it completely caught me off guard, and I briefly lost it.

Kelly appeared to be more perplexed than anything. Dead looked like sleeping, and she liked to sleep. I could tell she still hadn't accepted the situation as final and was looking for a work-around solution.

But both of them found their niche in greeting the mourners as they came through the receiving line. *Of course they did, their mother is The Mayor!* And they took particular pride when one of my mother's contemporaries would tell them that they looked just like their Gram did when she was their age.

The final party of Sarah Dunbar couldn't have come off any better, and was a smashing hit … except for the fact that she was still dead and I wasn't ready for her to go.

Afterward we went to JK's, which for my money has the best hot dogs in Danbury, and the girls are big fans of their milkshakes. We ate like there was no tomorrow. As we've learned; there's no guarantee there will be.

We planned to head home for the night, to get some rest in preparation for the funeral tomorrow morning. But Karen surprised me, telling me that first she needed to go to Mom and Dad's house.

Chapter 40

The house had ceased being a crime scene, and the media were no longer camped outside. It was just another empty home on a dark street.

Chris and I were three years old when we moved here, while Karen was eight. So when we stepped into the living room, it wasn't the same one where Karen had famously asked, "Where's Eliza's leg?"

"I haven't been here in a long time," Karen said, as she viewed the room.

Maybe we had a different concept of time. "You were just here last Fourth of July."

"That was different—we were visiting. Surrounded by everyone. It's been a long time since I've been here by myself—a lot of memories in this place."

Since my mother's death, the only memory I could muster in regards to this house was the last horrific one. But Karen's presence allowed me to travel back to a happier time. I recalled how old Karen always seemed to me—when I was Brooke's age, my sister was a teenager. I idolized her. Would I ever be that old? Would I ever be that cool? Well, one out of two, I guess.

"Moving here changed everything," Karen said, continuing to look around the room.

"For better or worse?"

She thought for a moment, before answering, "Neither really, just different. It just felt like we weren't the same family."

I thought her answer might be diplomatic. She always found excuses to not come back once she left for college. Summer classes, internships—all legitimate reasons—but I sensed this place didn't have the same magical pull it did for Chris and me.

We stepped into the hallway—the Dunbar Wall of Fame.

Karen stared glowingly at the painting of my parents on their wedding day. Her eyes then moved to a photo of her own wedding, which took place on their ranch—the Wyoming sun setting perfectly behind her and Trent—and commented, "It seems like yesterday."

Karen was twenty-two when she got married, right out of college, while I was twenty-four when Kirk and I got hitched. So the Dunbar girls didn't fool around when it came to tying the knot. Although, Chris seems determined to stop that cycle.

Mom used to refer to Chris as "my little devil's advocate" for her penchant to always be different from the herd. And while she was indisputably Dad's favorite, Chris and Mom also had a special relationship. They locked horns a lot—*who didn't Chris lock horns with?*—but Mom was also the first to see the fragility behind her tough exterior, and was her original protector.

"Your wedding photos seem to have disappeared," Karen continued inspecting the wall.

I smiled. "I think they sent them out to be touched up."

"Yeah, Dad was never a big fan of Kirk. Speaking of which …"

"We're not," I beat her to the punch.

"I was just going to say that he did a great job with the arrangements."

"No you weren't—you were wondering if we were back together."

"I was surprised that he's living with you, that's all."

"Just until the funeral is over, and the craziness dies down."

"He told me he's planning on sticking around—what do you think about that?"

"I think it will be good … for the girl's sake."

"For the girl's sake, of course," she made her point, although, I wasn't completely sure what that point was.

"I just hope one day I can find my cowboy, like you did, sis," I said.

"I did kiss a lot of frogs before I found my prince, so there is hope for you."

I had a good laugh at that one. "Tell me about it."

"What's that supposed to mean?"

"It was never safe around here when you were in high school. One false turn, into what I thought was an empty room, and there's my sister sucking face with some guy. And when you'd baby-sit Chris and me, and you'd sneak those guys in through your bedroom window."

"The great thing about nobody paying attention to you, is that you can get away with anything you want."

I wondered if her answer, meant to be flippant, contained more truth than she'd led me to believe. "Did you resent us for that?"

She looked shocked. "Are you kidding? Not in the least. I was nothing but proud of you two … although, sometimes I did feel a little bad for you—it was like they threw you into a fish bowl and nobody taught you how to swim. I left because I fell in love, not because I was running away."

We moved on to the less tense, and slightly humorous photos. Our proms. We had a few laughs at our dresses and hairstyles. Karen mentioned, "Our twenty year reunion is coming up next year."

"Are you planning to go?"

"I'm not sure—it would be nice to see some people, but I've never been big on looking back."

But she was tonight. That's why we were here. She needed to know what happened to our mother. The how … and the why.

Chapter 41

Karen just stared at the tub for what seemed like minutes.

When she was ready, I explained the story as best I knew it. Starting with Chris meeting Plato in a bar, which wasn't a chance meeting. She was forced to rob a bank and then make a scene in front of mom and dad's security cameras, looking desperate for money. This was the prep work, leading up to the home invasion, and eventually to Mom's final moments in this bathroom.

I pointed out the spot where Dad was shot, and allegedly lay helpless as our mother drowned.

"You and Dad aren't in a good place right now," Karen mentioned.

"He said that?"

"He didn't have to. You don't think he had anything to do with this, do you?"

"I don't think he killed Mom, if that's what you're asking."

"Do you blame him for not being able to save her?"

I shook my head. "I believe he did everything he could."

"Then what is it?"

"I just think Mom deserved better."

"What's that supposed to mean?"

"Just that he … I just think that … he cheated on Mom."

"He told you that?" she asked. And for the record, she didn't look that surprised.

"He implied that it happened a long time ago, and he and Mom had worked through it."

"Marriage is like life, and life is what you make of it. And they seemed very content the last few times I'd seen them. Mom was strong—she would have left if the marriage was broken."

It's not often that your murder-suspect sister would be the lighter subject matter, but in this case it was. We spoke in generalities this morning, and I provided a rosy-as-possible scenario, along with vague commentaries like "she's holding up well under the circumstances." But I could tell that Karen wanted the real scoop. And like myself, she didn't waste any time questioning whether Chris really did it.

"Her face was beat up pretty good. She'd been on the run. I'd never seen her so skinny—looked like she hadn't eaten in a month. She wouldn't tell me where she was staying, but I got the idea she was moving around, never in the same place twice."

"I'm glad she's planning on turning herself in—as long as she's on the run, she's in danger. But what do you think her chances are of convincing the police, or a court, if it comes to that?"

"Probably a lot better before her sister sabotaged her case."

Karen's face tensed. "I hope you're not talking about your article. I thought that was brilliant."

"You read my article?"

"I read them all—we do have the Internet out in Cowboy Country."

"And you thought it was helpful?"

"Absolutely. You took control of the story. You were able to speak for Chris when she couldn't speak for herself. Allowed her to be heard over the drumbeat of guilt." She smiled. "It was almost like you two were connected at one point."

I then reenacted what happened that night, based on what I had learned. I started with Mom and Dad in their room watching TV.

We moved from the bedroom to the kitchen, where there was a knock on the back door. It was Chris, even if my father didn't initially admit it to me. The men barged in with Chris acting like the leader, and first went after the safe in the hallway. When it was found to be empty, Dad made a failed attempt to get the gun from the safe in their bedroom. This led us back to the bathroom, where Chris was knocked out and eventually dropped off at Rogers Park, my father was shot, and my mother ...

We were again staring at the bathtub.

It was too much for us to take. Karen pulled me out of the bathroom and led me to the kitchen. She opened the freezer and removed a carton of Neapolitan ice cream. "I knew it!" she exclaimed.

Mom always kept a carton of ice cream in the freezer. This one was probably earmarked for the girls following their Monopoly game last Friday night, before I whisked them away.

"Should we be eating that?" I asked, as Karen searched the cabinets for two bowls.

"You think it's evidence?"

"No, I mean, she's ... I don't know."

"It's sealed," she said, "And I'm normally not one of those people who speak for the deceased, but I'm confident that Mom would want us to eat this ice cream."

She had a point.

Karen began scooping it out. Each of us had own preferred flavor. Karen liked the vanilla, Chris was all about the chocolate, and my favorite was the strawberry. So Neapolitan became a staple of the Dunbar household, with its blocks of vanilla, chocolate, and strawberry.

"Mom said she got it to please us, but it was her favorite too. She liked to mush the three flavors together."

"Sort of how she saw life—all happily mushed together."

"Variety was the spice of life, but ice cream was what made the dark days go away."

We both smiled, as we stirred our ice cream until you couldn't discern which flavor was which, and then dug in.

"I want to give the eulogy tomorrow, if that's okay," Karen again surprised me.

I'd planned to do it, but I would gladly hand it off. And I thought Karen was the perfect person. She was there with Mom in that period before our lives changed forever, when Chris and I entered the world conjoined. And the last few years she'd been far enough away that she could observe our mother like a reporter might. She had seen her life from every angle.

And while Chris and I have a bond that comes from our conjoined status, first-born children always have a special connection with their mother. I didn't understand this until Brooke was born.

As I happily ate my ice cream, I thought that if at the end of her eulogy Karen would offer one of her poignant questions, it would be something along the lines of, "Now what?"

Chapter 42

The funeral of Sarah Dunbar would take place at St. Francis church, on the grounds of the elementary school my children attend.

I was seated in the front row, along with my sister and Trent. My father was still too weak to attend, and Chris was doing her "fugitive-from-justice" thing.

In the pew directly behind us sat the five grandchildren, looking adorable in their Sunday best. Kirk was wedged between them, and with his freakishly long arms he was able to reach all of them, if perhaps they needed a poke to keep in line.

I viewed the standing-room-only crowd, which included many familiar faces from the night before. The most familiar were my friends, Connie and Jillian, who I traded quick waves with, and it was impossible to ever miss Beef. Tim was not present, but that was expected.

Just as the ceremony was about to begin, I swept the crowd one last time, and what I saw sickened me.

Part of me wanted to storm back to where Alexis and Niko had taken a seat in the back of the church, and personally escort them out … by their pretty hair. But in honor of my mother I would be the bigger person today, and chose to ignore them.

I remained strong during the ceremony, at least until my two girls did a reading, together, even though Brooke did the heavy lifting. Not only did

I find it very symbolic—the together part—but it also brought out my philosophical side. The whole "circle of life" thing was making sense to me at that moment.

Just as Karen was about to take the stage for the eulogy, a buzz could be heard throughout the church. When it began to sound like a beehive I turned to look.

I shouldn't have been surprised, since this had been the plan all along, but it was still quite a moment to see Chris walking up the aisle with all eyes upon her, Detective Ruiz at her side—no handcuffs, which was part of the deal. Perhaps the most shocking part of it was that she was wearing a dress and makeup. She looked stunning.

She continued cautiously like she were walking on ice—it was obvious she didn't have much practice in heels—until she reached the altar. She made a sign of the cross and moved to my mother's open casket. She looked down on her, as if lost in her own world. She leaned her face to my mother's, whispered something, before kissing her on the forehead.

Chris then made her way to the front row. Tim had waited behind to give her a private moment with our mother, but was again at her side. She warmly greeted Karen and Trent, and then turned to the pew behind us. She bumped knuckles with Kirk, and smiled at her nieces and nephews.

I couldn't wait any longer, gripping her with a hug. She latched on so tightly I thought she might crack my spine. "Nice dress," I whispered in her ear.

"Mom always wanted to get me into one of these things—it's for her."

"Are you okay?" I asked.

She looked at the coffin, tears in her eyes. "It's Mom's day—it's not about me."

Karen's eulogy hit all the right notes. How a free-spirited girl from Rockford, Illinois, who always dreamed of flying got to live out that dream, traveling the world as a flight attendant, which was how she met the man she'd spend the rest of her life with.

She included humorous anecdotes that highlighted our mother's quirkiness, and occasional forgetfulness. But made it clear that despite some bad breaks, she was *not* a victim, and that's *not* how she should be remembered. She lived life on her own terms, and that's all any of us could hope for.

Our mother found her most joy in family, and with that in mind, she could not have scripted her last day any better, spending her final hours playing games with her two beloved granddaughters. And Karen reminded the mourners of the Dunbar family motto, which grew out of the birth of her conjoined twins—always be proud of who you are. Never hide from it. "And as she looks down on her family today, she would be as proud as ever."

And since it was Karen, she had to end on one of her simple questions that perfectly captured the moment. "My mother is going to be just fine. That's not what this is about today. The question is: how are we going to make it without her?"

The burial was just for family. Detective Ruiz again hung back to give Chris room, as did her lawyer, Morgan Gregson. They would escort Chris to the police station to turn herself in as soon as she completed her final goodbye. For Chris, being allowed to be here with us today was the most important part of our agreement with the police.

As they lowered the coffin into the hole, and we tossed red roses onto it, everyone was bawling their eyes out.

"Good night, Mom. Sleep tight," I said softly, before recalling something she used to say to me right before I'd go to sleep, "and don't let the bedbugs bite."

Chapter 43

Beef stepped up to the table with a wide smile. "So this is what Dirty Martini Friday looks like. I came to see what I was missing out on."

The table was made up of the Friday regulars, Jillian and Connie, but also a couple of new additions. It was less festive than usual, as they'd come directly from Sarah Dunbar's funeral, but Beef could always light up a room no matter the circumstances.

He recognized one of the new additions. His old high school basketball teammate, Patrick Gibson, and they slapped hands, "What's going on, PG13?"

Beef reminded the rest of the table that they called him PG13, because his jump shot was so ugly children should not view it.

But added with a laugh, "We used to make fun of him being a bench-warmer, but now I see his strategy—he was getting used to sitting on the bench because he's going to be a judge some day."

"I don't know about that—judge is pretty far off from prosecutor."

Beef took a seat. "I'll take your word for it, PG, but I'm still going to suck up to you, just in case. You in town long?"

"Just took the train in for the funeral. I grew up across the street from the Dunbars, practically lived in their pool during the summers, so I wanted to pay my respects. She was so full of life, even after the stroke … it's hard to believe she's gone."

Jillian then introduced Beef to her boyfriend, Maxwell. They shook.

Wojo stopped by the table. "What can I get ya, Beef? Any friend of Eliza drinks on the house today."

"Thanks Woj, but brought my own," Beef held up a transparent plastic cup containing his latest health drink.

Connie looked like she was going to be ill. "That looks like the stuff we clean off our boat every year."

"Don't knock it until you try it."

"That's so not gonna happen."

Beef held up his cup. The others followed his lead, raising their glasses. "To Sarah Dunbar—a cool lady who deserved a hell of a lot better."

"Here, here," clank.

"And she raised an amazing girl—to Eliza!" Jillian added.

"Here, here," clank.

"She might be amazing, but also gullible," said the man in the expensive Italian suit—Jillian's boyfriend.

The comment received a glare from Connie. "What's that supposed to mean?"

"I'm not saying she should sell her sister up the river. Just that it's so obvious she's guilty, it's making Eliza look like a fool with her support, pretending to be an unbiased reporter."

"She's covered the story fairly—unlike those other papers that jumped to the conclusion about her father," Connie fired back.

Maxwell sipped his beer, unaffected. "I'm just stating the facts … no reason to get so emotional about it."

"Emotional? I think if it was your sister, you'd be singing a different tune. It's a lot easier to criticize when you don't have to walk in that person's shoes."

"If it was my sister I'd run away from it as fast as I could—before it started to affect my brand, and my clients realized I was backing a murderer," Maxwell said, his tone cold.

"There's more to life than business," Connie said.

"Maybe so, but if business goes in the tank, then there's a lot less to life than before."

Jillian stepped in on her man's behalf, "To be fair, the evidence is pretty overwhelming … fingerprints, the security video … if we didn't know Eliza we'd all be saying how guilty Chris was."

"I'm not casting judgment, either way. I'm just here to support Eliza," Connie said.

"So that's what I'm doing—casting judgment? Like you're doing to me right now?" Jillian came back at her.

Beef tried to intervene with a grin, "Ladies—if you're going to fight, can you at least have the common decency to oil up and pull some hair."

"Well, what do you think, Beef? It's not like you to not have an opinion," Jillian challenged.

"Chris is my guy, and I've always got my guy's back."

"From what I heard, she might actually be a guy," Maxwell said with a smarmy smile.

"Those rumors were shot down years ago. And for the record, she looked beautiful today," Connie said.

Everyone nodded in agreement, with one exception …

"Yeah, right before they hauled her ass off to jail. Doubt she's going to be looking very good in one of those orange jumpsuits." Maxwell looked to Beef, "And it's interesting, that you claim to have her back but you won't defend her—that speaks volumes."

Beef glared back at him. "I only talk when I know what I'm talking about. And last I checked, PG is the only one at this table who's an expert on the law. So if he'd like to speak, I'm all ears, if not, I suggest you zip it."

PG looked uncomfortable joining the fray, "From what I've seen on TV, sure, it appears to be an open and shut case. And Chris had her share of issues over the years. I always got along with her, but she isn't Eliza. If Eliza was accused of something like this, my first thought would be 'not a chance,' but Chris … I'm not as sure … we'll see how it plays out."

Jillian picked up, "It bothers me that Eliza and Chris are always connected. Why? Because they were conjoined as babies? Eliza is the sweetest person I've ever met, but Chris has always been about Chris—she's arrogant, and thinks she's above everything."

Connie snickered, "You're only saying that because Nelson Darby dumped you back in high school, for Chris."

"More like she stole him."

"That's not how I remember it."

"What are you like, her agent?"

"I support Eliza—and if Eliza thinks Chris is innocent, then I will too, until proven otherwise."

"If Eliza told you to jump off a bridge, would you? You're so desperate to be her best friend."

"It's not a competition, Jillian."

"Life's a competition," Maxwell interjected. "And unfortunately for Chris Dunbar, she was ill prepared for it. Her parents treated her like some science experiment. And why was she so special? Because she and her sister were born as genetic freaks?"

The audience was clearly not on his side, but that didn't stop him, "If the Dunbars had any decency they would have kept their condition as quiet as possible, instead of pimping their kids out—like some circus attraction. If you keep feeding the animals, the animals will eventually eat you, once they run out of food."

"You're seriously knocking the woman they just laid to rest? For real?" Connie said.

"I deal in facts, you deal in wishful thinking. That's the difference between us. I don't expect you to understand."

"I'll give you some facts …"

"If you cared at all about the truth, you would have been honest with Eliza. Tell it to her straight that her sister is a murderer and that she's embarrassing herself by defending her. But you're too worried about yourself, and having someone you can pretend is your friend to make you feel good about your sad life."

"You're a piece of work."

"But I'm right."

"We'll see how it all plays out. And you don't even know Chris."

He shrugged. "I didn't know OJ Simpson or Bin Laden, either, but I was able to see their guilt from a thousand miles away. It's not hard to do when you take off the blinders."

"All I'll say is, if I had to bet, I'd bet on Chris."

"Care to make it interesting?"

Maxwell took out his wallet and started peeling off hundreds, placing them on the sticky table.

"Maybe you should save your money and buy yourself a brain."

"Wow, that's a burn," he said with a jerky grin, and looked down at the money on the table. "Any takers? Going once …"

"I'll take that bet," came a voice over Maxwell's shoulder. They all looked to see Eliza standing there.

Chapter 44

"I guess you decided to have Dirty Martini Friday after all," I said, but my chilled stare told them what I was really thinking.

My family chose not to host a lunch or reception after the funeral. We made vague mentions of having some sort of get-together when my father was well enough to attend. But after my mother was lowered into the ground, and Detective Ruiz took Chris off to prison, I was in need of a drink. Kirk had taken the kids home, and Karen and the cowboy cousins would be coming over. So I wouldn't be missed.

When I entered Wojo's, I stood stunned at what I was hearing. It started well enough, with Beef toasting my mother, but it went downhill from there. People often desire to be a *"fly on the wall."* My advice: be careful what you wish for.

In some ways I can't blame people for suspecting Chris, and I understood how delusional I must come across. But that's the people who don't know her, like Jillian's crass boyfriend. The ones that do—my friends—I expected at least a smidgen of benefit of the doubt. It was disappointing that Beef didn't defend Chris with more vigor, but at least he didn't eviscerate her like Jillian did. On the other hand, Connie's strong defense was noted.

And while I hate to agree with anything Maxwell said, one thing was accurate—it was good for me to hear the truth. I now had a better idea of what Chris and I were dealing with. Yes, Chris *and I*. It would always be Chris and I to the bitter end.

I had nothing else to say, so I walked to the bar and took a seat. One by one, the Dirty Martini crowd got up and exited—I could really clear a room. Nobody came over to me—they knew better.

Wojo was working behind the bar. he offered me his condolences, along with a beer on the house. I probably could have used something stiffer, but free was free. I sipped on my drink, feeling the stares of the other patrons upon me. I came into this world as a circus attraction, so it felt quite natural.

I sat alone, wallowing in my beer, when a man approached. I was expecting either condolences or taunts, but instead I got, "We were never able to hook up—I thought you were blowing me off."

When I looked closer, I realized it was the guy from last Friday. Don the Chiropractor … the one who sent the drink over.

"I've been a little busy," I said, as he took a seat at the bar stool next to mine.

"So I've heard—I'm free tomorrow night if you're available."

Was this dude really hitting on me five seconds after I buried my mother? At least he could have played the sympathy card and offered me a shoulder to lean on in my rough time. Prey on my vulnerabilities. But Don the Chiropractor was just oblivious.

"I've got family in town, I'm sorry," I said.

Undeterred, "Bring them—I'd love to meet your family."

I looked to Wojo for help, but he was engaged with another customer.

"I appreciate the offer, but I'm not really in a place right now where I can think about dating."

"What the lady is saying, is that she is already taken," came another voice, this one accented.

When I turned, my emotions were mixed. I was happy to be saved from Don. But one of the last people I wanted to see right now was Niko.

Chapter 45

Niko straddled the bar stool that Don had vacated.

He was wearing a black funeral suit with his hair slicked back; his face stubble perfectly groomed. I decided you could add dapper, debonair, and dashing to his attributes, along with other cool words that begin with "D".

The only D-word I was going for at the moment was drunk, so I didn't appreciate the intrusion, even if he was smart enough not to bring his girlfriend with him.

"You shouldn't have come," I said, maintaining focus on my beer.

"I hear this is where all the beautiful women are, so I couldn't resist," he said with a confident smile. Don might want to start taking notes.

"I meant to the funeral—Alexis didn't belong there."

"That's what I tried to tell her, but she's an American woman now—never listens. We have a different culture in Greece when it comes to dealing with women."

"I think chauvinistic is the word you're looking for."

Wojo arrived to take Niko's order, "Whatever the lady is having." He smiled at me, as if that proved he wasn't a total pig.

Wojo slid a frosty mug in front of him and Niko took a long sip, before continuing, "Alexis had great respect for your mother, and was determined to pay homage to her. And today was about your mother, not you, Eliza, so it wasn't your place to object."

I didn't like the insinuation, but I also wasn't going to get dragged into whatever agenda he was here to fuel. "I'm not really in the mood for this … whatever this is."

"Did you know that Alexis and your mother communicated after she moved back to Greece as a young girl? I've seen some of the letters your mother wrote her. She was very fond of Alexis."

I did not know that, but I do recall my mother taking an interest in the girl, whose struggles with English caused her to shy away from the playing with the other children in the neighborhood. A few of the boys would even make fun of her, mocking her attempts to communicate. Lesson being: be very careful who you tease or bully, because they could turn out to be super hot.

While the other kids were playing in our pool during the summer, my mother would spend time with Alexis inside, helping her with her English. By the next summer she was practically fluent, and no longer shying away. In fact, she'd become the leader of the pack.

"She sure had a nice way of paying her back," I said, a bitter taste in my mouth, and it wasn't from the beer.

Niko laughed, which further pissed me off. "Please tell me that a smart woman like yourself doesn't believe those rumors about Alexis and your father."

"I've seen photos."

"What did you really see in those photos? And why would she be with an old man like your father when we both know she wants to be with me? At least she should choose someone to make me jealous."

Humility wasn't really his thing. "I stand corrected. You would know her better than me … being that you're her gigolo."

"I think you misunderstand our relationship. I went to work for her father back when I was a young man of twenty-two, and Alexis was but sixteen—I've known her for half her life."

"I stand corrected again—a *creepy* gigolo."

"She's more like a sister to me."

Only the fact that my soul had been completely squashed this morning kept me from laughing in his face. "So you're saying you two aren't ..."

"She chased me for many years. I resisted, but she's a beautiful woman and I'm an attractive man, so it was inevitable that we would be together that way. But our relationship has changed in recent years. It is now about business, not pleasure ... even if Alexis isn't so happy about that."

This guy really liked himself. "That was very courageous of you to hold out for so long, despite her advances. You're like the Greek God of Willpower."

He laughed. "In my country, women are often beautiful, but rarely funny. You are both, Eliza Dunbar."

"I've already heard the best lines from Don the Chiropractor, so I think you need to up your game."

His laughter built. "You make my case."

"So let me get this straight—you flew halfway around to world to spend time with your gorgeous, platonic, sisterly friend, who you have a history with, but nothing is going on?"

He turned deathly serious. "When her father died, he left two notes. One was his suicide note, the other was addressed to me. He asked me to take care of Alexis when he was gone, and also to run his businesses overseas—he didn't want Alexis involved in that. The restaurants in the States, yes, but not Greece."

"Was that more chauvinism? Or was it a father trying to protect his daughter from his shady business practices? The ones he fled back to in the US, instead of facing the consequences."

"That investigation was nothing but a vendetta by the Greek government."

Honestly, I didn't care—it's not like I worked for a newspaper in Athens. I just wanted him to leave, but that didn't seem to be happening anytime soon.

"Mr. Tskitapolis was good to me. He took me in off the street when I had nothing in my pockets. So I was determined to grant his final wish to run his businesses, and take care of Alexis. That's why I come."

"Well, in that case, shouldn't you be off babysitting her or something?"

"She doesn't need a babysitter, she needs a friend," he stared at me as he said it.

It took me a few moments to realize that he meant me. "She doesn't understand what it means to be a friend."

"I think you should cut Alexis a break. She only wants what's best for your family."

"And you say I'm the funny one."

"You're rational, because your family is that way. But she takes after her mother—she would lead with her heart and make emotional decisions. Alexis might do or say the wrong thing, but she means you no harm."

I do recall her mother, Macaela, being on the hot-tempered side. Sometimes we could hear the fights between her and her husband all the way down the block, especially those warm summer nights when the windows were open. Her father was the direct opposite. I found him to be cold, and I was always a little bit scared of him as a child.

But we all have our issues with family—*understatement of the year!*—so it was no excuse for Alexis' betrayal.

"Tell me about your mother," Niko said.

"You were there today. You heard my sister's eulogy."

"That's your sister's version—I want to know how you saw her."

And for some reason I opened up to this stranger. A stranger whose "little sister" was sneaking around parking lots with my father.

Niko listened intently, then smiled—add another D-word, devastating. "She sounds like an amazing woman. It's no wonder you grew up to be extraordinary."

He finished his beer and abruptly rose off his stool. He straightened his suit jacket and looked at his watch—a diamond-studded Rolex. "I have enjoyed our chat, Eliza, but I must catch a plane ... back to Greece. I apologize for our intrusion today, but I hope you understand that Alexis had the best intentions."

I didn't know if I should hug him or give him a swift kick in the rear, so I split the difference and went with a professional handshake.

"Just please give Alexis a chance, sometimes things aren't always as we first see them," he said.

I told him that I would, even though I had no intention to ever speak to her again. I watched Niko leave Wojo's, then returned to my bar stool with plans to cry in my beer ... literally.

I stared straight ahead, replaying Niko's words in my head. Something kept bugging me. Something wasn't right.

And then it clicked.

I ran out to the parking lot, but he had already gone.

Chapter 46

Officer Annie Sampson walked Chris Dunbar into the office. Her lawyer, Morgan Gregson, trailed closely behind. But the person Chris really needed was Eliza.

And even though she wasn't here, Chris could still feel her twin's presence, just like when she faced down hostile basketball crowds. It was Eliza, deep in her subconscious, appearing at the most important moments, which allowed Chris to keep her focus—block everything else out, so that it was just her, the ball, and the basket.

She would need the same focus here; this was the game of her life.

Chief Wallach sat behind a large oak desk stroking his mustache, with Tim Ruiz seated in a folding chair beside the desk. A window behind the desk provided a view of Main Street. Directly across the street was Easton Bank, which Chris had been forced to rob two weeks ago.

"Are you more comfortable?" Wallach asked, referring to the change of clothing they offered her—a *Danbury Police* T-shirt and a pair of loose-fitting sweat pants. Not one of those fashionable orange jumpsuits that she'd probably receive when she was transferred to state prison on Monday—the York Women's Correctional Facility in Niantic.

Chris would go before the judge on Monday morning and bail was a possibility, but Gregson cautioned her not to get her hopes up.

"Thank you, Officer Sampson," Wallach said to Annie, which was her hint to exit stage left. He then stared at Chris for a long moment. Chris stared right back at him. It was a showdown.

"I really hate the term 'good cop/bad cop'," Wallach broke the stalemate. "You see, most police officers are both. It all depends on how cooperative you are. If you work with us and tell the truth, we'll get along just fine. But if you lie, then you'll see my bad side, so it's really up to you, Chris … do you understand?"

Her natural instinct was to fight back, but she knew she had to keep her calm. Just take the abuse or it will make it worse—she had learned this lesson the hard way.

She briefly glanced in Tim's direction, and Wallach noticed. "I don't know you like Detective Ruiz does. He's told me a lot about you, but I'd like to see for myself."

He signaled Tim, who turned around the laptop that was set up on the desk, so that Chris and her lawyer could see.

He played a slide show for them. It was a compilation of Chris Dunbar's bad behavior. The first clip was of Chris and an opponent getting into a fight on the court back in college. The second was Chris' mug shot from her first DUI. The third was the security video of Chris threatening her father, a prelude to the break-in. She looked threatening, disheveled, and even Chris had to admit, a little scary.

"You have a history of violence and aggressive behavior when you don't get what you want. In this case, what you wanted was money. Which you'd later come back for."

Chris looked at Gregson, who nodded that it was okay for her to speak. "What you see on that video, I was forced to do. And when I initially refused, I was threatened."

It was like her words just whisked past Wallach without even a notice. "You appear to be acting erratically in the video. Were you on something?"

"I was sober."

"But you have a history of alcohol abuse."

"I don't see what this has to do with what happened to my client's mother," Gregson interjected.

"I'm looking for a reason that would explain her behavior. What would cause her to threaten her own father like that, and get to the bottom of why she was suddenly in desperate need of money." Wallach looked intently at Chris. "Are you an addict?"

"I have struggled with alcohol in the past. I spent time in a rehabilitation center."

"And have you been clean since?"

"For the most part, but I've had an occasional beer or glass of wine."

"When was the last time you had a drink?"

"A few weeks back—a friend of mine had returned from Europe, Kirk McCaffrey, and we went out."

"Which was the same night you supposedly met these men who forced you to threaten your parents—Plato and Socrates," he laughed to himself, "It's a good thing I took those philosophy courses in college. How about you, Detective Ruiz?"

Tim shook his head. "It wasn't required for a criminal justice degree."

"Well, it should have been. That way you'd know that the third masked man that night likely called himself Pyrrho. He was the philosopher who founded the Greek School of Skepticism. That would make the most sense, since I think we're all very skeptical of Ms. Dunbar's story."

Chris kept her composure. "He didn't provide a name, the third man."

Wallach again motioned to Tim, and the video picked up where it had left off.

"How come Plato and Socrates didn't accompany you to your parents' home?" Wallach asked.

"I was told to go alone, and given a script to follow. They said if I didn't, they would harm my nieces."

"Did you think to call the police? We could have provided protection for your family. We are trained in these sort of things."

"They said if I talked to anyone they would—"

"I know, I know, harm your family—kind of ironic, if you ask me—was that the same threat they made to you to get you to rob that bank?"

Gregson stepped in, "My client will not be making any comment on the robbery of the Easton Bank." Even if it was unrelated to her parents' deaths, it could put her away for a long time, and an admission would provide Wallach great leverage.

"We searched your apartment in New York, and found this," Wallach moved on, holding up the blonde wig. Chris hadn't stored it in her apartment, so either the Greeks had further set her up, or Wallach was bluffing.

Gregson scoffed, "Millions of people own blonde wigs."

"Ones that match the fibers at the bank robbery?"

"A match to a common style wig—the possibilities are endless. If you found hairs that belong to my client at the scene, that's a different story, but this is just a desperate stab."

Wallach again stared down Chris. "We do have a witness who claimed you were the one behind the robbery ... your own sister. Are you saying she lied in her article?"

Gregson grew irritated. "I guess you didn't hear me the first time—my client has nothing to say about the bank robbery. If that's all you want to talk about, then we're done here."

Wallach grinned. "I guess we'll have to wait for court then. But there is one other subject I'd like to discuss."

Chapter 47

"Take us through that night, Chris ... the night your mother was murdered."

Gregson sighed. "You have the security video, you have my client's statement. If there are any inconsistencies, fire away, otherwise let's move on."

Wallach threw up his hands. "Fine by me—I'm all for calling it a day and starting the weekend early. We have your client at the scene, and despite her claims, she can't provide any proof that she was forced, or tell us the identity of the men who threatened her. In fact, the video clearly shows that these men were following *her* orders."

"If she could do that, then we wouldn't be here wasting time, now would we?"

"She had previously threatened the victims, and has a history of aggressive behavior and addiction. So I'm just trying to do your client a favor, hoping she can provide just a shred of evidence that she may be innocent. This might be the easiest case we've ever had."

Wallach stood and headed toward the coat rack, acting as if he were leaving. Tim stepped in, "Listen, we've all had a long week, but if you could bear with me, there are a couple questions we really could use answers to."

Chris looked to her lawyer, and then nodded that she would.

"The three men who forced you into this—did you see them all without their masks?" Tim asked.

"Yes."

"Including the third member, who you hadn't seen prior to the day of the break-in?"

"Yes."

"So you could identify these men?"

"I believe so."

Tim rubbed his chin like he was thinking, and asked, "How did your prints get on the gun, Chris?"

"Like I said, I was knocked out the moment the bathroom door closed, so I have no recollection of any of the events that occurred after that, until I woke up the next morning in Rogers Park. I'm assuming they placed my hand on the gun while I was unconscious, but that's just conjecture."

"It's very convenient that your lack of recollection took place in the one room of the house where there were no security cameras," Wallach rejoined the party.

"I think that was their plan. They'd created enough incriminating evidence against me—why was I the only one not wearing a mask?—and without the cameras, there was no way for me to prove that I wasn't the one behind the murder. Especially with my fingers on the gun. They knew you'd be too lazy to look any deeper, so here we are, just as they expected."

Wallach smiled. "Except one thing. As far as we know, you were the only one present with knowledge of the security cameras."

Gregson groaned. "You're reaching, Bernie. My client's story is backed up by the statement of the victim … her father."

"Who lied in his original statement, claiming that Chris wasn't even there. So I don't know what to believe when it comes to Nathan Dunbar. Not to mention, he admitted his mind was hazy after being shot."

"He was obviously trying to protect his daughter. If Chris murdered his wife in cold blood, and severely wounded him, do you really think he'd go to these lengths to protect her, even if it is his own flesh and blood?" Gregson made the case.

"He could be scared to do so, we see it all the time with witnesses," Tim offered, but Wallach had a different theory ...

"If he was in on it with her, then he would. Come to think of it, Nathan Dunbar also had this knowledge."

"That's outrageous!"

"My father *was* in on it ... from the standpoint of these men who were after him," Chris interjected.

"And why would they be after him?"

"Their plan was to kill his wife and frame his daughter for the murder—that's not what you do when it's just about money. It was personal."

"And you can prove this, of course?"

"I can't."

"That's the problem, Ms. Dunbar—I *can* prove a lot of stuff. And you're just throwing stuff against the wall. It's not a strategy that's going to end well for you."

Annie Sampson knocked quickly and reentered the office. "I have Eliza Dunbar outside. She's demanding to talk to you, sir."

Wallach looked exasperated. "As you can see, I'm in the middle of interrogating a suspect."

"She's being insistent."

"Then please explain to her that I'm busy trying to solve her mother's murder, and I don't have time."

"Which is exactly the reason why I'm here," Eliza said, as she pushed passed Annie.

Chapter 48

Chief Wallach wasn't interested in what I had to say.

"I've had enough of the Dunbar sisters for one day," he said and headed for the door.

I didn't expect Wallach to hear me out, so no loss—Tim was my intended target.

I began talking a mile a minute, and Tim motioned me to take a breath and slow down. He then took me into his office, so I wouldn't be speaking in front of the arrested suspect, my sister.

"Who was there?" he asked.

I explained how Niko had approached me in the bar, and something told me I should keep a record of our conversation. So I reached into my purse and clicked on my trusty tape recorder, which I use to tape interviews for the paper.

He didn't say anything incriminating, at least on the surface, and mostly encouraged me to reconcile with Alexis. But it wasn't what he said—it was his voice. I had heard it before, and after replaying the tape, I was sure of it. It was the voice of the man on the security video from the night my mother was murdered. The third man, who Chris hadn't seen previously—the leader.

To anyone else I'd come off as the unhinged sister of a murder suspect, sinking further and further into deluded fantasy. But Tim knew me well enough to hear the conviction in my words.

I wished I had a photo of Niko that Chris could have identified for us. But Tim did the next best thing—he called a friend at the FBI who owed him a favor.

They ran the two tapes through "voice recognition" technology. And it came back as a match for a Greek national named Niko Gogan. Tim cautioned me that the technology was far from perfect, and would never hold up in court, but it didn't dampen my enthusiasm. I knew it was Niko, and this confirmed it. Of course, even if I proved he was there, Chris still appeared to be the ringleader. But it earned me enough credibility with Tim for him to hear me out.

Also, there was a reason why Niko was on an FBI list of possible voice matches. He had a long rap sheet in Greece, going back to when he was a teenager. I wanted to take what we learned to Chris, but something about sharing leads with the top suspect in the case was a big no-no.

Discussing it with Niko was also not an option, since he was long gone, having returned to Greece. But the bridge that connected him to my father was still very much here, and I pleaded with Tim that we needed to talk to her.

Minutes later, Tim and I were on our way to Skita's in Ridgefield, and we weren't going for a late lunch. We were told that Alexis was not expected in today, as she had some "personal business" to attend to.

My stomach sank. If Niko had left the country, could Alexis have been far behind? She had to know it was only a matter of time before we made the connection. Maybe they were traveling together, or perhaps Niko's sudden interest in me at Wojo's was to distract me while she slipped out of the country.

I grew hysterical, "We lost her ... she's gone forever ... there's no way we can save Chris now!"

Tim remained calm. "Let's go check her home—the farm in Roxbury, right?"

Roxbury was about ten miles outside of Danbury. It was a rural town made up mostly of local farmers, but it also served as a remote getaway for artists and celebrities. The writer Arthur Miller was once its best known resident, although his one-time wife, and infamous bank robber, Marilyn Monroe, was the one who put it on the map when she lived there with Miller in the early 1960s.

We drove up the long, gravel driveway, still lined by snow that remained from the brutal winter. We pulled up to a rustic farmhouse that looked like straight out of a Norman Rockwell painting.

I pulled my coat tight and wrapped my scarf around my neck. The sun was sinking behind the thick cluster of trees, and it felt like the temperature had dropped twenty degrees since I was at the cemetery this morning.

I followed Tim to the front door and stood impatiently as he knocked. When we received no answer, he knocked again, this time with more urgency. But not a creature was stirring.

Tim went behind the farmhouse to peer through the back windows, and check for potential hiding places like a storm cellar. What we couldn't do was just barge inside without a reason, or at least one that a judge would agree was a good reason. So if she decided to hide under the bed until we left, there was nothing we could do about it.

I checked out the small red barn that was a few hundred yards behind the house. The place where Alexis' mother took her life. An eerie feeling came over me as I creaked the door open and stepped inside. But my mind must have been playing tricks on me, because there was nothing in here— no Alexis, no Niko, no hanging ghost of Macaela Tskitapolis.

I took a moment to think of Alexis' mother. I remembered her as smart and beautiful and confident—much like her daughter. And she would never back down from anything, including her domineering husband. So it was hard for me to comprehend how she got to that point, feeling so sad or trapped that she thought this was the only way out.

But then again, I saw those days through the eyes of a child. And now as an adult, I realized that we never really know anyone as well as we think we do—our neighbors, our friends, our own family. I thought of the photo that Alexis had left for me, and how perfect I'd always believed that moment in time to be. But was it really?

I remained on edge as I stepped outside the barn. I felt a chill against my face, and the silence evaporated. I heard Tim shout, "Stop—police!"

I looked back toward the farmhouse and saw a figure on cross-country skis, zooming across the top of the snow-covered ground … and coming right at me!

I was too far away to stop the skier, who was headed towards the deep woods. I maneuvered as best I could over the icy terrain, almost falling a few times, but somehow maintaining my balance. I had changed into more comfortable clothing after the funeral, but my heeled boots weren't exactly ideal for chasing down runaway skiers.

The skier was coming fast, so I was forced to throw caution to the wind and sprint. More like fast hobbling. As I grew closer I saw the dark curls slinking out of the knit cap, and knew it was Alexis.

My adrenaline carried me the last twenty yards. I leaped and hit her with a perfect shoulder tackle, driving her to the ground. Beef would have been proud.

We were both momentarily disorientated, but Alexis was able to gather herself enough to roll off me, and attempt to run away.

Her poles had skidded away and she had lost a ski. She had to take a moment to rid herself of the other ski, so she could make a run for the path. It provided me enough time to remove my scarf, and use it to trip her up as she tried to dash off.

She scrambled to her feet, but she didn't get very far.

"Freeze," Tim's shout echoed off the woods, as he pointed his gun at her.

Alexis raised her hands in the air.

Chapter 49

We sat in the living room of the farmhouse in front of a crackling fire. It felt like a ski lodge in Vermont—a place where attractive people wearing heavy sweaters would regale listeners with tales of their day on the slopes, while sipping hot chocolate. But this was anything but a party.

"What's this about?" Alexis demanded from her seat on the couch. Her inner princess was coming out.

"With all due respect, I'll be asking the questions," Tim said, firm, but polite.

"Then ask."

"For starters, where were you going?"

"Going? I'm on my property. I do cross country skiing for a workout. Is that illegal or something?"

I snorted a laugh. "Do you really think we're that stupid?"

Tim hit me with a salty glance. He'd just given me the lecture about letting him handle this, and keeping my mouth shut. But to be fair, he'd known me way too long to expect that.

"Nothing illegal, but when I identified myself as a police officer, and asked you to stop, you didn't. That changed things."

"I didn't know for sure that you were the police, and I wasn't going to risk finding out that you weren't."

"Who did you think we might be?"

"You can never be too careful—my father had enemies. Sometimes that grudge is handed down to the children."

Enemies like Plato and Socrates and their buddy Niko. I really tried to hold back, but, "I had a little chat with your boyfriend today."

She blew out a frustrated sigh. "How many times do I have to tell you, Eliza? There was nothing going on between me and your father."

"She's referring to Niko Gogan," Tim said.

"Niko's a friend, not a boyfriend."

"Boyfriend … friend … it really doesn't matter. The only title Niko has that interests us is murderer. Which makes you an accessory to murder," I said.

Tim gave me another annoyed look—he was just mad I got all the good lines.

"What are you talking about, accessory to murder?" she said, frustration growing.

"Niko flew here to meet you last Friday night, correct?" Tim asked.

"Yes."

"And that night you went to a party in Manhattan?"

Her voice turned less sure, "No—I was busy at the restaurant that night, and Niko was tired from his flight."

"So you lied to us at Wojo's," I said.

"I didn't lie—we changed our plans. I didn't know I needed to clear that with you, Eliza."

"Was he with you at the restaurant?" Tim asked.

"No—he stayed here, to catch up on his rest. When I returned, he was sound asleep."

"What time was that?"

"Around 2:30 in the morning."

Just enough time to commit murder, drop my sister off at Rogers Park, and be tucked in when Alexis returned home. Not that anyone asked me.

"What if I told you I know where he was that night, and it wasn't here," Tim said.

"I told you we're just friends—if he met another woman, it doesn't affect things."

Tim took out his tablet and played for her the security video from that night. "Do you recognize anyone?"

"How could I recognize these men when they are wearing masks?" she fired back, flustered.

"Are you sure?"

"The only person I recognize is Chris Dunbar," she said, but she'd known Niko since she was sixteen. She could recognize his movements, his voice, his idiosyncrasies. She knew it was him.

The only question was whether Niko was frolicking with the enemy behind her back, or perhaps the princess was equally involved and was about to throw Niko under the proverbial bus to save her tiara. I wasn't falling for her sad words or trembling lips anymore.

I wanted to grab her by the throat until she admitted it was him, but Tim took a softer, and likely more effective, approach. "I can see why this is so hard for you, Alexis. You've known him most of your life."

"I'm not sure I really know him at all," she conceded.

"These other men he's with—Plato and Socrates—Eliza tells me are enemies of your family. The ones you worried had come for you when we arrived—that's why you tried to escape. And to see Niko with them …"

He let the statement marinate for a few long seconds, before, "You need someone on your side—let me be that person to protect you. There's really no way around the fact that you're connected to Niko, and he was behind the murder of Eliza's mother … who I know you were very fond of. So if you want me to bring you down to the station and charge you with accessory to murder, we can do that."

After a long tense pause, he added, "But I think it would benefit both of us if we worked together. You help us find Niko, so we can ask him the questions we need to ask him, and we'll protect you."

Her face hardened. "You think I'm that easily manipulated? I've been lied to by men my entire life—I can see right through you."

"But I'm not a man, and I've never lied to you," I stepped in. "You told me that you cared about my family, and that you understood my pain. You asked me if there was anything you could do for me. Well, what I need is to talk to Niko. He was there that night—maybe he was forced, just like my sister, I'm in no position to judge him, but the only way to find out is to talk to him."

Alexis appeared to be on the fence. "As far as I know, he returned to Greece this afternoon."

"Then we need to go to Greece … and you're coming with us."

Tim looked at me, as if to say; *and how exactly are you planning to do that?* The police weren't funding it, especially since they thought they had their killer, and the *Ledger* would be lucky to pay its electric bill this month.

"I'm not going to Greece, and you can't make me," Alexis remained defiant. "I've already told you that I'll be detained by the government if I do, which is why I took those flights with your father."

"You're right, I can't make you go, nor would I advise it," Tim said in a supportive voice, "but we're still going to need your help."

She looked hesitant at first, but I could tell that Niko's betrayal was eating at her. Or maybe she saw him as her big fat Greek liability and this was her chance to remove him … along with the pesky reporter and her cop friend. But regardless of her motive, she eventually agreed.

Which meant that Tim and I were going to Greece.

Chapter 50

Saturday morning, one week removed from the worst day of my life.

We were gathered in the driveway outside my house as the sun started to make it's rise over the lake. I was providing Connie last minute instructions, down to the minutest neurotic detail.

"You do know I have some parenting experience, Eliza."

"You have boys—you have no idea what you're getting yourself into with the Little Macs."

She stepped back and viewed me like she was looking at me for the first time. "I love the outfit by the way. The skirt is really cute, and the beret is so European chic."

More practical than anything. My prosthetic tends to set off detectors in airports, so I've learned from experience that it's much easier to clear up matters when wearing a skirt, than struggling to pull off a pair of pants in front of security. And the beret was all about not having time to do my hair this morning, plus, it's always been my good luck charm, and we needed all the luck we could get.

Connie continued grinning, unnerving me, "What?"

"It's just that a last minute weekend trip to Miami with a guy … that's so not an Eliza move."

I hated that I told them that I was going to Miami in search of the mysterious Plato, and not to the home of the original Plato, to hunt down

Niko. Especially after all my preaching over the years about the power of the truth. But I rationalized that I wasn't lying, rather, this was like the misdirection of a CIA agent for the good of the mission.

"It's not some guy ... it's Tim ... who happens to be the lead detective on my mother's case."

And speaking of "some guy" he pulled up the driveway in his custom Mustang. He wore a tweed jacket and glasses, looking more like a professor than police officer, a single overnight bag slung over his shoulder.

Kirk stepped out of the house in robe and pajama bottoms; a steaming cup of coffee in his hand. When I told him last night about our "Miami" trip, he was none too pleased. He appeared to be even less thrilled this morning. And when he laid eyes on Tim, it was like I'd poked him in the eye.

Despite my rugged independence, I always liked Kirk's over-protective side and never found it to be controlling. I thought of it more as chivalrous and old-fashioned. We all have our inner cave-woman.

And yes, it would be great for the girls if he stuck around. And he was a lifesaver with the funeral.

But.

And this was a JLO size but.

This was not his place. He had given up that right.

"Can I speak to you a minute?" Kirk requested, eying Tim as he did. "Alone."

We walked back near the entrance of the house. "This trip is a bad idea, Eliza—it's way too dangerous."

"I'll be fine—Tim will be with me. He's a police officer, it's his job to protect me."

"He's a police officer who is playing on your emotions."

"Not sure where you're going with that."

"His job isn't to protect you, but to get evidence that will help solve his case. And the top suspect in his case is your sister. He's using this trip to get close to you, so that he can get more information on Chris that will help put her away."

"You can't be serious."

"You're too trusting."

I thought for a moment. "You know, you're right—I hadn't considered that angle. I just thought he was trying to exploit my vulnerability to get me into bed."

I smiled, even if Kirk didn't see the humor.

But it did spark his thought. "What are the sleeping arrangements? Let me guess, he suggested that you get adjoining doors, just in case there's an emergency?"

I didn't have time to fight, or list out for Kirk the things that were no longer his business. "Your concern is noted, but I'm a grown-up. So you're just going to have to trust me. And if you don't, tough luck."

"Just like you trust me?"

As much as he was against the trip, he was just as offended that I put Connie in charge of the girls. So to repeat what I told him last night, "Of course I trust you with them—you're their father. But they have girl stuff lined up all weekend. Brooke has an art class and Daisy Scouts, while Kelly is going to a 'princess party' on Sunday. And besides, you're supposed to be looking for your hip bachelor pad this weekend—you promised you'd be out by next week."

He gave me a brooding nod, which was his version of a concession speech. I gave him a hug, which he didn't reciprocate. It was like a flashback to the last year of our marriage.

The Connecticut Limo pulled into the driveway. It sounds glamorous, but was really an oversized SUV that served as airport transportation. But it wasn't for Tim and me.

Karen and her crew exited the house, dragging luggage. She offered that we split the "limo" to the airport, but I wanted to avoid that awkward moment when they went to drop us off at the Miami terminal and we were like, change of plans, maybe a trip to Greece instead, we're kind of crazy like that.

We engaged in a mega group hug and tearful goodbye between sisters, cousins, aunts and cowboys, with so much love that I thought Hallmark should consider making a card for it. The Cowboy Kids and the Little Macs were already talking about their plans for next summer, since we decided to go out to Wyoming next July, instead of them coming here. It seemed like the right time to start a new tradition.

Tim and I then piled into my car, and drove off toward another day in the new life of Eliza Dunbar.

Chapter 51

When we stepped into JFK Airport, my first thought was that I had really missed the flying experience. It used to be as common for me as catching a movie, but I'd only flown twice in the last five years—once to Wyoming to see Karen and her family, and a trip to Florida last year with the girls.

The year I worked for the Cubs I would sometimes fly to three cities in a week. The veteran sports reporters complained constantly about the travel, but I would have done it for free. Even if the one-legged chick running through the airport wasn't always a pretty sight.

As children, with my father being a commercial pilot, we were able to fly for free, so we made many trips to Europe—Paris, London, Rome—but I had never been to Greece. And I doubted that I would get to see much of it this time. This was a business trip.

As we passed through airport security, Tim and I tensed. We didn't want to talk too loud—who was listening? Were we being followed? I've never felt so over-my-head.

We loosened up slightly once we boarded our flight. But when the plane took off, Tim grew quiet once again, and began nervously twisting his finger like something was wrong with it.

"Are you okay?" I asked.

"I think so," he said, but didn't sound convincing.

"Did you hurt your finger?"

He looked down, as if unaware he was doing it. An embarrassed look came over his face, "No … um … when I get nervous I play with my wedding ring. I guess old habits die hard," he said.

We both looked at the ring-less finger.

"You get nervous when you fly? That's a little surprising."

"Why so?"

"For starters, I went on that ride-along with you and your partner last year for a story. You guys dashed into the building on Beaver Street and took down that armed drug dealer without breaking a sweat."

"I can handle being shot to death, but not plunging to the earth from tens of thousands of feet. The good news is that it's just takeoffs and landings—I'll be fine once we get leveled off."

"The even better news is there's a 99.999% chance this plane lands safely to Athens. The bad news is that might be the safest part of our trip."

"I see what you're doing," he said with a small grin.

"You do?"

"You're trying to keep me talking, to distract me until we reach our cruising altitude."

I smiled. "I wouldn't waste my diversion skills on your mental health. If I was going to distract you, it would be to steal your wallet."

"With my police salary, I'm not sure that would be worth your effort," he replied with a laugh.

The ding indicated that the captain had turned off the *Fasten Seat Belt* sign, which meant Tim's nerves had a ten-hour reprieve before we made our descent into Athens. We floated through the puffy clouds—at 500 mph—somewhere over the Atlantic Ocean.

"So do you miss it?" I asked, noticing Tim still working on that finger.

"The ring or the marriage?"

"They sort of go hand in hand."

He thought for a long moment, as if choosing his words carefully. "Layna was pretty much all I knew. So the idea of us not being together took some getting used to. I mean, we'd been together since …"

As he struggled to remember, I thought I'd take a stab, "Dana DeCastro's party, the last weekend before sophomore year."

It started to come back to him, "That's right—wow, you have a really good memory."

"It's not always a good thing."

"You know when people say, 'we grew apart, and didn't even realize it until it was too late,' well, that wasn't the case with us. I felt Layna slipping away not long after we got married, and I tried to do everything I could to get us back on track, but it was like swimming against the tide—the harder I struggled, the more she drifted away."

He caught himself. "Don't get me wrong, I'm not trying to make myself the victim here. We were different people at that point, and we no longer connected in the same way. I dealt with it by clinging tighter, while Layna followed the current out to sea. I was trying to recreate something that no longer existed, and she accepted reality. There wasn't a right or wrong."

You could tell he'd done a lot of thinking about this. "Any regrets?"

"Just that I lost my best friend in the process."

"I'm sorry about that—you two were pretty inseparable for a long time."

After a brief pause, he said, "I meant you, Eliza."

Chapter 52

That could use some explanation.

"Your biggest regret about your marriage breaking up is … me?"

"What I meant is, Layna had issues with you right from the start. I guess she saw you, or our friendship, as some sort of threat. Whenever you'd come up in conversation, or she found out we'd talked on the phone, it turned into a fight. I should have stood up to her and said if she can't accept my friend then she didn't accept me, but I guess I was too afraid of losing her."

This was getting a little heavy, so I deflected, "I couldn't compete with those mini skirts. I mean who could, really?"

He smiled. "I'm just glad you came back home. Obviously I wish it was for other reasons than your mother's illness, but the place wouldn't be the same without you. I figured you'd end up staying in Chicago, and maybe I'd see you at the reunions, but that's it."

Is this what Kirk meant when he said that Tim was going to play on my emotions, so he could loosen me up to get information about Chris? Maybe so, but I was enjoying our conversation. We hadn't talked like this in a long time. Even that night at the hospital felt like we were talking through walls.

"Well, I'm glad I came back too. And when you think about it, Danbury is a lot like Chicago—diverse crowd, cool festivals, the lake rocks in the summer … they just have bigger buildings."

He smiled. "Never thought of it like that."

We hit a rough patch of turbulence, knocking the smile off Tim's face, and he went back to his ring finger.

When things smoothed out, I asked, "So do you keep in touch with Layna?"

"Not really. I had a call a few months ago at her aunt's house, who still lives in Danbury. She told me that she was living in Florida and had gotten engaged to some real estate tycoon."

"That was fast," I said, a little too snotty.

He shrugged. "Her life is her life. We played it out to the end, and it just wasn't meant to be. So there was no looking back and saying if we just did that, or tried a little harder. So it was a clean break for both of us."

"That's a really healthy way of looking at it."

"How about you and Kirk … any regrets?"

"Hey—I'm the reporter. I ask the questions."

"When I ask questions folks usually need their lawyer present, so consider yourself lucky."

"I think you're out of your jurisdiction, Detective Ruiz, but I'll make an exception for an old friend." My smile faded. "Well, we didn't play it out to the end like you—more like cut our losses—and we have two very cute reasons why we'll never have a clean break, so I guess I'll always wonder if maybe we gave up too easily."

"It looks like you'll get your chance to find out."

"Not sure I understand."

"I mean, you're living together again, so you're back together, right? You'll get a chance to answer those questions."

I almost choked on … not really sure what—some sort of cheddar chips and pretzel combo.

"Oh, no, no … no. We are definitely not back together. He's just been staying with us to help out with things. As you can imagine, it's been a little crazy this past week. He was actually pretty great with the funeral."

Tim didn't look upset by my answer. I was reminded of Beef's words from the other day, but then I recalled all the crazy things Beef had said over the years, and disregarded it.

With it being a ten-hour flight, there was no way we could small talk and reminisce our way through the entire trip, and completely avoid the reason we were here.

"Do you really think Chris killed my mother?" I got right to the point, and again grew concerned over who might be listening in on our conversation.

"Would I really be on this flight if I did?"

Good answer.

He added, "Like I told you at the hospital, I have to be a cop on this case, not your friend. But I'm human, and I've known Chris seemingly forever, so that does shape my opinion. And I can't imagine her doing something like that."

I would have preferred, *no way in hell your sister could do this, and I'll fight with you to the bitter end,* but an open mind was the best I could hope for. Wallach certainly didn't have one, and public opinion was hardly on Chris' side.

"Do you think Alexis will really help us locate Niko? She could just as easily tip him off that we're coming," I said.

"I think she's more foe than friend at this point. Although, she did look genuinely hurt when we revealed Niko's involvement."

I agreed. But just like I was betting on Tim's long history with Chris, Alexis had a long history with Niko. Sometimes those bonds are not easily broken.

"Then why are we putting our trust in her? It's likely to just scare him off."

"Because it's the best shot we've got."

"Ah, the old 'beggars can't be choosers' strategy. Sounds promising."

"I can paint you a rosier portrait if it will make you feel better, but the truth is, I'm completely out on a limb here—my boss thinks he has his killer, so he isn't even looking for other suspects. Alexis might not be on our side, but without her funding this trip, we wouldn't be able to follow up on our best lead."

"So what's our plan—jump Niko and drag him back to the US in chains? Maybe round up Plato and Socrates while we're at it. Good thing I brought those extra suitcases."

He lowered his voice, "Even if we locate Niko, the chances he will return to the US with us for questioning are less than zero. And I don't have the ability, or the extradition power, to force his hand. But if we can find that one item that gives Wallach some pause, then our mission was a success. And for some reason, I feel confident we will."

We ended the conversation on that positive thought, and I drifted off to sleep. But my dreams turned out to be much less optimistic.

I was at the edge of the water, while Chris was standing on what looked like an island, calling my name. I felt like I was close enough to grab her hand. I reached as far as I could, but I couldn't make contact. I had to get to her! To save her!

The water between us was filled with sharks—there was no way I could make it. And when I looked to Chris once more, I saw that she wasn't alone.

Niko was standing beside her, gun in his hand. He was daring me to jump into the shark-filled water. And even if I miraculously survived that, I would still have to go through him to get to Chris.

But if I could just make it, there would be two of us, working together, maybe we could hold him off. *Wonder Twin power!* I had to try.

I was about to make a swim for it, when I felt a tug on the back of my sweater. I turned to see Brooke. "Don't go, Mommy!"

I felt something wrapped around my leg. "No, Mommy—the sharks will eat you! We need you!" Kelly begged, while holding on tight.

I looked again to Chris. And then down at my girls. "Please don't go, Mommy!" And that's when I felt someone else grab tightly to my arm.

It was my father.

"It's important that you and Chris stick together," he pleaded, just as he had in the hospital. I wrestled my arm away from him and tried to make it to the water, but the girls were holding on too tight. I didn't know what to do—I needed to save Chris, but I also had to be here for them.

I was lost, and screamed out for the one person who could guide me.

And she appeared like a genie.

My mother looked me in the eyes. "I need you to guarantee me that both my girls will make it."

She held her gaze, until I finally called out, "I promise you that we will both make it!"

And I woke up.

"Are you okay? I think you were having a bad dream," Tim said.

I rubbed the sweat off my cheeks. "I'm fine," I said, my voice shaking.

But as we began our descent into Athens, I could sense the sharks in the water.

Chapter 53

I stumbled out of bed and did a zombie-walk toward the knocking sound. I opened the door to find Tim with coffee in hand, and sporting an eager smile. I accepted the coffee, but tersely let him know that he was in direct violation of the "Do Not Disturb" sign hanging on the door.

After a ten-hour flight and six hour time change, we had arrived at our hotel in Athens just before sunrise. And despite getting two hours of sleep, Tim looked no worse for wear, still wearing his tweed coat and glasses.

"I thought we were going to meet in the lobby at nine?" I said.

"Change of plans—my contact had to reshuffle his schedule, so he moved us up to fit us in."

Sounded reasonable. Tim waited for me as I retreated to the bathroom. I dressed in my "job interview" suit, which was getting a lot of work lately. And if Bob knew what I was doing, I might need to set up some actual interviews.

The temperature was expected to reach sixty degrees, but felt much cooler when I first stepped outside the hotel. The Athenians were out in force early on this Sunday morning. For some reason I expected the locals to be draped in togas, and the buildings to be built of white marble with magnificent columns, but it looked like any typical city in the US or Europe.

Tim flagged a cab, which took us to Vasilisis Sophias Avenue on the east side of the city. Under different circumstances, I could have spent an entire day along this street. It featured landmarks such as the Old Royal Palace and the National Garden of Athens. I would have loved to take in the National Gallery and the Benaki Museum.

It was also made up of prestigious mansions that housed embassies, including the French, British, and Byzantine. The US embassy was a modern, glass-fronted building, but the architecture was inspired by the Pantheon—so it was a mix of old and new. It was located next to the Athens Concert Hall, or Megaro Mousikis as our cab driver referred to it.

Tim did all the talking with security, sounding very official. He had set up a meeting with the US Legal Attaché, Larry Bradford.

Once all security badges were attached, and photos taken, a stout woman led us through the impressive hallways until we arrived at Bradford's office.

He greeted us with smiles and handshakes. "So you know Rob Anders?"

Tim nodded. "We went to college together back in Connecticut."

Rob was the FBI agent who hooked Tim up with the voice recognition identifier on Niko, and then helped broker this meeting with Bradford. The Legal Attaché was an FBI agent who works with the Greek authorities on areas of mutual interest to both the US and Greece, but doesn't have jurisdictional authority. Rob still thought he would be helpful in locating Niko.

I was expecting a middle-aged, vanilla-looking bureaucrat, and that's pretty much what we got. But one with a nice tan, having just returned from a family vacation. We engaged in some small talk, and found common interest in that he was a fellow New Englander, having grown up in Springfield, Massachusetts. His wife was Greek, and when her parents became ill a few years back, he put in for this assignment. It wasn't the best move for his career, but his family was happy in Greece and he hoped to stay here long term.

He shut the door behind us, and took a seat behind his desk. "We're looking for Niko Gogan," I got right to the point.

"Usually Niko is looking for people—not the other way around. What is your interest in him?"

"He killed my mother."

Always a conversation stopper.

"He's a person of interest in a murder back in the States, and we're looking to question him," Tim clarified.

Bradford leaned back in his chair and blew out a deep breath. "What type of evidence do you have?"

"We're still in the process of building a case," Tim said.

"We are hoping you can help us with that," I backed him up.

"I sympathize, I really do," Bradford began, which didn't sound promising, "but it's not like Greece is just going to hand him over to you without concrete evidence." He looked to Tim. "I don't think I need to tell you that you're well out of your jurisdiction, and my powers are limited within Greece."

"He killed my mother," I thought I'd remind him.

He gave it a charity ponder. "The best I can do is get the ball rolling at the Bureau. I can't guarantee anyone will run with it, and even in the best-case scenario, the process will take time. A lot will depend on the type of evidence you currently possess … I'm assuming you didn't just fly all the way to Greece on a wing and a prayer."

I explained the conversation I had with Niko in the bar, and how I recognized the voice from the security video from the break-in at my parents' house, which was confirmed by FBI voice recognition technology.

"Don't get me wrong, that's intriguing, but I've got to be honest—it's not enough to get the movers and shakers onto the dance floor."

He looked to Tim. "Do you have any type of physical evidence that ties him to the crime scene? A fingerprint? A hair? You know as well as I do that voice recognition will not hold up as proof."

Tim shook his head, and I could feel the air in the room deflate.

"Like I said, I'll pass your concerns along, but I'm afraid it won't be much of a help, at least based on what you've told me."

I abruptly stood. "Thanks for your help, Agent Bradford. It sounds like I'm just going to have to find him myself."

Tim calmly motioned me to sit. I decided against alienating the one person who might be on my sister's side, and returned my ass to the hard wooden chair.

He then addressed Bradford, "Our expectations are not an arrest or even to formally question him. I see our trip more as a fact-finding mission, to learn more about the man we're chasing in hopes of building that case, and Rob thought you'd be the right person for that."

Bradford nodded. "That I can help you with. But first it would be helpful to hear what you know about Niko, so I can determine what blanks need to be filled in."

Chapter 54

I took the lead, "He told me that he'd worked for Georgos Tskitapolis, and had taken over his Greek and European businesses since his death."

"And what do you know about Georgos Tskitapolis?"

"The Tskitapolis' lived down the street from my family when I was a child, prior to their moving back to Greece. His daughter Alexis *used to be* a close friend of mine. Our families were once tight, but had mostly lost touch until they returned to America in recent years."

"This might come as a surprise, but many of those businesses—the ones Niko claims to now run—aren't exactly on the up and up. And the restaurants are a front to launder money. His main source of revenue was gambling—Tskitapolis had been connected to numerous sports fixes in Greece, and throughout Europe. Futbol, basketball, and even to bribes in regards to the 2004 Olympics.

"To understand Niko, you must understand Tskitapolis, and their relationship. Niko was an up-and-comer in the gambling world, running a scheme out of Kos, when Tskitapolis took notice of him. He brought Niko in and made him his protégée. Because of this, there was much interest in Niko by the Greek authorities, hoping he could help them nab his boss and mentor. But once Tskitapolis died, that interest waned."

"I don't see why they'd back off. He's obviously running the same crooked businesses that Tskitapolis was," I said.

"Greece is in major financial straits. The pursuit of Tskitapolis was never about removing illegal gambling—that was the cover story—the true goal was an arrest of Tskitapolis, which would be of great financial benefit to Greece. It would give them the authority to confiscate his many properties, and his fortune. An arrest could also lead to bribe money—what would he be willing to pay for a lesser sentence? Arresting Tskitapolis could be a lucrative venture for Greece, but Niko was just another hoodlum they'd have to incarcerate. A more likely scenario would be to let him continue to operate, but the government would take a portion of the gambling revenue."

Bradford smiled slyly. "But of course, that's not the official position of the FBI when it comes to our Greek friends. We value our partnership and mutual interest in pursuing justice."

I saw an opening to make our case, "Niko might no longer interest the Greek authorities, but you represent the United States. And if he was involved in a murder on American soil, which could be connected back to this gambling business in Greece, you should be very interested in him."

Bradford didn't seem overly impressed. "Like I said, I will talk to people. But we're still talking about a foreign national and extradition treaties—it's more complicated than you're making it out to be."

"It's not complicated to me—he killed my mother, and he's going to pay for it."

"What I don't understand," Tim said, his calm voice contrasting from mine, "is with Tskitapolis' known criminal activity within Greece, why was he allowed to return to America?"

"Off the record—that's when the FBI was brought in."

"Why?"

"Tskitapolis had no prior interest to the US—he wasn't even on our radar when he lived there in the 1980s. So our first real dealings with him were when we worked with the Greek government to make sure he had safe passage back into the US."

Bradford saw that I was about to lose my mind, and put his hand up. "It was a joint venture with hopes of bringing him down. In Greece, he had many powerful protectors—the wealthy, the politicians, and the wealthy politicians. The thinking was if we could get him to the US, he'd lose his protection, and we'd be able to investigate him without interference."

"What was his incentive to return?" Tim asked.

"Times had changed—many of Tskitapolis' allies had lost fortunes, and therefore power. He was feeling vulnerable, so we spread a rumor that the Greek authorities were about to arrest him on tax evasion charges. With the state of the country, it was plausible. Tskitapolis bought what we were selling, and made a run for it ... back to the US. A move we helped make happen."

"I understand Greece's interest in him, but what was your motive?" I asked.

"That stuff goes way above me, but it could be anything from the US exchanging our help in order to have another criminal extradited back to the US, or something bigger, like needing to use Greece as a base to launch an attack into Syria. But I'm sure we got something ... that's how these things usually work ... off the record, of course.

"And so Tskitapolis continued his business tactics while in the US?" Tim asked.

Bradford laughed. "I've yet to meet one of these criminal minds that decides to find religion. The main difference was that Niko's role was expanded, since Tskitapolis needed someone to run his businesses overseas. And even more so after his death. Tskitapolis' daughter, Alexis, is technically in charge of the family business, but Niko is the one running them."

"What does Alexis know?" I had to ask.

"That's a good question—I believe she's savvier than most people give her credit for, so I doubt she was completely blind to her father's ways. But never underestimate what someone is willing to believe when it comes to family. My best guess is she's naïve on the basis of pragmatism."

"I'm not sure I understand what that means."

"If she believes her father was a crook, not only would that put her entire belief system into question—who she is, where she came from—but also her lifestyle. If the palace she lives in was obtained illegally, then it could be taken away. I think she likes living in that palace. So she convinced herself it is rightfully hers, and she'll do what it takes to protect her kingdom."

"So you *don't* think she could be involved in my mother's murder in any way?"

"That wouldn't fit her profile, but she's always had a strong attraction to Niko, and she wouldn't be the first girl to follow the wrong guy to a wrong place."

I wondered if I'd done the same thing by coming to Greece.

Chapter 55

"We cleared the way for Tskitapolis to return to the US. He re-started his American restaurants, and used them to launder money from gambling, etc. Things were going as planned, until they no longer went as planned."

"I assume you're referring to when his wife committed suicide," Tim said.

"That's correct."

"Was foul play ever considered—maybe she'd found out something about her husband she shouldn't have?" I inquired.

Bradford shook his head. "Nothing to indicate that. Macaela Tskitapolis suffered from depression for years, which was exacerbated by a bout of homesickness. It's probably why they returned to Greece years ago—happy wife, happy life, as they say.

"But her life was never as happy as it looked from the outside. To say her husband was controlling would be an understatement. Perhaps she thought suicide was the only way to escape him."

"So the story of the husband, who was so devastated by his wife's death that he eventually took his own life, was fictional?"

"I don't doubt that it devastated him, but it might have been more a case of losing his most prized possession, than love. And it wasn't the only issue he was dealing with at the time. The Greek government had made great strides in their case since he'd left, and word was that his arrest, and extradition, was imminent."

"Doesn't that make you wonder about his suicide—that he possibly faked his death to avoid being arrested? I mean, they never recovered the body, right?"

"Tskitapolis left a video, shot on the boat, which included his dying wishes. It also captured him committing the act. Without going into too much detail, the evidence removes any reasonable possibility of survival."

"So at that point, your job is over," Tim noted.

"Tskitapolis was NLOP," Bradford replied with a smiling nod.

"NLOP?" I asked.

"No longer our problem."

"But since his protégée murdered someone on American soil, it looks like you're back in business," I kept hammering the point.

"I think we've been over that—you're missing a little something we call evidence."

Now was the time to play our one card—the security video that showed Niko and his men invading my parents' home. Tim took out his tablet from his bag and played it for Bradford. We had hoped not to use it—something about taking evidence overseas on an unsanctioned trip.

Bradford watched intently, then looked to me. "I hate to break it to you, but this just makes your sister look guiltier, whether that's Niko with her or not."

"But it is him on the video, correct?"

Bradford shrugged. "It might be, but with the mask I can't say for sure."

"We're still off the record," Tim said. "How about your best guess?"

"Gun to my head, I'd say it's him."

I moved on to the accomplices. "My sister identified the other men in the video. One called himself Plato. She met him at a New York bar, and he later introduced her to his friend, who went by Socrates."

I thought it was a long shot, but Bradford reached into a desk drawer and took out a folder. He held up a photo of a man who fit the muscle-bound description. "This is Plato Kostas—used to work with Tskitapolis. We heard there was a falling out when Niko was chosen to run the businesses, and they became bitter rivals. But based on your video, it looks like they're playing for the same team again. Like I said, we haven't been following Niko that close lately."

"Plato is his real name, seriously?" I would have bet my kids' college funds that those were made-up names. "Is the other one actually named Socrates?"

Bradford nodded. "The Kostas brothers—Plato and Socrates. And yes, they had an older brother named Aristotle, who died in a Turkish prison years ago."

Bradford pushed another photo across the desk, this one of an unmasked Socrates. I looked at the photos of Plato and Socrates side by side, the first time I'd seen them without their masks. They were both burly Greeks with enough resemblance to tell that they were related. My mother always preached never to judge a book by its cover, but I would make an exception in this case, "These guys don't look very bright."

Bradford got a chuckle out of that. "Ironically, they aren't very philosophical either. They did collections for gamblers like Tskitapolis. Shoot first, ask questions later types. They have rap sheets a few kilometers long."

I used my phone to snap photos of the photos. I wanted to send them to Chris to confirm that these were the other two present that night, but obviously, she wasn't allowed a phone in jail. So I did the next best thing, and sent Plato's photo to Kirk, to see if it was the same man Chris left the bar with that night.

I didn't expect him to be up at this hour, but I'd forgotten what a night owl he was. He messaged me back instantaneously. "That's him—see what I mean? So not her type."

I agreed.

He then took the opportunity to text-lecture me—texture?—about being out at three in the morning, which was the current time in Miami.

I thought to tell him not to worry, because I met some guy in South Beach last night and he flew me to Greece in his private jet. And then I could spend the rest of the day sending him photos from Athens to prove it.

But I chose the more mature route, and texted back: *It's been a long day—Tim and I blowing off some steam. Heading back to bed now.* I thought that would sufficiently irritate him.

He was helpful though. Confirming Plato as a match meant it was more likely than not that the Socrates photo was also a match. So we now had the identities of the three other men with Chris that night. It was a start.

"We need to talk to Niko," I said to Bradford. "He told me he was returning to Greece, so if you could point us in his direction, we'd appreciate it."

"He did go out of his way to let you know he was returning, which makes me skeptical. It's like he wanted you to believe he was in Greece to create a diversion. In the past, he'd been known to hide out in Macedonia and Albania when the flames got hot. But we don't track him anymore, so I don't have a good read on where he might be."

I got the feeling that Bradford didn't want us to find him. "Where does he stay when he's in Greece?"

Bradford shrugged, acting like I was wasting my time. "The Tskitapolis family has a mansion in Kos, right on the water, nice digs—one of the few places the government hasn't been able to get their hands on."

I stood. "How far to Kos?"

"I doubt he'd be there," Bradford said, peering at me. "But on the chance he is, I wouldn't recommend it—Niko can be dangerous … especially if he feels trapped."

Chapter 56

We took the first flight out of Eleftherios Venizelos Airport, and just under an hour later landed on the Greek Isle of Kos.

The island dated back to 366 BC, and according to Greek mythology, it was once visited by Hercules. So I doubted that anyone was impressed by the arrival of Eliza Dunbar and Detective Timothy Ruiz.

The temperature was slightly warmer than Athens, with a nice breeze coming off the water. Tim flagged a cab and we were on our way to the Tskitapolis mansion, where hopefully we'd find Niko. What would we do then? We'd cross that bridge when we came to it.

It looked like a castle perched on a hill, overlooking the Gulf of Gökova. The entrance was gated and manned by an armed guard. Suddenly I wasn't so confident, but Tim showed no fear. He went right up to the guard and introduced us, "Hello, my name is Tim Ruiz, and this is Eliza Dunbar."

He looked at me with a death stare, to which I smiled nervously and waved.

"We are here to see Mr. Niko Gogan," Tim said. This seemed like the perfect time to whip out the badge, but it was pretty useless here in Greece. *We're a long way from Kansas, Toto!*

"He's not here," the guard grunted.

"We're old friends. He bought me a beer when he was in The States, so I was hoping to return the favor," I said.

"He's not here."

"Do you know when he'll be back?" Tim asked.

"No."

"Do you know where he is?"

"No."

"Can you elaborate on that?"

"No."

Tim casually reached into his jacket pocket and pulled out his card. He handed it to the guard. "Please let Mr. Gogan know we came by to see him."

The guard looked apathetically at the card, which I guess was better than tearing it to pieces.

As we walked away, I was feeling particularly despondent. "I'm sorry I dragged you halfway around the world. I just thought if we could get to Niko, it might be our chance to help Chris."

"No reason to apologize, and I think it's been a very productive trip."

I glanced sideways at him. "You can't be serious."

"Not to state the obvious, but to catch the bad guys you first have to figure out who they are, and we've done that. We confirmed the identities of all three men who were with your sister that night."

Not that I didn't appreciate the sunshine, but, "The bad guys also happen to reside in a foreign country where you have no jurisdiction, the FBI seemed to want no part of this, and were annoyed we were messing with their NLOP policy. But that's still an improvement over your boss, who's convinced my sister did it, and has stopped looking for other possible suspects."

"What we did by coming here is force the FBI into action. And our trip to Niko's home was a statement that we'll come after him on his own turf—that we're not afraid. Now we've got him on the run."

"On the run?"

"Okay, maybe more like uncomfortable."

"I'm sure he's real *uncomfortable* in his mansion overlooking the Gulf, with his armed guards out front. While my sister is spending her weekend in a jail cell."

"He can only hide in there for so long … or wherever he is. But we've put him on defense, and he's bound to make a mistake."

"I thought the over-confident ones make mistakes—maybe we warned him to be careful?"

"Can't you pretend I'm the expert, just once?"

I took from the comment that I should keep to myself the fact that I wasn't convinced we'd accomplished anything, and had done the equivalent of shooting a spitball at a grizzly bear.

My "expert" companion wasn't sure what our next move was, so we strolled around Kos Island like tourists. As we passed the famed tree that Hippocrates, the Father of Medicine, used to teach under, I said, "Why don't you just admit it, Ruiz."

"And what should I be admitting?"

"You knew all along that we'd never find Niko. And the only reason you came with me was because you have an ulterior motive."

"And what was that?"

"You were just looking for a free trip to Greece with the coolest carpool mom in the Greater Danbury Area."

He smiled at me. "I've had worse company."

Chapter 57

Tim's phone rang—the *Mission Impossible* theme, which I never would have guessed, but was a good description of this trip.

It was Alexis. She informed him that she'd just spoken with Niko. That he was in Kos, and he planned to eat lunch at a place called Lofaki.

My first thought was this was a setup, visualizing Chris being jumped in that alley by Socrates. But a public restaurant during lunch hour would seem like a strange place to ambush someone, and we hadn't eaten all day, so Lofaki's it would be.

"Did you tell her that I would be ordering the most expensive thing on the menu," I said as we took a seat at a table in the outdoor patio area. There was also an indoor dining area, but just a hunch, Niko seemed like a patio-dining kind of guy.

My quip barely registered with Tim, whose eyes were darting from table to table, searching for any sign of trouble.

It seemed strange to even think that something bad could happen somewhere like this. The word breathtaking might have been coined for this place. Our cab driver told us it was the "most privileged" spot on the island. I didn't really know what he meant until I saw the view from the patio.

It had a panoramic view of the harbor, which extended out to the many small Greek islands. The Kalymnos Mountains formed the background.

Three sets of people—cab driver, waiter, and couple seated next to us—informed Tim and me that we'd be doing ourselves a disservice if we didn't return to witness the sunset. I doubted we'd have time, so we'd have to take their word for it.

We hadn't been seated for more than five minutes when my hunch was proven correct. Niko strutted in with a stunning woman on his arm; her mini-dress was designer, and her handbag probably cost more than my mortgage payment. Niko looked his usual romance-novel-cover self, but left the fashion style to his date. He wore a tank top with tight jeans and sandals, and was perfectly unshaven, of course.

We peered over the top of our menus, observing the attractive couple across the patio. Whenever they'd look up, we'd duck down—it was like a scene out of a bad sitcom. But luckily Niko was too focused on his date to notice. He sure didn't seem like he was "on defense" or worried we were "onto him," as Tim claimed.

Our waiter arrived, and I ended my strike against Greek food. Why should my taste buds suffer because Alexis was a backstabber? It wasn't their fault.

When our food arrived, I literally drooled it smelled so good. But we barely got three bites into the meal before Niko was on the move. He made a big to-do to say his goodbyes to the restaurant staff, including hugs—appearing that he were a regular customer—so he wasn't exactly trying to sneak out unnoticed.

When he finally left the restaurant, his date stayed behind. I guess she was just the appetizer.

We followed as close as we could until Niko arrived at a docked ferryboat. We waited until the boat was about to leave and then we boarded.

The ferry was headed to Bodrum, Turkey.

Chapter 58

It was a serviceable looking vessel that called itself the Aegean Angel. The upper level was an open sun deck, while the bottom was closed ... with the exception of a small area in the rear where Tim and I stood.

We watched as Niko made his way to the top deck. Maybe it was a strategic move, so that he could view his prey from a perch. Or perhaps he just wanted to work on his tan. He was a tough one to figure.

There was no point in following him upstairs, although, there was a part of me that thought it might be fun to sit down next to him and offer him a drink. And he'd be stuck beside me for the entire fifty-minute jaunt across the Aegean Sea. *Now that would make him uncomfortable, Tim!*

Or get me thrown overboard.

I had to remind myself that things had changed drastically since our meeting in Wojo's. At the time he was just Alexis' himbo, but now I knew he was a coldblooded killer, and we needed to proceed with caution. Tim had also convinced me that we had the perfect spot to gain an advantage. We were out of his view, yet all passengers had to pass through this area to exit the boat, so he couldn't escape us. And the element of surprise would be on our side. Unless he jumped overboard and swam for it—sounded crazy, but I wasn't ruling anything out at this point.

Tim was also worried that if we came after him on the boat, we could be putting passengers in harm's way. Always thinking of others, that one. So our strategy would be to follow him once he got off.

I saw benefit in determining where he was going. He was up to something. Why else would he so abruptly leave his lunch ... and his fashion-model babe ... to head to Turkey? Was he going to meet up with Plato and Socrates? Was this connected to my mother's case, or some other shady, yet unrelated business dealing?

We bumped over the choppy water, the sky was clear, and the sharp breeze felt refreshing on my face. Tim and I stood by the railing and stared out into the sea, lost in thought. Tim was fidgety, and he kept looking at his watch. I was about to place my hand on his shoulder in an attempt to comfort him, but someone beat me to it.

Before I could even scream, the man's strong arms were holding Tim over the side of the boat.

It was Niko.

Chapter 59

I tried to pry him off of Tim, but he swatted me away like a fly. I lost my balance and fell to the deck.

He peered down at me and smiled, which pissed me off.

"Get off of him," I scolded like Brooke and Kelly had failed to properly clean their room. And rose to my feet.

"You shouldn't follow people—it's rude," he said.

Tim was still dangling perilously. I shouted for help, but nobody came.

"We need to talk to you," Tim said, as if he had say in the matter.

"What about?"

"Sarah Dunbar's murder."

"I didn't kill her."

"The evidence tells a different story."

Tim was either really brave or really stupid. But whichever one it was, it turned out to be effective ... at least temporarily. Niko reeled him back over the railing like a prize fish he'd caught. Tim reached for his gun, but it was just an instinct—he wasn't carrying.

Niko was—he removed the weapon from the waistband of his jeans and held it by his side; a reminder of who was in charge of this meeting.

"Alexis tipped you off," I said.

He laughed. "Of course she did—said you'd be joining me at Lofaki."

"Then why did you go? To trap us?"

"I went for the lamb chops—you're the ones who tried to ambush me."

"I'm just doing my job," Tim said. "I'm investigating the murder of Sarah Dunbar, and since you were there that night, it makes you a person of interest. But you ran off before we could speak."

Niko looked at Tim like he was having second thoughts about not sending him overboard. "I didn't run—I had business here."

"Once Alexis finds out about your new girlfriend, you better start running. And then you'll have lost the one person who is willing to lie and cheat for you," I said.

His laughter increased. "I keep telling you truth, and you keep choosing to no listen. My relationship with Alexis is not like that no more—it's strictly business. Did she mention that she's in love with another man? Maybe he's the one you should be talking to."

"You didn't tell the truth about my mother—we confirmed that it's you and your pals, Plato and Socrates, on the security video. You killed her!"

"Your father killed your mother."

"You're a couple weeks behind on your cover stories—he's been ruled out as a suspect. So stop the lies!"

"He got involved in something he couldn't escape. He was in over his head. And it got your mother killed. I was trying to help him, but I was too late."

"If you're so confident of that, why don't you come back with us and clear your name?"

"You can discuss that with my lawyer," he said, before letting out more laughter. "I almost forgot—I don't have a lawyer. I guess you have no one to talk to."

"You might want to think about hiring one," Tim challenged.

"The Greek government has been after me for years. If they can't get me, then I'm not worried about some American cop on a fishing expedition."

"They might not get you here, but the FBI is now involved, so don't be expecting to be making any further trips to the United States to see your *business partner* Alexis. You take one step on US soil and you're mine," Tim fired back.

The threat felt hollow to me, and Niko seemed amused by it. "You really don't know what you're dealing with here, do you?"

"Why don't you fill us in," I said.

"I would, but I can't trust that you're not taping me again. You'll twist my words with your voice-recognition gimmicks. You're just like the Greek government—you have no case, so you make things up. Do you at least have a fingerprint to prove I was there that night, or a credible witness? Someone that isn't a murder suspect like your sister."

I clenched my jaw so hard I'd thought I'd broken it. "The tough-guy act isn't fooling me, you're scared. Your castle is starting to crumble, and Tskitapolis isn't here to save you anymore. His daughter is about to turn on you, and just wait until we find Plato and Socrates. They strike me as the type that will go to the highest bidder."

He sent one of his devastating smiles my way. "I love a woman who's not afraid to speak her mind. Maybe when this is over, you and me can go out ... dinner ... dancing."

"This will *never* be over."

"Actually, this ends the moment the ferry docks. So you better ask me all your questions now, because once we arrive in Bodrum you'll never see me again. And if you do, that means things went very wrong for you."

I only had one question. "My father was willing to do whatever you said that night, and give you whatever you wanted, yet you and your men killed my mother anyway. Why?"

He shook his head. "You keep looking at me when you should be looking back."

"Someone once told me that you should never look back, because someone might be gaining on you."

"Then maybe they'll catch you. And that might be the only way to get to them."

I don't know what it was about Greece, but everyone here was a philosopher.

When the ferry docked in Bodrum, true to his word, Niko pushed by us and off the boat, knowing there wasn't a damn thing we could do about it.

"I'll never stop trying to save my sister," I shouted at him.

He just shook his head again, as if to say: *don't say I didn't warn you.* And then he disappeared into the crowd.

Chapter 60

We entered Bodrum with very little resistance. No stamp of the passport, no visa required.

Wikipedia told me that it was once a small fishing town on the southern peninsula of Turkey, but over the last couple of decades it had developed into a playground for the wealthy, and was very popular with the yachting crowd. My first impression backed up the description—it definitely had a glitz factor to it.

Luckily for us, it also spoke our language. Most of the signage was in English, and the shop owners at least spoke a broken version of it. And as was typical with the region, the place was steeped in history. Bodrum boasted the ruins of the original Mausoleum, which was considered one of the Seven Wonders of the World. *Yeah, but did they have the Danbury Fair Mall ... I didn't think so.*

There would be no sightseeing for us. That much was clear. But what wasn't so clear was what our next move should be. There was no reason to continue to follow Niko. What could we do? He had no plans to return with us, and he was done answering our questions. Plus, he had a gun and we didn't.

So we started with the basics—we needed to settle into a hotel before nightfall. I thought we deserved a very nice one ... on Alexis' dime ... and the Su Hotel located in Bodrum City fit the bill.

While in the lobby, waiting for Tim to check us in, I picked up a copy of the *Bodrum Voice* newspaper, printed in English. And if I thought the *Danbury Ledger* had gotten a little lean in recent years the *Bodrum Voice* was a glorified pamphlet.

I noticed a writer named Hedo Kantor, who was their version of me—the AP. He wrote on the usual stuff like crime and political scandals, but also covered sports. And when I browsed an article about the local basketball team, a bad feeling came over me.

Once safely in my room, I called Connie back in Connecticut, where it was now lunchtime. "I'm glad to hear your voice—your girls and I had been a little worried."

"Why is that?" I asked, searching out possible reasons in my mind. Could they have found out that I was chasing murderers across Greece?

"The storm in Miami—sounds like you guys are getting slammed."

I quickly checked the weather app on my phone. Sure enough, South Florida was in the midst of a tropical storm. But 64 and clear skies here in Turkey. It seemed we made the right choice.

"We've been stuck inside all day, but it's not as bad as they're making it out to be. You know how those weathermen like to hype things."

"Really? Because they said the governor is thinking about evacuating the area."

"Politicians—they're like weathermen with richer parents."

Connie chuckled. "Well, that's a relief. I talked to Kirk this morning and he said you had some luck locating Plato."

Sometimes it was what Kirk didn't say, more so than what he did. Which was the reason for my call.

"Locating him might be a little strong, but we were able to confirm his identity with a photo—Plato is his real name, if you can believe that."

"Do you think he's in Miami?"

"I doubt it. He's a Greek national, so I wouldn't be surprised if he went back. Maybe laying low until my mother's investigation dies down. Even so, the photo was worth the trip."

"That's good to hear—you guys should celebrate. Any plans for tonight?"

I sensed a friendly hint in there. I glanced at the newspaper, still open to the sports page. "It will have to be something inside, with the storm and all. We were thinking a basketball game if it's still on."

"My boys will be jealous—they love the Miami Heat."

I checked the ESPN app on my phone—luck was on our side for once. The Heat were scheduled to play a game in Miami tonight, and it was still on, nicely backing up my story.

Connie thought for a moment, and added, "Hold on—that was the team LeBron James left, right? I think they switched their allegiance to whatever team he's on now. I can't keep up. But you two have fun … and stay dry!"

I told her we would, but had one last request, "Can I speak to Brooke?"

"Sure thing, have a safe flight back," Connie said cheerfully, and then Brooke's little girl voice took over, "Hey Mom—how's Miami?"

"Bad storm."

"I know—we were watching it on the news. Kelly was getting a little worried."

Unlike her big brave sister, who surely took it in stride. "We're fine. We're staying at this really big hotel, so inside we can barely tell that it's raining."

"Mrs. Marchand says you're going to a game tonight."

"That's the plan. And it got me thinking about when your father played. What was the name of his team?"

"The Celtics," she said with a small huff, like she couldn't believe I even asked such a question.

"That was the NBA team he played with, I know that, but what about the team he played on this year … in Turkey?"

"Bodrum," she said, and my head almost hit the roof. Son of a …

"Where is your Dad now—is he there?" my concern growing.

"No—he stopped by this morning. Said he was going to dinner tonight at Skita's. You know, the opa place."

I knew it all too well.

I didn't want to hang up—Brooke's voice made me feel like everything was right with the world, even in times like this, when it was anything but.

I took one last glance at the newspaper, and I couldn't shake the feeling I was having. But I had an idea of who could make some sense of it for met.

Chapter 61

Tim suggested we meet up later, maybe grab some dinner, and if we got crazy, hit a local drinking establishment to unwind. I appreciated the offer, but I was working on two hours sleep, and I really needed to catch up on some shuteye.

That's how we left things when we headed off to our separate rooms, so he seemed surprised by my sudden urge to go watch the Bodrum professional basketball team play tonight. I explained that it was Kirk's old team, and Brooke had developed an interest in them, and I promised her I'd check it out while we were in town.

There were plenty of holes in my story, which could easily be picked up by my savvy-detective traveling partner, but he accepted my invitation to come along without raising an issue—I suspected he was just happy to get out of a night of Turkish television and room service.

"Maybe we could have dinner after," he offered.

"That sounds nice," I replied. Hopefully I'd still have an appetite if my suspicions were confirmed.

The venue was more gymnasium than a professional basketball arena. I could imagine Kirk being depressed playing here. The other places he played in Europe weren't the NBA by any means, but were the next step below, with quality facilities and thousands of fans attending games.

Tim and I had our choice of seats—to say the crowd was sparse would be an understatement. This made it much easier to search for the man I was looking for.

As I did, Tim focused on the game that had just gotten underway. "You know what I like about basketball?" he asked.

"I'm guessing the cheerleaders," I said, still searching the crowd.

"Basketball is like a metaphor for life. You take a shot—sometimes it goes in and you're the hero, but when it doesn't, you have to keep shooting. You miss 100% of the shots you never take."

I took a moment away from my search and smiled at him. "Very philosophical—this Plato thing must be rubbing off on you."

I returned to my search—the small crowd certainly was loud, sounding like a group three times their size. Tim continued talking, but I grew distracted. Because I found the man I'd come to see. "I'll be back," I said, and hopped out of my seat.

"I was just going to get some food. You want me to get you some popcorn ... or falafel?" Tim asked, but I was barely listening.

"Sure ... thanks," I said, as I made my way down to the man who was sitting courtside.

I recognized Hedo Kantor from his photo in the *Bodrum Voice*. He had jet-black hair and droopy eyes. He was younger than I expected, maybe late-twenties, thirty at the most.

I introduced myself as Eliza Dunbar from the *Danbury Ledger*, a newspaper from the United States, hoping to form a little journalistic bond. He didn't recognize my name, which I thought would be helpful in my pursuit.

I explained to him that I was from a far a way land called Connecticut, and was in the process of doing a retrospective on the University of Connecticut basketball team winning the national championship of my country, as it was the ten-year anniversary of their achievement.

"UConn," he said, displaying a knowledge of American college basketball, and a fluent understanding of English. A positive development.

"I'm assuming your interest lies in Kirk McCaffrey," he said.

"Yes—he was the star player of that team. And also recently played here in Bodrum. Quite a journey."

"Speaking of which, you've come a long way yourself. This must be an important story to tell."

I pointed up at Tim, who was looking curiously at me. I could only imagine what was going through his mind.

"I wish my paper had the budget to send me around the world," we traded knowing nods—the language of slashed newspaper budgets was universal. "But my husband and I had come here on vacation, and knowing that McCaffrey recently played in Bodrum, I thought I could get some firsthand knowledge from the reporter who covered him."

Kantor seemed like the type who would work during his vacation, so he understood, "I'd like to be helpful, but there isn't much to tell—his stay here was very short."

"It's not a fluff piece," I said.

He didn't appear to understand the term, so I followed up, "My story is about telling the good and the bad of the players on that team in the years that followed. Don't be afraid to tell me the bad—I know his time here didn't end well."

He nodded astutely. "He never seemed happy. It happens a lot with Americans who come here—it's not what they're used to, and it's usually about getting that last paycheck before they retire."

"But I sense there was more to it when it comes to McCaffrey."

"There were rumors."

"I like rumors. I can't print them, but I still like them."

"He got himself involved with some people he shouldn't have—gamblers. From what I'm told, he got deep into debt with people you don't want to be in debt to."

"I hear one of them was Niko Gogan," I played my hunch.

Kantor appeared impressed by my knowledge, his voice quieted, "A very dangerous man. And a man the Bodrum club didn't want to be associated with. It's been rumored that Gogan uses creative ways to have debts paid off ... ones that can reflect unfavorably on the club."

"You mean like fixing games."

He nodded.

"Was McCaffrey involved in anything like that?" I asked, and braced for the answer. Once you go there, hoping to make your debt go away, Niko owns you. *I have another job for you. Do whatever I say, or I'll make sure the police find out what you did, and you'll end up in a Turkish prison ... or worse.* And if that doesn't work, then he'll start threatening family members. I sure hoped this was all just a stupid coincidence.

"There was no proof it ever got that bad, but sometimes in these parts they always believe the worst about the American. My sources told me the debt was paid off by a mystery person."

"Do you know who this mystery person was?"

He shook his head.

"Could it have been paid by the club, to avoid the bad publicity?"

"It could have been. But my sense was that it was someone connected to McCaffrey. The club had been suspicious of the rumors, especially after he was injured, claiming to have fallen down the stairs in his apartment. They were worried about the bad publicity you mentioned, so if they were connected to any payment it would be harder for them to distance themselves from the situation."

"It sounds like you don't believe falling down the stairs was an accident. I'm guessing it was a message from Niko, delivered by his muscle, the Kostas brothers."

He again looked impressed by my insight, which once more, was just a hunch. On the downside, I could tell that he was also becoming suspicious of my interest in Kirk.

"That would be my estimate. The club also had their suspicions and launched an internal investigation. They suspended McCaffrey until it was complete."

"What did the investigation find?"

"The club worked out an agreement with McCaffrey—his contract became null and void, and he returned to the US. The official statement from the club said that McCaffrey had lost his desire for the game and wanted to return home to be closer to his family. That it was a mutual decision. It never mentioned the investigation."

It sounded like all parties wanted to keep this quiet, including whoever paid off Kirk's debt. But there would be no time for further questions, as Hedo had to hurry off in regards to another story he was covering. Before he left, I thanked him for his help, even though I didn't like the answers.

Alone again, I sat and stared at the court. I was overcome by the same sensation as I was at the DCHS game, when Beef first told me about Alexis and my father. The place went completely silent, except for the rhythmic pounding of the ball.

I struggled to get my mind around the many unanswered questions, but one thing was clear—Kirk was connected to the man who killed my mother. And I couldn't rule out the possibility that he was somehow involved in her death.

I felt sick.

Chapter 62

Tim and I had dinner at the hotel restaurant. We ordered numerous Turkish Meze, which was basically appetizers. They included fried calamari and squid, stuffed vegetables, and small fish dishes. We washed it down with well-earned beers.

I wasn't the best dinner partner, as my mind had wandered thousands of miles away.

"Ground Control to Major Tom," Tim broke my thought.

"I'm sorry, I just have a lot on my mind," I halfheartedly replied.

"Is it about that guy you met with? Something he told you?"

I hadn't exactly been forthcoming about my meeting with Hedo. I explained that he was a local sports reporter I'd recognized from his photo in the newspaper, and I was hoping to get the scoop on why Kirk suddenly left the club.

"Something like that."

"So your distractedness is connected to the reason Kirk left the club? That's a relief—I thought it was my boring conversation."

I smiled. Quite the opposite—it was so easy talking to Tim. "Just Kirk being Kirk," I said.

"You wanna talk about it?"

"Not really."

"But there was more to why he left the club than he had told you?"

"You could say that."

After a long pause, he asked, "How do you feel about him being back?"

Much differently than I did a few hours ago. "It makes the girls happy."

"What about you?"

"What's good for them is good for me."

I could tell he was gauging my answer, probing, and since Kirk was the last topic I wanted to discuss at the moment, I segued the conversation back to the case at hand. Tim continued with his sunshiny outlook, re-hashing our successes—identifying all three men, meeting with Niko, taking our case to the FBI. I chose not to be an eclipse and bring up the fact that we had limited support, and our two person international manhunt was pretty feckless.

What we did have was a string of connections. Kirk was connected to Niko through his gambling debts, Niko was connected to Alexis, who was connected to my father, who was connected to my sister, who was connected to me. But what was the link that brings it all together? That was the question. And one I'd likely have better luck with after a good night's sleep.

Tim walked me to my room. You could tell he was in cop-mode, as no detail was too small for him to notice. The truth was, we were dealing with some really bad dudes here, on their home turf, and we poked them today.

When we arrived at my door, he told me at least three times that he was right down the hall if I sensed even an inkling of trouble. I assured him that I would, we said an awkward good night, and I turned to open the door.

"One more thing, Eliza," he said.

When I turned, he kissed me.

And not the peck on the cheek, friends type of goodnight kiss.

I think I kissed him back, but I can't say for sure. When he pulled away, I attempted to gather myself.

"Tim … this isn't the best time," I was able to stutter.

He looked at me, and I thought he might kiss me again, but he didn't. "I know. That wasn't about tonight—it was what I should have done years ago. They say you can't go back in time and make up for what you missed out on, but I thought I'd find out for sure."

Um, okay. I stood silent, staring at him, leg trembling, nothing to hold on to, unsure what to do.

"We have an early flight tomorrow. We need to get our sleep," he said. Then turned and walked toward his room.

Chapter 63

As we began our journey home Monday morning, my ex-husband consumed my thoughts.

And yes, the kiss.

But thoughts of Kirk took precedence, because it directly affected Brooke and Kelly—always my top priority. No matter what issues I've had with Kirk over the years, there was never a moment when I didn't feel safe with him around them. Until now.

He was connected to this in some way, and until I figured out what that meant, I had to assume the worst.

I called Connie to check on them—it was Sunday night there, just past midnight. The girls were snug in their beds, feeling both apprehensive (Brooke) and excited (Kelly) to be returning to school tomorrow. The plan was for Connie to drop the girls off in the morning, then Kirk would get them in the afternoon, and watch them until I returned home.

The thought left a lump in my throat, but I didn't want to set off any alarms. I figured I would be home by dinner, and I could confront him then, head on, as has always been my way.

I also checked in with Bob, who no surprise, was still at the office. But with good reason this time, as he was pulling double duty, since his AP had jetted off to Miami for a weekend of fun.

I had told him that it was an impromptu trip planned by my girlfriends, as a way to try to get my mind off recent events. Bob had known me for five years, so he knew this was the last thing Eliza Dunbar would do at this moment. But he'd been bugging me to use my mounting vacation days for some time, so he couldn't take umbrage now that I was finally going to take him up on it.

He provided me an update on the reaction of my sister's arrest—to summarize: not good. Guilty as sin. And the way the arrest went down, it was thought that Chris had gotten special favor, and that she used her own mother's funeral as a publicity stunt to try to gain sympathy, which the public found appalling.

I checked the Internet to see what our competitors were saying. And they predictably ran with pun-filled headlines that accompanied one-sided articles. Some of them had moved past the particulars of the case, onto an analysis of how this cute "Conjoined Kid" we all rooted for had turned into an unimaginable monster.

Our main competitor went with "Mother of all Spectacles" splashed across the front page, and had gotten a photo of Chris from the funeral, standing over our mother's coffin.

"Killer Dress" chirped the *New York Globe* tabloid, and featured a photo of Chris in her flattering black funeral dress, walking awkwardly down the aisle in heels.

"Drowning in Guilt!" screamed another paper, similar to the "Drowning in Debt" headlines about my father when it was discovered he was having financial problems earlier in the investigation. No points for creativity. I assumed there were endless "Drowning in …" headline possibilities when it came to this case.

And of course, there had to be a basketball related pun when it came to Chris. "Slam Dunk! DA says open and shut case against Chris Dunbar."

I'm not sure why I kept reading. It was like one of those horrific twelve car pileups that you just can't take your eyes off. One article referred to Chris as a "modern day Lizzie Borden." Another said, "Sarah Dunbar was buried with the secret of what happened to her, but there has never been any question of who her killer was. Her own daughter, Chris Dunbar."

I had to commend Bob for going with the straightforward, "Chris Dunbar Arrested in Mother's Murder." I found the journalistic integrity of it a nice change of pace.

I thankfully lost service as we took the ferry back across the Aegean Sea to Kos. This trip was less eventful, but the customs on the Greek side were more thorough than they were in Bodrum, taking up valuable time.

We took a return flight from Kos to Athens, where we would pick up our plane to JFK. During our takeoff from Athens, I again noticed Tim fidgeting with his ring finger.

"Do you want to talk about it?" I said.

"I think we covered everything. It was a good start, but now we have to come up with something concrete that will force Wallach to reopen the investigation."

"I was talking about the kiss."

He reached for his finger again. "I think it's best we focus on saving your sister."

The answer made me smile. Not because he completely avoided the kiss subject. But for the first time, Detective Ruiz admitted that he believed in Chris' innocence. *Save your sister!*

When we arrived in New York, more good news. Tim had checked in with his department to find that Chris had been granted bail. This was a pleasant surprise, considering her lawyer didn't even think she had a shot. She would be ordered to wear a monitor to track her movements, so she wasn't completely free, but it was still better than jail. I wanted to rush to see her, but first I had to deal with Kirk.

Chapter 64

I entered home sweet home a weary traveler, feeling the effects of my new jet-set life.

But there's no better pick-me-up than my kids rushing into my arms. Kirk, wearing an apron, walked toward me with a smile. It was his peace-treaty smile. There would be no peace tonight, but no reason to rain on this parade just yet … at least not on an empty stomach.

"Welcome to Chateau McCaffrey—we normally require reservations, but we'll make an exception for the pretty lady," Kirk said. He and the kids then led me to the impressively set table, and Brooke and Kelly took my coat and hung it in the closet.

The meal lived up to expectations, and the kids went off to work on their homework—they had a lot to make up after missing time last week.

I retired to the couch. Kirk joined me with a cup of hot chocolate in each hand, and a satisfied look on his face.

"You need to be out of here by tomorrow," I said coldly.

He looked to be caught off guard. "I went to see a few places this weekend, like we talked about … it's not an overnight process, Eliza."

"That's not my problem."

"Is this about the other morning? I was just worried about you," he took a deep breath, "and fine, I'll admit it, I might have been a little jealous. I know I have no right to be, but—

"You're right—you don't."

"What's going on? Did something happen on your trip?"

"You could say that."

"What happened?"

"Gambling, Kirk—that's what happened. And then to drop in here acting all fatherly, while putting us all in danger."

"What are you talking about? I would never put you or the girls in danger."

"I know what happened in Bodrum."

"I got released from the team, it just wasn't working out. I don't know what you're getting at."

"Don't play dumb with me. I know about it—the gambling debt, the investigation—all of it."

"Have you been checking up on me?"

"I've been too busy trying to solve my mother's murder, but now that you mention it, that might not be a bad idea. Maybe the two are connected."

His face went limp. "What does my gambling have to do with your mother?"

"It seems you ran up this gambling debt with a man named Niko Gogan. Sound familiar?"

"Yeah, so. That was settled before I returned."

I glared at him, fire in my eyes. "Niko Gogan is the man who killed my mother."

I couldn't tell if he looked more shocked or confused. "Let me get this straight—Niko from Bodrum was one of the men with Chris that night?"

"He showed up the night of the break-in. You happened to return to the US around the same time, hiding out with Chris. What were you doing—getting intel for them on Chris?"

"That's crazy."

"You did owe Niko a favor—what a coincidence that your debt suddenly got paid off—maybe they found a better currency than money. And come to think of it, the night Chris ran into Plato at that bar, who was she with? Oh, yeah, you. Must all be a big coincidence."

"You really believe that?"

"Spill it," I said.

And he did.

Chapter 65

"I took a big cut in pay this year. But Turkey was the only offer I got, so there wasn't much choice. I tried to make up the difference by placing some bets, and a couple of guys on the team knew this guy."

"Niko."

He nodded. "It started out well—I was on a winning streak, but then I got greedy. Next thing I knew, I was ten thousand American in debt, and the more I tried to dig out from it, the worse it got."

Ten thousand dollars to gamble away, I pondered. And he had the gall to complain about the rise in tuition at the girl's school.

"When the bill came, I didn't have the money. The Bodrum club was notorious for being late with our checks, so Niko granted me an extension. But when I still couldn't meet it, he sent me a message."

"Did the message look like this?" I held up the photo on my phone.

He looked perplexed. "That's Plato from the bar. You sent me that photo the other day to confirm it was him." He thought for a second. "You weren't in Miami, were you?"

"That's not important—how about him?" This time I showed him a photo of Socrates.

His face filled with fear, like he was recalling their last meeting when he "accidentally" got thrown down the stairs. "Yeah, that's him—how did you—

I felt a shiver in my spine. "Did he threaten the girls—is that how he got you to go along with their sick scheme? That's how they got to Chris."

"Our girls? Hell no—he'd be dead if he ever threatened them. Or I'd be, but they would have a fight on their hands before I'd ever let him near them."

I believed him, but that wasn't the main issue here. "Go on."

"This Socrates dude beat me up pretty good. I missed a couple games. I claimed it was an accident, but there was this reporter—

"Hedo Kantor," I said.

"Yeah, that's him," he said, dumbfounded by my knowledge, but no longer questioning my sources. "He did some digging, and found out about the gambling debt. He went to the club, looking for comment. It was the first they'd heard of it, and they launched an investigation, suspending me until it was complete."

"Kantor never wrote a story on it. I searched the archives of his paper."

"Things work differently over there, Eliza. The team didn't want the bad publicity—they had enough financial problems as it was—so they likely paid off Kantor not to print it."

"The same way they paid you off."

"You make it sound like I got something out of this. Basically, they informed me that my debt had been paid in full, and my services were no longer needed. They ripped up my contract and handed me a plane ticket back to New York. They made it very clear that if I attempted to fight it ... let's just say, it was in my best interest to get out of Turkey."

We sat in silent thought for a moment, before he said, "I still don't see how this connects to your mother."

"You don't know who Niko Gogan really is, do you?"

He shrugged. "I just thought he was some thug running a gambling ring."

"You didn't see him at my mother's funeral?"

His face scrunched. "I was too busy keeping the kids in line to see who was there. What was he doing there? I don't get it."

"It wasn't so much *what* he was doing there, it was who he was with. Niko worked for Georgos Tskitapolis, and since his death, he runs many of his European businesses, while his daughter, Alexis, runs the restaurants here in America. They're a team."

"Niko and Alexis? That doesn't make sense."

"What doesn't make sense, is how you got mixed up with the people responsible for my mother's murder. Every road leads back to them," I wanted to shout, but had to keep my voice low, so as to not alert the kids.

"Alexis couldn't have been on the same team as Niko."

I shook my head with exasperation. "And what makes you say that?"

"Because Alexis is the one who paid off my gambling debt ... to Niko. Why would she do that if they were working together?"

Now it was my turn to be surprised. "Why would she ... she barely knows you. Is that why you've been defending her? Why you tried to strike that peace accord between her and me? Because you felt guilty?"

He stood. "Some people see others in need and they lend a hand, no questions asked. No judgment. No holding it over their heads. Maybe you could take a lesson from her."

And somehow I became the villain.

"I'll be back for my stuff ... I'll make a reservation," he said and slammed the door on his way out. The next sound I heard was the screeching of the Corvette's tires as he tore out of the driveway.

Welcome home, Eliza.

Chapter 66

I met with Bob first thing Tuesday morning; three cups of coffee counterbalancing my jet lag.

"So how was your trip?" he asked, settling behind his desk.

"Brief, but relaxing. I feel refreshed and ready to go."

But that might have been the caffeine talking.

He began to chuckle.

"Is something funny?"

"Just that I pushed you to get away for so long, and when you finally do, you run into one of the biggest storms of the year. Life has a sense of humor."

"It definitely put a damper on my beach plans, but it was still good to get away."

"So where'd you really go?"

"Greece."

He shook his head with a half smile, as if resigned to my lunacy. "If you think the paper will be contributing one dime, you've officially lost your mind."

I've heard Bob's lecture on numerous occasions—*freedom of the press isn't free, it costs money. And we don't have any!*

Once I was able to assure him that I'd found a donor to fund the trip, his interest-level raised. But not so much in my theories, or riveting tale about tracking down Niko on a ferry to Turkey. He wanted to know what I had that was concrete, and could be printed. And my answer was that we confirmed the names of the three men with my sister the night of the home invasion.

I told him about the FBI voice recognition that pointed us to Niko as the leader—at least according to my sister—and showed him the photos of the Kostas brothers, Plato and Socrates. Bob appeared to be intrigued.

"So did I miss any excitement while I was gone?" I asked.

"It's been all Chris Dunbar 24/7."

"My childhood in a nutshell."

"She has certainly riled up the emotions of the community."

"Because she got bail?"

"Partly, but more so that she decided to take refuge in the home of the woman whom she is accused of murdering. Has a very Shakespearean feel to it."

"Where else was she going to go? My father still owns the house, and he obviously believes in Chris' innocence. That should be the takeaway here. My father and I have had our issues, but if he'd really seen Chris kill his wife, do you think he'd let her stay there?"

"Sounds like her lawyer sent you the proper talking points."

"Please—it's just basic logic, which people seem unwilling to accept when it comes to this case."

"You're preaching to the choir, Eliza. But perception is reality," he thought for a moment, before adding, "I was hoping to come up with a third cliché, but I couldn't think of one."

"My sister has never been good with PR—being proficient in it requires one to give a crap what people think."

"I don't dance, but if I'm on hot coals I'd be Fred Astaire—sometimes survival takes priority over our ideals."

He was right. Chris was coming off as a spoiled brat sociopath. But she wasn't going to change, even if that meant a trip to the gas chamber, so we needed to clear her before this got to trial. She'd have no shot with a jury.

"Whether you agree with the public sentiment or not, the accused taking up shelter at the murder scene *is* the story here. So I expect that's what you'll be covering."

I thought we'd gotten past that.

"You mean it *was* the story. The new story begins tomorrow morning when we splash photos of my favorite new band, Niko and the Philosophers, on the front cover—identifying them as the men who were with Chris that night."

"You feel confident in making that assertion?"

"100%."

"Then run with it. But just remember that this won't help your sister. These men will not be considered to be alternative suspects, but Chris' team—the group she's ordering around in the security video. And when their rap sheets are revealed, it will look like she'd gotten mixed up with the wrong crowd."

"Or they would be the type of guys who could threaten someone into going along with it."

We had reached a deadlock, so we moved on to other business. There really was such a thing. Bob had taken over the coverage of the mayor's immigration bill. "A little rabble-rousing and racial tension makes me feel like I'm back in the 60s," he said with a burst of enthusiasm. "Back on the front lines."

I would cover the next DHCS state playoff game on Thursday, and I'd include some of the photos of my Greece trip in the *Ledger's* first ever Travel Section, which would appear Sunday. I would tie it in to the annual Danbury Greek Festival that was coming up in the spring.

When we finished, Bob leaned back in his chair and rubbed his eyes. "So what's your next move, kid?"

"I'm just going to keep following the truth, because that's what will set my sister free."

"You do know that many innocent people end up in jail … and that's the truth."

"I'm either going to get her out of there, or I'm going to end up in jail with her. We will never be split apart."

He smiled wryly. "I can see the headline now—*Cons Joined in Prison.*"

Chapter 67

I stepped into the gym and glared at Beef.

He stared right back at me. "Don't give me that look, Dunbar."

"What look?"

"Like you're all pissed off at me. I'm not the one who was talking that junk about Chris."

"But you didn't exactly defend her either. Sometimes that's just as bad."

"I said I wouldn't say anything about my guy, and when Jillian's douche boyfriend started talking nonsense, I directed him to an expert on legal affairs—PG13. So if you think I'm gonna apologize, you can kiss my ass."

I was all kissed out. "I'll pass, thanks."

"Good. Because we've got work to do. Gotta make up for you missing Sunday."

"I got my cardio in chasing the bad guys around Greece."

"I thought we'd switch things up today—start with a little boxing. Your training partner is already in the ring, so hurry it up."

"Training partner? I work with you only—that's our agreement."

"Plans change. It's called life."

When I arrived at the boxing ring and saw who was standing in it, if I wasn't so pissed at her, I would have laughed my head off.

"Now *she* wants to apologize, so you two go knock yourselves out," Beef said and left the room.

Even looking like the proverbial fish out of water, in her protective headgear and boxing gloves, Jillian still looked perfectly put together.

"I know you want to punch me, Eliza. So here's your chance. I deserve it."

"I'd settle for that apology."

"I'm sorry—Chris and I have always butted heads, but I shouldn't have piled on. I was wrong, and if I had something to say, a real friend would have said it to your face."

"Apology accepted."

"And I would also like to apologize on Max's behalf."

"Not accepted. If he wants to say something to me, he can tell it to me when I win that bet." And I would be remiss not to add, "I'm sorry, Jillian, but he's a total asshat."

"Yeah, but he's my asshat," she said with resignation in her voice. "Are you going to get into the ring and hit me, or what?"

"Your punishment will be much more painful. You're going to baby-sit my kids tonight when I go visit Chris."

Now she looked scared. "You know how me and kids are ... and you remember how that went last time."

"I've hidden the rope, and will let them know that it's not to happen again."

The last time Jillian babysat Brooke and Kelly, they tied her to a chair and poured water, milk, and whatever else they could find in the refrigerator, over her head. If Jillian was on the fence about ever having children, I think that sealed the deal.

She turned jittery. "I'll have to check my schedule. I think I might have a work thing tonight."

"I'll expect you at seven o'clock sharp."

Chapter 68

Beef and I did get an actual workout in, and I took out my pent up emotions on him. It had nothing to do with Jillian—it was all about my next stop.

It was the first time I'd seen my father since last Wednesday, when I walked out with no intention of returning. But I still had unanswered questions. Actually one question. I understood the *when* the *where* and the *how*. And thanks to my trip to Greece, I even knew the *who*. But I still couldn't answer the why. It was the answer that could unlock the mystery, and my father had the key. I was sure of it.

"Hello stranger," he greeted me. "I wasn't sure if I'd see you again."

"I meant to stop by, but I've been busy trying to keep my sister out of jail. It seems I'm the only one in the family willing to do that."

He didn't want to touch that topic. "I heard that your mother's funeral was worthy of her, which is saying something. You did right by her."

"Don't thank me—Kirk was the one who put it together."

"Kirk?"

"Yeah—learn something new about people all the time."

"And what did you learn about Kirk?"

"That you and him have more in common than I would have ever thought."

Another subject he wasn't interested in pursuing. "They tell me I'll be getting out of here in a few days."

"You do look a lot better. When I first saw you, I wasn't sure you'd make it out of here alive."

"That makes two of us. I'll be rooming with Chris—unlike you, she won't be able to run from me, with that ankle bracelet. Have you made any progress on 'keeping her out of jail'?"

"I identified the three men who were with her that night. You ever hear of Plato and Socrates?"

"I know it's been many years, but I did attend school, Eliza. I was actually going to be a philosophy major in college, before my parents set me straight."

I took out my phone and showed him the photos of the Kostas brothers. He tried to hide behind his reading glasses, but I could tell he knew who they were.

"Do you recognize them?"

"The men that night had masks on—it's hard to say if this is them."

"I asked if you recognized them—not if they were the ones there that night. I think you do. Along with this man."

I showed him the photo of Niko and he turned away.

This time he let down his facade. At least enough to peek over the top of it. "These are very dangerous men, Eliza—I'm begging you to stay out of it. I can't bear to see anyone else I care about get hurt."

"What did you get yourself involved in, Dad? What wouldn't they let you out of?"

He just stared straight ahead at the colorless hospital wall.

"If you won't, I'll take a shot—you were having some financial issues and your good friend Alexis was eager to help you out, so she introduced you to her guy Niko. Maybe win a few bets, pay off some debts."

"That's not what happened."

"Which brings me to what you and Kirk have in common. He also got into debt with Niko. But Alexis must be a better friend to him, since she paid off Kirk's debt. So either she didn't help you out, or it didn't matter, because this wasn't about money when it came to you—it was personal, and Mom and Chris would ultimately pay your debt for you."

He refused to look at me.

"Why was it personal, Dad?"

He finally turned in my direction. "You need to stay out of this, Eliza. I know your instincts are to not stop until you get your answers, but you're just going to have to trust me this time."

"That's the problem—I don't trust you anymore. And Mom shouldn't have either."

I turned and walked out.

Chapter 69

The girls and I had a sit-down dinner for the first time in what seemed like forever.

The main issue that needed to be dealt with was the sudden departure of their father. It seemed fatherly trust was an issue for all of us these days, and they were concerned that Kirk had gone back on his word and wouldn't be sticking around, as he'd promised. I assured them that while he had moved out of the house, he would be living nearby, and involved in their lives. Having said that, until I could figure out his role in my mother's murder he wasn't coming near them.

I could tell they really needed me tonight. They craved normalcy, and normal meant me being downstairs working on an article, while they were up in their room doing their homework, occasionally checking in on them when things got "too quiet." My life getting turned upside down had trickled down to them. But stability would have to be put off for another day—I needed to see Chris, and talk to her about what we'd found.

Jillian showed up promptly at seven with a hesitance in her stride. The woman has gone head-to-head with CEOs of Fortune 500 companies, but she was deathly afraid of children. At least my children. I promised her again that they'd be on their best behavior, but just to be safe, I advised her not to let the girls see the fear in her eyes.

I drove to Ridgefield, both wanting and not wanting to see Chris. I hated to see her caged like a bird, even if it was better than prison.

The media was camped out in front of my parents' house—Chris was the story, just as Bob stated. My arrival caused a glimmer of excitement—these news stakeouts could be an eleven on the boredom scale. But they weren't quick enough to block me from pulling into the driveway.

I casually strolled to the front door, acting confident—smiling and waving at the mob of reporters as they shouted questions in my direction. If my sister didn't want to play the PR game, I would pick up the slack for her.

Chris didn't exactly have the same response when she opened the door for me; greeting them with a one-finger salute.

She was in shorts and a tank top, and was sweating like she'd just ran a couple of miles in the summer heat. I also took note of her stylish, court-ordered ankle bracelet.

"How can you work in that profession?" she asked, taking one final look at the mob before slamming the door shut.

The moment the door closed we embraced, and held on as tight as we could for what seemed like an hour. It was always our most natural state, and one I felt most comfortable with. It's a conjoined thing.

"So how was your weekend?" she asked casually, tying to lighten the heavy moment, as was her style.

"You know, the usual—headed off to the Greek Isles for a little rest, relaxation, and chasing murderers. How about you?"

"I rented out this really trendy four-by-six cell at the Danbury police station. Kind of like a time-share, but without the high-pressured sales pitch."

I turned serious. "Did they treat you alright?"

"It wasn't so bad. The overnight cops were cool—ordered pizza from Sevaldi's. They were big UConn fans, so we talked a lot of hoops. And even if they weren't—Gregson came by every hour on the hour to check up on me."

"That's good to hear," I said with relief.

"And thank you for the care package—that was such a Mom move. Kirk brought it by on Saturday."

I didn't want to talk about Kirk just yet. "I'm just glad you were granted bail."

She smiled. "I expect you are—my decision to stay in this house will probably double the *Ledger's* sales the next few days."

"You know what I meant."

"I always know what you mean ... sometimes before you do."

I followed her into the living room, and immediately saw her workout of choice. Like my kids, Chris was in search of the normal tonight. And nothing was more normal to her than playing basketball. She had our old Nerf hoop attached over the door to the storage closet.

"I found it in a box in the garage. Luckily, our parents are part human, part pack-rat."

I thought back to some of the spirited Nerf hoop battles we used to have as kids in our bedroom. With my leg issue, I could never compete with Chris outside on the regulation-size basket, but in the confined space of our room, without much distance to cover, I could hold my own.

She tossed me the squishy orange ball, but I wasn't in the mood for the competitive battle she was seeking, and tossed it back.

Chris shrugged and began shooting, making one after another. She looked much healthier than when I saw her in the park. She was gaining her weight back and the black eye was healing.

"I don't blame you for not wanting a piece of me—Kirk came by earlier, and I kicked his ass," she said with a cocky grin.

Which brought me to what I needed to tell her. As gently as possible, I said, "I think Kirk might have been in on it."

Chris stopped in mid jump shot. "What the hell are you talking about?"

I proceeded to tell her everything I knew, starting from when I broke into her interrogation, to the basketball game in Turkey, and my subsequent showdown with Kirk. I then showed her the photos of Plato and Socrates, to get a final confirmation if they were indeed the ones who forced her into this.

Chris just nodded.

While I provided her a lot of information and possibilities, I really had no answers. I felt like I was looking at a pile of loose wires, which all somehow fit, but I just didn't know exactly how. But somebody did.

"Dad is the one who knows, but he'd rather let you go to jail than to reveal what he knows."

"He's just trying to protect us."

"Why do you always defend him?"

"I know I was his favorite, Eliza. He lived vicariously through me, while you guys were always up and down. And I know he screwed up a lot, but he eventually got it right in the end. No matter what, he's always wanted the best for us, *both of us*, and Mom. There is no way he'd purposely hurt our family."

"Maybe so, but there's always collateral damage from the bad decision. Getting it right in the end doesn't change that."

She smiled. "You don't think he's that bad."

"What makes you say that?"

"If you thought he was, I doubt you'd have married a guy just like him."

"You can't be serious. Kirk and Dad were like oil and water."

"In some ways, but they shared a few important characteristics. If I recall, Kirk also has had his share of screw-ups, but got it right in the end. Which I think is why he came back home. And he also would never intentionally hurt us—he and Dad aren't the bad guys here. Those guys in your photos are, and now we need to figure out a way to convince the police of it. Because if I ever have to go before a jury I'm screwed."

The last part we were in full agreement on. The rest of it, I wasn't so sure.

She let loose one final, ferocious dunk on the Nerf hoop, followed by a primal scream. She then made her way into the kitchen, mentioning, "I think better when I have ice cream in my stomach."

I followed her. "You know this doesn't make up for the Baskin-Robbins 31 Flavors you promised me."

"I can't believe you'd even question me—my word is like gospel."

"I'm not so sure about that—you did lie about going to Miami."

"So did you."

"Touché."

Chris scooped out the remainder of the chocolate for herself, and the strawberry for me. She left the block of vanilla in the middle of the Neapolitan for whenever Karen returned.

We sat at the kitchen table, just as we had a gazillion times as kids, and she said, "I think you're leaving something out from your Greece trip."

"I told you everything—FBI, Niko, Kirk's gambling connection. I did forget to mention we ate at this amazing place called Lofaki. Although, eat might be over describing it—I barely got three bites in before we were on the move."

"Stop holding out on me."

"That's everything, I swear."

"C'mon, Eliza—I'm your conjoined twin. You can't fool me."

Finally I smiled. "Tim kissed me."

"And you kissed him back?"

"I'm not sure, things got a little hazy."

Chris grinned from ear to ear. "I knew it ... and it's about time."

But it was time that we were running out of.

Chapter 70

I'd planned to drive by the media with another forced smile and wave.

But something compelled me to stop my car at the end of the driveway and get out. I walked directly toward the herd.

I proposed a deal—if I gave them a statement, answered a few questions, and provided a photo or two for their stories, would they give my sister some peace? It was the best offer they were going to get, and at least they'd have something to take back to their editors for time spent.

Cameras and microphones were shoved in my face, and I spoke with firmness and clarity. They were on my home turf—the place where I was raised—so I felt very comfortable.

I stated that I, along with the rest of my family, unequivocally supported Chris and did not believe she was the one responsible for my mother's brutal murder. I then took it another step, declaring that Chris too was a victim, of an extortion plot that she'd been forced to go along with.

I reminded them that they stood before the home that my father shared with my loving mother for decades, and he was a witness that night. The only one. And I wondered aloud if my father had witnessed Chris murder his wife, in such an egregious manner, does anyone really think he would let her stay in the house they shared? Or would feel safe living with her, as he planned to do when released from the hospital?

I took questions. Whenever I was on the other side of this, it seemed so easy for the interviewee to tell me no comment, or brush me off. But it wasn't as simple as I'd thought. Everyone was hanging on my every word, making me feel like the belle at the ball—it was quite seductive.

I was questioned on my claims of Chris' innocence. Asked to explain away her behavior on the video, and offer reasons as to how her fingerprints got onto the gun. But I had no plans to try the case in the press ... this time.

The question that got under my skin questioned the possibility that my longstanding relationship with Detective Tim Ruiz led to Chris getting preferential treatment. I vehemently denied this, and made sure they were aware that Chief Bernard Wallach was the one calling the shots at the Danbury PD.

They delved further into my relationship with Tim, specifically our trip to Greece. And suddenly the questions weren't as much fun. I knew they'd eventually connect us to the trip, but not this soon. Lying about it was the worst thing I could do, so I kept it vague, smiling, "I just needed to get away from you guys for a few days. Could you blame me?"

I braced, waiting for one of them to whip out hotel security photos of Tim kissing me, but luckily there were no Perry Masons in this crowd. The questions kept coming, but eventually I had to put an end to the madness, and played to the mothers in the bunch, explaining that I had two little girls—and an over-matched babysitter—that I needed to get home to.

And keeping with the deal we made, they retreated from the property. My faith in my profession had been restored ... for now. I watched as the vehicles dispersed. All was clear ... except for one car that remained parked along the street. I made eye contact with the driver, before they drove in the opposite direction of the other cars.

Chapter 71

Once the coast was clear, I followed in the direction of the car. I drove the short distance to the cul-de-sac at the end of the street—a place we spent much time as kids.

Alexis was standing by her car, smoking a cigarette.

"Stupid habit—picked it up in Greece. Everyone smokes there," she said. She tossed the cigarette on the ground and extinguished it with the twist of her boot.

I walked up beside her. The only lights came from the houses in the distance, but it shined enough light on her face to notice that she looked as tired and despondent as I'd ever seen her.

She viewed the cul-de-sac, surrounded by a thick forest of quiet pines. "I remember we used to play that game here as kids—when we'd hide in the woods and then run out."

"Kick the can."

"That's it—olly olly oxen free," she said with a smile. "Do children still play that game?"

"If it's not on a screen with a control stick, kids don't do it."

"That's too bad—we had so much fun. We'd play until dark. I can still hear your mother calling you: *Eliza! Dinner's ready!*"

I remained quiet, letting her continue, "She always called you, and not Chris. She knew you were the leader. That Chris wouldn't listen to authority, but she would listen to you. Your mother was a smart woman."

In another time and circumstance this would have been an enjoyable stroll down memory lane, but I wasn't going to let her soften my resolve. "Why did you pay Kirk's gambling debt?"

"Because I was in love with him."

I didn't see that one coming. "You and Kirk?"

"He was in town to visit your children last year, and came by the restaurant late one night. We were closed, and I was the only one there, but he looked so sad that I let him in. The two of you had had a disagreement, and he was really down in the dumps about it, so I struck up a conversation with him, hoping to cheer him up. The bottle of wine we finished probably helped more than my words.

"Maybe it was because we were both so vulnerable—my mother's suicide was still fresh—I don't know, but I've never felt instant chemistry with someone like that. It was like our bodies were on fire, and the only thing that could put it out was …"

I put my hand up—I didn't need the details. The shock was clouding my thoughts, but it did clear a few things up. When Niko said that Alexis was in love with someone else, he meant Kirk. And I now understood why he had invited her over that night, trying to broker peace. A rift between his 'ex' and his 'current' could be problematic. But most of all, her many trips to Europe now made sense. It was about Kirk, not business.

"One of the reasons he was so down was that he'd received no offers to play basketball. I knew the owner of a team in Bodrum, as my family lived nearby in Kos, and he did me a favor by hiring Kirk. I would go to visit, but I couldn't let the Greek authorities know I'd be so close by. So I would fly to Paris on the flight your father piloted, then another flight to

Istanbul, and a long train ride to Bodrum. But love is one long journey worth taking."

I got the sense that there was a lot more to this. "But you also introduced him to Niko, knowing that it would end up with Kirk being indebted to him. That doesn't really sound like an act of love to me."

She looked perplexed. "Kirk's gambling debt wasn't with Niko—it was those men Plato and Socrates … the ones who are the enemies of my family."

It amazed me how the mind works. Even after seeing the security video that showed Niko collaborating with these supposed enemies, she still remained in denial.

"With all due respect, Alexis, I have it from multiple sources that Niko was the one Kirk owed money to." Including Kirk himself.

"I went to Niko when Kirk told me of the threats, and he informed me that Plato and Socrates were the ones Kirk was in trouble with, and they were dangerous. He advised me to pay off the debt before they hurt Kirk."

How very convenient of Niko to get her to go along, since he'd be the one ultimately pocketing her money.

"So you paid off the debt … on Niko's advice … hoping to save Kirk?"

"I thought that would put an end to it, but it was just the beginning."

"How so?"

"They considered it a down payment on Kirk's life. But to keep it that way, I would have to assist them in a smuggling operation."

I thought of my father—*what did he get himself involved in?* I think I was about to find out.

"They needed a pilot," she said.

"So you offered my father to these men, knowing what they were capable of? How could you do that?"

"No, Eliza—they wanted your father. It was either him, or Kirk dies."

"Why him?"

"I wish I knew. I wasn't exactly in a position to demand answers."

"So that's what your meeting was about that night in the parking lot?"

"We had been talking about the Haiti idea, and I led him to believe that was my reason to meet. When I revealed the truth, he felt I'd tricked him into coming. That's why he left the restaurant in anger, and I followed after him. He eventually agreed to do it—that's what you saw in the pictures."

"But why would my father agree to help you—he couldn't stand Kirk?"

"He wasn't able to live with the idea of his granddaughters growing up without their father."

"According to Chris, my father offered to continue with this smuggling scheme in exchange for my mother's life. So why then kill her, and potentially the golden goose? There has to be more to this."

Alexis just shook her head. "I've thought about it so many times—we did everything they asked. And now to think that Niko was the one behind it …"

She paused for a moment, and choked up with emotion. Reality had finally defeated Delusion in the Battle of Alexis' Mind. For what it's worth, it seemed genuine.

She wiped tears away and found resolve. "I'm willing to do whatever it takes to find out the truth—wear a wire tap, whatever."

She looked at her watch like she had somewhere to be. "I need to get back to the restaurant. You and Tim are the only ones I trust right now—come by the restaurant after closing, just the two of you, and I'll fill you in on all the details of the smuggling operation, and anything else you want to know."

Alexis got into her car. Before she shut the door, she told me, "Just so you know—Kirk is staying with me at the farmhouse, since he can no longer stay with you."

The Kirk/Alexis thing was still not computing. "So you're together?"

She shook her head somberly. "No—he broke it off with me while he was still playing in Turkey."

"Yet you still paid his debt, and provide him shelter—why?"

"Because I love him."

She shut the door and started the car. But before she drove off, she rolled down the window and said, "In case you're wondering, the reason he broke it off with me was that he told me he was still in love with you, Eliza."

Chapter 72

I stood in the empty parking lot of Skita's awaiting Tim's arrival. The last patron left about twenty minutes ago, and I was eager to begin our meeting with Alexis. *Where are you?*

I pulled my jacket tight to my body attempting to fight off the cold. I almost reached for my phone to call Tim, when a black SUV pulled up alongside me. It appeared he was driving the Chief Mobile—I was impressed.

I hurried around to the driver's side, but quickly realized that it wasn't the Chief's Tahoe—the one they picked me up in the morning of my mother's murder. This was a black Suburban with tinted windows ... just like the one used in the bank robbery.

The door swung open. I only made it a couple of steps before a pair of strong hands reeled me in. I struggled to break free, but it was no use. The back door opened and I was unceremoniously tossed in. The door slammed behind me and the vehicle drove off.

I looked to the man sitting next to me. He was older with a trimmed white goatee, and was dressed in a dark pinstriped suit with a bright red tie.

"Don't look so surprised, Eliza—it's not like you didn't have thoughts. That's why you asked that FBI agent in Greece about the possibility," he said.

I found the courage to look the man in his sinister eyes, and held my stare. As a little girl I'd always turned away from him when he'd look in my direction. But he wasn't dealing with a scared little girl anymore.

It was Alexis' supposedly dead father Georgos Tskitapolis.

"I'm sure Agent Bradford told you that it was impossible for me to have survived, and he's right, based on what he saw. I wouldn't have been able to survive on my own."

I followed his look to our driver—his partner in crime. Niko.

I lashed out at him, "You're a liar—you said I'd never see you again!"

"You continue to twist words. I said, if you did, it no be good for you."

"What did you do with Tim?"

"He's fine, just ran into a little car trouble," Niko said with a grin. "I'm surprised he didn't call you."

I wanted to slap the pretty right off his face.

I checked my phone that had been stuffed in my jacket pocket, and sure enough Tim had left a message. But I didn't get to check it, before Tskitapolis swiped the phone away from me and handed it over the seat to Niko.

He patted my leg, which gave me the creepers. "I was just thinking back to those days when you were a little girl and our families were close. Do you remember those days?"

I nodded.

"The thing is, children view the world through idealism, while adults see reality. Do you understand what I'm trying to say?"

I had a pretty good idea, and also thought I was about to get an answer to my lingering question. "Why was it personal with you and my father?"

His face creased with anger. The wrinkles on his bronzed skin appeared to deepen. "He killed my wife."

I edged back in my seat. "I was under the impression that she took her own life." Of course, I thought he had as well.

He stared menacingly at me, before reaching into the breast pocket of his suit jacket. He took out a folded piece of paper and urged me to read it.

Within the first few sentences it was clear that I was reading his wife's suicide note. The basic gist was that when it became apparent to her that she couldn't be with the man she loved, she no longer wanted to live. That man was my father.

I should have been shocked that he had carried on an affair with Alexis' mother. He basically admitted he'd cheated, but she would have been the last person that would have come to my mind ... if it hadn't been for the photo Alexis had showed me.

It looked like an idyllic snapshot of childhood memories, but when I looked closer, I had noticed the shared look between my father and Macaela Tskitapolis. It was subtle, and you'd have to have really known my father to even pick up on it. It was the way I remembered him looking at my mother. It had been a long time since I'd seen that look. I'd always thought the stroke marked the time when things changed between them, but I was learning that it went back much longer than that.

Now it was my turn to be angry. "My mother and sister had nothing to do with this!"

"A father is supposed to protect his wife and children, but Nathan put his in danger. He took my wife, so I took his. Yet taking Sarah would just be removing a burden for him ... not providing justice."

"She wasn't a burden, she was my mother!"

"To you, perhaps. But your father's main concern has always been himself. In his eyes, your mother was holding him from the life he deserved. The only way to get through to someone like that is to make them suffer—to make him watch his pride and joy be destroyed. His own daughter. And with all due respect, Chris is the daughter he truly loves."

I went into reporter mode, piecing the story together. "You vowed revenge against my father, but you had a big problem—the Greek government was getting close to arresting you, and you would have been sent back to face trial, without your usual protectors in place.

"So you played the distraught husband, and made the world believe you took your own life, all while concealing the real reason your wife committed suicide. Then you created a smuggling scheme to lure my father into your web.

"You found your pressure point in Kirk's gambling debt to Niko. You claim my father is this evil man, yet you knew that he would put himself in danger to help Kirk, and protect his grandchildren. That doesn't sound like someone who is all about themselves."

"You're his daughter—children normally see their parents in a good light."

"Will Alexis see you that way? When she learns you used her to help along your sick plan of revenge, while letting her think you were dead?"

His anger returned. "I love my daughter! But she makes many poor decisions, and I need to save her from herself. Like getting involved with a lowlife gambler like Kirk McCaffrey. Or tonight—bringing you here to tell you details of the smuggling operation, and help you to take down Niko."

"At least she's willing to put herself on the line. Not some coward who hides in the shadows. Who in the end, didn't have the guts to go through with it."

"I think you're confusing me with your father's cowardice. Your mother is dead and your sister has been arrested for her murder. The plan is in motion, and there's nothing you can do to stop it. "

"I meant *you* didn't go through with it. You had your goons do the dirty work for you. No wonder your wife didn't love you—I'll bet she wanted a real man."

The slap happened so fast that I didn't see it coming. My cheek stung like never before, and my eyes welled with tears. But it was worth every throb.

"So why are you telling me this?" I asked, gritting through the pain.

"You keep digging until you get your answers—I thought I'd give you those answers."

What a swell guy. "And what do you get out of it?"

"You back off."

If my cheek didn't hurt so bad I would have laughed in his face. "You have to be kidding me."

"The more you dig, the worse it will be for your family."

I moved closer to him, making it clear I wasn't scared of him. "I will never back off, and I will never be silent."

He shook his head sadly. "I'm afraid you don't have a choice. I was just hoping we could do this in a civilized way."

The vehicle stopped and Niko got out. Seconds later, my door opened and he dragged me out.

I felt Tskitapolis' beady eyes on me, looking right through me like I was already dead. "I'm sorry this is how things must end between us, Eliza, but don't say I didn't give you a chance."

Chapter 73

I wasn't afraid.

But I was frustrated as hell. I could see my house lit in the distance as Niko forced me over the muddy terrain. It might as well have been a thousand miles away.

"You promise you won't hurt them?" I asked for the umpteenth time, and was still waiting for an answer.

"As long as you cooperate," Niko finally spoke. He nudged his gun into my ribs, inspiring me to pick up the pace.

I did my best to avoid tripping on the underbrush, concentrating on each step, until we arrived at a rowboat that sat on the edge of the lake. It was sort of a community boat for the neighborhood. The fact that he knew exactly where to find it meant that this moment had been meticulously planned. Just like my mother's murder.

He instructed me to get in and to row out toward the center of the lake. Unfortunately, he would also be coming with me. And like the chauvinist he was, made the woman do all the work.

By the time Niko demanded I stop rowing, my house was just a speck of light in the distance. I pictured Jillian and the girls inside, laughing and eating popcorn with extra butter, after they'd conned her into letting them stay up long past their bedtime. A tear trickled down my frozen cheek.

"So how are you planning to do this?" I figured there was no point in beating around the bush.

"To do what?"

"I doubt you're going to shoot me—too messy. My guess is your going to hold my head under water—drowning is sort of your specialty. And by the time they discover my body on the bottom of the lake, you'll be safely out of the country."

"I didn't kill your mother," he said, like it mattered at this point. "And I'm not going to kill you, Eliza."

"Can we stop playing games? I think you owe me that much. I've seen enough movies to know that when the bad guy surfaces, you better not be looking, or you become a liability. And now I know he's alive."

"You're no threat to him. What are you going to tell people—that you saw a ghost?"

"Are you sure you heard him correctly? Because it sure sounded to me like your boss ordered you to bump me off."

"You're starting to tempt me. But his instructions were to warn you off, scare you into cooperation ... and he's not my boss."

"I'm sorry—I forgot that we're still pretending. Tskitapolis is dead, and Alexis is actually in charge. Did that sound convincing?"

"The only person I answer to is Agent Larry Bradford of the FBI."

It was a good thing I wasn't standing, as I might have gone overboard. "Come again?"

"You heard me."

I tried to wrap my head around what he told me, and questioned whether it was some sort of mind game. "You're telling me that you're an FBI agent?"

"No—I'm an informant. Which means, like it or not, we're on the same team."

He could see the doubt in my eyes, and offered an explanation, "A few years back my gambling business was infiltrated by an undercover agent from the Hellencic Police in Greece. I was facing many years in prison, and I was willing to accept it, until I learned that Mr. Tskitapolis had worked with the Greek government to take me down, all in order to save his own skin.

"Suddenly prison didn't seem like such a loyal gesture. So I agreed to become an informant, spying on Mr. Tskitapolis in exchange for my freedom. He was under the impression that the case against me was dismissed due to lack of evidence, and he was impressed that I didn't give into government pressure to expose him. He welcomed me back with open arms.

"When he and his family returned to America, my role was now monitored by the American FBI. They essentially became my new boss."

This did explain how Tskitapolis knew I had asked Agent Bradford about his suicide. Niko likely claimed that he had a source inside the Bureau, making him even more valuable to Tskitapolis, but in actuality Bradford passed the information directly to his informant.

"So the FBI knows he's alive—Bradford lied to us?"

"There was a suicide video of Mr. Tskitapolis proclaiming his love of Macaela, cutting his wrists, and then tossing himself overboard. But it failed to show my arrival in a speedboat, saving him from certain death. The FBI played along, declaring him dead, and then stopped any official investigations into him and his businesses."

"No longer their problem."

"That was their public stance, but underneath the surface they were using me to continue tracking him."

"So now that he was 'dead,' he felt free to plot revenge against my family, including the scheme to lure him in. What was he smuggling?"

"The contraband was people—human trafficking. Many of them bad people who wanted to get into the US for an assortment of reasons."

"Terrorists?"

"Some were, I'm sure, but the focus was on repaying those who had helped protect him over the years. Many were now facing arrest in Greece and needed to escape, just as he had."

"And being the good little soldier that you were, you set all this up."

"My duties included producing false identification, paperwork, visas, passports, etc., here in the United States. I was also in charge of recruiting. For instance, he needed someone to deliver the items to the subjects, who could make constant trips to Europe without raising eyebrows."

"Like a pilot."

"Exactly."

"But not any pilot would do—he needed my father."

"The smuggling was very profitable—these men were willing to pay a high price for a new life—and Mr. Tskitapolis was in need of money, especially with the Greek government seizing many of his assets. But make no mistake, the true focus for this operation was revenge against your father."

"And he used his own daughter to do it ... how sick."

"It was actually my idea to bring Alexis into it—I had to convince her father to involve her. I had never seen Alexis so in love with someone as she was with Kirk. And his getting himself into debt was quite a stroke of luck, making it an easy sell. I convinced her that Plato and Socrates were enemies of her father, and the only way to keep Kirk safe from them was to get your father to go along. She didn't think twice about it."

"Why did she fly to Europe on my father's flights?"

"She was worried about Kirk's safety, and visited him as frequently as possible. She even continued to do so after he broke off their relationship. She really does love him—it's no act."

I seethed—and it had nothing to do with Kirk and Alexis. "So the FBI not only paved the way for this lunatic to re-enter the country, knowing his criminal history, but also helped him destroy my family!"

"The FBI liked the idea of the smuggling. It brought bad guys onto their turf where they could monitor them, watch them, and eventually arrest them. They are in the bad-guy business, and more bad guys meant more business for them."

"And in doing so, they basically looked the other way when they murdered my mother, and set up my sister to take the fall! Bradford knew this the entire time and lied to my face. He encouraged me to stay out of it to help protect his lies. Did they use one of their neat, pretty words to describe her murder, like collateral damage?"

"I'm not defending your government's actions, but nobody believed Mr. Tskitapolis' plan involved killing your mother. He never revealed this to me, and he had trusted me with his most sensitive information, like the plans for his suicide. If I thought someone might get killed I never would have agreed to be involved."

"You were *just* going to frame my sister for a home invasion, not murder. I guess that makes everything hunky-dory."

Niko inched back like he thought I might send him over the side of the boat into the chilly water. A complete reversal from our time on the ferry. "The FBI would have dropped all the charges against your sister in exchange for testifying against Mr. Tskitapolis, once they'd made an arrest. I was just doing my job … I was on your side."

"Bullshit. You were there that night—you could have done something. You're just as much responsible as they are!"

"I had no choice but to play along. I wasn't the one calling the shots."

"You say that, but according to Chris, you were the leader. You could have called off the mission."

"I thought so too, but that no turn out to be the case. Once Socrates shot your father, they decided your mother must be silenced. I ordered them to stand down, but I realized that had been the plan all along. And there was nothing I could do to stop it—I was severely outgunned, so I saved what I could."

"Chris."

He nodded, and blew out a smoky breath in the cold air. "After I punched Chris unconscious, I got her out of there, on the grounds that it would be best way to set her up for the murder. But I sneaked out the security video to thwart any attempt to frame her."

Until her twin sister handed it over to the police. But still, that didn't explain, "If you removed Chris from the scene, then how did her fingerprints get on the gun?"

"No idea. They must have lifted them previously. Maybe they were on a glass the night Plato approached her in that New York bar."

"And I assume you're the one who made that emergency call. Not a neighbor."

"I did—my only hope at that point was that the authorities might arrive before they killed your parents."

It turned out to be false hope. And it was looking like any new hope I felt from Niko's association with the FBI was going to have the same bad ending.

"If you weren't the leader, that tells me that Tskitapolis didn't trust you. He must have known you've been working with the FBI. Which means we're both going to end up on the bottom of this lake."

"If he doubted my loyalty, I'd already be dead. He's known me since I was young. I might be a liar and a cheat, but I'm no killer. I wouldn't have killed your mother, and he knew that. So he called on someone who would."

"Then why were you there at all?"

"Because he needed my leadership. I'm always calm under pressure—the opposite of Plato and Socrates. If he left it up to them, everyone would be dead or in jail. And he was determined to have your father alive, so he could see your sister suffer."

My anger continued to build. "You can go tell Tskitapolis that I hope he enjoys the front page story tomorrow, which will declare him as my mother's murderer. Do I have permission to quote you by name ... or should I use 'well placed FBI informant'?"

"You'll do nothing of the sort."

"You obviously don't know me very well."

"Maybe not, but I'm aware of the love you have for your children, and that you would never purposely put them in danger. I also know that you're smart, so you understand the odds. The FBI will be against you—they will never admit they knew of criminals being smuggled into the US with their assistance.

"Same with the local police—they believe Chris is their killer, and that they have an open and shut case. And if you start making accusations against a dead guy, trying to save your sister, you'll lose any of the credibility you'll need to try to help Chris win her case in court."

"I'm not letting her burn for this. Take me to Tskitapolis. If he wants to go after my family, he's going to have to deal with me ... face to face."

"I have no idea where he is. He contacts me when he needs me—like tonight."

"Then I'll find him myself."

"That will only make things worse. I would suggest you go home and hug your children, and consider yourself lucky. You're better off cutting your losses. Help Chris the best you can, but understand that Mr. Tskitapolis won't stop until he feels your father has properly suffered."

He was right—I didn't want to hear it.

And I wouldn't.

But I would take one piece of advice from him. Now that we were done here, I planned to go home and hug my Brooke and Kelly, and not let them go until the sun rose over the lake tomorrow morning.

Chapter 74

"We don't have to go to school?" Brooke asked with suspicion in her voice.

So I explained once more about their impromptu trip to Boston with their father, which would include seeing where Kirk had grown up, taking in a Celtics game, and eating all the clam chowder they could fit into their little stomachs.

"But the last time we missed school we had so much extra homework," Brooke continued.

"And today is the day Gramp is coming home. I wanted to see him," Kelly added.

Obviously they weren't getting the concept. If you're offered a day off from school to spend with the fun parent, you take it before someone changes their mind.

And they were going, whether they liked it or not. I didn't want them anywhere near here today. What I took away from last night was that we were alone in this—to save my sister, we would have to do it ourselves. And we needed to act before Georgos Tskitapolis was so far underground that we'd never find him.

Kirk pulled up in the Corvette, looking as confused as our children. He asked at least six times, "Are you sure?"

I'd never been so sure about anything. I would have preferred he took them completely out of the country, or to another solar system, but on short notice, Boston would have to do.

I played the role of the cool, "skipping school is no biggie" mom, up until it was time to part ways. My eyes welled with tears, blowing my cover, and I reminded them of things that wouldn't require reminding if we planned on seeing each other again in the future.

Once Kirk secured them in the car, he came over to me. "So are you going to let me in on what's going on? This is, let's say, very un-Eliza-ish."

"I can't," I said.

His face tensed. "Thanks for trusting me."

"I'm sorry, Kirk. I hope you can understand."

"I was being serious—thank you for trusting me. Whatever is happening, it's obviously important."

"I do trust you … with their lives." Especially now that I knew he was involved in this the same way we all were—dragged in unknowingly. Although, I had made it very clear that if he planned to be around the girls in the future, he would stop associating with gamblers.

"Just be safe," he said and we hugged.

I tried to look away as they drove off, and ignore those tiny hands waving at me. But all that mattered was that they were out of the line of fire.

After a quick stop for coffee at Luke & Jack's, I headed over to the *Danbury Ledger.* Bob looked up with surprise as I barged into his office, the glasses impressively remaining on the end of his nose. "What can I do for ya, Eliza?"

"I've got an idea for a new feature for the paper."

"And this couldn't wait until our Friday meeting?"

"I think it's imperative that it starts today."

He leaned back in his chair, waiting for me to wow him. "I'm all ears."

"A gossip section."

Unsurprisingly, this didn't excite Bob.

"You know, like *Page Six*," I added.

"I know what a gossip page is. I'm just curious why it's important for there to be one in the *Ledger* … and what makes it so urgent."

"A couple of high profile residents are engaging in a secret romantic tryst, and I don't want our competitors to beat us to the scoop."

"That would be a tragedy," Bob quipped sarcastically. "Would this involve a hunky policeman who recently went on a romantic getaway to the Greek isles with his journo cutie, gal pal?" He paused for a second, adding, "Did I get the gossip page lingo down?"

Actually, not bad. But no, our first edition would feature, "A hot romance between local restaurateur, Alexis Tskitapolis, and widowed, former murder suspect, Nathan Dunbar."

"And so soon after his wife's death. Quite tawdry … it must be especially hard on Mr. Dunbar's daughter."

"No, she's taking it just fine," I said with a smile.

His eyes narrowed, trying to figure where I was going with this. "I'm assuming you have proof of this affair. And by proof, I mean something that will keep us from getting sued."

"Oh, I'm not going to be on this story, Bob. I'm too close to it, and I have too many biases. I thought I'd leave it for you."

"Me? I'm a newsman. I wouldn't even know where to begin looking. And if you think I'm going to climb a tree outside their house with a camera, you've lost your mind."

"It shouldn't be that hard. My father is going to be released from the hospital today, and he and Alexis plan to hold a joint press conference to let the world know about their unbridled love."

He stared at me quizzically. "What are you up to, kid?"

"Just make sure you're there—and that the story goes up immediately on our website," I said as I walked away.

He smiled at me as I left. But it was a worried smile.

Chapter 75

My father looked much healthier than he had on previous visits. He was dressed in a flannel shirt and khakis, and looked like he'd taken a recent shower. As I stepped closer to him I could smell his cologne.

"This is a pleasant surprise," he said, looking up from the overnight bag he was packing.

"Surprises seem to be a theme lately."

"I thought the girls might have come to pick them up, so I left them out," he said, pointing at the framed photo of my mother, along with the model airplanes, which sat next to his bag.

"They're spending the day with their father."

"Just like their mother."

He smiled at me, but I didn't return it.

"I was wrong, Dad."

He paused for dramatic effect. "The gunshot must have affected my hearing because I thought I heard you say—

"I was wrong about your affair with Alexis."

"I told you, sweetheart—it was just business."

A business that included a smuggling ring, which helped bring numerous unsavory characters into the country, and could put him behind bars for many years, but I would get to that later.

"I had the wrong Tskitapolis woman. It was Alexis' mother, Macaela, whom you had the affair with."

My words stopped him in his tracks. Suddenly he didn't look so chipper. "I don't know what you've heard, but—

"Save it, Dad. I spent some quality time last night with our old neighbor, Georgos Tskitapolis, and his little buddy, Niko. You might remember him—he was there the night Mom died."

"It can't be," was all my father could muster.

"Oh, it can. He took me for a little drive to reminisce about the good old days. He had an interesting story to tell—it really hooked me in."

My father appeared to be lightheaded, and took a seat on the edge of the bed.

"He provided me a little reading material on the trip—Macaela's suicide note. She was pretty clear that if she couldn't spend her life with the man she loved, she didn't want to live at all. Do you want to take a guess as to who that was?"

"But that doesn't mean—

"It doesn't, you're right. But Tskitapolis holds you responsible. Did you know he was behind all of this? Is he the one you're trying to protect us from?"

He looked straight ahead at the sterile wall. "I assumed he was dead—I had no reason to think otherwise."

"Then who did you think was responsible?"

"Obviously there was a Greek connection—the guys that Kirk got involved with over there. I actually wondered if maybe Alexis was behind it—she was so desperate to involve me—but I never connected it to Georgos or Macaela."

"It didn't once occur to you that getting involved with people like this might put you, and those around you, in danger?"

"Of course it did. But when I thought of Brooke and Kelly growing up without a father, it wasn't that hard of a decision. I thought I'd fly a couple jobs for them and then it would be over—debt paid off."

"Did Mom know?"

"No—she had enough concerns just making it through each day, without having to worry about me."

"I meant about Macaela."

He nodded. "She knew very early on. She didn't catch us in the act or anything like that, but she knew. I eventually came clean to her, and we separated for a brief time."

This surprised me—I couldn't recall a time that my parents weren't together. My father added, "That summer you spent at Lake George."

My favorite summer, spent with my sisters on the lake. It was a magical memory that was now stained.

"When we reconvened that fall, she forgave me, not that I deserved it. I was determined from that moment forward to make sure she didn't regret that decision. I look back now and think of all the things that I would have missed out on, and just thinking about it scares me."

"Did Tskitapolis know about you and his wife?"

"When they so abruptly moved back to Greece, it led me to believe that was the reason. But I didn't have any contact with them until they returned."

"Did you see her again … when they returned?"

"She came to me, wanting to pick up where we'd left off. It was strange—for me, those days were a million years ago, but for Macaela, it was like only a couple days had gone by. And now that she'd returned, she thought things would go back to the way they were.

"I wasn't the same person I was back then, and there was no way I was going to risk your mother's trust again. So I turned her away, and told her that it would be best if we didn't meet again. That was the last time I saw her. I hate to think that might have contributed to her demise."

"You have many things to regret, Dad, but that's not one of them. She was a troubled woman, held prisoner by a monster." And since I always needed to know the why, I asked him why he would risk his wife and family for this woman, even if I wasn't sure I wanted to know the answer.

He thought for a long moment. "It all happened so fast. One minute I was this free bird, and like a snap of the fingers I had a wife and three children, two of them facing an overwhelming future."

"You're seriously putting this on us?"

"Oh, no," he backtracked. "It was my mistake and I own it. I'm just trying to give you an understanding of my mindset at the time. I was traveling so much and your mother was so wrapped up in the Conjoined business, that it was like we'd become complete strangers. It was as if we'd set out to separate our children, yet we ended up separating our lives."

"Did you love her … Macaela?"

"I thought I did at the time. She was intoxicating; I couldn't believe it could be anything other. But looking back, I had no idea what love was. Your mother, and you, and your sisters are the ones who taught me what it really is."

I sat next to him on the bed. "We have to put a stop to this, before anybody else gets hurt."

"I agree, sweetheart, but how do you stop a dead man?"

I took a moment to send a text, which would begin to answer his question. The door opened and Alexis walked in. I had a plan, and it was simple. My father and Alexis would appear at the press conference I'd told Bob about, and they would declare their love to whoever was listening … hopefully Georgos Tskitapolis.

Niko was right—we would never find him. So we needed to smoke him out from his cave, make him come to us, and there was only one thing that could spark him to surface—the sight of his flesh-and-blood joining his mortal enemy.

Alexis had been my first stop after my meeting with Bob. She wasn't exactly receptive to the idea that her father was still alive, or that he was the one behind my mother's murder. And if I was in her shoes, I doubt I would have believed it either.

But I received an assist from my favorite FBI informant—Niko—who had decided to come clean with her. People who have a long history together are hard to fool, and Niko convinced her that we were telling the truth. Not to say it was an easy truth.

The press conference took place on the steps of the hospital. My father and Alexis held hands and lovingly touched each other at every opportunity. They announced that they'd been in love for some time, but couldn't be together because my father was committed to my mother. And while they were thrilled that their love was no longer hidden in the shadows, my father reiterated that he, Alexis, or my sister had nothing to do with removing my mother from the equation.

They went on to say that they understood that people would not accept their love, and many would consider it a betrayal of my mother, but that wouldn't stop them. Because nothing could stop true love. But the most important announcement was that my father would be spending the coming days at her Roxbury farm, recuperating with her at his side. *Got that, Georgos?*

Even though I was the one who wrote the script, it was still hard to listen to. So I tried to divert my attention by viewing the crowd of reporters. I spotted Bob, and could tell that he still wasn't sure what I was up to, but my little caper had hooked him in.

I kept the rest of my afternoon as normal as possible. The kids were having a great time in Boston. Not only did they get to see where their father grew up, but also they got to go to the Children's Museum, and had lunch at the Flour Bakery. I kept it all business this time, displaying little emotion, which was much easier to do over the phone. Once we said our goodbyes, I made my way to Ridgefield.

Tim met me at my parents' house, and we found that Chris wasn't alone. Her bail deal had no restrictions on visitors—just that she couldn't leave the premises.

Beef was there with his son, Terrell, who was getting an intense coaching lesson from Chris. Just seeing the passion in the way she instructed him in the finer points of basketball, I could tell that she'd finally realized her calling. She was right—it wasn't working for Norby, or sitting in some office with a pretty view.

But for her to pursue it, at least outside of prison, tonight needed to be a success.

Beef read our serious looks, and sent Terrell away. "Practice is over—take the car home. Just don't let your mother know I let you drive."

He tossed him his car keys. Terrell appeared excited by the prospect, but Tim not so much. "Wait a minute—he's only fourteen. He doesn't have a license."

Beef shook his head. "You're always a stickler for the rules."

"I'm a police officer—it kind of goes with the territory."

I flashed Tim a look to let him know that we had bigger fish to fry … and laws to break. He finally relented, "Fine—but you better not mention my name if you get pulled over."

Terrell smiled and fist bumped with Chris, then did a drive-by hug with his dad, and he was off.

The moment the door shut behind him, Beef turned to us. "I'm down."

"On your luck? For the count?"

"Whatever you're up to."

Tim and I played coy, but Chris filled him in on the plan. She then added, "I'm in too."

Tim shook his head. "Beef's one thing, but you can't go. And it's not me saying it—it's that monitor on your ankle."

"Luckily for me, I know a police officer with the ability to remove it without detection."

"Not a chance."

"C'mon, Tim—it's my ass that's on the line. I at least deserve a chance to prove my innocence. I'm certainly not going to get it in a courtroom with a stacked jury against me."

"The minute I take that device off, I'm going to end up in jail right with you."

Chris made one final plea, "You guys have all been trying to save me since I got into this mess," she looked directly at me. "But now it's time for me to save myself. To be there for my teammates."

We were at an impasse. Beef was a yes, Tim remained a no. So they looked to me to cast the deciding vote.

It wasn't much of a decision. History had proven that separating us requires 31 hours and a lot of medical degrees, none of which we had. Whatever was going to happen tonight, we would do it together.

Chapter 76

I stepped out of the bedroom and shut the door behind me. The sounds of moaning and groaning were muffled slightly, but still audible.

"Sounds like someone is having a good time in there," Tim said to me.

Which was exactly the point. "I found it in Alexis' movie collection."

Beef smiled wide. "I'm really starting to like this Alexis."

"Not that type of movie collection. It's *When Harry Met Sally*, the restaurant scene with Meg Ryan."

Beef looked disappointed.

Tim, on the other hand, remained skeptical.

"So you really don't think Tskitapolis will show?" I asked him.

"It just hasn't been his style. He's been completely disciplined up to this point. And he's called on others to do his dirty work for him."

I countered, "The man is so consumed by revenge that he faked his death just so he could better take down my family. I'm willing to bet that seeing Alexis and my father together is the one thing that will get him to show his face."

That, and a well-placed source assured me that he was on his way, which I decided to keep to myself.

Chris arrived. "Okay, Dad and Alexis are locked safely in the storm-cellar—we're good to go."

Now all we could do was wait. When Tskitapolis arrived, we expected him to march directly into the house, and once they heard what was going on inside the bedroom, or at least thought to have heard, it would likely set him over the edge and they'd barge in. They would find nothing but an empty room and a scene from a movie playing on a loop. They would be trapped, and we'd have the element of surprise on our side.

But I had to consider what Tim said—that even though I was confident Tskitapolis was coming, he might send his men in first, with the orders to bring my father and Alexis back to him. If that occurred, the response would be trickier. But luckily for us, we had an FBI informant on our side.

Tim drew his gun, indicating we were ready. He offered me a weapon, which I declined. "I don't know how to use that thing, so I'd be more likely to shoot one of us."

"Which is why you should hide with your father in the storm-cellar. I've put myself on the line for you, Eliza, and I can't be responsible for putting a journalist in harm's way."

We had already been over this … twelve times. "I'm not hiding from him."

"I'm not asking."

"I'll sign one of those waivers like I did when I went on the ride-along with you and your partner last year."

"This is far from official police business."

"Then I guess it's settled—I'll be right by your side, partner."

He sighed. "That's what I'm afraid of."

Chris pulled out a gun of her own, surprising me … and Beef. "Where'd you get that?" he asked, his voice raising a couple octaves.

"I'm a single woman living alone in New York City. I needed to protect myself, and it's legally registered."

"The gun might be legal, but you ain't. You're a bail-skipping fugitive, so you might not want to get caught with that thing."

He nodded in Tim's direction, who acted like he hadn't seen anything.

Chris peered out the nearest window into the dark night, and ominously said, "My gut tells me that you're going to be happy I have it."

Maybe it was a conjoined thing, but I had the same feeling.

Tim offered Beef a gun of his own—the one that had been earmarked for me—but he informed him that his hands were registered weapons, and they were all he needed. We could only hope.

The last piece of equipment to check was our communication. And it wasn't exactly of the high-tech variety. We had found walkie-talkies in my parents' basement, which we used to play with as children. Not exactly ideal, but they still worked. We added new batteries, and they had enough range to cover the perimeter. We had left our cell phones behind, so they couldn't be traced—these weren't amateurs we were encountering.

Chris and I locked eyes as she headed out with Beef. I always struggled separating from her. I watched as she left the room, but the bad feeling I had remained.

Chapter 77

Chris and Beef stationed themselves behind a group of pine trees, where they had a view of the driveway. Dressed in all black, they melded into the night. They turned their flashlights off and waited.

When the large Suburban rolled down the gravel driveway, Beef squeezed his radio and simply said, "The Eagle has landed."

They watched as three men got out of the vehicle, none of which was Tskitapolis. With the combination of the darkness and the vehicle's tinted windows, it was impossible to see if he was present. But Chris could sense his presence.

She recognized the three men—Niko and the Kostas brothers, Plato and Socrates. The same group that accompanied her into her parents' house that night. She fought off the sickening flashbacks.

Just as Eliza had predicted, the men headed toward the farmhouse. They would follow behind them, so they would be able to warn Tim and Eliza as they closed in, and provide backup once they've trapped them inside the house.

But things went off course. The three men veered to the left and walked past the house. For a brief moment, Chris worried they knew of the storm-cellar location—fearing Niko might have double-crossed them—but they walked by it and continued on to the barn, a few hundred yards away from the house. Chris should have felt relief, but her bad feeling actually began to worsen.

They watched as the men disappeared inside. Chris and Beef discussed ambushing them in the barn, but Tim and Eliza thought it best to stick to the plan. So all they could do was wait. It seemed like that's all they'd been doing, and Chris and Beef weren't exactly the patient types.

"What are they doing in there?" Chris asked.

Beef just shook his head.

When they eventually came out of the barn, it was just two of them.

"They're moving toward the house, but no Niko," Beef relayed into the walkie-talkie.

There was a back entrance to the barn—perhaps they split up to attack the house from both the front and back. Chris continued to worry that Niko's loyalty to Tskitapolis had won out, and thought that maybe her sister had put too much trust in him.

They needed to check the barn, but fast. And then get back to help defend Tim and Eliza in the house. If this was a tactic to get them scrambling, it was certainly effective.

They entered the barn, Chris' gun drawn. And they immediately got their answer.

There was no need to check the back entrance. They had found Niko. He was right in front of them.

And he was dead.

His throat was slit, and a knife was plunged through his heart. They must have surprised him before he could call out, or fight back, which explained the lack of noise. A search of his pockets found nothing but a set of keys.

Beef spoke rapidly into the walkie-talkie, "Change of plans! Niko's dead!"

They dashed out of the barn, heading toward the house. Chris hit a patch of wet leaves and crashed to the ground.

She screamed out in agony, which caught the attention of the Kostas brothers. That was one way to stop them.

One of them shouted, "Who goes there?"

"Let's get out of here," Beef whispered as loud as possible, pulling Chris to her feet.

"I can't," she said, and fell right back to the ground. She pounded the terrain with her fist, frustration oozing out of her.

"Then I'm gonna have to carry ya—but we need to bail."

"All that will do is get us both killed—go on without me."

"This isn't a war movie—now get on!"

They could hear the heavy footsteps closing in.

Chris pulled her gun out and pointed it at Beef. "If you want to get us both killed, I can do it much quicker. Now get out of here!"

"You're crazy, ya know—you *and* your sister," Beef said, knowing he'd never won an argument with either of their stubborn asses. He ran off into the darkness, hoping to draw the men away from his injured partner. He shouted out, "I'm over here, ya big fat Greek toad! Come and get me!"

Chris struggled to her feet and felt a sharp pain through her knee like she'd been stabbed a thousand times over. She could feel the pounding of the earth as the men got closer. She tried her best to hobble away. She looked back and saw Plato—he was too close. She wasn't going to make it.

She turned and fired at him, but didn't come close. She was about to try again, when the other one, Socrates, blindsided her and she crashed to the ground. Her gun spilled away, out of her reach.

Chapter 78

Officer Annie Sampson walked into police headquarters. She spotted a couple of her colleagues—Gibbs and Delgado—and asked, "Have you guys seen Tim?"

"And what's your interest in the good detective?" Gibbs asked back.

Not that it was any of his business, but, "He left his sunglasses in my car earlier, and I wanted to return them." She held up the pair of aviators for them to see.

"In your car, huh?" Delgado said with his usual meathead smirk. "You two out for a romantic drive?"

Annie rolled her eyes. "More like working security for the Nathan Dunbar press conference, and then provided him and Alexis Tskitapolis a police escort to her home."

Delgado appeared physically angered by this. "Can't believe they're wasting our time … and taxpayer money … to protect some murderer."

"Don't know if you've been keeping up, but Nathan Dunbar is no longer a suspect in his wife's murder. And our job is to protect the citizens, no matter what we think of them—Dunbar had received numerous death threats."

"Wallach's convinced Dunbar's daughter did the deed, but I'm not so sure. Seemed like Daddy couldn't wait to run off with his hot young girlfriend once his old lady was underground."

It did seem a little odd to Annie, as did the sudden urge to tell the world about their relationship. She considered herself a good judge of character, and while her "look 'em in the eye" test wasn't infallible, and there had been many rumors circulating about Nathan Dunbar since that night, she really got the sense that he was committed to his wife.

She didn't want to debate the case with Delgado, and looked to the more levelheaded Gibbs, "So you haven't seen Tim?"

He thought for a second. "Saw him a few hours ago—he was going into a meeting with the chief."

Annie looked up to see that Wallach's door was shut. If he was still in there, it must be serious. She would return the glasses tomorrow … not that big of a deal.

Gibbs snapped his fingers. "I take that back. I did talk to him when he came out of his meeting. He was heading out to visit Chris Dunbar. I guess there was a problem with her ankle monitor."

"A problem?"

"I don't think it was anything serious. Something about the transmission going in and out."

Ridgefield was on Annie's drive home, so she could stop and drop them off on her way. But when she arrived, there were no cars in the driveway. She had likely missed him. Yet something was nagging at her— how still the house seemed.

She wasn't even sure what that meant—what did she expect, a party? But she decided to knock on the door. What could it hurt? She would just say she was looking for Tim, and had heard he'd been by. Seemed reasonable.

She got no answer on her first attempt. She peeked through a window and didn't witness any movement. Maybe Chris was sleeping. Or perhaps she saw it was her, and didn't want to deal with the police. Annie thought to announce herself, and make it police business—tell her Tim had asked her to double-check that the transmission problems had been fixed—but she decided against it.

What she should have done was get back in her car and continue on home. But her Spidey sense was going off, and her nerves bristled. She looked through the window once again, and this time she saw it.

At least she thought she did. It sure looked like it.

She needed to get inside to make sure. She recalled entering through the garage during the initial crime scene investigation. But it was locked. She got on her tiptoes to see through the garage window. And she was surprised by what she saw.

There were two cars inside. One was the Chevy Blazer that Tim drove when he was off-duty, as he only took his Camaro out on weekends. The other vehicle was a Honda Pilot that she recognized as Eliza Dunbar's car. She remembered from her first visit that the Dunbar parents owned matching Volvos.

It seemed like Tim and Eliza had swapped out their vehicles for the Volvos. *Or were they forced to?* She ran back to her car and got her gun, planning to break in through a window. She could visualize herself trying to explain this one to her boss. It wouldn't be pretty, but if she did nothing it could be much worse, and for all she knew, Tim and Eliza might be in trouble.

She found a better way in—one that wouldn't require broken glass and alarms going off. Thinking back to the investigation, she was reminded that the Dunbars had kept their spare key taped under a lounge chair by the pool. It caused her to wonder; if Chris wanted to rob them, why didn't she just use the spare key at a time when the parents weren't home?

She ran to the backyard and climbed over the gate. Sure enough, the key was still there. She removed it and dashed back toward the house. She entered, announcing herself as police, with gun drawn. She checked room by room, but it became clear that nobody was home.

She did confirm what she had seen. It was the ankle monitor. It was resting on a chair in the kitchen, no longer attached to Chris Dunbar.

Her mind swirled. Tim had been here, and he was one of the few people qualified to remove the monitor without it being detected. If Chris had done it on her own, alarms would have gone off, and this place would have been crawling with cops. And if someone had forced Tim to do it, he could have sent a signal to headquarters to let them know he was under duress.

Could this have been related to the transmission issues? Annie got the idea that there was no such thing. That Tim had made it up to provide a reason for him to come to the house and see Chris Dunbar. He was the one who had set her free.

She was about to call it in, then hesitated. She had learned a lot from Tim, especially about trusting her instincts. Those instincts had gotten her this far, and now they were telling her to trust him. There must be a good explanation for what he was doing. But she also felt he could be in danger, and she needed to get to him.

But where would he be?

She thought back to the reason she came here in the first place—the sunglasses that he'd left in her squad car when they escorted Nathan Dunbar to … *the Tskitapolis farm in Roxbury.*

Chapter 79

Being the chivalrous gentlemen they were, Plato and Socrates helped Chris limp back to the driveway area, where a man waited for her.

Georgos Tskitapolis was leaning against the large SUV smoking a cigarette. Chris hadn't seen him since she was a little girl. He looked mostly the same, just grayer.

He flicked the cigarette to the ground and smiled at her. "Little Christie Dunbar all grown up. How time flies."

"It's Chris," she stood firm.

She glared at the man who was behind the murder of her mother. She contemplated spitting in his face, but there was too much distance between them, and with a stiff wind, it was more likely to end up back in her own face. That would pretty much sum up her last couple weeks.

"I remember back when you were little, and how you and your sister were always together. It almost seems strange to see you apart."

Chris was in no mood for games. "I'm not going to tell you where she is."

"Oh, yes you will," he said with eerie calmness. "And also Detective Ruiz."

Chris paused momentarily, waiting for him to add another name. But he never mentioned Beef. A minor victory.

She shook her head. "Once I failed to contact them, they left. That's how we planned it. Better luck next time."

"Your sister would never abandon you in your time of need. Your bond is too strong. It's your greatest strength, but also your biggest weakness. So how about we try again?"

Chris refused to take the bait. But when Plato opened the back door of the SUV, she realized that she *was* the bait.

We arrived with our hands up—there was no other choice.

Tskitapolis' men moved in, searched us, and took control of Tim's gun.

Once they got their dirty paws off me, I made a beeline for the large Suburban, and the precious cargo it carried in its backseat. They could shoot me if they wanted, but it wouldn't stop me from getting to my girls.

I grabbed hold of them and tried to remain calm as best I could, "Wow—what a surprise. I thought you were going to spend the night in Boston."

"We got a little sidetracked," Kirk said, holding his gaze on Tskitapolis.

The usually chatty Little Macs were quiet, and their father, Mr. Cool, had a shake in his knees. I caught a glimpse of Chris out of the corner of my eye, and noticed her guilt. I flashed her a reassuring look—once they brought my children into this, she had no choice. She did the right thing.

I turned to Tskitapolis. "You son of a bitch."

It was like my words just bounced off him, and he coldly replied, "It's still preferable to being the daughter of Nathan Dunbar."

He motioned for Plato to shut the door to the SUV, and I felt my heart break as my children disappeared from view.

"You were warned to back off. And since you failed to listen, people are dead."

Niko had told me on the boat that if Georgos had suspected him, he'd already be dead. So despite the many years he'd spent with his mentor, he still underestimated him. I would learn from his mistake.

"I don't want to hurt anyone else, Eliza," he said, glancing back at the Suburban to make his point. "But that will be up to you, whether you are honest with me."

"Said the guy who's pretending to be dead," Chris could only bite her tongue for so long.

Plato smashed his boot into her injured knee and she went to the ground in pain. Not being able to help her was the worst type of torture.

"So here's your first question, Eliza. Where is your father?"

"She doesn't know," Chris interjected, struggling to her feet. I almost expected another kick, but none came.

Tskitapolis turned his attention to her. "Why do you say that?"

"Because I'm the one who hid them, and only I know where they are."

"Then I'm going to need you to take us there."

"She can't even walk," I protested.

"I'll go on one condition," Chris said.

"You're hardly in a position to be making ultimatums."

"I need Eliza to go with me."

Tskitapolis scoffed, "Aren't you two a little old for separation anxiety?"

"It has nothing to do with us being conjoined. I instructed Nathan and Alexis not to reveal themselves unless another one of the group confirms it is really us, and it's safe to come out."

Tskitapolis looked frustrated. "Then take Detective Ruiz—your sister stays with me." He looked to Plato. "If she's lying, kill him on the spot."

I could tell that Tskitapolis was keeping us apart out of spite. And I got the feeling that Chris had been counting on it.

"But make sure you bring the girl back to me," Tskitapolis warned. "I am going to savor the look on Nathan's face as he watches his favorite daughter die a slow death."

Chris seemed to take the threat in stride. We looked at each other, but this time I didn't feel the usual angst. I could tell that Chris had played it perfectly.

Chapter 80

Tim led the way with flashlight in hand, while Chris struggled to keep up.

"Hurry it up," Socrates demanded. Plato adding, "Maybe we should leave the cripple behind and let the wild animals get her."

Luckily, Tskitapolis had a much more excruciating death planned for her. So she had that in her favor. She continued to stare straight ahead as she limped along, and wouldn't even give them the pleasure of seeing even a slight grimace.

They arrived at the farmhouse, causing Socrates to say to his partner, "I told you they were in the house. There's no secret hiding place."

"So they lied."

"Which means we kill Ruiz—you heard Mr. T's orders."

They appeared quite excited at the prospect of killing a police officer, but Chris tossed a wet blanket on their fun, "Nobody lied—they're not in the house. Search it if you want, but you're wasting our time."

They continued to follow. Tim led them to the back of the house, where they arrived at the storm-cellar. All that was visible was a set of wooden doors built into the ground, which led to a concrete, bunker-like room. Very Wizard of Oz.

"They're in there?" Socrates asked.

Chris nodded. "But it's secured from the inside, so we need them to unlock it."

"You better be right," Plato warned.

Chris yelled through the door, "The coast is clear."

No response came, which made their trigger fingers very itchy.

"We told you, they won't act without a second voice," Tim said, then spoke into the door. "It's Ruiz—I need you to unlock the door so Chris and I can enter."

A short, tense pause took place, before they heard Nathan's voice through the door, "It's been unlocked. You may proceed."

Chris flashed an "I told you so" look. And when nobody moved, she questioned, "What are you waiting for?"

Plato wasn't falling for it. "You're pretty eager for us to go in. I think it might be a trap."

"Are you serious?" Chris said with a sigh. "You're the ones with the guns."

"You go first," Socrates ordered.

"Fine," Chris said and limped to the door. As she did she cupped her hands around her mouth and called out, "Terriers!"

Before Plato knew what hit him, Beef had stepped out of the shadows and sent him to the ground, dislodging his gun. *The pick.*

Chris dropped to the ground and scrambled to secure the gun. Her leg had become a liability, but being on the ground neutralized its importance. She'd learned this from her many Nerf games with Eliza.

Chris beat the stunned Plato to the gun, and knew exactly where Tim would be. Without looking, she tossed it behind her back, right into his hands. *The Orchestrator.*

"Terriers" was the call for their "pick and roll" offense—based on the Danbury Catholic school mascot, the terrier dog—that proved unstoppable during their basketball days, leading them all the way to a state championship. Beef would set the crunching pick, creating space for Chris. And when the defense converged on her, it would leave Tim wide open on the perimeter for his deadly shot. Their connection wasn't natural like the one she had with Eliza—it came from hundreds of hours of practice and repetition.

But the game was far from over. Socrates still had his gun, and was pointing at Tim, who was aiming right back. It was a standoff. Plato tried to rise to his feet and help his partner, but Chris hung on to his leg.

"He won't kill you—he only kills handicapped women in wheelchairs. Like a coward," Chris tried to distract him.

Socrates kept his focus on Tim, but spoke to Chris, "Your mother was a mercy kill. Just like it will be when I put you out of your misery."

The door of the storm-cellar flew open, and Socrates was too close. It clipped his ankle and sent him tumbling to the ground, the gun slipping from his grasp.

And when he tried to recapture it, Nathan Dunbar put his foot on his neck, stopping him cold. "You killed my wife, and you're not going to get any mercy."

Socrates continued to squirm, desperately trying to reach the gun, but another figure appeared from the storm-cellar and scooped it up.

Alexis.

"I need to talk to my father," she said in a commanding voice.

Chapter 81

I wanted to cheer when I spotted the figures heading back toward the driveway. It was Tim, and he had the Philosophers in handcuffs.

Of course, this would have been a much more pleasant experience if Georgos Tskitapolis didn't have me in his clutches, a gun in one hand and a knife in the other, positioned next to my carotid artery.

"You didn't live up to your end of the bargain. This is not good for you," he said.

"Circumstances changed," Tim said, his voice calm. "I want to renegotiate our deal."

"What terms are you proposing?"

"You let Eliza go in exchange for Tweedle Dumb and Tweedle Dumber. Then I'll release you, so you can slither back under that rock you came from."

He laughed. "You think I really care about those stupid brutes? You're going to have to do better than that."

"Those are my terms, and I would advise you to accept them."

He lifted his gun and fired in Tim's direction. I screamed.

Socrates slumped to the ground, a bullet between his eyes.

The circumstances had changed once more.

Tim did the math—the next person to take a bullet would be the kids or me. He had no choice but to lay his gun down. Then came the indignity of releasing Plato from the cuffs. Plato thanked him by delivering a punch across Tim's nose, causing it to bleed. His legs wobbled, but he willed himself to remain standing.

Tskitapolis was sporting an evil grin. "Now that I've got your attention, I want to make it clear that this is your final chance to bring Nathan and Alexis to me. If you don't, Detective Ruiz, you will get to watch Eliza die. Those are *my terms,* and they're not negotiable."

He pricked my neck with the knife. All I could hope was that the vehicle the girls were in was soundproof and that their father was somehow shielding them from watching this.

As if she'd heard him, Alexis stepped out of the woods, supporting my injured sister, helping her to walk. That might have been the reason for her late entrance, but I got the feeling the timing was choreographed.

Father and daughter locked fiery eyes. "Baba—you're alive," she exclaimed.

It was one thing for us to inform her that he was, but another to see the ghost in the flesh.

"What have you done, Baba?" she said through angry tears.

"Everything I did was to honor your mother."

"Killing Niko honored Mama?"

"He betrayed our family. He'd been doing it for years."

"This has nothing to do with our family, or Mama. Every day it hurts me that she's gone. I needed you, but you chose this misguided revenge over your own daughter. You let me hurt for you, grieve for you. You think others should pay for your pain, but who pays for the pain you've caused?"

Based on his grip tightening around my neck, I don't think he was moved by her plea. But with all his attention focused on Alexis, he never saw the man in the shadows move closer to us.

But Chris did. And she tossed the keys to him in a perfect pass. Beef caught them on the run and rushed to the driver's side. The tires shot up gravel as it tore out of the driveway. Plato took a shot at it, but it helplessly bounced off the bulletproof glass.

Beef had saved my kids! Everything else, including whether I made it out of this alive, was secondary.

Despite the chaos, Tskitapolis didn't budge. I remained in his clutches, but his entire focus was on his daughter. It was as if he was in a trance.

She stared right back at him. She wasn't afraid.

"Please let Eliza go ... I'm asking you as your daughter," Alexis said.

"You stopped being my daughter the moment you crawled into bed with that snake."

"I'm not with Nathan—it was an act to get your attention. You've told me in the past that sometimes you need to save me from myself. Well, this time, Baba, I need to save you from yourself."

"You have chosen the enemy. He killed your mother."

"No—you killed her."

I felt the tip of the knife digging deeper into my neck.

"Don't you ever talk to me like that!"

"Mama needed love, but instead of opening your heart to her, you caged her, just like you tried to do with me. Then you blamed it on the man you pushed her to."

She took out a gun and I let out a yelp—this was about to turn into one of those duels in the Old West, and I was square in the middle of it.

"Is that what you want, Baba? For me to end up just like Mama?"

She didn't point the gun at him; instead, she placed the tip on her own temple.

"Alexis ... no!" I shouted out.

I looked to Tim, hoping he might be able to get the gun away from her. But he was focused on Tskitapolis. "Put the gun down, and let Eliza go. It's the only way this can end without anyone getting hurt."

Tskitapolis dug in. "This will never be over until Nathan Dunbar pays for what he did."

"You want me Georgos, now you got me," a voice rang out from just outside the forest. I watched as my father stepped beside Alexis, and she lowered the gun to her side.

Chapter 82

Just the sight of them together might set Tskitapolis off on a shooting spree, I thought.

My father began walking toward us—he was pushing the action.

"Just you and me Georgos—leave our families out of this. I'm the one who did this, not them."

He stopped and knelt down. "I'm all yours. This is what you wanted. Fire away."

"That would be the easy way out for you—you wouldn't suffer enough."

"I made a mistake, a terrible one, and I live with it every day. But not as much as my wife and children have."

"It's too late for pity."

"I never wanted pity—I wanted a second chance. One that allowed me to see my daughters and granddaughters grow up. It's not too late for you to do the same, Georgos. It won't bring Macaela back, but it can be damn rewarding. They say revenge is best served cold, but it also means you're eating alone. And that can be a lonely way to live."

"All you did was delay the inevitable. And now it's time for you to pay up."

"Then you better hurry up. Beef will be back soon with the police. You're running out of time."

It was like he was begging him to shoot him ... shoot us all. *The kids are safe, the kids are safe, the kids are, hopefully, safe,* I kept telling myself.

Tskitapolis looked like he was contemplating the offer, when a sound stole our attention. A vehicle was speeding up the driveway. It was the Suburban. But there were no police accompanying it—no lights or sirens. There went that idea.

It pulled to a stop and Beef got out with his hands up. "What? You thought I'd leave my teammates behind? That's not how I roll."

Plato met him with another pat-down, then searched the vehicle.

Not bringing the police was one thing, and since we left our phones behind, I wasn't sure he was even able to call 911. But the good news was that my kids and Kirk were not with him, and out of harm's way. Maybe they could get to a neighbor's house and get help. The downside was that even if they did, they would likely be too late.

"Get over with the others," Tskitapolis ordered, sounding frustrated by Beef's arrival, while waving his gun at him. Beef obliged, with a little help from Plato.

Tskitapolis regained his bearings. "Now where was I?"

"You were about to let everyone go so you can shoot me," my father said.

"You have it backwards, Nathan. I'm going to shoot everyone else and make you watch. And *then* I'm going to shoot you."

"Nobody's shooting anybody," a voice echoed off the woods, startling me. It was a female voice; one I didn't recognize at first.

When my eyes adjusted to the dark, I realized it was Officer Annie Sampson, alternating her gun between Tskitapolis and Plato. I had no idea where she appeared from, but I was really happy to see her.

"Game's over. Let Eliza go, and put the gun down slowly."

Tskitapolis didn't budge.

Then of all the people to come to his defense … my father. "I appreciate what you're doing, officer, but this is between me and him. It doesn't concern you."

"I'm making it my business." She glanced at my sister. "I'm here to bring Chris Dunbar back into custody. She has not met her bail agreement and is considered a fugitive. And if anyone gets in my way, I'll bring them in on an obstruction charge."

The quarrel briefly distracted Tskitapolis, giving me the split-second I needed. I wrestled myself free and fell to the ground.

He looked down at me, just long enough to give Officer Annie the upper hand. She had a clear shot at him and she was going to take it.

Tskitapolis knew it too. And he was determined not to leave this world—for real this time—without taking his bitter rival with him. He turned and fired.

My father just closed his eyes, as if accepting his fate.

Chris had other plans—she found just enough strength in her knee to knock him out of the way.

But there was nobody to knock Chris out of the way. The bullet scorched her chest, sending her in a heap to the ground.

"No!" I screamed out.

Officer Annie emptied her gun into Tskitapolis, whose body crumpled next to me.

This time Alexis was the one to scream out, and began to run toward her father's bullet-ridden body. But Tim held her back. She fought him, but he wouldn't let go, and shielded her eyes.

For me, it all took place in painful slow motion, and once again my world went silent. The only thing I could hear was my sister's shallow breaths.

Chapter 83

Even in the dark of night, with the black fabric Chris wore, the blood soaking through her shirt was evident. When I got to her, I could see that it was also trickling out of her mouth.

"And my coaches used to say I never play defense," she said and tried to smile, but it came out as a wince. I could tell she was in a lot of pain.

For those who've called her selfish in the past, I just wanted to grab them and show her lying on the cold ground, her chest bloodied. She just stepped in front of a bullet to save our father. And I wondered if he was worth the sacrifice.

As if reading my mind, Chris said, "Take it easy on Dad—he messes up a lot, but he always gets it right in the end."

I looked to our father, also on the ground, about ten feet away. His head was buried in his hands, as if he couldn't even look at the scene before him.

"I think he's worth saving," she answered my question, even though I never asked it.

I wasn't so sure, at least not when the cost was factored in, but I did know one thing—if Chris didn't get medical attention fast, she was going to die. The blood kept coming, and her voice was losing steam.

"Somebody call 911!" I screamed out, but Tim had already radioed it in. "They should be here within ten minutes," he said back; his tone was urgent but not hurried.

I looked to my sister, and questioned whether that would be soon enough. "Hang in there, help is coming," I said in my most optimistic voice. But I couldn't fool her.

Chris slowly turned her head to where Tskitapolis lay dead. "At least that bastard won't get to hurt our family anymore. I guess we threw a wrench into his plans."

I thought of the plans that she had, that *we* had. Eating Baskin-Robbins until we puked, our trip to Wyoming this summer to see Karen, and Chris pursuing her passion of coaching.

She smiled up at me. "Don't tell Karen, but you've always been my favorite sister."

"That's a good thing, since you've always been stuck with me."

Her smile faded away. "They say I 'won' our surgery, but you really did, Eliza. Because you understood what it meant to be conjoined—the power of connection. And not just with me—with family, friends, community. It took me a long time to finally figure that out. Better late than never, I guess."

It didn't sound like Chris. She was giving up too easy. "Call them again, Tim! We're running out of time!" I shouted.

I grabbed Chris by the cheeks and made her look at me. Her eyes were fading fast. "Mom said we *both* live. That's the only choice. We came into this world together, and that's how we're leaving."

"You can't come with, Eliza ... not yet. You've got too much work to do here. I love Kirk, but do you really want him raising the girls alone?"

"Don't do this."

"They need you. And while you're at it, maybe find yourself a hot police officer to spend your nights with. Do you know any?" She smiled again, but it seemed so far away and distant.

"You can't go."

"I'd just be the third wheel. That's not my style."

Her words grew short and slow like her battery was draining. She never listened to me anyway—only actions work with Chris. So I wrapped my body around her and held her as close as possible, as if we were one. Our faces were just inches apart, staring at each other, just like the day we'd arrived.

"I love you, Eliza," her voice grew sleepy, and her eyes fluttered.

"I love you too," I said back, but her eyes were already closed.

Chapter 84

One Month Later

It was the opening Saturday of Little League baseball at Rogers Park. The sun shone brightly, the sky was a perfect shade of blue, and the emerald green grass was glistening. The sounds of children playing soothed, and the smell of spring was in the air. It represented a fresh start.

Except, there's no such thing.

"C'mon, Kelly!" I shouted out with the right balance of enthusiasm and support, but not so much that I'd embarrass my daughter on her first day of tee ball. It was an art.

Brooke sat next to me in the metal bleachers, more reserved. She wasn't interested in playing, but enjoyed watching and observing like her mother. I taught her to keep score, like my father had for me when I was her age.

"It seems archaic," she was resistant at first. I was impressed with the vocabulary, but not the sentiment. "You could just update it on the website. Why do old people need to write everything down?"

"You still don't play Monopoly on the computer," I said, and we smiled at each other, thinking of Gram.

Kelly took a big swing, and, well … she missed.

I was sure Babe Ruth did the same in his first try. "It only takes one, sweetie!"

I could see her bottom lip tighten and curl upward. According to my mother, I used to do the same thing when I grew determined. She swung again.

This time she hit it. And quite impressively. The ball flew into the outfield, waking up a couple of seven-year-olds who began to run after it.

Kelly stood and admired her blast, until she was pressured into running by our shouts of, "Go! Go!"

And once she started to run she didn't stop. Even when the third base coach—her father—tried to hold her up, she ran right by him and headed home. He looked baffled that she didn't listen to him. Welcome to my world, Kirk.

The rest of her team mobbed her after her home run and Kelly had the widest smile I'd ever seen on her face. Even Brooke couldn't act ho-hum-cool about it, and cheered wildly for her little sister. In honor of my mother, I performed a version of her happy dance.

"Maybe she should start playing with the boys," said the woman moving toward us on crutches.

I don't know what the happiest moment of my life will eventually be, but it'll be tough to beat the moment when the doctor informed me that Chris was going to make it.

She still had trouble breathing, recovering from the collapsed lung, and she just had her fourth knee surgery. She's never been the sedentary or patient type, so she's been cranky and irritable, but it has sounded like beautiful music to me. We hadn't discussed how close we were to losing each other, but we didn't need to—we already knew.

But just because there was a happy ending didn't make it a perfect ending to the story. I've always been a seeker of the truth, and never saw it as a negotiating tool. But as I've mentioned, the older I get the more complicated the truth gets.

The FBI swept in like heroes, and concluded what we already knew. That Georgos Tskitapolis had faked his death and was running a human trafficking ring. But here's where things turned fictional—when my father had found out about it, and was going to blow the whistle, Tskitapolis ordered him and his wife killed. And since my father had survived, he was able to back up their story.

I doubted that I would ever regain trust in my father. But that didn't mean I wasn't thrilled that he lived, and I still had a Dad, and the girls still had a Gramp. But the hero of the story? Really?

And Plato Kostas backed it up … in exchange for a cushy plea deal. In his version, the bad guys were his boss, Georgos Tskitapolis, Niko, and his own brother, Socrates. Quite conveniently, all were dead, and unable to say any different. Not to mention, a nice little thank you to Niko from the FBI for his undercover work. I'm not sure he was the good guy either, but he wasn't the killer he was portrayed as, and I thought he deserved better.

Someone had to take the hit for the smuggling ring, and that would be Alexis. Unlike my father, she didn't have any leverage, or a heroic whistle-blower cover story, and was threatened with an unpleasant return to Greece. So she took a two-year deal in American federal prison, and should be out in one.

We sent her off with a final Dirty Martini Friday salute yesterday, and all things considered, she was in pretty good spirits. We also took on a new member of the group. Officer Annie Sampson, who's smart thinking and bravery saved our lives. She had already arrived on the scene, unsure of her next move, when Beef drove away. She stopped him at the bottom of the driveway, put Kirk and the kids safely in her squad car, before returning to take down Tskitapolis, Annie was hidden in a secret compartment of the vehicle, which allowed her to avoid the sweep by Tskitapolis' men. For that, her martinis would forever be on my dime. Which goes down much better on a Friday afternoon than eternal gratitude, which I'd also pledged to her.

What didn't see the light of day, and never will, was the part about the FBI helping Tskitapolis and numerous other criminals enter the country, and that they were essentially complicit in my mother's death. And if it does come out, you won't be hearing it from me.

You're probably thinking, why don't you stop being such a hypocrite, Eliza, and shout the story from the rooftops like you claimed you were going to do? Expose the story, seek the truth. Be true to your journalistic roots.

I can't argue with that, but there is something that will always trump truth and justice, and that's family. And I got mine back. My mother's killer was dead, and no longer a threat to my children. So they would be able to live their lives with freedom, just like the gift my mother had given us.

Chris was cleared of all charges. Although, the bank robbery was still under investigation—her lawyer, Morgan Gregson hoped to have a positive result in the next month or two. Fingers crossed.

My father decided to move west near Karen and her family, hoping for a fresh start. I wish him luck, and hope he finds peace, if there is such a thing.

While I'm sure he never thought his choices would cost my mother her life, our actions, for better or worse, affect those around us. And they accumulate like a snowball rolling down the hill. They never get washed away, no matter how many years pass by. We can learn from our mistakes, grow from them, and change our path, but there are no do-overs or mulligans. No fresh starts. And as I raise my own children, I realize that what I do today can affect them tomorrow, or thirty years from now.

After the game, we were met by my little slugger, Kelly McCaffrey, and her father.

"Can Dad come with us for lunch?" she asked, the smile still plastered on her face.

Unfortunately, there would be no time for lunch. I had to drop Chris off at her physical therapy appointment, as she still couldn't drive. Brooke had a birthday party to attend, and then I had to get Kelly home so that she could change out of her baseball uniform, so I could drop her at … I couldn't even remember what she had going on, but I was sure it was something, and that it would be memorable and riveting.

"I've got to go anyway—have some business to take care of. But you're coming over tomorrow night for the barbecue, right?" Kirk said, and gave the girls a big hug goodbye. I was glad this goodbye wouldn't require a trip out of the country for the next six months.

He was currently sharing the Ridgefield house with Chris—roomies once again. There was much debate whether Dad should sell it after his move, but we decided that we're Dunbars, and we're fighters, so we weren't going to let anyone bully us out of the home we've built for three decades. There were a lot more memories to make there. For better or worse.

Brooke lit up. "I wouldn't miss it."

Kelly asked, "Can Mom come to the barbecue?"

Kirk looked at me with his boyish grin, "That's up to her."

Kelly then looked to me with her sad puppy eyes—she wasn't playing fair. "We can talk about that later—we need to get going," I said.

Our first stop was the physical therapist on Cole Street. But when I pulled into the parking lot, it was empty. A sign said it was closed.

"Oh, I forgot," Chris said. "We're doing an outdoor session today."

"An outdoor session?"

"Yeah—it's important for my lung function."

That sounded like a bunch of hooey, but I followed her directions to the place where this supposed session was to take place. And when we arrived, I knew she was up to something.

It was an abandoned lot on Bowman Avenue. It had been empty for years, and was an infamous Danbury eyesore. The city had attempted numerous proposals to fill it, but they all had fallen through.

"Hey, look—Dad's here," Kelly exclaimed.

As was Connie and her husband. Beef and his dog Boss. And Jillian pulled up behind us in her Mercedes. "So what's so important that I had to drop everything and drive up here on a Saturday?" she asked, as we got out of the car.

I was about to ask the same question.

Tim arrived in his Camaro—it was a casual, off-duty Saturday for him. I looked to him as if he might know what was going on, but he just shrugged. Everything was status quo with us, business as usual, despite my sister's claims that I told her on her deathbed that I would pursue something more with him. Maybe in time, once everything settles down, and can it still be considered a deathbed if she didn't die?

We followed Beef to the center of the property, which was nothing but some overgrown weeds and dumped garbage. He gathered us around and announced, "As you all know, my gym is on its last legs. And since I needed some new space, and Chris Dunbar was looking to go into coaching …"

Chris took over, "We thought we could create the best of both worlds. So we have purchased this land in order to build a recreational center, which will include basketball courts and a workout center."

"Along with an indoor track and tennis courts, and maybe a dance studio. All members will get top-level coaching and instruction, including former all-American basketball player Chris Dunbar," Beef continued with the sales pitch.

Chris added, "And to prove that we're serious about bringing in top flight instructors, we will also be joined by former college All-American, and professional basketball player Kirk McCaffrey, who has agreed to partner with us."

Kirk stepped forward and stood with them—I guess he really was serious about sticking around, since this was no short-term project in front of them. I was excited for all three of them, chasing their dreams.

And I wasn't the only one, because the rest of the group gave them a loud cheer. Chris added that they planned to name it the Sarah Dunbar Center. This time I didn't cheer—I cried.

Beef interrupted my moment, as I felt his glare. "And we're hoping to get a nice write-up in the paper."

"I'll see what I can do," I said, my smile overtaking my tears.

We all stood silently together, admiring the spot. It wasn't just an empty lot we were staring at anymore, but the future. And that powerful feeling of hope that comes with it.

Kelly broke the silence, "We should take a selfie!"

"Selfies are so narcissistic," Brooke countered, again with the big words, and I hoped that she remembers that when she's a teenager.

"How about just a regular photo from a professional photographer?" Connie said, and started to her car to get her camera.

"Sounds like you still will do anything to get out of a photo," Jillian said to her and they shared a smile.

The kids knelt down in front with Boss at their side. I had Kirk to my left and Tim to my right. The others flanked us, and we all wrapped our arms around each other.

Chris and I made eye contact, and at that very moment I realized that it's not how you come into this world. We all start with an empty lot. It's what you build when you get here. Family, friends, careers … and moments like this.

All of us were connected by our past, joined in our present, and staring ahead at our future.

We were conjoined.

Painless Excerpt—

Chapter One

Mitchell Jones' Labor Day wouldn't be filled with parades or barbecues, and he didn't get the day off from work. He was thousands of miles from home, sitting quietly at a kitchen table in a small house in Malmo, a city on the southern coast of Sweden.

His assassin-like stillness was only occasionally interrupted to check his watch, or dispassionately stroke his long, graying beard. The beard, along with his wiry frame and dark, vacant eyes, gave him a resemblance to a certain infamous terrorist. This made flying commercial virtually impossible. But luckily for his job with Operation Anesthesia, transportation was a much more private affair.

As Sunday night slowly morphed into Monday morning, he patiently read his favorite author—Herbert Spencer—while waiting for the Lerner family to return from the United States. The news that the Lerners received from the US doctors was no doubt life-altering, but little did they know that he was about to *really* change their lives forever.

Based on eighteen years of experience, he didn't expect a confrontation. He knew the Lerners' minds would be too cluttered to notice the obvious signs that someone had broken into their home, such as the left-on lights, or the lingering odor from his chain-smoking. But if an altercation did occur, he was under direct orders to take everyone alive.

This went against Jones' natural instinct to shoot first and ask questions later, a philosophy that got him fired from his old job at the CIA. But Operation Anesthesia didn't see it as a black mark on his résumé. In fact, it was the reason they'd sought him out those many years ago.

He took an extended drag on his cigarette, attempting to relieve some of the pain that was a souvenir from a recent mission in Iran. A mission that went awry, to say the least. Sixty percent of his torso was burned in the helicopter crash—the cigarette didn't serve as a very good anesthetic.

Not even the best spin-doctor could heal the colossal failure of Iran. Any mission where you are presumed dead, and that's the good news, was not one for the time capsule. But thanks to Jones' survival instincts, he and his boss, Franklin Stipe, were preparing a dramatic rise from the dead. A resurrection in which Stipe would likely portray himself as the brave hero, leaving out the part where Jones guided him to safety, allowing him to avoid the cruel fate of the others they left behind.

But he smiled anyway, exposing his cigarette-stained teeth. He knew Stipe wouldn't be in power much longer. It was dictated by the laws of nature, or what Spencer so brilliantly termed "the survival of the fittest"—a concept wrongly credited to Darwin and his theories of evolution. Herbert Spencer coined the phrase in his 1864 masterpiece, *Principles of Biology.*

In it, Spencer warned that humanitarian impulses had to be resisted, as nothing should be allowed to interfere with nature's laws. This is where Jones differed from Stipe, who sought useless elements such as glory, acceptance, and credit. As did the culture of modern America, which embraced concepts like love, happiness, and religion. It chipped away at its inherent survival skills, softening the society, and making it a target for its predators. But of course, that was the reason Operation Anesthesia was created in the first place.

The front door creaked open and a weary family entered, with two-and-a-half-year-old Petr sleeping in his mother's arms. Their bright blond hair didn't appear to be dimmed by the life-changing news they'd received on their trip, but each step they took was marked with exhaustion. Jones was sure the physical fatigue didn't even compare to the mental strain of trying to grasp Petr's diagnosis.

Upon reaching the kitchen, they were met by Mitchell Jones and his 9mm Glock. He coldly explained to the Lerners that their trip had just begun and it would be in their best interest to quietly cooperate. The father declined the offer, shouting, "Aldrig i helvete"—*no way in hell*—and Jones could *kiss his behind*, "Kyss mig i arslet."

Jones went right for his weak spot, knowing a little Swedish of his own. "Jagt skar av dina ballar om du inte haller kaft," he calmly threatened to remove the man's testicles.

The man stood down.

Predictable.

He knew the mother would be a tougher challenge. They always were. When it came to their children they were true survivalists, willing to fight to the death. So he went with a pre-emptive attack—threatening to kill Petr.

She cooperated.

There would be no need to bind and gag them. He used a concoction created for Operation Anesthesia by one of the world's leading neurologists, which would temporarily paralyze the body, including voice. And when Jones expertly injected each of the family members with a syringe containing the paralyzing drug, it didn't surprise him that young Petr didn't wake, or even flinch.

He effortlessly loaded the drugged family into the rented SUV that he'd parked two houses down on the quiet street. He then drove out of Malmo, over the modern Oresund Bridge, and into Denmark. In Copenhagen, a private plane waited to take them to the home base of Operation Anesthesia. It would be the Lerners' home for the rest of their lives.

It was the end of the road.

Chapter 2

It was the end of the road for Billy Harper, both literally and figuratively. From the literal standpoint, the end of the road was a well-groomed cul-de-sac in New Canaan, Connecticut, with stately mansions staring back at him. The figurative was much more complex and hurtful.

His old high school football coach used to drill into his head that you should never look back because someone might be gaining on you. And whenever Billy glanced into his rear-view mirror, what he always saw gaining on him was his past. But ironically, as he looked through the front windshield at the children playing on the lush lawns, his past was straight ahead, mocking him, and the pain began to rumble.

He gathered his emotions as best he could and drove his Jeep Cherokee down a dirt driveway, which was hidden between two majestic mansions that anchored the cul-de-sac.

The Cherokee was a lot like him—it wasn't *that* old, and still looked pretty good on the outside, but had a lot of hard miles on it, and had the potential to break down at any moment. He bounced along the strip of gravel, kicking up dust and rocks, and rattling his few remaining possessions that were strewn throughout the vehicle. Billy glanced into the rear-view mirror and saw the cul-de-sac disappear from view.

The gravel turned to pavement as he pulled to a stop in front of an arch-shaped, red barn, typical of the New England countryside. A large silo stood next to it like an overprotective big brother. A sign welcomed him to *Bevelyn Farms*—his new home.

Billy stepped out of his vehicle and into a sun-drenched afternoon—a record high temperature for the tenth of September. In a dramatic twist from the morning rain showers, the sky now looked like Monet had brush-stroked it with oranges and reds, and the smells of Saturday afternoon barbecues filled the air. It was as if the once-dreary day was given a fresh start. Billy took a deep breath, before heading toward what he hoped would be his own fresh start.

He passed an 800-series black BMW, confirming that this place might be *just a bit* out of his price range. He still wasn't sure why they had rented the cottage to him at such a bargain cost. Just rich people doing some charity work, he guessed.

Chuck Whitcomb answered the door, wearing a *Speak Slow I Only Speak Canadian* T-shirt and mesh baseball hat. Standing almost six-foot-two, Billy didn't have to gaze upward to look many people in the eye, but Chuck was an easy six-six. He reminded Billy of many of the people he encountered growing up in Johnstown, Pennsylvania. Honest working-class folks who slaved in the local mill all week so that they could spend their Friday night cheering-on Billy Harper, the local hero of the moment. Billy was surprised when he'd first met Chuck—based on the ritzy neighborhood, he'd expected someone more resembling his former in-laws.

Chuck greeted Billy enthusiastically and led him into the barn, which actually had been converted into an exquisite home. Billy was just as impressed as he was last Monday, Labor Day, when he came to view the guest cottage the Whitcombs were renting.

He trailed Chuck into an expansive open area. The interior was dominated by heavy, honey colored timber. Large wood beams shot horizontally across the room, giving it a secure feel. A cathedral ceiling soared up two stories, arching at the top. To his left, a spiral staircase led to a second floor overhang that reminded Billy of a balcony in an old-time movie theater. On his right was an elaborately decorated, but comfortable looking living room area that featured a large fieldstone fireplace.

"Carolyn's upstairs with a little fever and Beth is setting up for the birthday party tomorrow. So it'll be just you and me," Chuck said as he pulled Billy toward the kitchen.

Billy nodded hesitantly, still expecting Chuck to come to his senses about renting him the cottage.

The country-style kitchen was an impressive blend of wide-beamed wood flooring and whitewashed wood trim. An adjacent breakfast nook ushered in streams of powerful sunlight through oversized windows, which reflected off a cluster of copper pots and pans that hung over an island stove.

Beth Whitcomb stood at the kitchen sink washing a plastic cereal bowl. She was in her mid-twenties, about ten years Chuck's junior. Her strawberry blonde hair was cut into a simple bob with box layers, and light freckles dotted her fair skin. She wore a flowered sundress filled with pinks and greens, but while the dress was soft and breezy, her demeanor was anything but carefree.

Chuck walked to his wife and hunched downward to give her a kiss on the cheek. "How's my girl?"

She surprised with a smile. "Do you mean me or Carolyn?"

"I know how amazing you are—how's she doing?"

"Fever's down—taking a nap upstairs."

Chuck pulled out two perspiring bottles from the refrigerator, receiving a dirty look from Beth. At first glance, they made for quite an odd couple. Chuck was the affable working-class man, while Beth was the icy heiress to the Boulanger Kingdom. But then Billy recalled where he'd seen this story before, and felt a sour taste in his mouth.

"Beer, eh?" he offered in his Canadian twang, and Billy accepted the bottle of Klein's. Noticing the label, he almost laughed out loud at the irony—he just couldn't escape from the past.

He twisted off the top and took a swig, washing away that sour taste. As he did, he could feel Beth's glare on the back of his neck. When they met last week, her first words to him were, "When I pictured who my sister would send to look at the cottage, you are exactly what I imagined."

"What's that?" Billy had asked.

"The good looking, T-shirt and jeans type. The wavy hair, the charming smile, and oh, Dana loves a cute dimple."

Billy touched his dimpled chin, briefly impressed with himself, before noticing Chuck's slumping body language, indicating that he was about to take a punch-line across the nose.

"But of course there is the other side to Dana's men," Beth continued.

"Her men? She's my agent, not my girlfriend. I think you have the wrong idea."

Beth rolled her eyes, as if to say she'd seen this movie before. "Dana's men are always starving artists who end up living off of her like parasites. They also just got out of some complicated relationship, and have a fifty-fifty shot of having a drinking problem."

It was obvious to Billy that she wouldn't rent him the cottage at gunpoint, even if he could afford it, which he clearly couldn't. So he decided he was done being shit on.

"Divorce became official about a year ago. I do have a job at the *Shoreline Times* here in New Canaan, which Dana got for me, although I don't have the four thousand a month you're asking for rent, not even close. And lastly, I don't have a drinking problem. I happen to like drinking—it's not a problem!

A sudden thunder boomed through the air, and cascaded down from the balcony overhang. Billy looked up to witness a small girl running down the stairs like a precocious barrel of energy. As she did, she let out an innocent giggle that bounced off the acoustics. She wore a denim dress with butterflies embroidered on it, and her tiny sandals looked as if they'd fly off her feet as she excitedly bounced down the stairs.

The first thing Billy noticed was her eyes—two big saucers of hazel. Her brown hair was in double ponytails that jutted from both sides of her head. Her apple cheeks resonated with joy. When she reached the bottom, her eyes locked on Billy and her face scrunched, seemingly in deep thought.

They stared at each other for a long moment, before she finally asked, "Who are *you*?" She spoke with a slightly muffled lisp, and when she opened her mouth, exposing her tongue, Billy understood why.

"I'm Billy, what's your name?"

She stuck her chest out proudly and stated, "I'm Carolyn Whitcomb, but you can call me Princess."

There was nothing pretentious about the statement. It reminded Billy of an innocence he once knew. Their bond was instant, and the princess would eventually cast the deciding vote as to whether Billy would be offered the cottage. Or at least that's the way that Chuck had portrayed it to him.

Even with a few days to ponder it over, the decision still baffled him. Not just because he couldn't afford the rent, but part of his rental agreement was that he would care for Carolyn during the day. By the looks of things, the Whitcombs could afford a team of nannies, but that still wasn't it. What he found most odd was that they never asked him the basic background questions—the ones about being arrested for a violent crime—that would have ruled him out of any such responsibility.

Now less than a week later, he was preparing to move in.

Thunder once again crackled from above, and in a repeat performance from his previous visit, Carolyn scampered down the stairs, her voice booming off the acoustics, "Billy—did you come to play with me!?"

Chuck impeded his daughter's dash, swooping her into his arms. "Billy is moving into the cottage today, princess."

"Can I help?"

"Are you feeling better?"

"Yes."

"Tell Billy how old you're going to be tomorrow."

She flashed the three most inner fingers on her small hand, and then took attendance. Upon discovering she missed one, she manually raised her pinky finger. "I'm gonna be foe."

Billy smiled to match hers. "Four? And not even one gray hair?"

She laughed. "You're silly."

Still holding her in his huge arms, Chuck planted his face into hers. "And not even one wrinkle."

"That's cuz I wear sunblock so the *ubee* rays don't get me!" she exclaimed, her voice climbing octaves in a scale-like cadence: d*o-ra-mi-fa-so.*

Beth walked to her daughter, all business, and placed the palm of her hand on her forehead. "Fever's gone," she announced to Chuck.

He nodded, as if it were the expected conclusion.

"Can I help Billy move in, Mom, can I?" Carolyn pleaded.

Her mother refused at first, but Carolyn once again proved to be a tough negotiator. It seemed that she truly was a princess, and always got her way in the end.

Chapter 3

With Carolyn's birthday party planned for Sunday, and Chuck scheduled to leave for a hunting trip Monday morning, Saturday was the logical day for Billy to move into the cottage.

Chuck assumed the role of muscle, while Beth spent most of her time scurrying around the yard setting up for the party. But she did find time to neurotically check on Carolyn every fifteen minutes.

"Look, Mom—I'm the momback," Carolyn said to Beth as she approached once again. Carolyn returned her attention back to Billy, who was slowly backing up the Cherokee to the front of the cottage. She started waving her arm like she was directing traffic.

"The momback?" her mother inquired.

"I wave to Billy to tell him if there is enough room to back up and say momback … momback!"

Chuck grinned, which received a stern look from his wife. "I hope you're watching her," she warned.

He nodded away his grin.

Carolyn, wearing a backwards baseball cap and a white T-shirt saluting the fictional minor league hockey team, the Charlestown Chiefs, suddenly threw up her hands and shouted, "Stop Billy!"

Not completely trusting the soon-to-be four-year-old, he sought out a second opinion from Chuck, who confirmed his daughter's diagnosis. Billy threw the truck into park and hopped out. He slapped Carolyn five and she flashed him a toothless grin. It exposed the grisly, stitched tongue he'd noticed during his initial visit.

Carolyn moved to her mother, who first inspected her arms, and then under her shirt.

"She's checking me for the lime," Carolyn explained to Billy.

The response didn't clear it up.

"Actually, I'm checking for ticks so she doesn't get Lyme disease," Beth clarified, and then checked for a fever by pressing her palm to Carolyn's forehead.

"Maybe you can put her in a bubble," Billy remarked snidely.

Carolyn appeared excited about the idea—mentioning her fondness for bubbles, whether it be blowing them or in a bath—but Beth seemed less than impressed, and stormed off without a word. He was not off to a great start with his new landlord.

On the next trip, Billy and Chuck moved his mattress and bed frame. Carolyn asked to help them move the large items, looking for a promotion from the momback.

"Princess, you carry the small stuff. Billy and I will get the heavy things," Chuck instructed.

She looked dejected, but remained defiant. "I'm a big girl."

"I know you are. Carrying the little stuff is a big girl job."

After a moment of tense reflection, she appeared to accept her fate. She grabbed a pile of folders and manuscripts and marched them into the cottage.

Billy and Chuck had just begun hooking the bed frame together when they heard Carolyn let out an ominous "uh-oh!" They looked up just in time to ...

Acknowledgments

As I've mentioned in this spot, on previous books, I am very lucky to work with the best team in publishing, independent or traditional (Yes, I know I'm biased!). But for the most part things have gone smoothly on the first ten books, considering how many obstacles there are on the road to publishing. But for whatever reason, this book hit a perfect storm of everything that could go wrong, pretty much did. With some team members having their own "thrillers" going on in their real life lives. When things don't go smooth, that's when you truly learn about the people around you, and how much they care about the books. And what I learned, was what I already knew! So I take extra pride (and a sigh of relief) that these great folks were able to find the time and make the extra effort to make sure this book got to you, for which I'm very appreciative. Especially my great editor Charlotte Brown. Fantastic proofreader Sandra Simpson. Best cover guy in the business, Carl Graves, thanks for another great one. And Curt Ciccone, with his usual expert work on digital formatting.

Until next time ...